MARSHALL RYAN MARESCA

People
OF THE
City

A Novel of the *Maradaine Elite*

DAW BOOKS, INC.

DONALD A. WOLLHEIM, FOUNDER

1745 Broadway, New York, NY 10019

ELIZABETH R. WOLLHEIM

SHEILA E. GILBERT

PUBLISHERS

www.dawbooks.com

DAW TRADEMARK REGISTERED
U.S. PAT. AND TM. OFF. AND FOREIGN COUNTRIES
—MARCA REGISTRADA
HECHO EN U.S.A.
PRINTED IN THE U.S.A.

Acknowledgments

This has been a journey, friends.

In 2007, sitting in a bookstore café, frustrated that the novel I was trying to write wasn't coming together, I had a strange idea. I wrote it out in longhand:

- Four series
- Magic student/secret street thief?
- Traditional knight/paladin/elite warrior
- Police detective partners
- Thieves—brothers?—pulling heists together
- Interconnect in same world

There, in twenty-odd words, the seed that became the Maradaine Saga was planted. It took time and a lot of work to cultivate that seed, grow it into what would become *The Thorn of Dentonhill, A Murder of Mages, The Holver Alley Crew,* and *The Way of the Shield*, as well as the further development for all the other Maradaine novels, leading to this book in your hands.

More than once over the course of writing this book, I whispered to myself, "I'm actually getting to do this." Because with this, finishing the first phase of the Maradaine Saga, I've accomplished something beyond what I thought I'd, frankly, be allowed to do.

But I actually got to do this.

Let me clarify what I mean. This saga, comprised of four series that interconnect with each other, all while laying the foundations of larger plots that reach a climax in this book in your hands, started with *The Thorn of Dentonhill*, which was released in February 2015. I'm writing these acknowledgments for the twelfth book just five years later, with the book being released before the end of the year. Twelve books, in a span of time where it's rare for a writer to put out more than three. Twelve books, in a span of time where it's not uncommon for someone to go from "debut author" to "retired author."

I actually got to do that. I was *allowed* to do that. I had this mad, absurd plan, and enough people nodded their heads and said, "Yes, do that," to put this in your hands.

Thanks to so many people lending help and support along the way.

First and foremost, I have to talk about my absolute rock of support, my friend since middle school, Daniel J. Fawcett. So much of the worldbuilding and big ideas behind Maradaine were shepherded by long conversations and email chains with him over the past thirty-plus years. His influence is woven into the very DNA of the work. The books—and I—would be lesser without him.

A lot of my development as a writer can be tied to the ArmadilloCon Writers Workshop, which was run by Stina Leicht for several years. Stina's been a friend and mentor for years, first with critiques of my work when I was a student in the AWW, then bringing me up to help her run it. She continues to be one of my favorite people in this business.

Being a student in the AWW also helped these books with critique and guidance of several other generous folks who volunteered as instructors and administrators, including Julie Kenner, Kimberley Frost, Anne Sowards, Patrice Sarath, and Melissa Mead Tyler. The first books, and consequently the saga as a whole, were improved by the early reads from several peers I had critique exchanges with, including Abby Goldsmith, Ellen Van Hensbergen, Katy Stauber, Nicky Drayden, and Amanda Downum.

Of course, there have been two people who were deeply consequential as first-readers for every single one of these books: Kevin Jewell and Miriam Robinson Gould. I've been incredibly graced to have their insight throughout this whole process.

This isn't even counting all the people I've been privileged to talk craft with, and through those conversations, build long necklaces out of their pearls of wisdom. I could not, in any fair or accurate way, name them all, but I would like to single out my podcasting co-hosts Alexandra Rowland and Rowenna Miller. They're brilliant and insightful and just a damned delight to talk to about the process of writing fantasy.

I can't emphasize enough how much is owed to my agent, Mike Kabongo. He's handled with grace and humor the arduous task of dealing with my constant harassment while shopping my work in the early days, not to mention just plain keeping up with me continually going, "OK, now here's what's next" at the, frankly, absurd pace I've been maintaining. Years ago, when he first read the then-too-short draft of *Thorn of Dentonhill*, he told me, "Clearly you are a writer I want to watch. Even if you decide I'm not the agent for you, do let me know when you hit the shelves, I want to buy something with your name on it." That's the kind of faith you want to see in a future agent.

Way back when I first started talking my Big Plan with Dan Fawcett, he said, "That's fantastic, but for it to work, for you to be able to do what you want to do, you're going to need the right editor and the right publisher." Fortunately for me, Sheila Gilbert and DAW Books were very much the right editor and the right publisher. Were it not for Sheila—two-time Hugo winner for Best Editor, so very well earned—and her astounding faith in this work and my big plan, we wouldn't be here. How *absolutely blessed* I am to have her at my back and in my corner, I cannot adequately express.

Everyone at DAW and Penguin Random House—Sheila, Betsy, Katie, Josh, Leah, Alexis—have been fantastic partners on this endeavor. Another person I should thank is Paul

Young, who has done such gorgeous work on the covers for these books. I've always been thrilled to see his interpretations of each of these stories and characters, as well as Maradaine through his eyes.

Further thanks are owed to my parents, Nancy and Louis, my mother-in-law, Kateri, and my son, Nicholas.

And highest and first in my heart, my wife, Deidre. None of this, absolutely none, would have come about without her. Deidre has been a beacon of strength and support who has always believed that I could be successful as a writer. She has been an anchor in my life for the past fifteen years, giving me the ability to pound away at a keyboard day after day and making this book happen. But more importantly, she got me on task in the first place, moving me from being that guy who just talked about "writing a book at some point" to actually making all of this happen.

She's the north star by which I can always navigate my way.

And, of course: you, with this book in your hand. It's for you, and I am so very grateful to have you join me on this adventure, and everything still to come.

PEOPLE
OF THE
CITY

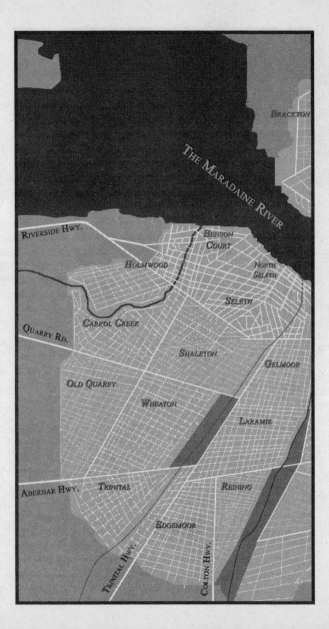

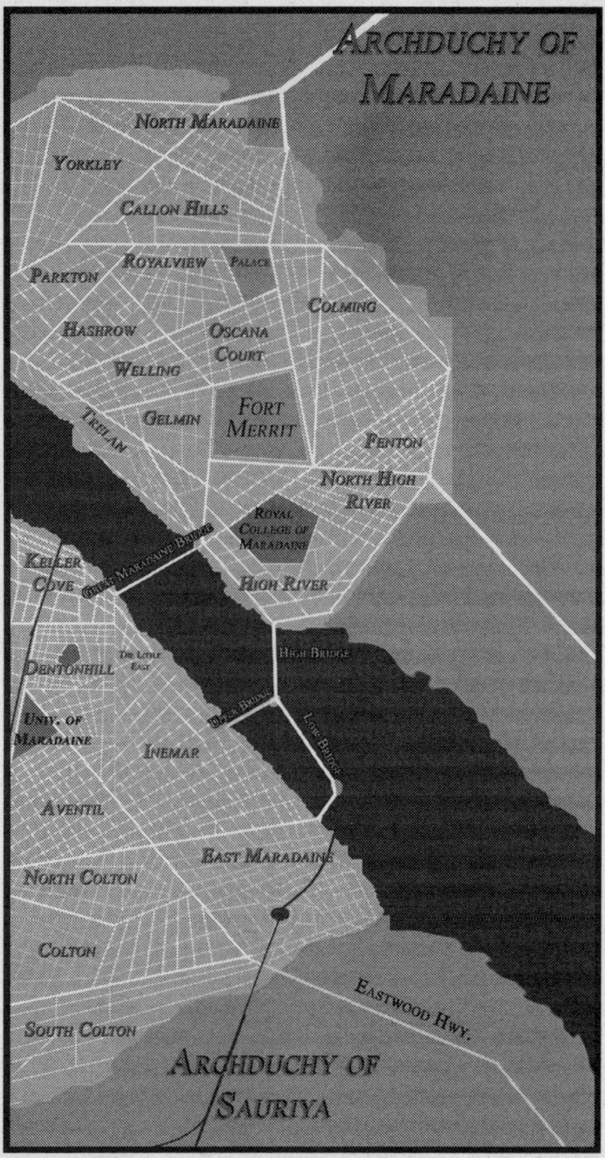

ARCHDUCHY OF MARADAINE

NORTH MARADAINE

YORKLEY

CALLON HILLS

ROYALVIEW

PALACE

PARKTON

COLMING

HASHROW

OSCANA COURT

WELLING

TREHAN

GELMIN

FORT MERRIT

PENTON

NORTH HIGH RIVER

ROYAL COLLEGE OF MARADAINE

KELLER COVE

OLD MARADAINE BRIDGE

HIGH RIVER

DR. LITTLE EAST

DENTONHILL

HIGH BRIDGE

UNIV. OF MARADAINE

INEMAR

AVENTIL

EAST MARADAINE

LONG BRIDGE

NORTH COLTON

COLTON

EASTWOOD HWY.

SOUTH COLTON

ARCHDUCHY OF SAURIYA

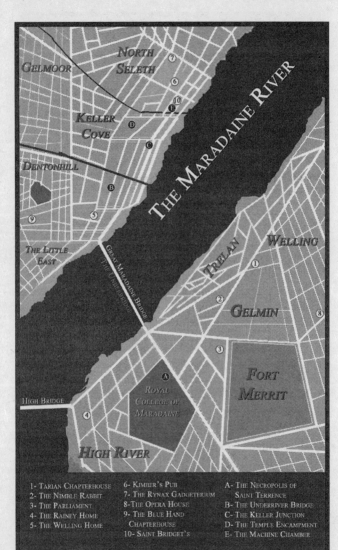

1- Tarian Chapterhouse
2- The Nimble Rabbit
3- The Parliament
4- The Rainey Home
5- The Welling Home

6- Kimber's Pub
7- The Rynax Gadgeterium
8- The Opera House
9- The Blue Hand
   Chapterhouse
10- Saint Bridget's

A- The Necropolis of
   Saint Terrence
B- The Underriver Bridge
C- The Keller Junction
D- The Temple Encampment
E- The Machine Chamber

Chronological Note

THE THORN OF DENTONHILL (Maritan 7th–14th—mid-spring)

Veranix Calbert, magic student at the University of Maradaine and circus-trained acrobat and archer, waged a vigilante war against Willem Fenmere's drug empire. He stole two magically empowering items, learned about missing children in Dentonhill, fended off assassins, and stopped Lord Sirath and the Circle of the Blue Hand in their nefarious magical plans, earning the sobriquet, "the Thorn." In his final moments, one of the Blue Hand mentions having failed "the Nine."

A MURDER OF MAGES (Maritan 19th–22nd—mid-spring)

Satrine Rainey—wife, mother, and retired spy—faked her way into an Inspector Third Class position with the Inemar Constabulary, and was partnered with **Minox Welling**—outcast and an untrained, Uncircled mage. Together they investigated the ritual murders of several mages—especially from the Firewings—that used strange magic-draining spikes, until Minox was nearly the last victim. Satrine rescued him, but his arm was broken by the spike. The killer mentions having taken the spikes from "the Brotherhood of the Nine."

THE HOLVER ALLEY CREW (Maritan 27th–Joran 5th—mid-spring)

Asti and Verci Rynax—a broken spy and a brilliant gadgeteer—lost their home and shop to the Holver Alley fire, and gathered a crew to steal a statue for an unnamed buyer. They learned the fire was set on purpose, and have their revenge on the man who arranged the fire, only to learn he was part of a larger plot.

THE WAY OF THE SHIELD (Joran 10th–15th— late spring)

Dayne Heldrin—Second-year Candidate for the Tarian Order—returned to Maradaine and befriended Tarian Initiate **Jerinne Fendall**. Together they helped foil a plot against members of Parliament, captured failed Spathian Tharek Pell, and were publicly lauded by *The Veracity Press*. They didn't know that a deeper conspiracy drove that scheme, run by the Grand Ten—power players of Maradaine, including Tarian Grandmaster Lon Orren, Dayne's beloved Lady Mirianne Henson, and Major Silla Altarn of Druth Intelligence.

THE ALCHEMY OF CHAOS (Joram 18th–22nd— late spring)

Veranix dealt with an alchemical prankster seeking revenge on campus, multiple assassins, and final exams, and shattered the fragile alliance between Fenmere, the Red Rabbits, and the alchemist Cuse Jensett. Veranix also found a savior and ally in Reverend Pemmick of Saint Julian's Church.

AN IMPORT OF INTRIGUE (Erescan 13th–15th— early summer)

Minox and Satrine investigated the murder of a Fuergan *lavark* in the Little East, which led Satrine back to an old rival, Pra Yikenj of Lyranan Intelligence, and to her old spymaster Major Grieson, and the reminder that her daughter Rian is also the child of the current king of Waisholm. Minox's attempts to learn about his magic and his injured hand from the Tsouljans led him into their underground chambers, and triggered a magical transformation of his hand. Pra Yikenj told Satrine she was working with a traitor. Minox also learned the spikes have vanished from the Constabulary evidence lock-up.

LADY HENTERMAN'S WARDROBE (Erescan 18th–24th—early summer)

Asti and Verci's investigation of the fire led them to Lord Henterman, and inadvertently to Liora Rand, the spy who betrayed Asti to the Poasians. Their final confrontation left Liora severely injured, but she was able to control Asti's broken mind, and escaped with a statue similar to the one they stole before. Major Grieson—Asti's old handler—confides in Asti that Liora is part of a corruption in Intelligence. Liora has been working with Major Altarn, and is also connected to the Brotherhood, Lord Sirath, and someone called Crenaxin, the Dragon.

SHIELD OF THE PEOPLE (Erescan 26th–31st—early summer)

Dayne and Jerinne, with the help of Amaya Tyrell, prevented the corruption of the Parliament election by rescuing the Scallic ballots from the Deep Roots. The largest surprise was the election of Ret Issendel, of the separatist movement the Open Hand, which troubled Dayne due to Ret possessing a terrifying mystical power. Altarn was promoted to colonel, and prepared to begin the "Altarn Initiatives," which included working with the Brotherhood, Crenaxin, and Ithaniel Senek.

THE IMPOSTERS OF AVENTIL (Soran 11th–19th—late summer)

At the Grand Collegiate Tournament, Veranix struggled to keep drugs off the U of M campus, but two imposter Thorns created trouble for him, including attacking the local Constabulary. Minox and Satrine came to Aventil to investigate, and became intertwined with the Thorn. Veranix discovered he can control Minox's altered hand, and Minox can use it to control the Thorn's rope. Minox learned Veranix's identity as the Thorn, but decided to help him by providing files about Fenmere's operation. Fenmere's Poasian smuggling connections brought him a new drug, the more potent *efhân*. Satrine learned of the Altarn Initiatives, somehow tied to changes in the magic curriculum at the U of M.

A PARLIAMENT OF BODIES (Oscan 3rd–5th—early autumn)

Minox and Satrine investigated the Gearbox Killer, who left a monstrous device in the Parliament, which brought them to Dayne and Jerinne. Minox and Dayne were able to rescue most of the victims, and with the help of Verci Rynax, dismantled the device. Dayne knew the Gearbox Killer was Sholiar, but Sholiar outmaneuvered them all, escaping after torturing Minox's Uncircled mage friend Joshea Brondar. Sholiar told Satrine the Brotherhood commissioned him to compose "a symphony of fear." Minox faced an inquest regarding his untrained magic, especially his powerful altered hand, and was restricted from active duty. When Minox's cousin Nyla was threatened by Sholiar, Satrine found Verci with odd help from Sister Myriem. Satrine stopped the abduction of children bound for someone named Senek, but Minox's sister **Sergeant Corrie Welling** was taken and put on a slave ship bound for somewhere far from Maradaine. The slavers and the abductors had connections with Vice Commandant Undenway, who was behind much of the corruption in the Constabulary, including having Inspector Kellman under her control. Grieson told Satrine he had lost standing and resources in Intelligence, and to seek Verci's brother if something happened to him, but Satrine had her own crisis with the release of her mother from prison. Jerinne learned the secret of Rian's parentage, and Dayne, Minox, and Satrine agreed to work together to investigate the deeper corruption in the Constabulary and Maradaine.

THE FENMERE JOB (Oscan 13th–17th—early autumn)

Asti and Verci tried to keep Fenmere's Poasian smugglers from using their neighborhood as an entry point, which connected to the Firewing mage house that had been built in the wake of the Holver Alley fire. Veranix came to their neighborhood to cut off Fenmere, and after an initial misunderstanding with the Rynaxes, worked with them to stop Fenmere and the Firewings. Asti's mental state continued to deteriorate, drawing the attention of Poasian spies who believed he knew of a mysterious list. Verci built a special new bow and arrows for Veranix as thanks. The brothers learned that a project behind the fire involved building underground machine carriages, and began a plan to infiltrate and sabotage the project. Tarvis and Telly, street boys in the neighborhood, were grabbed by a monstrous beast calling itself Gurond, who brought them into the underground tunnels for the Brotherhood. . . .

PRELUDE

THEY HAD SHACKLED TARVIS TO the wall, in a dark stone cell, deep underground. Tarvis had no idea how deep. The giant bastard had taken him and Telly down, down through tunnels and steps, through places darker than any night Tarvis had ever known in the six years of his life.

That giant bastard. Gurond. Taller than anything Tarvis had ever seen. Skin that his knives just slid off of. Tarvis tried to kill him. Couldn't. Couldn't kill him, couldn't save Telly.

There were voices in the dark, in the distances. The beast, with a voice like scraping a knee on the street. Other voices, old men. Couldn't make out what they were saying.

And the other kids. Crying whiners, the lot of them. Tarvis could hear them, couldn't see them.

The shackles were hard and cold. Small. Made to hold children. But they wouldn't hold Tarvis. He was smaller than most, small even for a kid his age. He liked that. The bastards always underestimated him. Never expected someone like him to fight back. Never expected a kid as young and small as him to win.

He pulled in his thumb as hard as he could, twisted his wrist. Scraped the skin, hurt like blazes, but Tarvis didn't give a rutting hole. Pain was nothing. After what the bastards had done to Jede, he didn't give a rutting hole about anything, especially not getting hurt.

But he wasn't going to let these rutting bastards win. No damn chance of that.

Skin scraped, blood flowed. Made his hand slippery. Slipped through the rutting shackle. One hand free, he got out the knife he kept hidden in his skivs. They had taken his others, but they didn't bother searching for more. What little kid would hide a knife in his skivs?

Tarvis rutting would, and they wouldn't forget it when he was done.

With the knife, he was able to pop open the other shackle.

"Telly," he said in the darkness. "We're getting out."

No response.

"Telly, you here?"

"Are you free?" some kid asked.

"Get us out," another said.

"Help us!"

More kids, more voices. No idea how many.

"Shut it!" he shouted.

The other kids started crying more.

Another voice in the distance. Then sounds of a door opening, light searing Tarvis's eyes. Shadowy figure of a man, dragging a kid with him.

"Silence!" the man hissed.

Tarvis didn't waste any time. Dove in low with the knife. Knee. Knee. Tenders. The man screamed, blood flowed. Tarvis grabbed the lamp as the man fell. Another stab in the neck to be sure.

The kid he was dragging—prim little bastard, dressed like a swell—just stared blankly.

"Run, you nit!" Tarvis hissed. The kid dashed off.

"Help us!" the kids all shouted, those who weren't just screaming. Tarvis ignored them, went into the hallway.

"Telly!" he shouted. "Where are you?"

"Tarvis!"

Another door. Tarvis went to it, tried to pull it open. No rutting good.

"Telly, you in there?"

"Tarvis, run!"

"I ain't leaving you!"

"Just run!"

Some more shouts down the hall. More figures coming toward him.

The giant. And two more, almost as big. From their shapes, just as monstrous.

"I'm gonna kill them all, Telly," Tarvis said.

"Run!"

"Naughty boy!" the giant bellowed.

Tarvis threw the lamp at the bastard, and flames burst forth from it as it shattered. The giant was covered in the fire.

And he kept coming.

Everything hard and cold and broken in Tarvis melted away, and for just a moment, he was the terrified little boy he'd sworn he'd never be again. In pure, uncut fear, he ran.

He ran like he'd never run before, through hallways and tunnels until he couldn't hear or see anything but his own pounding heart in the darkness.

Alone in the dark.

Saints even knew how far down.

He needed to get out. Needed to get help. Needed to go—

"Up!"

The screams echoed through the cloistresses' residential wing of Saint Limarre's. Sister Alana got to her feet as soon as she heard them, knowing exactly where they were coming from.

"You have to do something about that girl!" Sister Enigaria said as Alana came out of her own cell. "She's—"

"She's leaving today, Sister," Alana said. "Go back to sleep. I'll take care of it."

Enigaria glared, as did the half-dozen other cloistresses, all sticking their heads out of their rooms. None of them were happy. None of them had gotten a decent night's sleep in weeks. Alana waved them all off.

"Up! Away from the beasts and the fire and to Saint Jontlen!"

The door to her cell was shut—latched with a key. A step that Alana wished wasn't necessary, but the poor girl kept ending up in the streets in the middle of the night, pounding on the door of the local post or a bookseller.

Alana opened the door to see Sister Myriem—poor young girl, no clue how old she was, but certainly no older than nineteen—in just her nightshift, pounding on the wall with her copy of *Testaments of the Saints*. When Myriem had come to Saint Limarre's as an angry orphan, raised by the church, Alana had seen something of herself in the girl. She had hoped that the faith and discipline of the Sisters of the Blue would have had the same impact it had had on Alana, tempering the rage. But the day she took her vows had been the beginning of something harder and darker. Myriem had faith and discipline, but also an infliction that could only be madness, losing all connection with the present moment and any and all times. Even when she was lucid, there was a sense her mind was always tuned in elsewhere.

"Myriem!" Alana said sternly.

Myriem turned to her, eyes blank and glassy, and charged at her. "I have to find Saint Jontlen!" She grabbed Alana with both hands and lifted her off the ground, carrying her out of the cell.

Saints almighty, the girl was strong.

Alana didn't waste any more time, knowing what had to be done. As best she could with Myriem gripping her, she slapped the girl across the face. Then once more for good measure.

Myriem shook for a moment, and then her eyes focused on Alana.

"Sister," she said calmly. "I presume I was unseemly again?" She put Alana back on the ground.

"Quite," Alana said. "I don't know the hour, but it is still some time before sunrise."

"I'm sorry," Myriem said, smoothing her nightshift with her ink-stained fingers. "I wish I could—"

"I know, sister," Alana said. "I wish we could be more help to you."

"You have been," Myriem said. "I—I know this is where I needed to be until now. And now I will go to Saint Julian's."

She was confused again. "You mean Saint Bridget's."

"Yes, what did I say?"

"Julian."

"Why would I—" She paused, and then nodded like she understood. "Because I must seek Saint Julian."

"Seek him?" She had said Jontlen before. Myriem was often very focused on specific saints, including Jontlen and Julian. Alana had often found her sketching pictures of those saints, though the finished works were nowhere to be found.

"The one with the shield!" Myriem snapped with irritation, pushing Alana out of the room.

"What?"

Myriem stormed out into the hall, but as soon as she crossed the threshold, her expression changed to confusion. "What . . . I was telling you about . . . someone. The tall one . . . with the shield. He comes here to see you. I saw him . . . in water, in fire. In agony. Weeping in defeat."

Sister Alana wasn't sure how to respond to that. She

knew who Myriem meant: Dayne Heldrin, of the Tarian Order.

"Did you need me to tell him something?" Alana offered.

"No," Myriem said. "I don't . . . I cannot put that burden on you. I . . . I don't understand why I am so driven but I do know it is mine alone to bear."

"Myriem, whatever plagues you, I want to—"

Myriem didn't let her finish. She put the book into Alana's hands, her expression one of steely resolve. "I'm afraid I have damaged my copy of the *Testaments*. It will be of no use to whoever inhabits this cell next. Inspector Rainey should receive it. It will give her guidance." Her hands trembled as she let go of the book. Tears formed at her eyes, and the steel in her jaw fell apart. Suddenly she wept like an infant.

"Myriem, what—"

"I need to pray, Sister Alana," Myriem said through her tears. "Pray that what guides me is truly godly. Pray that the fight ahead of me is for the light."

"Fight?"

"Please lock me in until it's time for me to leave."

"But, Myriem—"

"Please!" Myriem went back into her cell and slammed the door.

Alana latched it with a sigh. She looked at the copy of the *Testaments*, and to say it was damaged was an understatement. Some stories were torn out, words crossed out in others, ink splattered on the pages. What horrors befell Myriem in these waking nightmares that compelled her to do this? And why would she want to give the book to Satrine?

And what, in all of that, made Myriem think of Dayne? What horrifying vision did she have of him?

Chapter 1

"**Y**OU AREN'T SUPPOSED TO BE here."
Jerinne Fendall felt the glare from the marshal
at the palace gate even stronger than the hot autumn
sun overhead. He tried to look down at her, but he
wasn't anywhere near tall enough, so he craned his neck
in an attempt to intimidate.

"I don't think you're right about that," Jerinne said.
"I've been invited."

"Nonsense," the marshal said. "Pips on your collar
clearly mark you as an Initiate, and only Tarians and
Spathians of Master rank are invited to the Royal Authentication. That's how it is."

Jerinne reached into the coat of her dress uniform
and pulled out the letter. "That might be how it is, but I
was still invited."

Another marshal came up behind him and gave him
a disapproving knock on the shoulder. "Kasmar, open
your damn eyes. Miss Fendall is a special guest. Don't
you recognize her?"

"Am I supposed to?" Kasmar asked.

"Don't you read the newssheets?"

"Not much, no, sir."

The other marshal—a chief by his rank insignia—shook his head. "Come along, Miss Fendall. I apologize for the inconvenience. Dayne's already here."

"My apologies, Chief," Jerinne said as they walked onto the palace grounds. This was the first time she had ever even been near the Royal Palace, let alone on the grounds, and her heart was fluttering despite herself. "If we've met, it escapes my memory."

"Perhaps briefly, but not formally," he said. "Chief Donavan Samsell, but feel free to just call me Donavan."

"Samsell, yes," Jerinne said. He had been the one in charge of administrating the election a few months back. "I thought you were assigned to another city now."

"I was in Marikar for about a month," he said. "But after the latest atrocity and the scandal with Chief Quoyell, I was recalled to Maradaine."

Scandal was selling it lightly. Quoyell had orchestrated mass murder on the Parliament floor, and was assassinated after his arrest. Needless to say, his tenure as head of security for the Parliament was disastrous.

"You're head of Parliament security now?" she asked. "Or the Palace?"

"Well, the Palace marshals and the Parliament marshals need to work together on a day like today," he said with a chuckle. "But—sorry, I thought Dayne might have told you."

"I've not seen Dayne much for the past week or so," Jerinne said. Both of them had taken a battering at the Kittrick Hotel, and Dayne seemed to be overwhelmed with duties at the Parliament since the atrocity incident. Jerinne thought it best to give him some space for a bit.

"Ah, of course. Well, you should know that Parliament security will no longer be handled solely by the

King's marshals. Instead it will be a joint operation of the marshals, the Tarians, and the Spathians."

That explained why Dayne had been busy. As the liaison between the Orders and the marshals, his hands would be kept full setting up something like that.

"That's why he's here already."

"Perfect aim on that," Samsell said.

Jerinne followed him down the walkway, already crowded with people. Most of them were high-class swells—nobility, high-ranking officers in the military, members of Parliament—all of them in elaborate suits and exquisite dresses. Her own dress uniform, as crisply as it was pressed and as shiny the buttons, seemed shabby in comparison.

He led her around a hedge wall down a marble stairway, and her breath was almost taken away.

The royal courtyard was a splendor of colors in bloom. Jerinne had never learned anything about flowers, but now she was overwhelmed by the beauty and spectacle before her.

"You all right, Miss Fendall?" Samsell asked.

"It's a lot to take in." Amaya Tyrell, Adept of the Tarian order, was at her side. "I mean, I've never seen its equal."

"That's for certain," Jerinne said.

"Miss Tyrell," Samsell said, "I never had the opportunity to personally thank you for your role in defending the integrity of this election."

"I appreciate your thanks," Amaya said with a nod. "That's pretty much why Jerinne and I are here. Though if you ask me, the entire third-year Initiate cohort should have been invited."

Samsell gave a weak smile. "I was not consulted, on many things."

"Not blaming you," Amaya said. She hooked her arm around Jerinne's. "Shall we, Initiate?"

"Of course, Madam Tyrell," Jerinne said.

The sun was already high and unseasonably warm for the end of Oscan. Usually by now the trees would be resplendent with golds and reds, but many were still bright green.

"You're slightly out of uniform," Amaya said once they were away from Samsell and down the walkway, to the area where many of the guests were milling about with drinks and food, chattering away about whatever the gossip of the day was.

"I'm of the opinion that the dress uniform could use gloves," Jerinne said, holding out her hand for Amaya to inspect. "I think they go quite nicely."

"I don't disagree," Amaya said. "But the Grandmaster is here. He will also notice, and he will probably say something."

"Oh no," Jerinne said flatly. "Perhaps I'll lose ranking among the third-years."

"Don't joke," Amaya said. "You haven't been ranked on the bottom in two months."

While true, she had still been in the lower half. Jerinne's time of being repeatedly ranked dead last ended shortly after mentors had been assigned. She had assumed it had been an orchestration to specifically deny her a formal mentor.

Dayne's position as her mentor was, after all, unofficial and informal. Denied a proper mentorship with one of the Masters or Adepts, Madam Tyrell—

Amaya, she corrected herself.

Amaya wanted Jerinne and Dayne to work together, away from the rest of the Tarians at the chapterhouse. She had been vague about why, but Jerinne trusted her.

Jerinne spotted Dayne across the courtyard next to Lady Mirianne, looking slightly uncomfortable talking to several nobles. She noticed that Mirianne was not dressed like most of the noblewomen present, at least the older ones. No flowing dress with crinoline petticoats or whalebone corsets. Instead Lady Mirianne wore a deep blue suit jacket, tight-fit trousers, high boots, and a leather cap.

A glance at the crowd showed that many of the younger noblewomen, while not matching Lady Mirianne's defiant style, wore the same cap.

"We seem to be out of the fashion," she said to Amaya.

"Ah, the Marikar suncap," Amaya said. "She did say she would make it the thing for ladies in Maradaine this season, didn't she?"

Jerinne tried to make her way toward Dayne, but the crowd between them started to move together toward a raised platform. Jerinne didn't see for what purpose at first, but then she noticed several people stepping up on the platform. Including a young man who was devastatingly handsome.

That was not a thing Jerinne had a habit of noticing in any man. That's how pretty he was, that even she had to acknowledge it.

Then she saw the silver circlet he wore on his head, and realized who he was.

"Ladies and lords and gentlepersons of all persuasions," Prince Escaraine said with a voice that washed over the crowd like it was carried by doves. "Thank you all for joining us on this glorious day. We are here, of course, to formally give the royal blessing to the newly elected members of Parliament, so they may start to do the good work of the crown and throne in the name of the king."

The crowd gave a polite smattering of applause.

"Normally, this benediction before the ceremony is given by my sister, but unfortunately she was unable to return to Maradaine at this time."

Jerinne noticed that a few of the noblewomen near her whispered to each other, usually with a throaty chuckle or a sigh of exasperation. Perhaps there was some gossip or poorly kept secret about Princess Carianna. Jerinne didn't know it, nor did she feel a burning need to know it.

"Needless to say, I'm sure she would echo my sentiments on this day, as my cousin the king does, of how blessed we are in this country, that we have stood together for over two centuries, with a continuity of the throne, and continuity of the Parliament. That we have a civilized rule of law, governed by the people, presided over by the blessed line of Maradaine. This is what makes us Druthal, the great jewel in the crown of the world."

More applause, now thunderous.

"And now, can we have the new and re-elected members of Parliament come forward."

The men standing on the back of the platform—twenty-three of them—stepped forward. Jerinne only recognized one of them: Ret Issendel, the former bishop whom Dayne enjoyed arguing with. The rest were just a sea of pompous-looking men in suits.

Jerinne realized she was stuck in the middle of the crowd, no easy way to escape without making a scene. Yet another slog of political theater to endure. She glanced about to see where Dayne was. He, smartly, had placed himself at the back of the crowd. Of course, at his height, standing in front of anyone would be rude. Dayne was many things, but rude was not one of them.

"Now take a knee for his Royal Majesty, King Maradaine the Eighteenth."

Jerinne presumed that was for the prospective members of Parliament, but then everyone in the crowd dropped to their knees as well. Jerinne quickly did the same, as Amaya half-pulled her down to the ground.

The king was so very normal, so average. Prince Escaraine stood on the stage like a presence, as if the light of the sun shone inside him. King Maradaine XVIII walked up in a half slouch, in somber gray clothing that matched his energy, violet mourning sash lazily draped over one shoulder. He just looked exhausted.

"Thank you, cousin," he said quietly. He clapped his hand on the prince's shoulder, and the prince reached up and squeezed the hand briefly. The king stepped away and went to the first new member of Parliament. "Do you pledge to serve this nation, to honor the Rights of Man, to be deliberate and wise as you serve the people, and honor the trust put into you with their just and true votes?"

"I do, in your name, and in the name of God and every saint," the parliamentarian said. The king touched his thumb to the man's forehead and moved on to the next. This ritual continued with each one, with quiet dignity and respectful efficiency. In just a few minutes, they were all pledged and blessed.

"Thank you, all," the king said as he came to the center of the platform. The prince had taken a few steps back to yield the stage to his cousin. "I happily bless these good and true men to serve the office they have been elected to, this great Parliament to serve my throne and my people, to join the other good and true men who continue their diligent work of governing in my name."

"Rise and hail," Prince Escaraine called out. "Welcome these good and true men, and praise be the name of Maradaine the Eighteenth, may his reign be long and grand!"

"Hail!" the crowd called as everyone got to their feet. "Hail Maradaine the Eighteenth, King of Druthal!"

"Never!" a voice shouted from the back. "The True Line lives!"

With a piercing *thwang*, a crossbow bolt flew toward the stage, toward the king. Marshals—unobtrusively on the stage all this time—acted in a snap, grabbing the king and the prince and pulling them off the platform before anyone was hit by the shot.

Jerinne looked around, trying to spot the shooter. Not that she could do much: no shield or sword on her at the moment.

That didn't stop Dayne. She saw him charging across the lawn, running ahead of the swarm of marshals toward the would-be assassin.

Dayne was well aware that the crossbow was aimed right at his heart.

"Friend," he said, holding his hands out and open. "There's no need to do this."

Dayne had been able to get to the young man who had just taken a shot at the king before he could load another quarrel in his crossbow, but only just before.

"The True Line . . ." the young man said, his hand shaking. He didn't look like an assassin at all. If anything, he looked like he barely knew how to hold the weapon. He looked more terrified than anyone.

"You've never taken a life," Dayne said. "I can see that. I can see you believe in your cause, but it doesn't have to make you a killer."

"But the kingdom needs—"

"It needs you to put the crossbow down. No one needs to die today. No one needs to kill today."

Dayne noticed the marshals out of the corner of his eye. All of them had their crossbows trained on the boy. "No one needs to, hear?"

"Get out of the way, Tarian!" one of the marshals said.

"We need a strong hand, a pure throne!" the young man shouted.

"This won't do that," Dayne said. "It will taint the throne with blood. It will taint you with blood."

"No!" the young man said, though now his hand lowered a little with the trembling. "I don't have a choice. I have to."

"Why?" Dayne asked.

"I . . ." His voice cracked, like he was fighting to get the word out. "I . . . have . . . to."

"You can't," Dayne said. "You fire, you won't kill the king. Marshals have already pulled him away." Dayne hadn't seen that, but he assumed that would have been the first thing they did. "All you'll do is hurt me. I don't want you to do that. I don't think you want to do that."

"Please," he said in a hoarse whisper. "I have to. They said that . . . the True Line . . ."

Dayne took a step closer. "That doesn't matter. The only thing I care about is—"

That step panicked the young man, and the crossbow went back up at Dayne. But as soon as it did, no fewer than nine bolts fired into his body. Dayne tried to grab him, grab the crossbow away, but he dropped like a sack.

"Get a Yellowshield!" Dayne called out, looking to the marshals behind him, all of their crossbows expended.

The young man still held up his crossbow as he died, wheezing out one last "The True Line . . ." before he passed.

"Dayne." A hand touched his shoulder. "The rest of you, back away, give him space."

Dayne looked up to see Chief Donavan Samsell. "That didn't need to happen."

"I'm sorry, Dayne," he said. "But it did as soon as he raised his weapon." He guided Dayne away from the scene.

"We could have taken him alive," Dayne said.

"I know. I would have liked to know how he got on the grounds, with the crossbow. There's no reason he should have gotten close enough to take a shot."

Dayne glanced around at the crowd, still watching the scene in shock. Over on the platform, the king and the prince were being taken inside, while the newly sworn members of Parliament came down, marshals standing watch over each of them.

"I meant we don't sentence people to death in this country. And we don't do that if we can help it."

"I know this was unpleasant," Donavan said. He shook his head and sighed. The other marshals were cleaning up the scene, removing the body with quiet efficiency. Dayne was more than a little disturbed by how easy it was for them. How eager the nobility and power players seemed to be to get back to their festivities. He turned back to Donavan.

"Why are you here? I thought you were at the Parliament."

"I should be," Donavan said. "But the High Lord Marshal thought I was needed here, so here I am."

Dayne let a smile come to his lips. Despite the differences between them, he knew Donavan Samsell was a good man who tried to do his job well, miles away from the likes of Chiefs Toscan and Quoyell. "And I think the marshals need you."

"And I'll be needing you," Donavan said. "In just a moment, over there."

Over there, meaning where the members of the press were gathered.

"This role, still?"

Donavan shrugged. "They do like you, and you're good at it." Holding a hand out to keep Dayne from commenting, he added, "We all have so much to do. There is a lot of work ahead right now."

"Good," Dayne said. "Frankly, with Quoyell at the Parliament, I was largely without purpose."

"I won't have it that way," Donavan said with a clap on Dayne's shoulder. "Others want your attention. I'll call you when I'm ready for you."

He walked away as Jerinne approached. "You always find the excitement."

"I was just in the right place," he said. "I'm glad you were invited."

"I'm not," she said. "I'd rather be training. Why are they honoring us this time? We didn't capture Quoyell or the other people behind the atrocity on the Parliament floor."

"For the election," Dayne said. "I know it was a few months ago, but today it matters."

"New Parliament, same as the old one," Jerinne said.

"It is important. And who knows what these new voices will bring."

"Hopefully some new ideas." Bishop Ret Issendel—or rather, Good Mister Issendel, 10th Chair of Scaloi—approached with another one of the new members. "It's good to see you, Dayne."

Dayne took his hand warmly. Despite not agreeing with Ret's politics, Dayne liked the man quite a bit. They both had one strong piece of common ground: they believed in peaceful solutions.

"How was your trip home?" Dayne asked.

"My affairs are in order," Ret said. "Though I will miss the hot rains of Korifina."

"It's pretty damn warm here," his colleague said. "Ain't right." He had an unusual accent for a member of Parliament—no sense of educational refinement. He talked like a stevedore from the Kyst docks.

"But right now, Korifina is hot, and it's a luscious, moist heat that fills your bones. Maradaine is dry."

"Also ain't right."

"Dayne, have you met Golman Haberneck? The new 10th Chair of Sauriya?"

"I have not met any of the new members, save you," Dayne said. He offered his hand to Haberneck. "Hi, I'm Dayne. Dayne Heldrin of the Tarian Order."

"I know who you are," Haberneck said, taking Dayne's hand with a grip that matched his dockworker accent. He then pointed a meaty finger at Jerinne. "And you. You two get things done, and that's what this city needs. What this whole blasted country needs. With your pardon, Rev."

"I'm not a member of the clergy anymore, Golman," Ret said. "Feel free to speak as profanely as you please."

"Tenth chair of Sauriya," Jerinne said quietly. "It's a pleasure to meet you. If you'll excuse me." She went off toward the banquet table.

"I say something wrong?" Haberneck asked.

Dayne realized exactly what had upset her. "You're replacing Mister Seabrook. She was . . . he was killed under her protection."

"Oh, I'm a rutting fool," Haberneck said. He looked over to where Jerinne went. "Apologizing would just make it worse. I'll let her be."

Ret cleared his throat. "Golman wanted a word with you about a security concern."

"I don't know much about that yet," Dayne said.

"It's not about the Parliament itself," Haberneck said. "But rather—"

"Dayne!" Donavan Samsell came back over, taking Dayne by the shoulder. "My apologies, gentlemen, but duty calls us."

"Of course," Ret said.

"I'll find you later," Haberneck said.

Donavan guided Dayne over to the podium where members of the press were gathered about. "I know you hate this, but about the assassin—"

Dayne sighed. He understood exactly what was expected of him. "I'll say we are pleased a greater tragedy was averted but we will need time to investigate before we have any further answers."

"Perfect," Donavan said. "See, you are very good at this."

Dayne refrained from sighing. Donavan was right, and that was probably a good thing. Dayne was well aware he would never be a true member of the Tarian Order. His mistakes had already made him enemies, and in a few months, his third year of Candidacy would end, and he would leave the Order forever.

In that time he needed to reconcile what meaning his life would have without it.

Hemmit Eyairin never would have imagined that when he launched *The Veracity Press* with his two closest friends, it would reach the point where he was covering the Royal Authentication of the Parliament. He had written about it before, of course. Last year he had published a scathing piece on how decadent and depraved the event was, how it showed the royal and ruling classes as more concerned with their own comforts than the needs of the people.

Now he was an invited guest. Now *The Veracity Press* was backed and funded. It was still the same newssheet, no change in tone or viewpoint. They continued to call out the Parliament, the nobility, the corruption against the people of Maradaine and Druthal. But now they could print more, pay the paperboys better, reach far more readers. Thanks to Lady Mirianne Henson.

Thanks to her, and thanks to Dayne, they had funding and they had access. Which gave them the opportunity to ask hard questions of the powerful.

"These pastries are incredible," Lin said as she took three more off the tray. Lin Shartien, reporter, dancer, and mage. Always brilliant, beautiful, and hungry. She was enjoying the decadence of the event far more than she probably should, but Hemmit could hardly blame her for that.

The Royal Gardens of King Maradaine XVIII were quite spectacular, and while the expense that went into cultivating and maintaining them had to be enormous, Hemmit had to admire the craft behind it. That money, he told himself, was providing jobs for common people who worked the grounds. They were skilled craftspeople and artists, and patronage of such people was for the common good.

Just like their own patronage was.

"You've got a guilty face," Lin said, her typically rich Linjari accent subdued.

"Don't you think we've gone too far, being at something like this?"

"You're sounding like Maresh," she said. "There's no purity in not getting our stories out there."

Maresh Niol, who handled the art for the *Veracity*, had opted to stay at the press office. They had a proper office now. Maresh had been increasingly vocal about his discomfort with being funded by a member of the peerage. Hemmit understood where he was coming from, but it wasn't as if Lady Mirianne had ever asked them to change a story or curb their rhetoric. If anything, she encouraged them to write exactly what they wished.

"Is there a risk of getting corrupted, though?"

"For you? Never." Amaya Tyrell, the young Adept of the Tarian Order, had approached quietly. She looked stunning and powerful in her dress uniform, her dark hair artfully styled to cascade down one side of her face.

"Good to see a friendly face," he said.

"I am surprised to see you here," she said. "But it's good to see you as well. Both of you."

"We hear the Tarians will be more active in the security of the Parliament," Lin said. "Any thoughts?"

"I hadn't heard about that myself, but it makes sense," Amaya said. "You have to ask yourself how many failures the marshals would oversee."

"Quote you?" Hemmit asked.

"I would prefer not," she said. She pointed across the lawn. "It looks like the other members of the press are gathering over there, near Dayne. I imagine he's going to make an official statement in a moment."

"We should head over," Lin said, eating another pastry. She started to walk over, and Hemmit made to follow her before Amaya put a hand on his arm.

"I'd like to get a word with you alone later," she said.

"You found something?" he asked. About what did not need saying—the two of them had had many words alone in the past months, including several conversations about what they had been calling the Conspiracy of the Grand Ten. They still had no hard evidence that such a conspiracy truly existed, but despite that, they were both convinced it did.

"Maybe," she said. She pointed across the crowd to a woman in a gray uniform. "You know who that is?"

"No," Hemmit said.

"Possibly the most powerful woman in the country right now. Colonel Silla Altarn of Druth Intelligence. Mage on the Colonel's Table."

"All right," he said. "What about her?"

"Not sure yet. But I'm watching her, and who she's watching." She shook her head. "Maybe nothing. Your apartment, this afternoon?"

He nodded, and she gave his arm a friendly squeeze before walking off. Hemmit ran to catch up with Lin, and the two of them reached the gathering around Dayne and a handful of marshals.

"Going forward, we will have the manpower to better provide both security for the members of Parliament and the facility itself, while also being able to oversee each other, and prevent further incidents."

"What about the incident today?" Harns from *Throne and Chairs* asked. "Was that a failure of the marshals?"

"The incident today was not a failure, at least in terms of security," one of the marshals said. "Isn't that right, Heldrin?"

"An attempt was made on the king's life, and it was prevented," Dayne said. "While it would have been preferable to capture the man alive, it demonstrated how capable the marshals are at the task of protecting their charges. The Tarian Order is looking forward to the partnership with them."

"Mister Heldrin, you took personal action at this incident," a young woman stated. Hemmit knew her by reputation—Cairns, from the *High Maradaine Gazette*. "Just as you did with the incident with Tharek Pell, the rescue of the Scallic Ballots, the atrocity on the Parliament floor."

"Is there a question?" Dayne asked.

"Do you feel a personal charge to take such action? Do you feel like you, Dayne Heldrin of the Tarian Order, are the one single hero in this city who can save us?"

"Of course not," Dayne said. "This city—it's full of so many good people. People who are fighting every day to make it better, make it safer. People who reach out to help their neighbors, people who extend a hand to whoever needs it. This city is full of heroes, both in the light and the shadows. Every part of this city, every alley and neighborhood, has a champion ready to rise up and do what's right. I'm honored if you count me among them, but I would honor every one of them as well, wherever they're found."

Chapter 2

"**T**WO RASPERS, EXTRA MUSTARD."

Veranix Calbert looked a little conspicuous ordering sausage sandwiches from a Dentonhill food stand in his University of Maradaine uniform, even if he was just a block from campus. He was the only student in the line, the rest were workers from the chicken house. He was amazed those folks could even eat, given how they stank of chicken filth and blood.

He wasn't the only student in the square, even if he was the only one in uniform. While he paid for his sausages, he kept his eye on the two he came here to watch. Fourth-years, boy and girl together, both from the social houses. They were dressed like they were trying to fit in with the Dentonhill crowd, but they were too clean, clothes looking like the fashionable idea of working class. They stood out easily, not that anyone here really cared about the two of them.

Anyone except Veranix and his friends.

Veranix watched the pair as they approached a fellow

leaning against a lamppost. He kept his attention on them while eating his raspers—dry and overcooked—as they had a brief conversation with the fellow. Things exchanged hands and they left, heading back to the campus gate. Veranix ate the last bit of sausage and started walking, so he'd go right past them. He charged up just a bare hint of magic, drawing the *numinic* energy around him and channeling it into his hands. As he passed the couple, he sent that energy out. No color, no flash, no sound, just a wash of *numinic* energy over them. He glanced back at the campus gates, where Delmin Sarren was chatting up one of the cadets on guard duty. Delmin looked up for a moment and nodded. Delmin wasn't a very good practical mage, but he was an excellent magical tracker. This was a new trick the two of them had been practicing: Veranix "tagging" someone magically, and Delmin tracking them afterward. Delmin had these two in his sights, and he'd find where they went, where they lived, and then he'd use his authority as prefect to bust them for trafficking *effitte* onto campus.

Veranix often leaned toward using force to stop the *effitte* trade, but not against students on campus. Delmin insisted that they be dealt with through the proper system, until it proved corrupt.

Force was what he had in mind for the fellow who sold them the *effitte*. Now he had identified the dealer, the next step was Mila.

Mila Kendish, new first-year at U of M, street girl from the west side of town, was pretty damn incredible. She had disguised herself as one of the chicken house workers, unrecognizable as a student or even as herself, and was walking past the lamppost. She didn't even slow down, and to Veranix's eye, never touched the seller. Despite that, she gave Veranix a quick nod. She had grabbed the fellow's *effitte* stash.

The girl had hands like magic, and quite the devious

mind, since she had come up with this plan. Veranix knew she had learned her craft with the Rynax brothers, a pair of real schemers from the west side who worked elaborate heists.

As quickly as she had brushed by the dealer, she was out of sight.

Someone else came up to the dealer, and after their brief exchange, he was looking put out. He checked his coat pockets, and then again, and looked all around him. Veranix pretended not to make too much note of him as the dealer, swearing a hot streak, stormed off down the road.

Veranix followed, but not as Veranix Calbert, magic student at the University of Maradaine.

He slipped into an alley, and with a magically powered bound, leaped up to the top of the roof while shedding the illusion of his uniform.

Now he was the Thorn—crimson flowing cloak and hood, shading magic hiding his face. Fighting staff and a quiver of arrows on his back, magical rope at his belt, and his brand-new bow in his hand.

He was excited to try the new bow, finally.

From the rooftop he stalked after the dealer until he went down another alley. He knocked on one basement door and then went in.

Veranix dropped down to the ground, and drawing two arrows—normal ones, not the gifts from Verci Rynax—he kicked the door open and went in.

A small storeroom, and four guys, including the one he had followed, standing among crates of *effitte*.

Perfect.

"Gentlemen," he said as he drew back the pair of arrows. "I'm the Thorn. Perhaps you've heard of me."

He loosed the arrows, and allowed a smile to come to his face. He was going to enjoy knocking these dealers about, and destroying the poison they were selling. He'd keep doing that until it, and the entire empire of drugs and death Willem Fenmere was running, were wiped out of the city.

Inspector Second Class Minox Welling needed more lamp oil.

Whoever designed the archive room at the Inemar Constabulary stationhouse clearly did not expect anyone to be staying in the archives for extended periods. There was almost no natural light. The few windows were small and at the top of the wall—street level in the basement—and were on the north side of the building. It seemed an absurd design for a room devoted to finding and reading written records.

Even more absurd was the limited budget for lamp oil, and despite Captain Cinellan's promises that he would try to get Minox more, he had almost run out for the month, and today was only the twenty-fifth of Oscan. In addition, his extended time down here had begun on the sixth. Without a significant change in the near future, his coming months would be largely in the dark.

His exile to the archive room—technically to desk duty, but that translated to him being down in the archives much of the day—was to be one hundred days, of which nineteen had passed. And he was already feeling his grip on normality slipping away. He needed the work, to be on the streets, dealing with cases and, hopefully, making the city safer.

But instead he was down here, him and his dangerous magical hand.

Minox decided to solve at least one problem by using his hand as a light source. It wasn't efficient—the use of magic taxed him, and he couldn't efficiently use his hand to look through files and as a light source at the same time. If he had received proper training in magic, he might be able to create the light without it having to come from the hand itself. But he remained untrained, Uncircled, and outcast among mages and the Constabulary.

Despite all that, he was determined to make the most of his exile, to use it as an opportunity. The archives were in a frightful state—the chief archivist clerk had passed away six months before, and no one had been hired to take her place. Plus, she had clearly grown negligent in her later years.

Minox had been spending the last nineteen days making some sense and order out of things, organizing the files that represented over twenty years' worth of investigations, cases, and arrests. He found a letter detailing the process of sending files to the City Archivist— that must be an astounding library of records, over on the north side of the city—but those protocols had not been followed for some time. He had hoped for some assistance, but no one was available.

His cousin Nyla hadn't been back to work since her encounter with the killer called Sholiar. And his sister Corrie—

Corrie was gone. Maybe dead. He was holding out hope that she was alive, and that somewhere in these files was the clue that would help him find her.

"Welling, you down here?" That was Inspector First Class Henfir Mirrell, currently the Chief Inspector of the Grand Inspection Unit. A post that was far from deserved, but he had been promoted to it nonetheless.

"The light must make that apparent," Minox called back.

Mirrell came around the file cabinets to Minox, discomfort plain on his face. Probably from the bright glow emanating from Minox's left hand.

"Everything all right down here?" Mirrell asked.

"Lamp oil is, apparently, at a premium, but I'm making do," Minox said. "Do you need me for something?"

"Yeah, something scratching at the back of my head. We busted up that ring that was abducting kids, working out of the docks, right?"

"There was an arrest of a group of abductors, yes," Minox said. "Let me guess—a new surge in missing children."

"Yeah," Mirrell said. "Maybe it's connected, maybe it's not. But it's again mostly focused in Dentonhill, though I've sent inquiries to other stationhouses. A few similar reports." He held up a handful of files.

"Are you asking my opinion?"

"Well, I think they could be more connected with the old cases, not sure. There's some fanciful stories, of course."

"A great giant taking children?" Minox asked.

Recognition flashed over Mirrell's face. "Yeah."

So there was something connected. "I'll look it over, see what I can determine."

"Good," Mirrell said. "And if you figure something out, I'll send Kellman and Tricky out to run it down."

Minox scoffed reflexively at that. Of course, he would be asked to do the deduction work, even stuck in here. Others would actually be in the field.

"Sorry," Mirrell said. "I know you and Tricky are still at odds. Just let me know what you find."

"Always," Minox said, taking the files to the archivist desk he had claimed.

Mirrell believed that Minox and Inspector Rainey were at odds. That was their current subterfuge, a ruse for them to privately investigate the corruption in the Constabulary and the city, by giving the appearance of division.

Unfortunately, over the past nineteen days, that investigation hadn't progressed much. Minox had largely been sorting through files, earmarking the ones that could apply to such corruption, or to cases he had considered unresolved. Inspector Rainey had had her own problems to deal with.

Satrine Rainey was an Inspector Second Class, and she shouldn't have to deal with an altercation in a corner grocer like she was a fresh-from-cadethood footpatrol officer. Of course, she never had been a cadet or served as footpatrol, having started her Constabulary career late in life as an inspector, so perhaps this was some act of balance. A test the saints or sinners were putting on her to teach her humility.

Satrine was not interested in having divine humility thrust upon her.

She ran to the corner of Jent and Tannen on the summons of a winded and terrified page. He had found her all the way in Hashrow, on the north side of the city, where she and Inspector Kellman had been working another crime scene that was beneath their skills. Old man, killed in an alley over the coins in his pocket. The only reason why they had been called out at all was because the man had been a retired inspector, but there was no reason to believe there was a case there.

This was an emergency that had required her, so she had whistle-galloped back to Inemar, until her horse had given out on her at Promenade. She had run the rest of the way while Kellman dealt with the exhausted horses.

She got to the grocer shop, finding a small crowd formed around the place. They gave a wide berth to the door and the patrolmen.

"What do we have?" Satrine asked the two patrol officers who were outside the grocer, both of them with their crossbows up and their fingers on the trigger. "And put those down."

"But—"

"You're likely to fire by accident and hurt a by-stander," she said.

They lowered their weapons. "Fight broke out between the proprietor and a customer. We think they're both armed. Another customer had run out and called us, and when we tried to come in, the customer shouted they'd shoot anyone but you."

"Any stick besides the 'dirty spec Tricky Rainey,'" the other officer said. "Not my words, ma'am."

"Not the worst I've been called this month," Satrine said. "So the proprietor and the customer are in there? No one else?"

"As far as we know," one said.

"All right," Satrine said, pulling out her crossbow. "Call for a Yellowshield. Someone will probably need them in a minute."

She checked her crossbow—loaded with a blunt-tip. She might need to incapacitate someone, but she didn't want to go further than that.

"This is Inspector Rainey!" she called out. "Coming in!"

"Trini, you tell this rutting posk to get off my neck!"

"This old lady—"

The proprietor and the customer were both on the floor in the back, like they had wrestled each other into a lock and now had blades at each other's throats. Satrine was tempted to let them finish the job, but that wouldn't be fair to the grocer.

"Mom, drop the damned knife."

"He tried to kill me!"

"She tried to rob my store!"

"Those rutting kids were—"

"Mother!" Satrine shouted. "Drop the knife or by every saint I will shoot you with this crossbow and iron you and drag you down to the stationhouse. Are you going to make me do that?"

Her mother let go of the knife.

"Sir, now disentangle yourself from her and step away."

The grocer pulled himself off of Satrine's mother and scurried behind his counter. "You take her out of here."

"I will," Satrine said. "Get up, Mother."

Berana Hace, once Berana Carthas, got to her feet, looking like she wanted to slap Satrine. She was gray and drawn, but still looked like she could scrap like she used to. Satrine was perfectly eager to give her a scrap right back, but her mother didn't start anything this time.

"What did you take?"

"Nothing! It was those kids!"

"You told them to take it," the grocer said.

"I did not," she said. "Like I'd bother."

"What does she owe you?" Satrine asked.

"Twelve ticks," he said.

"Pay the man, Mother."

"I ain't got that."

"What happened to the money I gave you?"

"Spent it."

Satrine sighed. She had gotten a raise with the promotion to Inspector Second Class, and with her mother released from Quarrygate around the same time, brand-new expenses.

"I don't even—" Satrine pulled three five-tick coins out of her pocket and put them on the counter. "Keep the change and keep this to yourself."

"She can't come in here anymore," the grocer said.

Satrine grabbed her mother by the arm and dragged her out.

"We done?" one of the patrolmen asked.

"Handled," Satrine said. "Back on your beat."

The patrolmen, thankfully, didn't argue.

"And you," she said to her mother. "You go back to Phillen's apartment and you stay there."

"I'm not doing what you tell me—"

"You stay there, or I will iron you up and drag you

in," Satrine said. "I'll come by day after tomorrow and take you to church."

"I ain't going to church."

"You and I will go to weekly service at Saint Limarre's," Satrine said. "Don't make me waste time hunting you down, because Phillen will get every page in Inemar to All-Eyes you."

"Rutting blazes," her mother said. "What did I do to deserve two rotten children who are both rutting sticks?"

Satrine could provide her with a list, but held her tongue. Her mother stomped off down the street toward Phillen's place.

"Everything all right?" Inspector Kellman asked, looking harried as he guided two spent horses to her.

"Fine as can be expected," she said. Kellman had been more than accommodating about the new situation with her mother since they had partnered up. He was a dull block compared to Welling—just about anyone would be—but he was decent enough. There were worse fates than partnering with him.

Like whatever happened to Corrie.

"We got something?" she asked, noticing he was holding a new page note.

"Some window-cracking on the east side."

At least it wasn't another murder. The last thing Satrine needed was for today to be any more gruesome.

"All right, Kellman. Let's get to work."

"Let's get to work!" Verci Rynax called out to his brother as he came down the back stairway from the apartments to the workshop in the back of the Rynax Gadgeterium. He actually hoped Asti was in the shop. Asti was supposed to be out front, taking care of customers, while Verci was building and repairing in the back.

That's how it was supposed to be. But Asti would still

slip out for extended periods to "check on something" or "keep an eye on a situation." The neighborhood was relatively calm, no one was trying to kill or muscle them, at least not today, and they weren't directly planning to go at anyone in the near future. Right now, it was legitimate business for two reformed thieves.

But Asti was Asti. As much as he talked about "clean, honest lives," Asti wasn't handling the day-to-day of it well.

"Are you talking to me?" Raychelle, Verci's wife, asked as she came in from the front.

"I hoped I was talking to Asti, but I'm guessing he stepped out. Did you just come in?"

"I did," she said.

That meant there was something wrong with the bell on the door, which was the most basic bit of gadgetry in the whole place. For that to not be working was downright embarrassing. Verci grabbed a couple tools and went to the front of the store. Everything looked in order, nothing missing. The lockbox under the counter was in place.

Verci tried the door. The bell rang just fine.

"Did it ring when you came in?"

"Yes," Raych said. "Maybe you just weren't paying attention?"

"Possibly," Verci said. "I had told Asti I was going upstairs for a bit. Where did he go?"

"I saw him go past the bakery," Raych said. "Which is why I came over. Where did he go?"

"Asti being Asti," Verci said, hoping that would explain it.

"I think," Raych said carefully, "that Asti likes the idea of going straight, having a nice, normal life as legitimate shopkeepers. But the reality of it—"

"Drives him crazy?"

"I wasn't going to say that, exactly."

"Because he's already crazy?"

"I definitely wasn't going to say that," she said. "He's troubled, of course, but—"

"You're trying too hard to be kind," Verci said. Asti was far from stable, still occasionally having violent blackouts, muttering to empty air. Verci knew there was more to it, but Asti wasn't telling him.

Maybe that's where Asti was going all these times. Maybe he had someone to talk to.

"How's today been?"

"Actually pretty good," Verci said. The Rynax Gadgeterium had only been open for a few days, but with Terrentin coming up, there were people looking for toys and other gadgets to give as gifts. "We actually got a pair of fellows who came out here from across town. So word is getting out."

"Legitimate business is a beautiful thing," she said. She glanced at the satchel behind the counter. "So does that have to be there?"

The satchel had Verci's darts, his spring gauntlet and the various chemical-filled shots for it, as well as climbing tools, window-cutting and lockpicking tools, a bandage kit, a few other helpful gadgets, and a leather coat with iron plates.

Everything Verci might need if things went bad.

"Where would you want it?" Verci asked.

"I don't know, I just—I wish it wasn't necessary."

"Someday it won't be, I hope. But in this neighborhood, in our lives, love," Verci said, coming closer to her and wrapping his arms around her waist, "I'm afraid that day might never come."

"I hate living our lives afraid."

"Think of it as 'prepared.'"

She kissed him quickly. "I can live with prepared. I would like a less bloody version of prepared, but, well . . ."

"You know what our lives are like."

"But that's only there for emergency, right?" she asked. "You're not going out looking for anything?"

"I definitely am not," Verci said. "I really hope that bag stays right where it is."

Though he couldn't speak for what Asti hoped.

"I see her, you know," Asti Rynax said quietly. "Sometimes right in front of me, sometimes in the corner of my eye. But she's there, all the time."

Kimber, the sweet-faced proprietress of her namesake tavern, came a little closer to him, not saying anything. This was what she had done for him for months, since the night at Henterman's, since the fire, since . . . really since coming back from Paktphon. She hadn't pushed for anything from him that he wasn't ready to give—which he appreciated—but she had been there, with quiet reserve, always ready to listen. And usually bring him to Saint Bridget's Church afterward.

"It wasn't always like that," he went on. "But it started after Henterman's, and it's been pretty constant for the past few days."

"You mean the woman who betrayed you," she said.

"Liora Rand," Asti said, as if saying her name out loud would deny her power. "She didn't just betray me. She traded me to the Poasians, who tortured and broke me. And put something in my head."

He hadn't told this to Kimber before. He had barely told anyone—Verci, Mila, that was it, and neither of them knew all of it. But he needed to say it. And Kimber had already seen the worst of him, what he became when he let go, and she was still here with patient kindness.

"What does she say?"

"Things I already know. Things I don't want to admit to myself."

"Does she tell you that you've saved this neighborhood?" Kimber asked. "And the people who live here?"

"No, of course not."

"Then she tells you lies," Kimber said. "That's all she is. A liar."

Liora—the one he saw out of the corner of his eye, sitting in a chair with a glass of wine—just raised her glass quietly.

"I should get back. Verci will wonder where I am."

"No church service today?" Kimber asked.

"Maybe tonight," Asti said.

She gently touched his cheek. "Maybe. I'll be bringing Jared Scall as well." She pointed to Jared, sitting at a table in the corner. The neighborhood butcher was easily on his third beer, despite it only being early afternoon. He sat slumped. Asti couldn't blame him. He had lost almost everything in the fire.

"At least he's not still carrying his mace around."

"He is," Kimber said. "I take it from him when he comes in here, though."

"Wise," Asti said. "I'll try to come by later."

"I'll be here for you."

Asti left Kimber's and went down the alley that was the fastest route to Junk Avenue, to the Gadgeterium. He had only gotten a few steps when he heard a wheezing voice.

"Help—you gotta—"

A tiny person lay in the refuse—Asti wouldn't have even noticed him if he hadn't spoken. Asti knelt down and turned him over.

"Tarvis," Asti said. He hadn't seen the angry little boy in months, and now he looked worse than ever. Pale, down to his bones. Scrapes and scratches all over his face, dirt and filth on his scraps of clothing. "What happened?"

Tarvis's eyes focused on him. "Rynax," he whispered. "You gotta—stop—giant."

Asti didn't know what had happened, but he cradled the little boy in his arms and ran back to Kimber's.

Chapter 3

THE PARLIAMENT BUILDING WAS A chaos of functionaries and staff, marshals and Tarians and Spathians, and the actual members of Parliament themselves. They all went through the administrative work of assigning offices, coordinating security schedules, and for the custodians, trying to keep the floors clean through it all.

Dayne went down to the marshal offices briefly, but there the chaos was at its peak. Donavan was keeping charge, giving out assignments, and talking with the two elite masters about chain of command and oversight of the joint force.

Dayne watched that from a distance, as it seemed clear his input would not be welcome from either Tarian Master Gerald or Spathian Master Meralister. Which showed him just how empty and feckless his posting as a "liaison" really was. They were liaising just fine without him.

If all they needed was someone with a strong jaw and

clean uniform to talk to the press, Dayne would serve as he was ordered. He knew it was a waste of his time and his talent. He thought he had proven that enough, proven his value to the Tarians, to the august body of the Parliament.

He was reminded how little his efforts mattered as he went back up the stairs toward his apartments. He passed three members of Parliament: the 5th, 7th, and 9th Chairs from Yinara, respectively. Ruprect, Jude, and Samuel Benedict. Cousins to each other, uncles all to Lenick Benedict, the young boy who would spend his life in rolling chairs thanks to Dayne's failure. They all looked upon Dayne with utter contempt. They didn't speak. They didn't have to.

They still held such resentment for Dayne, even after he had saved Jude's life on the Parliament floor. Surely the heart of the 1st Chair from Yinara, Wesley Benedict, hadn't softened either. He was the one who led the Parliamentary Committee overseeing the Elite Orders, he was the one who would prevent Dayne's advancement to the rank of Adept, forcing him out of the Tarian Order forever.

Dayne slipped through the crowds as best as a man his size could, to make his way to his own apartments. If he was needed to talk to the press again, he could be easily found. That was why he was quartered here instead of at the Tarian Chapterhouse, after all.

Though he wondered if he just moved to Lady Mirianne's household, would anyone even care?

"Heldrin!" someone called. Dayne turned to see that new Member of Parliament—Haberneck?—approaching him.

"Good Mister Haberneck," Dayne said. "Are you lost? I know the corridors can be a bit confusing, but this area is mostly quarters for the building staff."

"No, Heldrin, I was looking for you."

"For me?" Dayne asked. He had wanted to tell Dayne

something before he was pulled away to talk to the press. "Is there something I can help you with, sir? I'm really not . . ."

"Don't call me 'sir,'" Haberneck said. "I'll tell you, this whole business is pretty strange, but the strangest is how everyone's talking to me. I ain't seen anything like it."

"There is a protocol of address, Mister Haberneck," Dayne said. "It's supposed to prevent—"

"I know the why of it, Heldrin. It's mostly hot wind off a stinking sea. But you . . . you seem like the sort who has his head on straight, not like the rest of these folks. They all got their cravats a little tight."

"I don't know about that," Dayne said. "But there's something you need? Perhaps you should go to the marshals or—"

"No, I . . ." Haberneck shook his head. "I already tried that. Let me start from the top. I know most of the folks in here, they're living in fancy houses that are gifts from barons, or something like that. I ain't going to do anything of the sort. I got some kin who live on the south side, so I'm staying near them, helping them out. Nice enough flop in Dentonhill, rent is a tenth of the place I was told to get."

"And you're worried about the security for the house?" Dayne asked.

"Nah," Haberneck said. "I mean, this is not for me. Like I said, I got kin there, they got neighbors, and they're talking to me. Things are going on, and apparently the sticks are no help. I asked around, no official on this level wants to help, because it would be Constabulary jurisdiction. I realized, I needed to be talking to someone who might be a little more . . . unofficial."

"Which brought you to me."

"Ret told me what you've done. You saved the ballots, you stopped Tharek, you rescued the folks down there on the Parliament floor when the marshals had their thumbs in their ears . . ."

"That isn't fair to—"

"Point is, you're a guy who *does*. Maybe you can come and do something down there."

Dayne was certainly interested, and there was nothing else of value being asked of him. "What's going on?"

"Kids are going missing," Haberneck said. "Apparently, it's always been a thing, but in the past week, it's spiked up something fierce. And nobody gives a damn."

"Children?" Dayne asked. "You have my attention."

Jerinne found the Tarian Chapterhouse oddly subdued when she returned to it after the Palace Garden event. Normally in the afternoon there was a fair amount of activity going on, both on the grounds and in the training room. Instead the place was nearly deserted, save for the staff going about their tasks of cleaning and preparing meals.

Even the baths and bunkrooms were empty.

She took off her dress uniform and put on her cottons, contemplating how nice it would be to just lie down on her bunk with no one else around. She almost never got a chance to do that.

But that also felt like wasting daylight.

She made her way to the training room, which she had all to herself for once. She started with a series of stretches, and then cycling through the calisthenics routine the Initiates had been doing each day. Then she took a quarterstaff off the wall and went through her paces. As strong as she could, as fast as she could, not letting up or slowing down. She pushed herself, pushed through the pain, let herself feel it in her bones, revel in it.

She swept the staff out, and to her surprise it made contact.

"Intense," Vien Reston, first-year Candidate, said with a wicked smile, having blocked the sweep with her own staff. "You didn't even notice me come in."

"Probably not wise," Jerinne said, "to be so in the moment to ignore my surroundings."

Vien brought up her staff, circling it around to then sweep at Jerinne's feet. Jerinne dove over it, rolled onto her feet, and spun on her heel to strike Vien. Vien was already there with the block. Then they started to spar in earnest: full strength, full speed. If either of them missed a block or a dodge, they could end up in the infirmary.

"Where is everyone?" Jerinne asked.

"Where were you this morning?" Vien asked back, not losing her pace for even a breath. "Oh, right, you were at the Royal Gardens. How was that?"

"Boring and intense at the same time. Assassin tried to kill the king. But yet, so many speeches."

"Assassin? That's exciting."

"Dayne and the marshals stopped him. And Madam Tyrell was there, but she went off somewhere else afterward." Jerinne stopped herself from saying "Amaya" in front of Vien. As far as Vien, or anyone else in the order was concerned, there was no familiar relationship between Jerinne and Amaya. Nor did she have the informal, unofficial mentorship under Dayne.

"She didn't tell me," Vien said. Hard jab. Low swipe. Kick. Perfect form, no pattern. Savage poetry.

"So where is everyone?"

"Most of the Adepts and Candidates are getting assigned details for security of the Parliament, and members of Parliament. And that meant the other third-years went with their mentors."

"No assignment for you?"

Overhead hammer. "I have an assignment. Initiate Drill."

"So where are the first- and second-years?"

"Took them for a run," Vien said. "A good ten-mile one. Most of them are collapsed on the yard now."

"And you came in here to spar?"

"I came in here for a cool down," Vien said. "But I couldn't pass up the spar."

Jerinne signaled she was done and hopped back a few steps. "I appreciate that. I missed morning training, and—"

"And you don't have the mentor for the rest," Vien said. "Sorry."

"No need," Jerinne said. "It is what it is."

"I'll be gathering the first- and second-years in here in a moment," Vien said. "You're welcome to stay."

She didn't phrase it as an order. Vien had cooled from her initial overzealousness in her position as Initiate Drill. Maybe being a bully lost its appeal when she got beaten by the traitor Osharin.

"I'll pass," Jerinne said. If the other third-years were with their mentors, she'd go seek out Dayne. "I think I'll clean up and do some reading."

"Mind and body," Vien said. "Keep it all sharp."

Jerinne put her staff back on the wall and made her way to the water closet, passing the heaving and wheezing first- and second-year Initiates as she did. After washing off her face, she changed into her regular uniform, belting a sword but forgoing the shield, at least for today. Dayne would be at the Parliament. Maybe he had something interesting planned.

Veranix was quite pleased with how lunch had gone. A storehouse of *effitte* and *efhân* wrecked, the sellers thoroughly chastised and magically tagged so Delmin could track them later. Their funds stolen, which Veranix would discreetly donate to the Lower Trenn Ward, where *effitte* victims were being treated.

Victims like Veranix's mother.

He even had time to drop all the gear back at the safehouse—Mila's term for the hidden bunker Kaiana had found to replace as their headquarters after she moved out of the carriage house—and get his school uniform on before going to class at two bells.

This was his Practical Use of Magic class, first one of the new semester, but it was already shaping up to be radically different than earlier years. Practicals had normally been small, personalized lessons with Professor Alimen in his office in Bolingwood Tower. This class was meeting in the Curtin Forum, a lecture hall that had been repurposed over the summer for the Floor and Beam Competitions of the Grand Collegiate Tournament.

He arrived at the Curtin Forum, a wide-open room with bleacher seating at the edges. Many students were gathering at the bleachers, most of whom Veranix knew in passing.

Magic students.

All of them, it would seem. At least the third- and fourth-year ones.

Veranix went up to Delmin, who was talking to two others that Veranix knew but couldn't remember the names of. Two fourth-year boys, a tall one and a blond one.

"So this is even stranger than I expected," he said to them.

"That's what we were saying," the blond one said. "I've never seen anything like it."

"Even the ladies' school magic students are here," the tall one said, gesturing toward the cluster of young women who kept themselves at some reserve from the boys. "That's never happened."

"I've never had any class with the girls," the blond said.

"It's very odd, indeed," Delmin said. He looked at Veranix, and his eyes went wide for a second. "Been busy?" He made a gesture to his cheek.

Veranix touched his own cheek and felt something slightly wet. He wiped it on his sleeve and realized it was a bit of blood.

"A bit," he said, sending a surge of magic to the sleeve of his shirt to clean the blood. A little trick he had gotten quite good at.

"Everyone, please sit down!" Professor Alimen approached the group with six men and women flanking him. Some of them, Veranix knew as other members of the magic faculty, including Madam Castilane, but others were strangers. Strangers with an odd bearing. "I apologize for the confusion, but if you can all sit and quiet yourselves, we can begin."

The magic students went and sat on the bleachers. Veranix found a place between Delmin and the tall fellow.

Alimen cleared his throat. "I'd like to thank you all for coming here today. I know that none of you are used to this method of doing things, but . . . things are changing. And perhaps that change is for the best. We've been teaching magic the same way for decades, and when 'tradition' is the only reason not to do something, we should take stock in—"

"What Professor Alimen is saying," one of the men behind him said, stepping forward. He wore something that put Veranix in mind of a Constabulary uniform, but gray and with a high collar. "Is we are no longer treating magic studies, in your practical usage here, like some sort of dilettante art."

Veranix and Delmin shared a confused look. That would not be how he would have described the last three years of study.

"But rather," the man said, "a craft that must be honed and tempered."

Alimen coughed. "Students, this is Mister Dresser, he will be—"

"Major Dresser," Dresser said. "I served seventeen years as a specialist mage before retiring from His Majesty's Intelligence Service. I have earned my rank just as surely as you have, Professor, and I expect you to use it."

He looked to the students. "Children, you should also address me as 'Major' or 'Major Dresser,' although 'sir' is fine in a pinch."

That was the bearing of Dresser and the two new instructors. Military.

Delmin's hand went up, and he spoke before any of the faculty called on him. "Professor, is the major a member of the faculty, or is he here as some sort of consultant?"

"Name, son?" Dresser asked.

"Delmin Sarren, fourth-year and prefect. And my question was for Professor Alimen, sir."

Alimen coughed uncomfortably. "Major Dresser, as well as Lieutenant Goodman and Missus Jacknell, will be teaching here as if they were visiting faculty, and will be treated with the same honors and respect due to anyone of professorial rank."

"Now," Dresser said, "this is how things are going to go. There are fifty-five of you, so you will be broken into eleven squads of five."

Veranix immediately disliked the use of the word "squad" in this context.

"You will train every class day with your squad and your designated squad drill instructor."

"Drill instructor" was even worse.

"You will learn to work as a cohesive unit, and you're going to be training together in magical applications that can be used offensively, defensively, and comprehensively."

"I like nothing about this," Delmin whispered to Veranix.

"Your effectiveness will be scored and ranked. You will also be in direct competition with each other, as squads will go head to head in exercises."

Veranix looked to Professor Alimen, who appeared pale and sickened over what was being said.

"Pardon the interruption," Veranix said. "But all of

this sounds explicitly militant in application. How is that appropriate?"

"You all could use a bit of military discipline, for one," Dresser said. "I won't tolerate another untimely outburst."

"You are correct, Mister Calbert," Alimen said. "We are adopting certain techniques, and while they will have a variety of applications for a professional mage, these . . . initiatives will give each of you certain tools which may empower you, should you seek a career as a mage militant."

"And successful completion with acceptable scores will entitle you to an officer's rank," Dresser said.

"Entitle or obligate?" one student asked.

Dresser snapped his fingers, and with a flash of light, that student's mouth was gone. Nothing but unbroken skin on the bottom half of his face. He clawed at the spot where his mouth should be.

"I said no further outbursts," Dresser said. "Consider that an opportunity for advancement. Figure out how to repair yourself."

Alimen waved his hand and the student's mouth reappeared, with a sudden and desperate gasp.

"We do not do that to the students," Alimen said. "Not even under the edicts of the Altarn Initiatives."

Dresser shot Alimen an ugly look when he said "Altarn Initiatives." Perhaps the specific name behind these changes was supposed to be kept secret.

Which made Veranix far more curious about what that meant.

A mystery for the future.

"Come on," he whispered to Delmin. "If we're getting broken into squads, let's make sure we're together."

Amaya Tyrell lay back on Hemmit's bed, perfectly content, if physically drained.

"So, you have something interesting for me?" Hemmit asked.

"I thought that was rather interesting," Amaya said. "If not, I'm doing something wrong."

"Nothing wrong," Hemmit said, leaning over to kiss her. She was no longer in the mood to have that beard in her face, though, and blocked him with her hand.

"Let's not dally all day," she said.

"Right." He took the cue and moved away. "You did say you had something."

"I have thoughts," she said. "Suspicions about this Grand Ten conspiracy that I cannot substantiate."

"All right," he said, getting out of the bed. He went across the room, to a large slateboard that Amaya had always found a little odd for him to own. She suspected he had pilfered it from the Royal College of Maradaine when he was expelled. He wiped the random notes off the board and picked up a piece of chalk. "Let's go over it fresh."

"Right," she said. "We've got reasonable suspicion that there is a group of conspirators in the city who fashion themselves after the original Grand Ten. So, ten players, using the ten titles."

He proceeded to write: Parliamentarian, Man of the People, Lord, Lady, Duchess, Priest, Justice, Soldier, Mage, and Warrior. "And from there?"

"The Warrior we suspect is a Tarian. Likely someone at the Master level. Or Grandmaster Orren himself." She pushed her way through that last sentence, as distasteful as it was. "I don't want to believe it is him, but . . ."

"It can't be discounted," Hemmit said. "It has to be someone with the ability to have Master Denbar sent to Lacanja. Who else can do that?"

"Really just the Grandmaster. But he could be influenced by someone else."

He wrote the Grandmaster's name under "Warrior," followed by "other Masters."

"And then what?" he asked.

"For the mage, I feel like it's got to be someone in Intelligence, in the Red Wolf Circle. Those are the most politically powerful mages."

"You know Lin is in Red Wolf," he said.

"And can we completely trust her?"

"She's not in Intelligence," Hemmit said. "Red Wolf is the largest Mage Circle in the city, and while members do serve in Intelligence, they aren't a Circle with an agenda. Half the members are like Lin—low skill mages who just need Circling to avoid legal trouble."

Amaya wasn't entirely convinced, but said nothing more. Something about Lin Shartien put her on guard. Perhaps it was the her strong Linjari accent, or how easily she dropped it when talking to a source. Lin had a great capacity for deception. Hemmit had told her the whole story of their subterfuge as Wissen and Jala, which led to their infiltration of the Haltom's Patriots.

"But that's why my eye was on Colonel Altarn today," Amaya said. "She's had an unprecedented rise in the past few months. Hardly anyone knew her name a year ago, and now she's seen in the halls of power more and more. Today I watched her intently."

"At the garden?"

"Maybe it's my own suspicion, but I swear, during the ceremony, she looked like she was waiting for something. When the assassin shot . . . it was almost like she was smiling."

"You think she was behind it?"

"There's no way that kid got on the grounds with a crossbow alone."

"The Altarn Initiatives," Hemmit said, snapping his fingers.

"What's that?"

He went to a box behind his desk and thumbed through newsprints, copies of *The Veracity Press*. Taking out a copy, he handed it to her. "Both the University of Maradaine and RCM have had some upheaval in their magic programs. New faculty this semester, and talk of significant changes to the curriculum. I couldn't find anyone to speak on the record, but several members of Lord Preston's Circle expressed concern that these 'Altarn Initiatives' were damaging the core purpose of teaching young mages."

"She's driving curriculum changes at the universities?" Amaya asked, getting out of the bed as she looked over the story. "Put her down. She's a primary candidate for the Mage."

He wrote her name. "What about outside of the realm of political power? There are small Circles that have strong agendas. I've dug up some troubling things about the Firewings, Light and Stone, the Blue Hand . . ."

"Write it all down," she said.

He did, and then under the Parliamentarian, wrote several names. "These are members of Parliament that I definitely have my suspicions about."

"All Traditionalists?" Amaya asked. She put the newssheet down and started stretching her back and shoulders.

"Maybe that's my bias," he said. "But these are the members I have some degree of suspicion about. The kind whose character indicates they'd be involved in something underhanded." He finished writing the names: Vale, Mills, Pollinglen, Bishop, Pike, Millerson, Tellerson, Calinar, Corvi.

"That's a decent list."

"They're also members whose influence stems from connections to the nobility," he said, pointing to the Lord, Lady, and Duchess on the board. "So that's the source."

"How many Duchesses are in the city?" Amaya asked. "I mean, in the whole country, there's, what, forty?"

"Fifty-one," he said. "Four live in Maradaine. But that's presuming our Grand Ten are being that literal about their titles."

"Right," Amaya said. She rotated her neck, and it gave off a few too many pops for her taste.

"Soldier?" he asked.

"Let's find a list of every major, colonel, and general in the city," she said. "If we're being less than literal . . ."

"Naval officers as well," he said. He then wrote on the bottom half of the slateboard. "WHAT DO THEY WANT?"

"Good question," she said. "That's what troubles me."

"That we don't know?" he asked.

"No," she said. "I've been thinking about what the name the Grand Ten implies. The original one, at least in terms of legend, protected the integrity of the Line of Maradaine during the Incursion. Protected the city, protected the young prince when the rest of the royal family was captured or slaughtered—"

"And authenticating his claim to the throne afterward," Hemmit said. "Not to mention building the current government we have."

"So, presuming that they need to have a conspiracy because their intent is revolutionary . . ."

"The True Line nonsense," Hemmit said.

"That is very troubling," she said. "Especially in light of today's assassination attempt." She shook her head, and started gathering her clothing off the floor. "I should be getting back."

"And I should get back down to the press," Hemmit said. "Maresh and Lin will be cross if I'm gone this long."

"Always duty," she said, getting her uniform coat on. She kissed him on a part of his cheek with no beard. "But it's good to get out of my head now and again."

"Pleasure to serve, madam," he said with a mock salute.

"Hush," she said. "I'll keep my eyes open and stay in touch." She left with that. There was still so much they didn't know, but she was certain that Colonel Silla Altarn was someone at the center of the problem.

"We have an Amaya Tyrell problem," Colonel Altarn said.

Lady Mirianne Henson did not care for her tone or her intrusion. No one was even supposed to know about the secret stairwell from the Grand Ten meeting room to Miri's office in Henson's Majestic, but yet Colonel Altarn emerged from Miri's private door with this pronouncement.

"We would have a real problem if one of my managers or secretaries came in and found you," Mirianne said.

Altarn waved her hand, and the door shut and latched. "There. No mundane person could get that door open. And if they did, they'd see an empty room."

"Colonel," Miri said sharply, "we have established rules of contact, which you are breaking."

"Because I don't want a meeting with all ten of us. I want to talk to you about our Amaya Tyrell problem."

"Oh?" Miri asked, closing her books of accounts for the store. It was clear that Colonel Altarn would not leave without some satisfaction, so she wasn't going to get other work done until this was handled. Altarn made that point all the more clear by sitting in the chair opposite Miri's desk. "Is this one of those situations where you act like you are in charge of things, and give me orders, and expect me to take care of them?"

"It's a situation where I have seen a problem, and it's one that you are in a position to handle. I come to you directly to not embarrass you in front of the others."

"So considerate," Mirianne said, standing up from the desk and smoothing out her coat with her hands. "Those uniforms don't do anyone justice, Silla. Do you want me to have one of my designers make something for you?"

Altarn looked down at her gray Intelligence uniform. Miri had noticed that she had taken to wearing it far more often since her promotion to colonel. Like a trophy pelt. It was an odd choice, indeed, since the Intelligence uniform was rarely worn outside of the hallways of the central office. Plus, the cut was deeply unflattering.

"It's perfectly comfortable," Altarn said.

"At least let me have one of my girls measure you and properly fit it," Mirianne said. "I mean, you're already skinny enough. You look like a child playing soldier."

"Stop that game, Lady Mirianne," Altarn said firmly. "I'm not some insecure baron's daughter you can manipulate."

"The offer is open," Miri said. "Though you are the one who mentioned embarrassing me in front of the others."

"I said I didn't want to do it."

"And why would I be embarrassed?"

"Because Amaya Tyrell is directly—even intimately—connected with your paramour, Dayne Heldrin."

"They haven't been intimately connected in years," Miri said. Though frankly she found the idea of Dayne and Amaya intimately connecting again quite invigorating. She would enjoy seeing that. "But I get your point. You feel a problem with Amaya is my problem, specifically. Though I would argue it would be the Grandmaster's."

"He's not quite ready yet to accept the solutions we'll need to use," Altarn said. Miri found that phrasing more than a little troubling, especially given the resources Altarn now had at her disposal. "Amaya Tyrell has been working with one of your newsmen, also. So she's very much your problem."

"I thought she had just taken him as a lover," Miri said. "So the two of them are, what, finding their way into your dirty business?"

"My dirty business is all of ours," Altarn said, though Miri had her doubts about that. There was definitely other business that Silla Altarn had her fingers in, and Miri didn't want to think too much about that.

"Why do you think she's now a problem?"

"I know when I'm being watched. And her attention was firmly on me at the palace today."

"I didn't notice," Miri said.

"She was close to Master Denbar, after all."

That was a point. Master Denbar had gotten too close to the Grandmaster's involvement, to the Grand Ten as a whole. Perhaps he had passed some information on to Amaya before dying, and she had been searching for them all.

They had been careful, but Miri was well aware that no amount of care was foolproof.

"You think she knows about all of us?"

"I think she suspects there is an all of us. As does Hemmit Eyairin—"

"You have an odd love of using full names."

"And we know he's got a connection to that fool from the Patriots who traced his way back to Millerson!"

That was a cause for worry. That boy definitely had figured out far too much, and he had gone completely to ground. And it put Millerson—who thought himself as being in control of things as The Man of the People—in a precarious position. That would require adjustment. "I'm handling Hemmit and the *Veracity*. It's all part of the plan."

"Well, the plan will have to eliminate Miss Tyrell."

"Eliminate?" Miri asked. She went back over to her desk. "No, that would never do. She dies, we might have a martyr. That will drive Hemmit further toward conspiracy."

Not to mention Dayne. She knew, as much as Dayne loved her, his bond with Amaya was deep. He would not let her death go.

"So what do you suggest?"

"If the problem is what she might know, then the solution is simple," Miri said. She unlocked one drawer, and from there, released a panel underneath her desk. She thumbed through the folders inside that secret niche, finding the right one. A plan to handle Amaya, as well as several other problems that had been brewing. If Altarn was so intent on action, now was as good a moment as any to move forward. She handed it over to Altarn. "We discredit her, and thus disempower her. And from there, she will be easy to discourage from further prying. Why kill her when we can make her feckless?"

"This is why I like to deal with you." Altarn took the folder as she stood up. "You always have a plan, and I do relish the way your mind works."

"Here to serve, you and the country, however I can," Miri said. "Please leave the way you came and try not to disturb me here again."

"I do not promise," Altarn said. She looked back down at the uniform. "It's not that bad, is it?"

"I'll arrange for a seamstress to visit your home, discreetly," Mirianne said. "She will be efficient. I know you have many initiatives on your plate right now, and your time is always something I respect."

Altarn shrugged and went out the secret door.

Miri sighed. She knew something like this would come, but it didn't matter. She had plans in place for all of them. Amaya, Jerinne, the ones at the *Veracity*, and of course, Dayne. Especially Dayne. It would break her heart, but when she needed to destroy him, she was prepared.

Chapter 4

DAYNE DID NOT HAVE A proper shield. He had the one the Parliament had given him, hanging on his wall. Far more useful as art than as protection. It was metal, and it was painted in Tarian gray and silver, but it was cheap, light, and flimsy. Dayne would still put it on his arm when he dressed in uniform, for no other reason than it did look appropriate. But he hated the thing. It was a reminder of his counterfeit posting. Still, he was going to meet Haberneck's people in Dentonhill, so it was best to look the part.

He was putting it on his arm when a knock came on the door. "Come," he called, expecting Haberneck. Instead, Jerinne came in, in her full uniform, but lacking the shield.

"It looks like you're about to get into some business," she said. "Need some company?"

"You looking to make yourself useful?" he sent back at her. "Shouldn't you be—"

"Every other third-year is with their mentors, who are getting protection details with Parliament members."

"Ah," he said. "Well, I'm about to head across the river with—ah, there you are."

Haberneck had walked in. "Are we ready ... oh, Miss Fendall. Are you joining us?"

"Where are we going?" she asked.

"Dentonhill," Haberneck said. "And I should apologize for earlier—"

"Not your fault," Jerinne said, her tone a bit clipped. "Don't worry. What's in Dentonhill?"

"Missing children," Dayne said.

Jerinne nodded. "Of course, however I can help."

"Glad to have you," Dayne said, double-checking the strap on his sham of a shield. "Let's go."

Haberneck had arranged a carriage, which took them across the river and dropped them off on a drab-looking corner, with high, windowless brick tenements in every direction.

"Dreary," Jerinne said. "But nothing is on fire."

"On fire?" Haberneck asked.

"I helped out the Constabulary in Aventil a few weeks ago. The gang war going on there leaves some buildings just ... smoldering. It's very strange."

"Aventil has a serious gang problem," Haberneck said, as if it was a fact. "It's rather tragic."

"That's what I saw," she said. "But I heard Dentonhill was a lot more crime-ridden."

"It's not that simple," Haberneck said. "It does have a drug problem, but that stems from the lives of the people here. Most of them are just desperate folk, trying to do good work, but the work isn't there. So, they turn to ways to escape their pain, and that leads to the drugs."

"I'll never understand that," Jerinne said.

"So who are we seeing?" Dayne asked as they approached a tenement.

"This is Elvin, distant cousin, and his wife Gabrelle. Well, it's their home, but I wouldn't be surprised if they have other neighbors in their flop."

"They know we're coming?" Dayne asked. "I don't want to impose."

"I've warned them," Haberneck said. "Which is why I expect there will be others there. Several kids have gone missing, so the parents are gathering together."

"Have you gone to Rainey about this?" Jerinne asked. "She was—"

Dayne shook his head. "I know she was working on a case that led to missing children. This may be connected. If it is—"

"I was going to visit her place later tonight," Jerinne said. "I'll tell her what's up."

Dayne gave her another look. "Why are you going there?"

"Her daughter's my friend," Jerinne said. "I like to see her."

Dayne understood. "Her daughter is the glove girl at the Majestic," he said. "You're sweet on her."

"That—" Jerinne said, her voice instantly defensive. Then she softened her tone. "That isn't the only reason. Not that anything is happening there. Or even would. I don't know. It must be easier for you."

"I don't know about that," Dayne said. "Saints know, I feel at sea with Lady Mirianne."

"I thought you two were great," Jerinne said. "I mean, she dotes on you."

"And I adore her," he said. "But that doesn't change the fact that our worlds do not align. I definitely feel she is keeping me at length from part of her life. I don't know how to reconcile that."

"Love finds a way," Jerinne said. "Isn't that what all those pennyhearts say?"

"Yes," Dayne said quietly. He had read too many of them, first when he was learning how to read with Miri as children, and now as a way to fill the time in the long hours where nothing was asked of him.

They approached the apartment door, where Haberneck knocked before entering. Dayne and Jerinne followed him into the place: a tight, warm home, with cracked plaster walls and a ceiling slightly too low for Dayne's comfort. He needed to crouch down to enter.

The place was also full of people—at least twenty, plus small children. Everyone was talking, drinking cider or beer, children running about.

"Hey all," Haberneck called out. "I brought some friends."

All eyes went to Dayne.

"Saints, he's a big one!" one person called.

One of the running children crashed into Dayne's leg. She looked up at him, her eyes wide, and then screamed, "It's the giant!"

More children screamed.

"Hey, hey, settle!" Haberneck said. "My friend's a big guy, but he's not a giant. He's a good guy." A few of the adults gathered up the children and brought them to the other room.

"Sorry," Dayne said as one of the men came up to him, handing him a beer.

"It's nothing. Kids being kids. Wow, look at you two. Actual Tarians, swords and everything. You said, Gol, but I didn't believe it."

"You're Elvin?" Dayne said, offering his hand. "Hi, I'm Dayne. This is Jerinne. I understand there are children missing?"

Elvin took his hand and led them to chairs. All the adults in the apartment gathered around, crowding into every space they could to see Dayne.

"So, friend," Elvin said. "What can you two do about this?"

"I can't promise anything," Dayne said. "But start with telling me what's happening."

Elvin looked to Haberneck first, who gave a nod, and then he started. "So, kids go missing here. That's been a thing, especially the doxy kids in the park. It happens."

"Doxy kids?" Jerinne asked.

"The street ladies," one of the women whispered. "They're too, you know, fallen to have proper homes. They camp in the park with their children, poor things."

"Tragic, tragic," other women said.

"I'm standing right here!" one woman shouted.

Elvin continued. "You'd hear about those kids going missing, other ones on the block. Always seemed too much, but the sticks, they said it was a thing that happened."

"Stupid sticks," another man said.

"They're in the pocket, they are," one woman said. "We all know it."

"But something changed?" Dayne asked.

"The last two weeks, it cranked up. Not a thing that just happens."

"All the kids in the doxy camp," the woman who shouted before said. Her eyes were red and tearing. "In one night, all of them. Gone."

"Then more in the neighborhood," Elvin said.

"At least twenty," someone else said.

"Twenty!" one woman said, her voice breaking. "My Molly!"

"My Astin!"

"Oscar!"

"All right, all right," Elvin said.

Dayne's heart was breaking. "I'm so sorry. And the constables didn't say anything?"

"Took reports," the woman whose daughter Molly was missing. "Said they would look into it."

"Ain't no one look into anything."

"What should they look into?" Jerinne asked.

A hushed silence fell over the room.

"Fenmere," the doxy woman said quietly. "Every dark and twisted thing in this part of town, he's the seed of it."

"Who's Fenmere?" Dayne asked.

No one looked like they wanted to answer.

The doxy woman answered again. "He's the man behind the drugs here. The *effitte* and the *efhân*. He runs that, he runs the dox houses, he's got the sticks under his thumb."

"He's taking kids?"

"I didn't say that," she said. "But nothing happens in Dentonhill that he doesn't touch." She glared at the other people. "I know one or two of you have coin in your pocket from him. Or a vial."

"Like you never did, Maxi," one woman said.

"I've been clean since spring," Maxi said.

"So he knows something?" Dayne asked. "Maybe someone he can't buy should have a word."

"You?" Elvin asked.

"Where do I find him?"

Again, the silence.

"Rutting sinners, all of you," Maxi said. "If Elvin won't take you—"

"One thing," Jerinne said. "Tell me about the giant."

"What giant?"

"The little girl said Dayne was 'the giant.' As in a specific one. What did she mean?"

The adults all shrugged.

"I saw it."

A little boy in the doorway to the back room. He shuffled forward, with an older girl standing behind him, hands comfortingly on his shoulder.

"What did you see?" Dayne asked.

"When Jilly and Goady were taken," the boy said. "I saw it. They had gone into the crushed house together, and I went with them, and they yelled at me to go away."

"Crushed house?" Dayne asked.

"An empty tenement a block away," Elvin said. "It's half collapsed, and we tell kids to stay clear, but . . ."

"Kids go play in there anyway," Maxi said.

"I stayed in the corner," the kid went on. "I was mad,

I wanted to play with them. They went in the basement, and I heard them scream. I went halfway down the stairs, and I saw him. The giant."

"Tell us about him," Jerinne said.

"Bigger than him," the kid said, pointing at Dayne. "And his skin was shiny. He scooped up Jilly and Goady, and went in a hole in the wall."

"A hole in the wall in the basement?" Dayne asked.

"And I heard him," the boy said in whispered horror. "He said . . . he said, 'Gurond take. Take the children. Children for the Dragon.'"

"Why didn't you tell us this?" Elvin asked.

"He told us all before," the girl behind the little boy said. "We tried to tell you."

"Can you show us this 'crushed house'?" Dayne asked. "And where we can find this Fenmere fellow?"

Elvin got to his feet. "We can do that, yeah. You're going to do something about this?"

"I promise you I will try," Dayne said, taking the man's hand. "I don't know where it will lead me, but I will look for your children, and do what I can to bring those responsible to justice."

Verci arrived at Kimber's not sure what he was going to find. Asti had sent a note that he needed to come urgently, so he locked up the shop and came.

"Your brother isn't about to drag you into some other scheme, is he?" Raych asked as they came in. "We're finally settling into normal."

"I don't know," Verci said. "I know that Enanger Lesk has been dying in one of the beds upstairs. Maybe this is it for him."

"What's he dying of?"

"Asti stabbing him."

"And Asti has been watching over him or something?"

"Well, Nange apologized," Verci said.

"For being stabbed?"

"For the reasons Asti stabbed him. It's complicated."

Raych sighed, a deep, exhausted sigh. "Most things are with the two of you."

They didn't even get into the taproom. Asti came down the stairs two at a time. "Took you long enough."

"What's going on?" Verci asked.

"Tarvis," Asti said. "I found him in the alley."

"His body?"

"No, he's alive," Asti said.

That was surprising. The violent little boy had launched himself into a rampage of rage and revenge that Verci was certain would end in self-destruction. "So what happened?"

"I'm not sure. He could barely talk. He was parched, half-starved. Exhausted. I got him in here and Kimber has been taking care of him."

"You said it was an emergency."

"He was rambling, surely out of his mind," Asti said. "But he said something about the other kids. Stolen kids."

"Stolen?" Raych asked. "By who?"

"He was probably delusional," Verci said.

"Maybe," Asti said. "But remember the Thorn asked if we had heard anything about missing children?"

Verci nodded. "You think this is connected?"

"I think I want to do right by that kid," Asti said. Verci understood why. Asti felt an odd kinship to the boy, and guilt over the death of his brother. "And if there are other kids, and the Thorn knows something? If those kids are from our neighborhood?"

"Right," Verci said.

"How can you do anything?" Raych asked.

"Well, we've got to get word to the Thorn," Asti said. "The only way I know how to do that is through Mila."

Verci sighed. "So, let's pay her a visit."

The collapsed apartment building had been a waste of time. Dayne and Jerinne, with the help of Haberneck and his cousin, searched through the parts of the basement they could get into. If there was a passage for a giant to come from, Dayne couldn't find it, and the unstable nature of the building made him uncomfortable with pushing around too much.

"It looks like the ceiling over there collapsed recently," Jerinne said, pointing to a section of the basement they couldn't get to. "Maybe there's something more there."

"If there is, we can't get into it," Dayne said. "Let's go see this Fenmere fellow."

It was already nearly evening by the time they got out of the building, brushed themselves off, and let Elvin lead them to the house.

"What's the plan here?" Haberneck asked.

"Not entirely sure," Dayne said. "This man is supposedly a crime lord, but he lives in this large, well-appointed home, in the open. I need to get my own sense of him. He lives in this neighborhood, as well. Maybe his humanity can be appealed to when it involves missing children."

"Barring that, we have swords," Jerinne said.

"No," Dayne pressed. "We're not going to resort to violence here. We'll see if we can have a civilized conversation."

"Right," Haberneck said. "I'm wondering if it's better or worse for me to join you here."

Dayne understood. "Your presence could make us seem like we're formally representing the government here."

Haberneck chuckled. "I was actually thinking if someone saw a new member of Parliament visiting the home of a known criminal boss, but I like how you think."

"Perhaps we should handle it alone," Dayne said.

"I'll talk to you later," Haberneck said, shaking Dayne's hand. "And I really thank you for your time and effort."

He went off with his cousin.

"Isn't he a Traditionalist?" Jerinne asked once they were gone. "He doesn't seem like one."

"He is," Dayne said. "But something like this goes beyond partisan opinions."

"No, it's just, I'm surprised to . . . from what I've seen, a fair amount of Dishers talk a good talk about the needs of the common man, but what they actually do . . . they stay at quite a remove. This guy, he's really in it."

"As are we," Dayne said. He had to admit, he was excited to be out and about, doing something that mattered. It was far preferable to being stuck in the Parliament, with no role beyond passing official reports to the press.

He went up to the door of the house, noting that there were more than a few folks with crossbows on the roof, and other fellows with handsticks on the grounds. One of those gentlemen was at the door.

"What do you think you're doing?" he asked, holding out his hand to block them.

Dayne took that hand in a friendly shake. "Hi, I'm Dayne, this is Jerinne. We were hoping for a word with Mister Fenmere."

"Mister Fenmere isn't going to see you."

"That's surprising," Jerinne said. "Saints, this morning we were on the palace grounds. Now some choad thinks they're too good for us."

"Shut that mouth, girl," the man said.

"Make me," Jerinne said.

"Don't think I won't," the fellow said, drawing his handstick.

"Jerinne, there's no need for a fight."

"I agree," Jerinne said. "How about a bet?" She pointed her finger at the man. "I'll give you ten tries. If you land a hit, we walk away. But I say you'll swing at air ten times, and if you do, we go in to see Fenmere."

"It's your teeth, girl." The man made a show of flipping the handstick around for a moment to get it in position to punch with it like a knucklestuffer. It was a bit of silly excess, as if flamboyance could stand in for technique. He took a sharp, heavy jab at Jerinne, which she dodged easily. She took two steps back.

"That's one."

The guy charged at her, throwing several more punches that failed to connect.

"And six, seven, eight," Jerinne counted. "Two more."

"Hey, Deggie, what are you doing?" one of the other guards shouted. "Just flatten her!"

"The girl moves like a mouse!" he yelled back. He tried to feint a punch with his right before bringing in a sucker shot with his left, but Jerinne saw it coming and stepped out of its way.

"I'll be kind and call that nine," she said. "But really that was two punches at once."

"Damn it!" he yelled, charging to tackle her, but she rolled out of the way.

"And that's ten," she said. "I win."

"Win this!" another fellow yelled, bringing up his crossbow. He fired in a snap, but Dayne was there with his shield. The bolt clanged off it and dropped to the ground. The other men brought up their weapons.

"That's enough!" a man at the door in an expensive suit said. "This has been quite entertaining, I'm sure, but there's no need for such foolery. Mister Fenmere would like a word with these two Tarians."

"Spirited," Jerinne said. "I appreciated the spar."

"Come on," Dayne told her. "You can play later." He was glad the conflict had ended here—the cheap shield he was carrying had been dented by the crossbow shot. He'd be hesitant to rely on it in a real fight.

"Yes, Dayne," she said in a mocking tone.

They went inside, following the well-dressed man, and were led to a sitting room. Dayne had seen more of his share of rooms like it, but it was surprising in contrast to the cramped, shabby apartment three blocks away. Here, the furniture was impeccable, imported from the Kieran Empire if Dayne's eye was correct. Several paintings hung in the room, including what looked like a Garston.

The well-dressed gentleman left them alone in there for a moment.

"This room is a brag," Jerinne said. "He's showing us how rich he is."

"If we didn't grow up in noble households, we might be impressed," Dayne said. He and Jerinne were both unusual within the Order, having been children of household staff, growing up in the presence of conspicuous wealth. Jerinne leaned in to the Garston, inspecting it as close as she could without touching it.

"Do you like that one, young lady?" An older man, with a tightly trimmed graying beard, stood in the doorway. "*The Last Stand of Queen Mara*. I find it a good reminder that no amount of righteous fury can match the strength of numbers."

That was an interesting interpretation of the history. Mara, Druthal's only female monarch, was ousted from her throne in a brutal insurrection, at one of the lowest points of the Shattered Centuries period. According to legend, she killed twenty of Lord Ferrick's soldiers before dying, sword in hand, still sitting on her throne. Queen Mara was the inspiration for quite a few pieces of art, including Whit's historical play, and the poem *Killed but Never Defeated*.

"Interesting," Jerinne said neutrally. "Queen Mara was the last monarch of the Line of Halitar, but quite a few nobles trace their heritage back to that line."

"Do they?" the man said with no sense that he was interested in what Jerinne was saying. "I under—"

"Including Baron Fortinare, which is why his great-grandfather commissioned the *The Last Stand of Queen Mara* from Garston."

"Did he?" the man asked, now with an edge in his voice.

"He did. That's why the Baron has it proudly hanging in his study. But this, sir, is an *excellent* forgery."

The man's jaw set, and he forced a smile to his lips as he looked to Dayne. "You're Dayne Heldrin, of course. It's a pleasure to meet the hero of the Parliament, the savior of the elections. We don't get any *real* heroes in this neighborhood."

"You must be Mister Fenmere," Dayne said.

"In the flesh," Fenmere said. "Though I am puzzled why two members of the Tarian Order would come to see me, just a simple businessman. It can't just be for art criticism." He looked over to the doorway, where the man in the suit was waiting. "Ask Olliman to come join us."

"Yes, sir," he said, and he went off.

"We're looking into some trouble here in the neighborhood," Dayne said. "Apparently there's been a rash of missing children in the area."

"And you come to see me? Surely you don't think I'm abducting children."

"We were given to understand you have some influence in this neighborhood," Dayne said. "Thus you might have . . . knowledge or resources outside of more conventional avenues of investigation."

"What a very diplomatic phrasing, Mister Heldrin," Fenmere said. "It's true, I am aware of quite a lot of the things that happen in this part of the city. I've heard some stories, of course. Quite a few of the people here work long hours at the cannery or the chicken house, and then drown their sorrows in beer. Or stronger substances."

"Stronger substances, indeed," Jerinne said.

"And in the midst of all that, they lose track of their children. It's quite a tragedy,"

"If only that tragedy had an architect," Jerinne said.

Dayne gave her a little scowl. He understood where she was coming from, why she was needling Fenmere, but it wasn't very helpful right now.

"Every person makes their choices," Fenmere said. "They'll leap into danger and death without a thought, it seems."

The man who led them in came back with another man, also very well-dressed. "Willem, were you going to come back—oh."

"Olliman," Fenmere said. "I'm afraid I'm going to have to ask you to help these fine people find their way back to their part of the city. They've clearly been in Dentonhill a little too long."

"Yes, of course," Olliman said. "I'll convey your regards to the High Lord."

"Please," Fenmere said. "I've enjoyed this little lesson on history and art, but it's not something I need to repeat." He left the room.

Olliman looked at Dayne and Jerinne like he was their father, angry and embarrassed by their behavior.

"What did you two do?"

"Do we know you, sir?" Dayne asked.

"No, but I know who you both are. Come on, we need to get out of here."

"We don't know you," Jerinne said. "And I don't think we're in any danger."

"It's because people don't know me that I can even be here," he said. "Let's go."

"What High Lord?" Dayne asked.

"Let's get out of here," Olliman said. "I'll explain as we go how badly you just screwed up."

Veranix had made a nightly ritual of patrolling Dentonhill, especially since the stories of the missing children had ticked up again. More and more of them.

He still didn't know what to do about it, but he felt if

he took some time each evening, watching from the rooftops, he might see something. The stories persisted of a giant taking children. That should be easy to spot.

Between that, shutting down the *efhân* dealers, and his classwork, he was close to the edge of his endurance. But he'd endure.

Tonight his patrol included the Fenmere mansion, in the heart of Dentonhill. He knew where it was now, thanks to Inspector Welling's records. Not that knowing made a difference. The house had dozens of guards on the ground, more with crossbows on the roof, and most troubling: dalmatium pylons at regular intervals. If he tried to assault it, he'd be massively outnumbered and magically hobbled.

He couldn't just charge in there, he'd need a plan. For now, he'd scout it and form that plan. Maybe he could call on the Rynaxes for a favor.

He watched as the front door opened, and three people came out. Clearly not from this part of town. One of them looked very official, with his suit and cravat. The other two looked like soldiers, matching uniforms and swords at their belt.

And the big guy had a shield.

Very big guy.

A giant, one might say.

He was tempted to follow them, but he had been out too late already. He was already drained from today's earlier fight and the magic class. If he had learned anything, it was not to push his limits when it wasn't urgent. The last thing he needed was to follow this giant warrior farther away from campus.

That didn't mean he'd just let them go.

He shrouded himself to be nearly invisible, and leaped off the roof, landing with soft magic half a block from them. Then he pushed just a little bit of speed into himself, and darted past the big fellow, tagging him with a magic charge as he passed.

Just enough to track him later.

He watched as the big fellow looked about to see what brushed him, and they all went on their way.

That needed to be enough for tonight. Time to get home, get something to eat, and sleep. And probably study a little as well. He did have classes in the morning.

Chapter 5

"**S**O WHO ARE YOU AGAIN?" Jerinne asked as Olliman, the strange, officious man, led them through Inemar.

"Unofficial," Olliman asked. "I don't have a title or a position in the government or the nobility. But my brother is the chief of staff to the High Lord of Diplomacy."

"And it's in that capacity you were in the home of a drug smuggler and crime boss?"

"Yes," Olliman said. He stopped, lighting a taper from a street lamp and using it to light his pipe. "All right, you two, since you're both so smart, let me ask you a question. You were at the Royal Gardens this morning, right?"

"Yes," Dayne said. "You were as well?"

"I was," Olliman said. "But you wouldn't have noticed me. The point is people don't notice me, and if they do, they only see two brothers talking. I'm never seen talking to anyone else in power. But to my real point. Did you see, for example, an ambassador from the Kieran Empire?"

"Maybe," Jerinne said. She wasn't sure where this was going, but Olliman looked terribly agitated about it. It was also a little hard to hear him, with him speaking in a low, smoky whisper. Maybe that was his intent.

"And an ambassador from the Imach Nations? From Tsoulja? Acseria?"

"I'm not sure," Jerinne said.

"You may not have noticed, but they were there. Do you know who was not there? An ambassador from Poasia. Because that doesn't exist."

"We have a treaty with Poasia," Dayne said.

"We have a peace right now, but we don't have relations with them. We do not have any sort of embassage with them, we only had one diplomatic mission where foreigners were allowed to step foot on Poasian soil, and that was ten years ago."

"But there are Poasians in Maradaine," Dayne said.

"There are, which we allow because we're trying to demonstrate how open and tolerant a nation we are, the crossroads of the world. It drives Intelligence mad, let me tell you."

"What does that have to do with you being at Fenmere's?" Jerinne asked, annoyed with this odd man and his roundabout explanation.

"We do not have relations with Poasia," he said. "We have, instead, a smuggling kingpin who specializes in Poasian goods, who has established roads of contact with influential people in the Poasian Pankchamnta."

"That's your diplomacy?" Dayne asked.

Jerinne couldn't believe her ears. "Is that why he lives in that palace amid a crumbling neighborhood? So he can be your contact with Poasia?"

"I'm saying, for now, the Druth government has a vested interested in letting Willem Fenmere continue his operations. If that means some drugs get into the city, and some people choose to get addicted to them, that's the price we pay."

"That's monstrous," Jerinne said.

"It's what's been accepted," Olliman said. "The two of you are both well regarded in the public eye thanks to your service, and whatever else may happen in your careers, you should bear in mind you both need that good esteem, and what might happen if you lose it."

"Is that a threat?" Dayne asked.

"Not from me," Olliman said. "I'm not a person who can do a thing about that. I'm just the brother of a minor official. But I do know that people who have threatened Fenmere's position, his ability to do what we need him to do . . . those people have found trouble for themselves. I would not wish that for the two of you."

"But what about—"

"Is your mission specifically about Fenmere? Are you trying to take him down?"

Dayne scowled. "Well, no, but—"

"Then find something else," Olliman said. "Find a way that doesn't involve Fenmere." He shook his head. "I trust I can leave you on your own reconnaissance. I would like to just get home, have a nice supper with my brother, and we can talk about our day."

"Yes," Dayne said through gritted teeth. He looked very unhappy, but he nodded. "We'll not harass him further."

"Good. Have a good evening." He went off toward the river.

"Now what?" Jerinne asked.

"You should probably get back to the chapterhouse for supper," Dayne said. "They'll be expecting you."

"And you?"

Dayne looked down the street. "One more stop."

"Saint Limarre's?" she asked.

He nodded. "I'll leave word for Welling and Rainey, maybe they know something we don't, and maybe we can do something they can't. I'll see you tomorrow."

He went off toward the church, and Jerinne decided

he was right about one thing: Inspector Rainey needed to know what they were looking into. One more reason to go to her house. Not that Jerinne didn't already have a very good reason to visit.

Satrine had finished her shift having accomplished very little. Two new murder cases, neither one very elucidating. Theft in East Maradaine, where the victim had been evasive about what exactly was stolen. They were very interested in finding the thieves and reclaiming their property, though balked when Satrine and Kellman pointed out that identifying the property was the best way to find the thieves. There wasn't much to go on.

Still, that was the case that stayed in her head as she came home, looking forward to having a hot meal, and falling into her bed. She was pleasantly surprised to hear warm laughter as she opened the door to her apartment.

"What's going on?" she asked as she came in. Down the hallway to the sitting room, where her daughters, Rian and Caribet, were cackling with Jerinne Fendall, the young Tarian warrior.

"Mother," Rian said, catching her breath and looking slightly guilty, like she had just been caught in something inappropriate. "Jerinne was telling us about her day."

"Must be a good story," Satrine said, sitting at the table where they were all drinking tea. "Your day had to have been better than mine."

"It started at the Royal Gardens," Caribet said. "She saw the king!"

"And that was funny? Could I get a cup? And is there supper?"

Rian grabbed a cup out of the cabinet. "Missus Abnernath stewed some lamb ribs with root vegetables, and there's bread."

"Lovely, yes," Satrine said. As annoying as her new partnership with Kellman was, the promotion to Inspector Second Class, compounded with Rian's work at the Majestic, meant they had more money, and the meals had been far more satisfying of late.

"I don't want to impose," Jerinne said.

"Nonsense," Satrine replied. "We love having you visit." She wanted Jerinne and Rian to be close. She wanted to know Rian would have a friend, a protector, in case anything ever happened to her. "So, what was the funny thing?"

"She told a crime boss that his beloved painting was a fake," Rian said.

That was intriguing. "How did you know?"

"I don't," Jerinne said. "I made it up. But his face was priceless."

"Girls, why don't you serve supper," Satrine said, looking to her daughters. Rian and Caribet both sighed, but got up from the table. Satrine looked to Jerinne. "Crime boss?"

"Fenmere?" Jerinne said. "Pompous git, but he's apparently protected from on high."

Satrine scowled. "I know the Dentonhill office won't touch him, but on high?"

"He has diplomatic value, or something," Jerinne said.

Satrine found herself laughing. "Of course a sewage crime lord has 'diplomatic value.' I swear, this country is run by feral pigs."

"The kids you rescued. What did you know about who was taking them, where they were going?"

"Some were put on a boat," Satrine said. That boat had made it to sea, probably with Corrie Welling on it. "And the rest, in crates on the cart with me. I heard them saying we were going to someone named 'Senek.' He needed children and mothers."

"Mothers?" Rian asked, coming back over with bowls. "As in, people who are mothers, or people to be mothers?"

"That's a disturbing question," Jerinne said with a shudder. "But you never found out more about this 'Senek'?"

"Just the name," Satrine said. "Maybe that'll help." She ground her teeth for a moment, unsure if she should even say the next part, burden Jerinne with it. The girl was so young, and constantly took on more than she ever should.

You were the same age in Waisholm, literally shaping the direction that kingdom would go.

"There is something else. Chief Quoyell was assassinated by a mage that night, so we couldn't question him further."

Jerinne nodded. "I think Dayne mentioned that."

"I found out later the assassination may have been ordered by a member of Intelligence." She leaned in to whisper, as if even the name reaching Rian's ears would put her in danger. Rian took the cue and went back into the kitchen with Caribet. "It was Colonel Altarn. You know who that is?"

Jerinne took that in, but if it gave her further clarity, Satrine didn't see it on her face.

Rian came back with a bottle of wine, pouring a glass and putting it in front of Satrine. "You look like it's been that sort of day."

"It has been that sort of day," Satrine said. She still hadn't yet told the girls about Mother. She didn't know how to tell them, what to tell them, about that awful woman who was now back in Satrine's life. Or that they now had an uncle who was only a little older than Rian. She knew she needed to tell them that before Rian accidentally started kissing him.

But seeing how Rian and Jerinne looked at each other as they started eating, it occurred to Satrine that Rian kissing boys wasn't a thing she should be worried too much about.

A young blond woman, in a cloistress habit and with a serious face, sat on the steps of Saint Limarre's with a valise next to her as Dayne approached. She seemed lost in thought when Dayne went up the steps, her eyes locking on him.

"A champion!" she said. "I've been here waiting for my champions. They . . ." She looked around in confusion for a moment. "They didn't . . . is this the wrong church?"

Dayne wasn't sure how to take that. "Miss, can I help you with something?"

"You're not helping me, you're serving the will of God," she said. "I am his vessel but you will be his arm."

"I'll be his what?"

"His mighty sword, raising up . . . no, that's not right." She shook her head. "No, no, no, I . . . wait. It's not Erescan, is it?"

"It's Oscan. Oscan twenty-fifth."

Her eyes went very wide. "No, no, then it's too late, much too late and we have—" She looked around the square surrounding Saint Limarre's. "No, that's not right. Wait. Is it Oscan in 1215?"

The girl was asking the year. Dayne had heard Sister Alana mention the troubled cloistress in her care. This must be her.

"Yes, that's right," Dayne said.

"Too soon. But yet you're—" She looked off to her left for a moment, and then turned back to Dayne. "I'm sorry, I get terribly confused some times. What did I say I was waiting for?"

"Your champions?"

"Silly of me. I'm waiting for my *carriage*, to take me to my new assignment." She paused, looking down the road, and then continued with a voice that was almost haunted. "At Saint Bridget's."

"Is everything all right, Sister?"

"Definitely not," she said. She looked at Dayne carefully. "You, my dear friend, should remember the parable of Saint Keller. Namely, the seventeenth verse."

"I've read it, but I don't know the—"

She reached up and touched his cheek—which was quite a stretch for her—and the contact briefly made Dayne feel compelled to look her in the eyes. "Hold close those that are dear, thy beloved friends, and do not fear to share your burdens with them, for their counsel and wisdom shall guide you through the darkest places."

Dayne suddenly wanted to cry, but had no idea why, how this strange young woman had unlocked something in him with those simple words. It was as if she had relieved him of a burden he had been carrying for years.

She stepped away and picked up the valise. "I think I don't wish to wait for the carriage. I will find Saint Bridget's of my own accord. You will find Sister Alana inside."

With that, she walked off to the west.

Dayne went into the church, back toward the living quarters, finding Sister Alana in the kitchen with two other cloistresses.

"Dayne," she said kindly as she came over to him. "Are you here for . . . absolution?"

"Yes," he said, and she led him out of the kitchen to one of the private chambers off the chapel.

"What's going on?" she asked, taking out her journal.

"I've been looking into a large number of children going missing in Dentonhill."

"You think it's connected to the children Satrine rescued from Quoyell?" she asked.

"Possibly," Dayne said. "They were providing children for someone's nefarious purposes. Maybe with Inspector Rainey stopping one source, they've resorted to a new one."

"All right. What else?"

"One child saw an inhuman giant take children, in

the basement of a collapsed, abandoned house." He gave her the address.

"In the basement?"

"That's what the child said. I checked it out, but it wasn't safe to look around too much."

"I'll pass it on to Satrine and Welling," she said. She thumbed through her journal. "Minox is wondering what you know about a member of Parliament named Chestwick Millerson."

Dayne scratched his chin in thought. "He's one of the chairs from Sauriya, I believe. Traditionalist. I don't know much more off the top of my head, but I'll look into it. Did he say why?"

"He did not," Sister Alana said. "I recognize this partnership of ours is new, but he's yet to be very open in his discoveries. I get the impression he wants to put together complete information before sharing it. And he's hurting over his sister."

Dayne remembered—Minox's sister had gone missing, and presumed dead, on the same night Rainey had stopped the child abductions. Probably due to the same people.

Dayne thanked her and made to leave, then added, "Oh, and that young cloistress outside? She decided not to wait for her carriage and just walk to where she was going."

"She wasn't waiting for a carriage," Sister Alana said. "She was supposed to go hours ago."

"Well, she's gone now," Dayne said.

Sister Alana scowled and nodded. "Thank you, again."

Dayne left the church, but the words of the young cloistress still rang through his head. And he was hungry. So it made sense to head to the Nimble Rabbit and seek out the counsel of some beloved friends.

Veranix returned to campus, more than ready to get back to Almers Hall and rest. Switching his shroud to an illusion of a student in a campus cadet uniform, he made his way across the grounds. Over the months of being the Thorn, he had tried a few different methods of going unnoticed as he made his way to his lair—Mila liked the word "safehouse" but "lair" was much more fun—but just looking like the very people who patrolled the campus for its safety was easily the most effective.

The entrance to the lair was not in the most convenient place, in terms of proximity to Almers. But it was close to the Dentonhill wall, and it was nearly perfect in so many other ways. It was a large underground room with a hidden entrance that no one else on campus had used for decades. How Kaiana had even found it was a mystery, but he did not complain. He slipped into the shed that housed the hidden entrance, opened it, and dropped down to the next level. He could see the flicker of lamplight in the chamber, heard voices. Kaiana was obviously there, possibly Mila and Delmin. He wondered what they were up to.

"I might know who this giant is," Veranix said as he came in. "It might be a coinci—"

"Thorn," Kaiana said as she came to the doorway. Her face was tense, her jaw grinding. "We have guests."

Veranix jumped forward, drawing an arrow and nocking it as he came into the room, shifting his appearance to cover his face with shadow again.

"Ease down, Thorn. Just us."

Sitting at the table next to Delmin and Mila were Asti and Verci Rynax, the brothers from North Seleth. Mila had a cat-like smirk on her face, but Delmin looked terrified.

Veranix put the arrow away. "What the blazes are you two doing out here?"

"Nice to see you, too," Asti said.

"Didn't we say let's not do this again for a while?" Veranix asked them. "It's only been a week or so."

"You do know them?" Kaiana asked.

"The Rynax boys. I presume you showed them down here, Mila?"

"They said they needed to see you."

"So we let anyone down here now," Delmin said. "I mean, that's very good to know."

"They are fine," Veranix said, taking off his quiver and putting it on the table. "I mean, Verci built the bow and the arrowheads here, I think we can trust them."

"How are they working out?" Verci asked.

"Excellent," Veranix said. "I like the knockout smoke a lot, it's very nice."

"Isn't it?" Verci said, wide grin across his face.

"Why are you here?" Kaiana asked sharply. "Do you need him to do something for you?"

"It's not like that," Mila said. "They've got something you might want."

"What's that?" Veranix asked. He hung the rope in its case, but didn't take the cloak off. The Rynaxes still hadn't seen his face, no need to change that yet.

"One of our local kids was abducted last week," Asti said. "You were asking about abducted kids."

"Yeah," Veranix said. "More and more in Dentonhill. With stories of a giant."

"Well, this kid got away," Asti said. "And he's got a story about a giant. And tunnels under the city."

That got Veranix's attention. "Who is this kid? Where is he?"

"He's at Kimber's, sick as all blazes. I barely got anything out of him."

"If any kid could get away, it would be him," Mila said quietly.

Veranix nodded. "That's good. Let's go and—"

"Hey, hey," Delmin said. "I can tell by looking at you, you're pretty spent. And we've got classes in the morning."

"Classes?" Verci asked.

Mila slapped him on the arm. "Classes matter, all right?"

"Sorry."

Asti nodded, taking it in. "When are you free tomorrow?"

Veranix looked to Delmin. "About one bell in the afternoon?"

"You're asking me?"

"I might need you," Veranix said.

Delmin's eyes widened a bit, but he nodded. "Yeah, that time works for tomorrow."

"Then that's what we'll do," Veranix said. "One bell-half at Kimber's?"

"I have class then," Mila said. "So I can't come with you."

"Sorry," Veranix said.

"No, it's fine," she said. "It's probably best that I don't see Tarvis."

"All right," Kaiana said. "If there's nothing else?"

Asti got to his feet. "This is a nice safehouse."

"I like 'lair,'" Veranix said.

Asti sighed. "I suppose you would. We'll see you tomorrow, and from there, figure out what we can do next."

"This is a we?" Veranix asked. "I thought you were staying out of this sort of thing."

"We're out of revenge and robbery," Verci said. "Clean, honest lives."

"But this involves boys we looked after," Asti said. "And hardly seems like we're dealing with decent people."

Dayne was fascinated how, despite the fact that Hemmit, Maresh, and Lin had a proper office for *The Veracity Press*, they still worked at the Nimble Rabbit half the time anyway. Dayne arrived to find the three of them in deep conference with several empty plates and bottles of wine around them. Joining them was Lady Mirianne, dressed in a deep red waistcoat and long skirt, with a suncap to match. He had to admit she was a vision, and it was easy to see how she had, in just a few months, become an icon of Maradaine fashion. Her signature looks were copied all over the north side of the city.

"What luck to find you all here," he said as he approached.

"Dayne!" Miri exclaimed, kissing him boldly. "Sit, join us."

"I hope I am not a disruption. I know you are working."

"Pish," she said. "We welcome your company."

Hemmit poured a glass of wine and passed it to Dayne. "The paper is already printed and ready for the boys to sell in the morning. We're talking long-term stories now."

"Long term? Such as?" Dayne asked.

Maresh answered. "We want to really profile each member of Parliament. Get a sense of who they are, what they stand for. Ask them hard questions."

"If they'll take it," Lin said.

"Can you help arrange some meetings?" Hemmit asked. "If that's not imposing."

"It's not," Dayne said. "My role is largely liaising with the press, so I might as well make the most of that." He let his voice be marinated with his sour feelings.

"I touched a nerve," Hemmit said. "I'm sorry." He signaled the waiter to bring a plate over for Dayne.

"It's a nerve that's been exposed for some time," Dayne said. "It's not your fault."

"If you don't like it, just stop," Miri said.

"Continuing in this assignment is the only chance I have at becoming Adept, or at least finishing my Candidacy with honor. I will endure."

The waiter came over with a plate of mustard-and-onion-slathered sausages and potatoes fried in duck fat, which was just the thing to take Dayne's mind off his troubles.

"What else bothers you?" Lin asked.

Dayne took a bite of his sausages. "I went over to Dentonhill with Haberneck—"

"Disher from Sauriya," Maresh said with a scowl. "What did he drag you over there for?"

"Didn't drag me. There are a number of children in the neighborhood who have gone missing."

"Dentonhill's a mess," Maresh said. "I imagine the kids are lost all the time."

"This is something serious. Even nefarious," Dayne said. "Someone is taking these children. One witness even saw a giant."

"A giant!" Mirianne said. "Are you sure?"

"That's what he said, but it was a small child. I would be a giant to him. Who can say what they really saw?"

"It's just . . ." Mirianne looked off in thought for a moment. "I'm sorry, I just recalled something. I must be off." She got to her feet.

"Are you all right?" Dayne asked.

"Yes," she said firmly, kissing him again. "I just remembered I needed to call upon a friend in Callon Hills tonight. It would be very improper of me to ignore them."

"Can't have you being improper," Dayne said.

"Hardly," she said with a smirk. "But in this case, I have made promises." A last kiss. "I don't know how late the evening will go, but if you wish to go to the house and wait for me?"

"Wish," he said lightly. "But I imagine I should get back to my apartments in the near future, in case I'm needed."

"I understand," she said. "But I'll call on you in the morning."

That was odd. Usually the shop kept her busy in the morning. Today had been an odd exception for the event at the palace. "All right."

"Good night, all," she said. "Good work, see you soon."

Dayne sat back down and got back to eating.

"So what are you going to do?" Hemmit asked.

"It's a good question," Dayne said. "I want to take immediate action, but I don't know what it could be. I should just go home and sleep, and hopefully figure out what I can do in the morning."

Minox should have just gone home. He knew he should have. The day in the archives—both at Inemar and the Dentonhill Stationhouse—had taxed him considerably. Even still, the work had proven fruitful. For one, by stringing together items in three separate reports at the two stationhouses, he had found the solution to one of his old "unresolved" cases: Endle Gibb's missing sister had actually faked her own disappearance so she could run off and marry someone in secret, only to be murdered by her secret husband some weeks later. The husband was then arrested and sent to Quarrygate on an entirely different matter.

Not a happy solution to the unresolved case, but now he could reach out to Endle Gibb and close the matter. He had written the letter and delivered it to Gibbs's home, placing him just by The Lower Bridge.

Despite being exhausted, there were too many other revelations in his research today to ignore, and there was only one person he wanted to talk to about it. The knowledge burned in him, and simply sharing it with Sister Alana to then share with the others would not suffice.

He had to talk to Inspector Rainey.

He made his way across the bridge, buying a pair of crispers from a cart vendor on the High River riverbank. He personally found the north side version of the hot lamb sandwich—cooked in red wine and onions—inferior to its South Maradaine equivalent, the striker. But he didn't eat for the flavor, he ate to fill the unending ravening of his magical body. A hunger that had only grown worse since his hand had changed. He finished the first by the time he reached 14 Beltner and knocked on the door.

In a few moments, Satrine Rainey opened up, in slacks and shirtsleeves, crossbow in her hand.

"Minox," she said, stepping out and closing the door behind her. She glanced around cautiously, but her front door was at the bottom of a stair, below street level. It was highly unlikely they would be observed. "Why are you here at this hour? We agreed—"

"Shared messages at the church is nowhere near as effective as direct conversation," he said. "Especially ones where we can spark inspiration in each other."

"Missed you, too," she said. "I have to tell you, pretending to hate you at the stationhouse is exhausting."

"Surely that endears you with our fellows there," Minox said.

"Oddly, it's eased their enmity of you," she said. "They think I'm being too cruel."

"Fascinating," Minox said. He had had enough of pleasantries. "Children are going missing again."

"I've heard," she said. "Dayne is looking into it in Dentonhill."

"That's good," Minox said. "Dentonhill is part of the problem."

"Part of it?"

"The patterns have been clear. There are three parts of the city where there have been spikes. Dentonhill, where the house is fully corrupt and under the thumb of Willem Fenmere."

"Right," she said.

"North Seleth, which seems to suffer from laziness and bureaucratic oversight. And Callon Hills, where the city-dwelling nobility tend to rely on private guards over the city Constabulary."

"All right, what's the connection?"

"All three areas have had reports of missing children

in the past few weeks. We have to presume that, due to the intrinsic flaws in reporting in those three areas, that the actual number is much higher."

"As in, you think areas are being targeted where missing children would be the most unnoticed. Or at least, where no larger pattern would be noticed."

Except by me, Minox thought. "I wanted to talk to you about that night."

"I've told you everything about Corrie—"

"Not about Corrie," he said sharply. Far harsher than Rainey deserved.

"Sorry," she said.

"You heard a name, who Quoyell was delivering you and the children to. Senek, correct?"

"That's right. Though Jerinne told me of a witness who saw the giant taking children. He said the children were for the Dragon."

That struck an old memory. "That was the word she used? Dragon?"

She nodded. "I wasn't familiar with the term. Is it meaningful? Like a title or something?"

"It's . . . a creature in an old Kellirac folk tale. My mother used to tell me it as a child." The story "Aladha va calix" always terrified him, yet as a small boy, he wanted to hear it again and again. He had always appreciated how the beast was beaten with cleverness. The trickster who managed to bind him up and drag him back to his cave.

"Does that connect to Senek?" she asked.

"I don't know how it could. But I think I've determined who Senek is," Minox told her. "In the Mage Rows in 1211, several arrests were made at the Inemar stationhouse of mages involved. Dismissed, Circle Law protecting most of them. But one had his case kicked up to the Archduchy Courts: Ithaniel Senek of the Blue Hand Circle."

"Why does Blue Hand sound familiar?"

"The day we met, I was connecting two separate cases about dead constables in Dentonhill, two dead assassins, and three mages from the Blue Hand Circle."

"Right," she said. "In retrospect, that was probably all to do with the Thorn."

"True. I'll want a word with him about that, but there is something else. The Blue Hand's chapterhouse was in Dentonhill. Perhaps that is exactly where the children are being brought."

"Perhaps," she said. "Though getting writs, working around Circle Law, based on supposition . . ."

"I know," he said. He swallowed hard. He knew what he had to say, but it was so very difficult. It went against every value he had been raised with, but he knew it was right. "I have built up a store of unclaimed personal days. I will be using at least one tomorrow. I've already left word at the station."

"What do you mean?" she asked.

"I mean . . . tomorrow . . . tomorrow I will not be in uniform or acting as an officer of the law."

Her eyes narrowed. "Are you sure—"

"I'm certain that someone must give this deeper investigation, and given the nature of it—in Dentonhill, with fetid corruption, as well as a mage chapterhouse protected by Circle Law—then that investigation must be done outside the bounds of the law."

"Do you need me—"

"No," he said firmly. "Satrine, I—you have a much heavier burden of home and family, and that weight is on you. I know you cannot risk your position or your salary."

She took that in. "And are you prepared to?"

"My position is tenuous as it is. I have examined the risk versus the benefit. I have a bit more investigation I wish to do first, for I have additional theories of connecting circumstances I wish to research, but . . . if there are children who require rescue, and they are in that house, I will take whatever punishment the city metes out to me as fair exchange."

She nodded. "You remember, though. You need help—"

"I cannot place that—"

"If you need help, Minox," she said firmly. "I'll always come for you."

He made a smile come to his lips, so she could see it. "I do miss your partnership, Satrine."

"Get home," she said. "Get a proper night's sleep, and I'm going to do the same. There's a robbery that's not sitting right with me, going to look back into that. That's my day tomorrow."

"Of course," he said. "My . . . my best to your family, Satrine. Take care of them."

She went in and latched the door.

That would do. He'd go home now, sleep in his bed, have breakfast with his family in the morning. And tomorrow . . .

Tomorrow would bring what it would.

Antepenultimate Interlude

"**C**OME ALONG, JARED."

Kimber had decided to make Jared Scall—pulling him away from the precipice, saving his soul—her own dedicated project. While most of the former residents of Holver Alley had recovered from the fire, or at least moved on, Jared had sunk further and further. She couldn't stop him from drinking—she knew if she cut him off, he would just go somewhere else. But she could temper it, and get him back on his feet and starting his day as soon as possible. That was her new strategy with him. Transform him into a man who was up with the dawn and ready to face the day.

He had made it clear he wouldn't sit at a service at Saint Bridget's, but he had agreed to go with Kimber and pray with her at the statue in the narthex. Going right at dawn, they were almost certain to have it to themselves.

They didn't.

Kimber was surprised to find a Cloistress of the Blue

at the foot of the saint in the narthex. But she wasn't praying; she was curled up, asleep on the ground.

"That usually happen?" Jared grumbled out.

"First time," Kimber said. She gently touched the cloistress on the shoulder, triggering a far more sudden and aggressive reaction than Kimber was ready for. The girl screamed, her hand shooting out to Kimber's neck, her eyes bloodshot and wild.

"None of you will pass these doors, foul—" She blinked, her eyes focusing on Kimber. "No, sorry, sorry, what— I—" She looked around, noting Jared. "And you. You are not in service of Saint Alexis."

"No," Jared said. "Girl, I think you should let her go."

Kimber wheezed out, "Please." The girl looked back at her, and seemed to only now realize that her hand was at Kimber's throat.

"I'm very sorry," she said, letting go. "I don't know— where even—was I asleep?"

"Yes," Kimber said. "Are you all right?"

"No, I most certainly am not," the girl said, anger rising in her voice. Her attention turned back to Jared. "And you, I—you're not the—" Suddenly she stopped, her face going pale. Her eyes welled up with tears. "I'm so sorry. I've lived through so many tomorrows that should not be, and . . . I'm so sorry."

"Sister?" Kimber asked. She was very confused and concerned. "Does Reverend Halster know you're here?"

"Here as in this church, or here as in sleeping in the narthex? Yes, and probably not. And I—what day is it?"

"The twenty-sixth of Oscan," Jared said.

"Twenty-sixth. Good. Good. I'm actually here. I'm actually now. Tomorrow is coming so many ways, and I must have the wisdom to guide it." The cloistress got to her feet and brushed her habit off. "I am very sorry, I'll leave you to your prayers. Be in grace, as Saint Alexis calls to you."

"Saint Bridget," Kimber said, pointing to the statue.

"Yes, I—" The cloistress stopped. "I'm sorry, I am— called, I believe. And I must act. I have much to do." She went out of the narthex into the street square.

"Are you all right?" Jared asked Kimber, his hand gently touching her shoulder.

"Yes, just . . . just surprised. Who is that girl?"

"I've never seen her," he said, looking out to the street, watching where the girl went.

Nor had Kimber. She didn't even know there was a cloistry here at Saint Bridget's. But she did not know all things; that was on God and the saints. "Are you ready for our prayers?"

"I am," he said, turning back to her. "More than I've ever been, I think."

That was a start. Perhaps there was salvation, even for his soul. For every soul the saints watched over.

Though as she knelt at the foot of the saint, Kimber wondered who was watching over the clearly troubled soul of that cloistress.

Chapter 6

DAYNE WOKE TO FIND LADY Mirianne making tea in his Parliament apartment, which was quite a surprise.

"You didn't stay here, right?" he asked. "I would have remembered that."

"No, but I wanted to be here when you woke," she said. "Something very important happened and you'll want to know about it."

That cleared all the cobwebs out of his head. "What's going on?"

"I went to visit Baron Vollingale, who has been going through quite an ordeal." She poured the tea for Dayne and handed him the cup. "His son is missing."

"What?" Dayne asked. "You think it's—"

"It definitely is," Mirianne replied. "I heard about it a few days ago, as he had confided in a few close friends. He's not involved the Constabulary or marshals or anyone, because he's terrified of public scandal."

"What?" Dayne couldn't believe that. "Surely the safety of his son would be more important."

She shook her head. "It's more complicated than that, but he's willing to explain it to you. That's why I raced off last night. You mentioned the giant, and so had he—"

"He's seen this giant?"

"And that's, apparently, part of why he's avoiding the authorities." She gestured to the teacup. "Drink up, get yourself together. I imagine you don't want to waste any time on this."

"Not at all," Dayne said, blowing on the hot tea. "Thank you."

"No need," she said. "I just hope you and I can do something for him, and hopefully help that poor boy."

Dayne took a sip and put the cup down on the table and went to his wardrobe. "I'm just hoping he—and all those other children—are alive. Though I think they must be."

"Why is that?"

"Should this be dress uniform or simply tunic?"

"Tunic is fine. Why is that?"

Dayne came out with his tunic in hand. "When Inspector Rainey rescued abducted children, they were still alive. Assuming the underlying cause behind these abductions is the same, they want the children alive."

Miri's brow furrowed. "Those were all orphaned or street children, yes?"

"As are the Dentonhill ones. Well, not orphaned, but definitely underprivileged."

"Odd," she said. "I mean, Baron Vollingale's son fits the same pattern, but he is far from that."

Dayne paused while he pulled the tunic on. "Maybe it's not connected, save some coincidental similarities. I want to hear more, regardless. Even if it's not connected, I want to help, and—"

The words caught in his throat, his heart flooded with

an intense need to find this boy, so strong it almost made tears burst forth.

He knew saving this boy wouldn't redeem him. Wouldn't change what he did to Lenick Benedict. Wouldn't change his fate in the Tarian Order.

He had to do it anyway.

Miri was on her feet, hand on his shoulder.

"Of course. Are you ready?"

"Almost," he said. He took his sword up and belted it, and looked at the dented, cheap shield on the wall. Taking that with him would be an insult.

No shield on arm today. Fitting.

"Let's go," he said, turning to Miri. "A child's life is on the line."

Satrine left for Inemar early, wanting to spend some time at Saint Limarre's with Sister Alana before having to go to the stationhouse, let alone stop at her mother's flop with Phillen Hace. Talking with Sister Alana was one of the few bits of solace she had outside of her family, the oldest friend she had.

For once, Sister Alana wasn't waiting outside the church's quarters with tea and pastries, so Satrine knocked on the back door. After a brief pause, Alana opened the door, looking slightly bleary-eyed.

"You beat me today," Alana said. "That's a first." She stepped back to allow Satrine in.

"Won't happen too often," Satrine said. "Couldn't sleep."

Alana took the teapot off the stove and brought it to the table. "I actually got to sleep through the night for once. The other cloistresses aren't up and about yet, so we have a bit of time. Though Sister Enigaria is stirring, and she's always putting her nose in business."

"I know the type," Satrine said. "I can sit?"

"Please," Alana said, getting out bread and preserves. "Just because she's got her opinions doesn't mean I'm not the ranking Cloistress of the Blue here."

"Does rank mean higher salary for you?" Satrine asked.

"We are in service of god and the community," Alana said. "But it does mean I get to be bossy. But hopefully all the ladies here will be a bit calmer now."

"What's now?" She had slept through the night, so something had changed.

Alana sighed and sat down. "Sister Myriem is gone, left for Saint Bridget's yesterday."

Satrine's own interactions with Sister Myriem had always been disconcerting—the girl was somehow both completely in her own world and eerily in tune with whoever she was talking to. Her words made no sense, but yet could cut straight to the heart.

Somehow, Sister Myriem had led Satrine directly to the trapmaster right when she needed to find him, just with a pastry wrapper.

"Are you relieved?"

"No," Alana said. "I can't help but think I failed that girl."

"How so?"

"She needed help," Alana said. "I thought through faith alone, I could, I don't even know, save her. But this cloister wasn't suited to her problems."

"But Saint Bridget's is?"

"Maybe," Alana said, shaking her head. "I mean, Reverend Halster offered to take her in, knowing her history. But in my soul I know she—" Alana trailed off. "She asked me to do something, and, I don't know if I should."

"What is it?"

Alana got up and went to a cabinet. With a glance down the hallway to check if any other sisters were coming, she took out a book. "This is her copy of *The Testaments of the Saints*. She's . . . she's torn pages, written in the margins, blotted out words. I don't even dare let any of the others see this, they'd think it was—"

"Blasphemy?" Satrine offered.

"At the very least. But she gave it to me, and . . . she said she wants you to have it."

"Me? Why?"

"I have no idea," Alana said. "But you don't need to—"

"I'll take it," Satrine said impulsively, reaching out for it.

"Really?"

"Lannie," Satrine said. "I don't know if I can explain it, but that girl—she's . . . she's guided by something. Whatever it is, I'm not saying I understand it, but—and I'm amazed I'm saying this—I have faith in it."

"I *want* to have faith in it. In her. Even in this torn-up book." She thumbed through the pages. "I can't even imagine—she actually rewrote the first part of the Testament of Saint Jesslyn, so it opens with 'listen to the gardener, seek answers when she calls.'"

"Listen to the who?" a voice called from down the hall. Satrine reached out and grabbed the damaged book from Sister Alana before the other cloistress came into the kitchen.

"Listen to the wise men, but seek shelter from their lies," Alana said a little louder, correctly citing the passage.

"That's my daily life," Satrine said as she stuck the book inside her coat. One of the other cloistresses stumbled into the kitchen.

"I must be losing my ears," the cloistress said. "Are we hosting the Constabulary in here?"

"Council for every citizen is our mandate," Alana said. "Especially old friends."

"These are our sanctums, though," the cloistress said.

"I'll go," Satrine said, getting up.

"I'll see you out," Alana said, taking Satrine out the back door.

"That was Sister Enigaria?" Satrine asked when they were outside.

"The very same," Alana said. "You're to work?"

"I must," Satrine said. "I now have more family to support."

"Dayne was concerned about children missing from Dentonhill."

"Minox is as well," Satrine said. "Whatever I stopped earlier this month, it wasn't enough."

"Should I tell them anything from you?"

"I talked to Minox last night, and today he's—" Satrine wasn't sure what to say. She understood exactly what was going on in Minox's head, and in her heart, she was with him. She wished she could be there with him. "If he comes, tell—remind him that he's not alone. Especially when it comes to acting outside the law."

"Outs—" Alana gasped. "I guess I didn't think it would come to that so soon. Of course I will."

"Thank you."

"Walk with the saints," Alana said, embracing Satrine. "Have a blessed day."

"And you," Satrine said.

It wasn't much, but the blessing and friendship would have to be enough to get her through the day.

A burning instinct told her today was going to be a bad one.

Minox knew he would endure some difficulty coming down to breakfast with the family out of uniform.

"Are you all right?" his brother Jace asked amid the shocked expressions. Almost the entire household was already at the table—some ready to go to work, some having come in from a night shift. Corrie's seat remained empty, though Mother had set her place anyway, as was Nyla's. Nyla had rarely come out of her room in the past two weeks.

"In many ways, the answer is no," Minox said. "I could catalog them if you want, starting with the loss of our sister."

"Foul, unfair," his cousin Davis said. "That's hitting all of us, and you know it."

"True," Minox said, taking bread and butter from the basket in front of him. "But I also have several other issues in play, including being removed from my duties. I need to deal with those personal matters, and I have banked the time to take off."

"That's good," Aunt Emma said. "All of you bottle yourselves up too damned much and work yourselves silly." She pointed an accusing finger at Ferah and Edard. "I heard you two talking about Nyla not going back to work."

"I'm just worried about her," Ferah said. Someone knocked at the front door, and Jace left the table to get it.

"She needs to rest is all," Emma said.

Minox's mother came and served him eggs and sausages with Kellirac spiced cream. "It's nothing dangerous, is it? You shouldn't—you shouldn't do anything alone."

"It's personal business, Mother," Minox said. "Mostly in the City Records, legal concerns for my status." He hated to lie to her, but he could not have her worrying. Her heart couldn't bear it.

Jace came back from the door, his face screwed in thought.

"Who was at the door?" Minox's uncle Cole asked.

"Strange bird," Jace said. "Cloistress, about my age."

"What did she want?" Davis asked.

"Nothing, really. She said, 'Tell unto your brothers to be guided by those who tend the path.' And then she walked off." He shrugged and pointed to Minox and their brother Oren at the far end of the table. "So, I told you."

"It's from the Testament of Saint Deshar," Ferah

said. Everyone looked at her with raised eyebrows. "Am I the only one who's paid attention to the parables?"

Minox saw no need to answer. Where he planned to go today, it was likely no saint could help him.

Amaya made a point not to show any favoritism toward Jerinne Fendall during the morning training. It was the same principle Master Denbar had treated her with during her Initiacy. They wanted no suspicion placed on her, no suggestion that her place at the top of the cohort was anything but earned. No one ever knew that Master Denbar was her mother's cousin, not even Dayne.

That wasn't the reason behind the facade between her and Jerinne in front of the rest of the Initiates. Jerinne had been consistently ranked near the bottom of the cohort, undeservedly, because that's what Grandmaster Orren and Master Nedell decreed. Amaya was certain that one of those two men were The Warrior of this Grand Ten conspiracy, and they were punishing Jerinne, drumming her out of the Order, for the part she played in the Patriot's Ordeal and the Election Crisis.

Amaya knew damn well Jerinne should be a Tarian. That was clear every morning. Most of the third-year Initiates were now up before the dawn, joining Amaya on her run up the Trelan Docks and back, and Jerinne was the one who always kept pace with Amaya. They'd get back to the chapterhouse and go through Vien's Spathian-inspired calisthenics, Jerinne pushing harder and stronger than anyone else in the cohort. Not that any of them were slacking or falling down. Some of them—like Iolana and Tander—had lost a certain spark after the fight in the Miniara Pass, but that didn't mean they held back when it came to the physical conditioning. These third-years, every one of them was dedicated and intense and put all of themselves on that training room floor.

And they were there for each other in ways that

Amaya had never seen an Initiate cohort be before. That was because of Miniara Pass, of course. All sixteen of these kids had been in an honest-to-the-saints fight where their lives were on the line, and that taught them more than any amount of training room exercises had. They helped each other, they encouraged each other, they lifted and supported, and hardly paid any attention to ranking anymore.

Amaya loved every one of those kids, but she definitely loved Jerinne the most. She couldn't show it on the floor, though. At least, not explicitly.

She showed it in her spar with Jerinne this morning, both of them with wooden practice shields and swords, both of them going full speed and strength. Amaya went at Jerinne brutally, attacking with every bit of skill, savagery, and subterfuge that she had. Jerinne gave just as much back.

She could see, in the spark in Jerinne's eye, in that sly tug at the corner of her lips, that she felt Amaya's love, and was giving it in return. She knew that this was how they respected each other, fighting this hard in an exercise spar, trusting that they wouldn't get hurt.

Amaya feinted to one side, and then dropped to sweep Jerinne's leg out from under her. Jerinne missed the step, and was knocked down on her back. Amaya sprung up, bringing her practice blade down on Jerinne's face, sure to break the girl's nose.

But it was blocked, another practice sword there for the parry. But it wasn't Jerinne's weapon—Enther was there, protecting his friend from the blow.

Saints, these kids were all Tarians.

"Good," she said, stepping away and wiping the sweat off her brow. "Well done, Enther."

"Between her and harm," he said, helping Jerinne to her feet.

"Lethal sweep, ma'am," Jerinne said. "I should have been faster."

"Damn right, you should have," Amaya said. "All right, break down, third-years. Weapons away, go get water and food, and meet up with your mentors. See you at Contemplation Exercises after supper."

The kids all went to work cleaning up the training room, filing out the door.

"Anything for me?" Jerinne asked.

"You tell me," Amaya said. "What's Dayne up to today?"

"Not sure," Jerinne said. "Yesterday we looked into some missing kids on the south side; he's probably planning on keeping a nose in that. It's the most interesting thing he's got going on."

Poor Dayne. Amaya knew the "liaison" position at the Parliament had already been a waste of time, and it seemed that with Tarians and Spathians taking an active role in the security of the Parliament, it would be even more pointless. And Dayne was stuck. But at least he was staying engaged.

"So are you going to help him with that?" Amaya asked. "If so, you can't be getting back in so late like last night." She noted most of the other third-years were out of the room, or paying them no mind. "At least a couple Adepts noticed and thought it was odd. Be sharper."

"Yes, ma'am," Jerinne said. "But this thing with the kids, I think it ties to the atrocity at the Parliament. Quoyell's arrest and then assassination."

Amaya gave Jerinne all her attention. "How so? There were kids involved in that?"

"Quoyell was involved in a ring delivering kidnapped kids to someone. Don't know why. But my inspector friend? She tells me that his assassination was orchestrated by Colonel Altarn. That was the woman you were interested in yesterday, wasn't it?"

Amaya resisted the urge to grab Jerinne by the arm. "You're certain?"

"I'm certain Missus Rainey thinks so."

Altarn was almost definitely The Mage. It all added up too well, especially with her sudden rise to the highest prominence in Intelligence and political circles.

"All right," Amaya said. "You find Dayne and you stay on that. Let me know if you need anything."

"Shield and sword," Jerinne said.

Amaya nodded. Raising her voice a little so the other Initiates could hear. "After you eat, go over the Armory, Initiate, and oil and sharpen blades. I'll personally inspect your work tonight."

"Ma'am," Jerinne said with a salute and a slight wink. She understood. She was on it.

Amaya wasn't going to waste any more of the day. She made her way to her quarters, brushing past the black-haired servant coming to clean the training room floor. She needed to change into civilian clothes. She had her own leads to investigate, and for this, she should not be in a Tarian uniform.

The household of Baron Vollingale was somber and quiet as Dayne and Lady Mirianne were led to his study by one of his underbutlers. They were brought tea and pastries in utter silence, to the point where Dayne felt awkward even speaking to Miri while they waited for the baron. She quietly accepted the tea and didn't break the silence herself until the baron came in.

"This must be the famed Mister Heldrin," he said as he crossed the room. "Thank you so much for coming, and thank you, Miri, for bringing him."

"Of course," Miri said, taking the baron's hand as he came over.

Baron Vollingale was a relatively young man, only a few years older than Dayne and Mirianne at best, but he had the harrowed look of a man who had aged years in the past few days. His fair hair was unkempt, his eyes were cast with dark circles, and he was wearing only a dressing gown, belted at the waist.

He sat down at the desk. "My gratitude cannot be adequately expressed, regardless."

"I don't want to get your hopes up too high, sir," Dayne said. "I am happy to help you in any way I can, but—"

"Of course, of course," Vollingale said. He sighed, and that sigh broke into sobs. "I'm sorry."

"Take your time," Mirianne said.

Neither of them spoke for a moment, and Dayne felt as if it was on him to prompt the conversation. "So I understand your situation might be connected to the ones I'm already looking into?"

"Yes," Vollingale said, dabbing his eyes with a kerchief. "Which surprises me, because until Miri talked to me last night, I thought—we had been explicitly targeted."

"A ransom situation?" Dayne asked.

"We presumed," Vollingale said. "This happened three days ago, late in the evening. I had been at the Hardicher Club, playing cards, and came home just around one bell. And I found my wife at the bottom of the main stairway, an absolute wreck, and one of the footmen badly injured."

"So, your home was invaded?" Dayne asked. "The person came here to abduct your son?"

"Person," Vollingale said with a scoff. "According to my wife's maid, it was some sort of monster, enormous. Taller than you, my friend. Skin of scaly gray. The sort of thing confined to Waish country stories. I couldn't believe such tales, but . . ."

"But?" Dayne asked.

"My wife, she could barely communicate with me. Whatever she saw, it terrified her."

"So what did she see?" Dayne asked. "Can I speak to her?"

"She is in no state, I'm sorry. She's only said one word since that night. 'Gurond.'"

That was of note. "That's a name another witness heard."

"Where?" the baron asked. "Who?"

"In Dentonhill."

"Who was taken there?"

"Children of factory workers," Dayne said.

"That makes no sense," he said, agitation rising in his voice. "Don't you know who that must be?"

"Gurond?" Dayne shook his head. "Should I?"

Vollingale sighed. "Maybe not. The Barony of Vollingale is in the eastern part of the archduchy, near Itasiana. It used to be two baronies, until about fifteen years ago. My family's, and our rivals, the Gurond family."

"Rivals?"

"Ugly, petty business that went back generations. Squabbles over land, over money, over anything. Too much blood spilt in the process, and so many lives destroyed, in both families. Not to mention the havoc it wreaked among common folk who were our tenants and residents. Nothing I am proud of, or ever had any part of myself."

"What happened fifteen years ago?" Dayne asked.

"I don't know all the details, as my father took them to his grave, but he had finally crushed the Gurond family. Devastated them utterly. They lost their land, their fortune, everything. Lord Gurond went to prison for years, ended up begging in the streets before he died. The lady killed herself, and their son—"

He faltered, his voice cracking. Mirianne reached across the desk and took his hand.

"It's all right."

"They had a son. Pendall. I'm given to understand he fell into a life of crime. An enforcer or assassin. He was a large brute of a boy to my memory. I imagine he grew up to match you in height."

"You think he's the giant we've been hearing tales of?" Dayne asked.

"I mean, this is—I only met him a few times, when I was about eight. I remember him as a cruel bully who had a . . . flair for the theatrical. He wouldn't just hurt you, he wanted to scare you."

Dayne understood. "You think the 'monster' is some sort of disguise he's adopted? And he took your son for . . . revenge?"

"Exactly," the baron said. "But how does that track with the other things you've heard?"

"I'm not sure," Dayne said.

"It's rather simple, actually," Miri said. "You say he became a criminal. Clearly, he's been drafted to abduct children, for a purpose we don't understand. He's largely been targeting vulnerable children in poorer neighborhoods. But the opportunity came to also make it personal, and he took it."

Dayne nodded. That made sense.

"Does this help you, Mister Heldrin?" the baron asked.

"It's another piece of the larger puzzle," Dayne said. "I'm afraid I don't have sight of the whole thing yet, and I know that's no comfort in terms of getting your son home and safe."

"No," Vollingale said.

"But I will keep working on this," Dayne said. "I will do whatever I can."

Vollingale got to his feet. "I appreciate that. Anything you need—money is no object, of course."

"Not necessary," Dayne said.

"Take care of yourself," Miri said to the baron. "You need to be strong for your family right now. You haven't slept, have you?"

"Not a drop," he said.

"I have a doctor who is very good," she said. "Should I send him to you?"

"Please," he said. "Thank you both so very much."

They were led out to Miri's carriage. "What are you going to do now?" she asked as she got in.

"I'm not sure," he said, staying on the walkway. "See what I can find out about this Gurond fellow, how it all connects."

"Aren't you getting in?" she asked. "I need to go to the store, but I can drop you, leave you the carriage if you need to get around . . ."

"No," Dayne said. "Like I said, I don't have sight of the whole picture, and . . . I think I want to walk so I can think it through."

"Of course," she said, leaning out of the carriage to kiss him. "Be kind to yourself, my love. It's not on you to save everyone."

Minox had spent the morning preparing himself. He first waited for most of the household to go to work, or, for the ones who were working moonslight shifts, to go to sleep. By nine bells, the only ones up and about in the house were Mother and Aunt Zura, both of them in the kitchen.

Confident he would not be interrupted, he went into his mother's room, and, more specifically, to his father's trunk. There he found what he would need: his father's old riding coat, as well as his crossbow and bolts. Sharp, deadly points. Not the Constabulary blunt-tips. Minox put it all together and put it in a knapsack with his own handstick.

In a few hours he would break law and convention, and force his way into the chapterhouse of the Blue Hand Circle. He might find nothing. He might find himself in the fight of his life against a well-trained mage. He might find children in need of rescue. He really had no idea.

He went downstairs, ready to face whatever it would be.

Mother was waiting for him at the front door.

"I really must be—"

"I'm not sure what you're doing today, Minox," she

said. "But, I've . . . I've lost a husband and a daughter already."

"I'm taking care of some personal business."

She gently touched his arm. "You're so smart, but you are not good at lying. I don't know what you have planned, and I won't try to stop you. There's nothing I could tell you that you haven't argued against yourself already."

He nodded. "I have thought through my intentions."

"Fine. But I have two requests."

He couldn't deny his mother that. "Yes?"

"Go tell Evoy. Don't leave here without seeing him."

Minox accepted that. "And the second?"

She picked up a paper bag. "I've wrapped up a few of Zura's spiced pork sandwiches for you. I . . . I have a feeling you might get hungry today." Her eyes welled with tears as she handed the bag to him.

"Thank you, Mother," he said, accepting an embrace from her. "Do you remember that story you would tell us when we were children?"

"I told you a lot of stories."

"'Aladha va calix,'" he said. "The creature was called a dragon. Was that also a title or rank of some sort?"

"I don't know," she said. "It was just one of the stories my grandmother used to tell me. Is it important?"

"I'm not sure," he said. "Part of what I'm doing today is looking for answers."

"Be smart," she whispered. "And come home."

"That is my intention," he told her. She wiped her face and went back to the kitchen.

He went out the door, and to the back of the house, to the stable. He knocked gently and went in. His cousin Evoy was there, as he always was, looking like only bones and hair and smelling of death. But, for once, Evoy was alert and active, reading through old newssheets.

"Minox," he said calmly. "And in daylight hours. Something is very afoot. Is today the day?"

"That depends what you mean."

Evoy chuckled. "The day they finally decide to bring me to join Grandfather at the hospital. But, no . . . that's likely not for another couple months, right? I assume my mother stops the discussion every time it is broached. And Corrie's disappearance has muted anyone's desire for further upheaval. For the time being."

"There's been no discussion in my presence," Minox said.

Evoy nodded, going up to the wall where several articles had been affixed, as well as chalk scrawls of Evoy's random thoughts. All of it madness, even though every time Minox looked at it, it made some small scrap of sense. He wished he could see what Evoy did, understand the grand picture that drove Evoy to spend all his time in the stable trying to figure it out.

"Then today . . ." He spun on Minox, eyes wild. "You're about to do something bold. Which makes sense. Things have been moving faster and faster, especially since that happened to you." He pointed to Minox's magic hand. "I didn't understand that at the time, and . . . all right, I still don't, but . . . I think how it happened is very important. What did that do to you? Where were they from?"

The spike. One of eight spikes Nerrish Plum had used to neutralize the mages he had killed, and nearly killed Minox with. It was surely the exposure to the spike that had catalyzed the change in Minox's hand, making it this unhuman, blackened non-flesh, holding immense amounts of magical power.

What had Olivant said of it? Unholy power. Enough magic to destroy the city. Perhaps he was right.

"Where had Plum gotten the spikes?" Minox asked Evoy.

"Yes. And what were they truly for?"

"Plum said something then. He was expecting retribution, from the Brotherhood of the Nine."

Evoy laughed. "Yes, that was why you wrote that there, right?" He pointed to that very name written on his wall. "The spikes had belonged to them, for whatever reason."

"Do you know who they are? I've dug through files, through newsprints. I've found nothing at all."

"I don't," Evoy said. He pounded on his bony sternum. "But I feel this . . . shadow moving over us all. The Grand Ten, the Brotherhood of the Nine, the eight pins, it's counting down and . . . today isn't the day for that, but it is a day for you."

"The missing children," Minox said, hoping that would make it clear.

"Yes!" Evoy shouted. "What did you find out?"

"Inspector Rainey was being taken to someone named Senek. He's a member of the Blue Hand. So that's where I'm starting."

"Dentonhill," Evoy said with understanding. "The giant taking the children. The reasons are all intertwined, a rope wrapping around the entire city choking . . ." He shook his head. "No, you interrupted my line of thought. That wasn't it."

"I didn't—"

"You're about to do something foolish, Minox," Evoy said. "But you know you need to."

"I do," Minox said.

"Then . . ." Evoy glanced around the barn for a moment. "No, that's not it. I remember. Don't go alone."

"What do you mean?"

"I can't go with you," Evoy said. "I can't—" He looked at the sunlight streaming through the open door. "I'm not ready yet. Soon. So today, whatever you have to do, I beg you, find someone who can be at your back."

Minox wished he could. Who would he even ask? Inspector Rainey was not an option. That was a shame, because there was no one else he would prefer.

He also considered Joshea Brondar—with his military skills and magic, he'd be very helpful in any emergency. But Joshea had definitely not recovered   physically or emotionally—from his ordeal at the hands of Sholiar. Minox had only spoken to him in brief moments since, and while Joshea was putting on a brave facade, it was clear he had been deeply affected.

Joshea would say yes if asked.

Minox would not put that on him.

He briefly considered someone else in his family, perhaps Jace. Edard knew Dentonhill, as did Ferah. But he couldn't bring himself to ask. Almost all of them would say yes, but he would be asking them to step outside the law. He was willing to take that step himself. He couldn't ask it of them.

Then the answer was clear: he had to seek assistance that operated outside the law. It was so obvious who to ask, he was embarrassed to not have already thought of it. Especially after thinking about the story "Aladha va calix," and the aptly named hero of that story.

He went out of the barn and got on his pedalcycle. The next stop was the University, to find Veranix Calbert.

Chapter 7

VERANIX PACKED HIS THORN OUTFIT, bow and arrows, and the napranium rope and cloak into a rucksack, changed out of his school uniform into normal city clothes. He wasn't sure exactly what was going to happen right now, but he wanted to be prepared. His fighting staff, though, he'd leave behind. It was just a bit too conspicuous for a walk out west, and since he was going with Delmin, it was best to walk appearing as normal looking as possible.

"So we're really heading out to the west side of town?" Delmin asked when Veranix met him outside Almers Hall. "You and me, together, to meet those . . . friends of Mila's?"

"They're fine," Veranix said. "I may need your tracking skills. If the giant is that Tarian fellow, I've got him tagged."

"You really think a member of the Tarian Order is involved in this?" Delmin asked. "You did pass Druth History, didn't you?"

"Yes," Veranix said. "I only know I saw him leaving Fenmere's, with that official I've seen come and go a few times. Something hinky is there, my friend."

"Maybe," Delmin said. He took a deep breath. "But, if you think I'll be useful, and if this is about helping children, I'm there for you."

"I appreciate it," Veranix said. "Besides, when we're out there, you have to try this Fuergan restaurant . . ."

They took a tickwagon through Gelmoor and Seleth, then walked the rest of the way to Frost Lane. At the corner of Ullen and Frost, a young Cloistress of the Blue, her blond hair tied back in a braid, walked straight into Veranix's path.

"You, young man, I need your help."

"Sister," he said, taken aback by her abrupt approach. "How can—how can we help you?"

She glanced at Delmin for a moment, as if his presence confused her. "I have an assignment to hear absolution from a man staying at Kimber's Pub. You will guide me to this place."

"Of course," he said. "That's actually where we were going anyway."

"Good," she said, taking his arm and starting to walk with him. "Earlier, I was reading the Testament of Saint Benton. You are familiar with it?"

"I'm not, actually," Veranix said.

"Standing on the bridge—" Delmin started.

"I was not asking you," the sister snapped.

"Benton isn't my saint," Veranix said.

She looked at him with a puzzled expression. "No, that can't be right."

"Always more of a Saint Senea fellow."

They reached the front door of Kimber's and the cloistress stopped and faced Veranix. She cupped her hand on his head and said, "Then pray to her with me."

Veranix almost pulled away, but something about the touch of her hand filled him with a sense of pure calm.

The instinct to withdraw fell away. He closed his eyes and bent his head down, and she touched her forehead to his.

"Give me your blessing, Saint Senea," they said together in reverent whisper. "Put your eye upon me, protect me, as I act in the name of the right. Give me your strength, to fight against the unjust, to stand for the oppressed. If my body is broken, guard my soul and deliver it to stand before judgment, which I will never fear as I act in your name."

He opened his eyes to see hers piercing into him: cool, blue, and strong. "Go without fear today, my friend. You are watched over."

She let go and went inside, leaving Veranix standing in the walkway, not even sure why he was crying.

"I am very confused," Delmin said.

"You're not alone," Veranix said, wiping the tears from his face. Despite that, he felt more peace than he had in months. He didn't know who the cloistress was, or what the day was about to bring, but he knew he was ready for it. "Let's do this."

Asti was in the taproom, nursing a cider while two pairs of strikers sat in front of him.

"I figured I had a couple of mages coming," Asti said. "So I thought I'd be prepared."

"Thank you," Delmin said as he sat down.

Veranix took a seat. "The kid is upstairs?"

"Verci and his wife are with him now," Asti said. He was looking at Veranix with an odd regard, and Veranix realized why. It was the first time Asti had seen his face. Blazes, for all Veranix knew, Asti didn't know his name. Perhaps it was best to keep it that way. "He's not in a good way, let me tell you."

"How so?"

"Let me tell you about this kid. I've known my share of tough kids on the streets out here. I was one of those tough kids. Verci and me, we ran our share of scraps back then."

"All right," Veranix said, not sure where Asti was going with this. He started eating one of the strikers to give the man a chance to talk.

"This kid, he puts us all to shame. I ain't never seen one this tough, this angry, this willing to fight. He's only six, best we figure, and he's a downright terror."

"Lovely," Delmin said.

"And whatever he saw, whatever he went through, it's scared him to his core. Maybe that's a good thing. It's the most normal, human thing I've seen from him."

Veranix understood. "What did he lose?"

"Everything," Asti said. "I mean, I've only known him as a street orphan, so I don't even know if he had parents around. But he had a brother. A twin brother. He—he got his head split open in the Election Riots here."

Verci came up to the table. "When Tarvis saw him, he made a sound like . . . I've never heard a person make that sound."

"So what's going to happen to him, once he's recovered?" Delmin asked. "There's orphanages, or the church, or—"

"He won't take any of that," Verci said. "I mean, his instinct is to escape. That's probably why he got away from whoever took him. He's ready for you all."

Veranix finished the strikers—which were quite good, he had to admit—and followed Verci upstairs to the room. The little boy—and saints, he was tiny—was lying on the bed, pale as a Poasian, while a woman sat next to him holding a damp cloth to his head. Asti said this boy was six years old? He looked like he was four.

"Hey, Tarvis," Asti said. "How are you?"

"Angry," Tarvis said. "I rutted up and lost Telly."

"Who's Telly?" Veranix asked.

"Who are these ninces?" Tarvis asked.

"We're here to find out what happened to you, stop the people who did it," Veranix said.

"You ninces?" Tarvis asked. "You ain't got nothing that can handle these rutters."

"That guy's the Thorn," Asti said. "He's in disguise."

Tarvis peered at him. "I don't see it."

Veranix remembered this kid now. He was with the other kids who had helped him and Mila. So was Telly. "Telly got taken, too?"

"Got taken. Couldn't get him out. Him or any of the others." Tarvis whimpered a little. "He told me to run, so I ran. Shouldn't have left him. But that guy, that giant, I couldn't kill him. Couldn't even hurt him."

Veranix sat down next to him on the bed. "What do you mean?"

"I stabbed him," Tarvis said. "My knife didn't even go through his skin."

"Wait, was this a person?" Veranix asked.

"Didn't seem like one. Barely spoke like one."

"He spoke?" Verci asked.

"Yeah. 'Gurond take children. Take them for the Brotherhood.'"

"The who?" Asti asked. His face looked like it was ready for violence.

"You heard me," Tarvis said.

"All right," Veranix said. "And he was the one who grabbed you and Telly? Where? And where did he take you?"

"We were by the abandoned factory, across the creek," Tarvis said. Veranix glanced to Asti and got a small nod—he knew where it was. "The bastard just came out of nowhere, grabbed us both, and took us into a tunnel to the sewers. Kept going, deeper."

"How deep?" Asti asked.

"I don't rutting know, deep," Tarvis snapped.

"When you came up, did you go up a slope, steps, a ladder?" Asti asked.

"All of 'em," Tarvis said. "Like I said, deep. I don't even know all of how I got up. It was a blur. I just knew I had to—"

He paused and looked at Asti.

"You found me, didn't you?"

"Yeah, in the alley."

"Dumbest thing," Tarvis said. "I was down there, hungry, dying, blind in the dark. Lost. But I knew I had to get out to find *you*." He growled a little. "I don't even like you, Rynax."

"You remember where you came out?" Verci asked.

Tarvis shook his head. "Nothing. I was down in the dark, and it's a blur 'til I woke up here." Another growl, this one more aimed at Veranix. "I'm tired. Get out. Let me sleep."

Veranix got up off the bed and went to the door, everyone else following behind him, none of them speaking until they returned to the taproom.

"So what's the plan?" Delmin asked when they sat down.

"What does he bring to this?" Asti asked, pointing to Delmin.

"He's the best damn magical tracker in the city," Veranix said. "If any of this involves magic at all, Delmin can sense it."

Delmin shrugged. "I mean, maybe. Is the idea we go to this factory, find this sewer entrance, and . . . see where it takes us?"

"Sewers and tunnels under this part of town are extensive," Asti said. "I mean, the city has got all sorts of catacombs and quarry digs, and . . . around here, some of the old street bosses built all sorts of tunnels and passageways using them. Nobody knows it all."

Verci nodded. "He's done a bit of mapping."

"I know enough to know there's a lot I don't know," Asti said.

"Right," Veranix said. "But I know one thing: Telly and who knows how many other kids are still down there. I'm going to try to find them. The question is, am I doing it alone?"

Delmin grabbed Veranix's arm and squeezed. "No, you stupid fool."

"I'm with you," Asti said. He had clearly been stewing on something Tarvis said, either Gurond or the Brotherhood. He glanced at Verci and his wife. "You stay up here, though. I'll mark our path on the way down and if we're gone too long, you get everyone you can for a rescue party."

"That's a good plan," Verci's wife said.

"That's what I'm good for, right?" Asti said.

Veranix stood up, feeling flushed with the same serenity he had received from the cloistress's prayer. This felt right, and now was the time to move. "Let's get to work, then."

Satrine couldn't think at her desk, partly because Kellman was tapping his stylus while he read over the report on one of the murder cases they had caught yesterday. It had been a straightforward investigation. The victims had been identified, and with a few choice questions to the folks in their lives, it had been simple to ascertain the guilty party: one victim's husband. The husband had tried to run when they confronted him, so Satrine had to tackle and restrain him. That was engaging.

"Yeah, I think this is good," Kellman said. "I think Protector Hilsom will agree it's a solid case."

"Of course it is," Satrine said. "What's next?"

"There's the Landorick murder," he said, holding out the file folder. The other murder from yesterday.

She scowled as she took it from him. "I don't think there's anything there. It looks like he was stabbed by a purse thief. I mean, tragic, but there's nothing to work with."

"Commissioner's office asked that someone here look into it."

"That's just because Landorick used to be an inspector. Retired a couple years ago. Drop it on one of the new folks. Benson or Careese."

"Fine."

She knew what she needed to do. Exactly what Minox would do if he was here. "You want to head out to East Maradaine?"

"What for?"

"That robbery," Satrine said. "There's something hinky there."

"Sure there is," Kellman said. "I mean, the guy refused to tell us what was stolen."

"You don't think that's odd?"

"Course I do," Kellman said. "But that means we've got no chance of breaking down the rest of it. I mean, maybe Welling would look at it and see some sort of pattern in the roads or the phase of the moons and figure it all out, but . . ." He shook his head. "I know I ain't like that."

"It's fine," she lied. "I'm tired of his sewage, anyway."

"Well, it's safe to go into the archives today," Kellman said. "He took the day off."

She shrugged, acting like she didn't care. Her whole body was filled with worry for him. She hoped he was right, whatever he was planning. She got up from her desk. If nothing else, some activity would occupy her attention.

"Have we eaten?" Satrine asked. "One thing about working with Minox, you never missed a meal."

"I could eat," Kellman said, putting the finished report on a clerk's desk. "Anything in mind?"

"Somewhere between here and East Maradaine," she said. "I want one more round of talking to the staff. Maybe someone saw something. Maybe someone will let it slip what was taken."

"I like where your head's at, Tricky," Kellman said. "Let's do it."

She got up and double-checked her handstick and crossbow. Ready for anything.

She was certain Minox was as well. She trusted he knew what he was doing.

Minox found the grounds of the University of Maradaine fascinating. On some level, he envied these children, being able to study for its own sake, but he knew
that he would not have been happy in this environment.
He could dig through records, research and analyze, but
he needed that to have a practical end. The abstraction
of university study never appealed to him.

But if his magic had developed at a normal age, he
would have been obliged to have come for study, to master his magic, to join a Circle. He wondered if Veranix
Calbert bristled at being here, or if he relished it. But
since the young man used his magic to fight the drug
lords and Fenmere as the Thorn, he suspected that Veranix wasn't a pure academic in his outlook.

After a few minutes of walking through the grounds,
Minox realized he had made a gross tactical error. He
did not know exactly how to find Veranix on campus. He
was here as a civilian, so he had no authority as an
officer of the Constabulary. Even if he had tried to exert
his authority, it could easily be called into question. Investigating on campus required writs and permissions,
and since he was not operating in an official capacity, he
could hardly call upon that authority.

So he needed a different way to find Veranix, and
before the campus cadets became too suspicious of what
he was up to.

Veranix had that rope, which was magical in nature,
that he used in his fight as the Thorn. Minox had formed
a connection to it, was able to use it much the same way
he was able to use his magical hand. Perhaps he could
sense it, and that could lead him to Veranix.

He closed his eyes and tried to reach out with his
magical senses. Feel his way to the rope, get any sense
of direction or location.

"Sir, what are you doing?"

Minox opened his eyes to see a young, dark-skinned woman standing in front of him, long-handled gardening tool in her hand.

"Sorry, miss, I—"

"You're standing in the pathway. My crew needs to work here."

"Your crew?" Minox looked to where she gestured, a few young men in work clothes.

"The grounds crew, sir. We've got to clear the weeds on the pathway, tend to the—"

"Of course," Minox said, stepping out of her way. There was something familiar about her, but he couldn't quite place it. "It's just—"

The words his brother had quoted this morning came to him. "Be guided by those who tend to the path."

"I'm looking for Veranix Calbert."

She startled for just a moment, then turned away. "I don't work with the students, sir. I'm just in charge of the grounds."

Dissembling.

"No, you know him," Minox said, moving closer to her. The twitch of her eye, the tightness of her jaw, it all spoke volumes. "You know he's the—"

"Keep that up, all down to the south gate," she ordered her men. Then she spun on her heel to face Minox, her grip on her tool tightening to strike. "You better walk away, mister, or I—"

"I need his help," Minox said, sensing she was protective of Veranix. Now he remembered why she was familiar. When he and Veranix stopped Enzin Hence in his monstrous form, she had been there. She was his friend. "I'm In—Minox Welling, I—"

Her grip relaxed. "You gave him the files." She grabbed him by the arm and led him away from the walkway, to the shade of a tree. "What's going on?"

"I've been tracking a lead, which involves the missing children of Dentonhill, and I suspect it is tied to the

Circle of the Blue Hand. I was going to investigate their abandoned chapterhouse, but thought it unwise to go alone. I had hoped—"

"Veranix would join you," she said. "And he would, but he's not around. He's—he's taking care of something else."

"When will he return?"

She shook her head. "You think it's urgent?"

"I think lives are already at risk, yes, but I—" He hesitated. "I can't involve the Constabulary on this. It's—"

"I get it," she said, pursing her lips in thought. "Give me five minutes."

"What will happen in that time?" he asked.

"I'll be ready to come with you," she said. "Where's this chapterhouse?"

"Price Street. Number 106."

"Wait here."

She jogged off, and he waited as instructed. She came back in five minutes, having changed her outfit to something that looked almost like the Thorn's outfit without the cloak—maroon canvas slacks, leather boots, and a maroon vest. She had tied back her thick, dark hair, and was carrying something wrapped in cloth.

"Let's go," she said. "I left him a note about where we're going."

"Miss," he said. "I asked for him because it is likely to be dangerous . . ."

"I'm aware," she said, holding up the bundle.

"And what's that?"

"My father's sword," she said. "In case of trouble."

He couldn't argue with that, though he had some small discomfort with any civilian walking about armed, especially with a sword. While he didn't know her or her capabilities, he could tell she was determined. She didn't hesitate at the idea of coming with him. "And you're prepared to use it?"

She narrowed her eyes at him. "Did you hear about

the guy who killed everyone at the Letters Ceremony last spring?"

"No, I didn't," Minox said.

She gave him a slight smirk. "Because I stopped him. All right?"

Fair enough. "I didn't get your name."

"Kaiana," she said as she led him toward the east gate. "Kaiana Nell. You say we're going after the Blue Hand?"

"That's where this investigation is starting."

"Then let's go," Miss Nell said. "I have my own account to settle with them."

Dayne's walk led him to the history library at the Royal College, and some brief discussions with the librarian there and a bit of unsatisfactory research. The problem was he wasn't sure what he needed to look for, but a nagging voice in his head told him it was something in the history of the city.

The words of the parable of Saint Keller came to him again. "Hold close those that are dear, thy beloved friends, and do not fear to share your burdens with them, for their counsel and wisdom shall guide you." Maybe he needed to talk it out. It was already past midday, he should eat something as well. So, even though it felt like he was admitting some sort of defeat, he went to the Nimble Rabbit.

"There you are!"

Sitting around the usual table were Hemmit, Maresh, and Lin, with Jerinne planted at the end, a wide grin on her face.

"What are you doing?" Dayne asked.

Jerinne shook her head. "Waiting for you to work your way over here, I think. I had checked over at the Parliament and you were gone, and I left you a note, and came here. Took you long enough."

"I've—I've been thinking about the missing children," Dayne said, confused by what was going on. "It seems to be more widespread than we—or at least there's a specific incident."

"What's up?"

"The giant took a child—a baron's child—and it's possible the giant has a grudge against the baron's family."

"Personal?" Hemmit asked. "How is that?"

"Someone named Gurond?" Dayne asked. "A noble family that lost their fortune?"

Hemmit shook his head. "I don't know the name."

Lin scoffed. "So this giant goes through Dentonhill, and Callon Hills, and saints even know where else, but no one sees him? How?"

"Sewers?" Jerinne asked. "We heard he used a passage in that basement. Maybe he mostly stays underground."

"There's a whole slew of tunnels, catacombs, and quarry digs beneath the city," Hemmit said. "Who knows how those interconnect?"

Lin shook her head. "Yeah, but he'd need a bridge or a boat to get across the river. He'd be seen."

The answer was on the edge of Dayne's memory. He knew he had read something, a story, a piece of the nation's history, that was exactly what he was looking for. But he couldn't think of it.

"The Necropolis of Saint Terrence Cathedral," Maresh said quietly while sketching.

That was it.

"Yes!" Dayne said.

"The what?" Jerinne asked. "Is this something to do with Terrentin? Are we doing gifts?"

"Lady Mirianne has made it very clear she's doing gifts," Lin said.

"No, no," Dayne said. "Saint Terrence Cathedral, it's part of the Royal College campus. So, during the Inquest, and then the Incursion of the Black Mage, Reverend Ottom Elt was sneaking people out of the city, and then when Oberon Micarum was captured—"

"And held prisoner in the Bench," Jerinne said.

"Elt helped sneak Xaveem Ak'alassa, Hanshon Alenick, and . . . the Ch'omik warrior—"

"Nancel-akra," Maresh offered, looking up from his sketches. "The three were able to secretly enter this part of the city to rescue him. The details weren't in any of the accounts, save Xaveem's journal, where he notes coming through a passage. An 'underbridge' across the river and through—"

Dayne jumped in, very excited. "Through the Necropolis of the Blessed House of Reverend Elt, which later became—"

"Saint Terrence Cathedral," Jerinne said, her face showing the same excitement Dayne was feeling. "So you think this Gurond came to the north side through that 'underbridge'? You find it, maybe you find the way to him."

Dayne's heart fell. "Except entrance to the Necropolis is forbidden to all but the clergy of Saint Terrence. And maybe the underbridge is just a legend. There's no way we can—"

"I've been there."

They all looked to Maresh.

"Been where?" Lin asked.

"The Necropolis. The underbridge. All of it." Maresh poured himself another glass of wine and casually sipped at it.

"What do you mean you've been there?" Hemmit asked, his voice jumping an octave.

"It's not like we were joined at the hip at RCM," Maresh said. "Art students had access to certain archives, and . . . it was not unheard of to make an . . . excursion. Especially for the Charcoal Club."

"The what?" Lin asked.

"This is the first I've heard of this," Hemmit said. "What is the Charcoal Club?"

Maresh gave a sly grin. "It's . . . it's kind of a secret

society of artists at RCM, going back for generations. And part of the rite of passage is to sneak into the Necropolis and make a sketch by candlelight."

"Of one of the tombs?" Dayne asked.

"Sure, of the tombs," Maresh said, in a tone that implied that was not the correct answer at all.

"I have a new level of respect for you," Hemmit said.

"Here's the point," Maresh said. "I've been down there. I know how to get down there, and how to get to the underbridge."

Hemmit threw back his glass of wine and stood up. "Then what are we waiting for?"

"Wait," Dayne said. "This is an illegal trespass."

"Dayne," Jerinne said. "We're talking about missing children. Who've been gone for days. And we don't have a better lead. Shouldn't we try?"

Dayne hesitated. "Maresh, you're certain you can get in there safely?"

"Absolutely," Maresh said.

"All right," Dayne said. "And you're willing to guide me?"

"Guide us," Hemmit said. "You shouldn't go alone."

"I'm in," Lin said.

Jerinne just smiled. Of course she was committed.

"All right," Dayne said. "Though I don't have a—"

"Stop," Jerinne said, going under the table. She came up with a shield, and Dayne knew exactly which one it was. The shield he had done his third-year trials with. The shield she had when she faced Tharek Pell. She handed it to him. "You've got a proper Tarian shield now."

"But—"

She pulled another one out. "I may have been instructed by Amaya to be properly armed. And she might be covering for me at the chapterhouse for the rest of the day. So you're stuck with me."

"Thus I asked the question," Hemmit said. "What are we waiting for?"

Chapter 8

THERE WAS AT LEAST ONE thing they needed
to wait on: being properly dressed and equipped for
a venture into underground tunnels. Hemmit was ready
to head out straight from the Rabbit, but Maresh quickly
corrected him about that notion. They needed water,
lamps, and oil at the very minimum, and Hemmit's soft
shoes were probably ill-suited for the journey. Lin insisted she go home to change as well, so they had agreed
to each get what they needed and meet back at RCM
campus in half an hour.

Hemmit raced to his flop to change to something appropriate, wondering what exactly he had that would fit
the bill. He had the boots and the heavy canvas slacks
he wore for his Wissen disguise. That and a work shirt,
a canvas coat, that should do it. Was it cold in the tunnels? Hot? He had no idea.

When he got into the flop, Amaya Tyrell was waiting
for him, out of her usual uniform. He almost didn't recognize her in civilian clothes.

"Did we plan to meet?" he asked.

"No," she said. "I just—I'm not here for that."

He had been taking off his clothes.

"Oh, no, I—sorry. I came here to change quickly."

She laughed. "Right. What's going on?"

"Briefly, Dayne is hunting a giant abductor of missing children, and Maresh knows where to look, and Lin and I will go along, in part because it's a great story."

Amaya raised her eyebrow. "Is Jerinne with you all?"

"Yes," he said. "Should she not be?"

"No, she . . . she should," Amaya said, a bit lost in thought. "Stay close with her. All of you, watch each other's backs."

"That's the idea," he said, finding the pants and shirt he wanted. "So what did you want?"

"Kemmer," she said. The surviving Haltom's Patriot, who had supposedly learned the identities of the Grand Ten. He had reached out to Hemmit months ago, but had since gone quiet. "No more tiptoeing around it. I need to find him."

"I haven't had any luck," Hemmit said. "I think he's gone to ground."

"Well, I need to try. What can you tell me?"

Hemmit scratched at his beard. "Braning. He and Kemmer were tight, and he also got away from the Parliament without being arrested. He was a brick and pipe man with his brother, and their father before. So maybe you can ask around those circles to find him—"

She nodded. "Yes. I can work with that."

"What's the urgency?"

"I've got a hunch," she said. "I think there's more connecting the Grand Ten to the missing kids and everything else you're looking at. But the only one with answers—"

"Is Kemmer. If you need, I could stay with you—"

"No, go," she said, almost too quickly. "I've got this. Try to keep Dayne out of trouble."

The way she said Dayne's name there, filled with affection and concern. He knew they had been lovers, and he never cared about that, but for a moment her obvious strong feelings for Dayne were so plain and raw, it stung. He knew there was no emotional bond between him and Amaya, and he accepted that. Even though he had not been taking their liaison too seriously, it was suddenly very clear where the depths of her heart still lay.

He wasn't surprised, or even jealous, but yet it stung. He would have to live with that.

"All right," he said. "If you don't hear from any of us by tomorrow, though—"

"I'll call out the whole Order," she said. "Where do we start looking?"

"The Necropolis of Saint Terrence," he said. "And then deeper into the catacombs."

"Exciting." She blushed a little.

"What?"

"It's nothing, just—" She sighed, looking away in embarrassment. "I got you something for Terrentin."

"You did?"

"It's nothing. Little thing. Silly—"

"No, I'm touched," he said. "I should—"

"You don't need to as well," she said, kissing him as she went to the door. "Just try not to get hurt."

"Yes, ma'am."

"See you soon," she said, and left.

He sighed. She was far more woman than he was worth. He was lucky to have any time with her.

But for now, he needed to find his boots and get to campus.

Asti still had a room at Kimber's, where he kept some of his gear. For some reason he had felt more comfortable with it here, away from the shop, away from Verci and Raych and the baby. It felt like a way to keep his promise to keep them away from a life of danger and violence. That was why he wanted Verci out of this action today. Perhaps dredging through the tunnels would be nothing. Perhaps it would be the death of him. Verci shouldn't take the risk. Shouldn't take any more risks. He had a family to care for.

Asti put on some good solid boots, a decent heavy coat, and Pop's set of knives at his belt, with another set in the boots and a couple throwing blades squirreled away in the coat for good measure.

Even still, the fact that Tarvis had said the Brotherhood couldn't be ignored. That was what Liora had said. That was who she worked for. When she took over his head, she told him to "serve the Brotherhood." Asti still had no idea what that was, but he was ready for answers.

Asti came back out of the room, ready to leave with the Thorn and his gawky friend, when a cloistress came out of Nange Lesk's room. Nange was taking his time dying, and Asti felt more than a little guilty about that. He was the one who had stabbed Nange in the belly, after all. Nange had asked for someone from the church to come see him, give his last Absolution.

"How's he doing, sister?" Asti asked.

"A troubled life," she said. "A long Absolution. We will not get through it all."

Saints, she was young. Somehow her face was both innocent and weary at the same time.

"He's had his share of trouble," Asti said, making for the stairs.

She put her hand on his shoulder. "He's not alone."

Asti stopped mid-step, her touch freezing him in place.

"Red-eyed and anointed in blood," she said in a low voice. "And a gift from God."

How did she know about that? How could she possibly? Asti wanted to turn to her, demand an answer. Instead, not even sure why he was saying it, Asti said. "I wish I could believe that's true."

"It is," she said. Her hand went to the back of his head, and she whispered ever so quietly in his ear. "Sleep, for he has much work to do."

Asti turned to her, but no one was there.

"Hey, Rynax?" the Thorn called from the bottom of the stairs. "You all right?"

Asti looked around, wondering what the blazes just happened. "I think so," he lied. "Just—"

"You were standing there in a daze for about a minute," Thorn said. "Ready?"

"Yeah, yeah," he said, coming down. "Let's get on with it."

Asti led them down through the street and across the creek to the abandoned factory. From there, the signs of a scuffle, the tracks to the sewer pipe, they were all pretty obvious. While Asti checked that out, the Thorn rifled through his pack, getting on his gear, including the bow and arrows Verci had made for him.

"What about you, kid?" Asti asked the friend while the Thorn readied himself. "You gonna get suited up or anything?"

"I don't really have anything special to wear," the kid said. "I mean, I'm *really* not supposed to do this."

Asti pulled out a small dagger and flipped it over to hand to the kid hilt first.

"I wouldn't know what to do with it," the kid said.

"Pointy end hurts people," Asti said. "Just in case."

The kid took it and shoved it into his belt.

"All right," the Thorn said, his face covered in shadow. "Down and deep."

"Is that really necessary?" Asti asked. "I mean—"

"There's chances I shouldn't take," he said. "I've already extended a lot of trust to you and yours, Rynax."

"All right," Asti said. "Down and deep."

He took them down into the sewer pipe, and took a piece of chalk out of his pack. Mark on the wall for Verci. Then he lit a lamp and went deeper in.

"All right, kid—"

"It's Delmin, you know." Asti found it amusing how guileless this kid was. A strange contrast to the Thorn. Saints, Asti still didn't know the Thorn's actual name. Probably best that way.

"What are you feeling down here?"

Delmin closed his eyes for a moment. "There's definitely . . . something odd."

"Odd how?" Thorn asked.

"I mean, it's like . . . can you feel it?"

Thorn shook his head. "You know my senses aren't like yours."

"If I had to put it to words, it's . . . like the *numina* equivalent to taking a sip of milk that's about to go bad."

"Soured?" Asti asked. "Can magic be soured?"

"I mean, that sounds right, but I've never read anything like that. I've never—but it's definitely a thing that happened here." He walked down a way, turning a corner into one of the red-bricked tunnels that were not part of the sewers. Many of Josie's secret tunnels looked like this, and Asti had made an attempt to map them to little avail.

"Whatever it is, it's stronger below us," Delmin said. "Down and . . . north."

"North it is," Asti said. "Let's keep moving."

Dayne had known fear, he had been afraid many times. Each year he went to his Initiate trials. Facing Sholiar, both times. When he fought Tharek Pell on the Parliament floor.

But none of those moments of fear felt as raw or as visceral as standing outside the gate behind Saint Terrence Cathedral while Maresh jimmied the lock open.

"Is this really safe?" Dayne asked. "What if we get caught?"

"Saints, Dayne, you sound like a first-year heading to the girl's dorms," Maresh said. "Relax." He clicked something and the gate opened. "Let's move."

Maresh went in, and Dayne followed his lead, with Hemmit, Lin, and Jerinne taking up the rear.

"Are we sure no one's down here?" Dayne asked.

"No," Maresh said. "There might be priests, or other art students, or you know, the giant we're looking for."

"I don't like these jokes," Dayne said.

"This is what I've got," Maresh said. He took a lamp out of his bag and lit it. Jerinne did the same, while Lin held up her hand and gave off a glow.

"Cheater," Hemmit said.

As they entered the Necropolis, Dayne's fear changed to disappointment, and then annoyance.

The Necropolis was nothing close to what he had imagined.

In his head, it had been a pristine mausoleum, a sanctum of rest for the regal and sacred who had been laid there. Instead it was dank and dusty, with far more skulls lining the walls than he had been prepared for.

"So many skulls," Jerinne said.

Among the skulls were marked coffins embedded in the walls, as well as niches where unadorned half-skeletons lay in twisted positions.

"I was expecting—"

"Tombs befitting a king?" Maresh asked. "Afraid this place has been vandalized and looted for years."

"Tragedy," Dayne said.

Maresh led them down a cramped, dark hallway, and Dayne had to crouch down to make it through. Whoever built this place did not think about a man his size. He pushed his way through, his heart pounding as they went.

Maresh went on as they continued. "For example,

down there is the tomb of King Maradaine the Tenth. But it's been stripped clean, and the plaques have rather nasty things painted on them."

"What sort of things?" Hemmit asked.

"Nothing I care to repeat," Maresh said. "But some people had strong feelings about his failure to hold off the Black Mage and General Tochrin."

Dayne's heart continued to pound like a Linjari drumbeat, even as the tunnel seemed to get narrower and narrower. "Why haven't the priests cleaned it up?"

"I think they did, and it keeps coming back. Strong feelings last a long time, apparently."

"But . . ." Dayne sputtered. He couldn't say more than that, not with the walls pressing into his shoulders.

The tunnel opened up to a wide chamber. Dayne felt his heart calm down, and he went to sit on the stone ground for a moment.

"You all right?" Jerinne asked.

"Wasn't prepared for it to be this cramped," Dayne said. "Glad to be out of that passage."

"And what's this room?" Hemmit asked, holding up his lamp. Lin lifted her hand up, and a soft glow came from it. Here the skulls and other morbid imagery were gone. Instead, the walls had faded imagery of the sigils of each archduchy in Druthal.

"The Chamber of Unity," Dayne said in a low voice. "As Druth was reunified, one hero from each archduchy was honored to be put to rest here, together, on equal ground."

But the ten sarcophagi were cracked open and broken. The bones of these heroes, their relics . . . all gone.

"What happened?" Dayne demanded of Maresh. "Where are Lief Frannel and Sammin Kinnest and . . . great blazes, Saint Alexis?"

"This place has been ransacked for decades," Maresh said. "Have you not been listening to me?"

"I'm just . . ." Dayne shook his head. "I'm disgusted.

In the people who would do this—you didn't have any part in that?"

"I leave things like I find them," Maresh said. "Most of the Charcoal Club folks do. Though you know how it is with some folk. They come down here with a few bottles, things get out of hand."

"Horrible," Dayne said.

"All right," Maresh said. "If you thought that passage was tough, this next one will be very bad." He pointed to a cut in the wall that was little more than a hole that came up to Dayne's hip.

"That's the tunnel under the river?" Dayne asked.

"No, it leads to it. About a quarter of a mile of that, elbows and knees, sloped down. It's not going to be easy."

Jerinne went and looked down the hole. "There's no way this giant went down there."

"We don't think he necessarily did," Dayne said. "But the tunnel under the river. You've seen it?"

Maresh nodded. "Didn't go very far, because it was pretty damn late the time a few of us went down there. But that's a sizable passage. Like, big enough to roll wagons through."

Hemmit scratched at his beard. "That . . . that seems like a lot of work to build."

Maresh shrugged. "I don't know why it's like that. I'm just telling you it is."

Jerinne took off her belt and scabbard. "Dayne, shield and sword."

"What are you thinking?" Dayne said as he took his off.

"We're not going to be able to crawl through there with them strapped on. Give me your belt as well. I'll lash them all together and drag them behind me."

"I can—"

"Dayne," she said, looking down the hole again. "You're going to have a hard enough time getting through that passage. You shouldn't have to worry about anything else. I've got it."

He fought through his usual urges to take care of everything. Let himself accept the help. Jerinne was more than capable. "All right. I should go through last."

"Yeah," Lin said, coming over. "I'd say me first, then Jerinne, Maresh, Hemmit, and you."

"You don't want me to take the lead?" Jerinne asked.

"I mean, you all would have to try and hold a lamp while crawling along, and that's going to be a challenge. But if I go first—" Her whole body started to emanate a warm glow. "Then I'm your lamp."

"Brilliant," Hemmit said. "In every sense."

Jerinne finished lashing the shields and weapons together with the belts, wrapping the whole thing in her uniform jersey, and tying it to her ankle. Standing above the hole in her shirtsleeves, she asked, "Are we ready?"

Lin answered by crawling down and going in. Jerinne followed, and Maresh gave Dayne a sympathetic pat on the shoulder before going in himself.

"I mean," Hemmit said with a self-deprecating chuckle, "it would hardly be seemly to let them go without us at this point. Even if it is . . ." He stopped himself. "Fear is nothing but an enemy to be conquered, right?"

"You've been reading Escarian, haven't you?" Dayne asked.

"Guilty," Hemmit said. "I've actually been digging through all the Elite Order narratives. Have you read—"

"Start crawling!" Maresh yelled from inside the passage.

"Another time," Dayne said.

Hemmit got on his knees, and with a deep breath, went in.

Dayne blew out the lamp that Maresh had left on the desecrated tomb of Saint Alexis, leaving himself in the darkness save the faint glow coming from the narrow passage. He was glad to not have to look at this room any longer. He couldn't believe that such a rich part of Druthal's history, the legacy of the nation and its founding, the sacred rest of some of the people who died for the nation—that all of that would be so callously treated, desecrated. It broke Dayne's heart, more than almost anything he had ever seen. What had become of these bodies, the relics and artifacts that had been interred with them? Were they lost forever? Dayne hoped they could be found again, placed somewhere with care and security, but he feared that there was no chance of that. Kinnest's helmet was probably being used to hold down papers on some desk somewhere.

Tragedy.

"Dayne!" Hemmit called from the passage.

The light was fading. He needed to go, move forward. The only way out was through, now. Taking a few deep breaths, he got on his hands and knees, and started to crawl into the tiny space.

It was tighter and harder than he had imagined. He pushed and crawled; every inch was a struggle. There was almost no space to move his arms, no way to slip through without scraping his body against the stone. Every breath was a struggle.

He could barely force himself forward. There was no way to go back. The light from Lin had vanished. He was in darkness, pressed on every side. His friends' voices were far in the distance.

Nowhere to go.

No one with him.

He pulled himself another inch. Another impossible victory. This all was impossible. There was no way he could possibly—

Darkness.

Alone.

Pressing down.

Crushing his chest.

Can't breathe—

Can't survive—

"Dayne!"

A hand curled itself into his.

He opened his eyes. He didn't remember closing them.

Jerinne facing him, a soft glow of light coming from behind her.

"Why are you—" He had to force the words out.

"You were screaming, I came for you," she said.

"You shouldn't have," he said. "I . . . I'm going to die here. I failed . . . I always fail."

"Don't say that," she said. "You're closer to the end than you think."

He heard her, but his thoughts dwelled on all his failures. Lenick. Master Denbar. Sholiar "No, no, I let so many people down, Master Denbar would be alive . . . ."

"Dayne," she said quietly, squeezing his hand gently. "You remember the contemplation exercises? Calming your mind at the end of the day?"

"Always hated those."

"Same," she said. "But right now, slow your breath, hold the flame in your thoughts. Keep it controlled. Breathe through the fear. Let the calm fill your body."

"Those aren't the words," he said.

"Still," she said. "That's what I need you to do. Then I'm going to start to go down; you're going to come with me."

"I can't—" He closed his eyes again, trying to hold back the tears.

"Eyes on me, Candidate," she said. He opened them again, focusing on her caring eyes, her kind face. "I've got you. We're going to move together."

"I—"

"Tell me about the Line of Cedidore," she said as she moved back, still gripping his hand. "Kings at the beginning of the Shattered Kingdom. River Wars, Quarantine Wall, all that?"

"Right," he said, letting her strength help pull him forward just a bit. "Of course, Shalcer was the king at the actual shattering of Druthal, and when he died the lords of Maradaine and the ruling council wanted to find someone strong to rule them. Shalcer's son, Prince Malceen, was considered completely unfit. Some sources say he was even dumber than Shalcer, unable to speak in complete sentences. The court sequestered him off in a forgotten wing of the castle, and the lords selected one of their own, Cedidore, the second cousin of Shalcer, to be the new king."

"Cedidore the Mad," she said.

"The great tyrant," he said, telling her everything about Cedidore's reign, how he decided that rather than trying to reclaim the parts of Druthal that had broken into new kingdoms, he would consolidate his power and cleanse his nation of any "subversive elements." He hadn't even gotten to the true start of the Quarantine after Count Rowland's failed coup when suddenly Jerinne was pulling him to his feet.

"See?" she said. "You made it out."

He was out of the tunnel, now in a grand chamber that arched twenty feet high, a hub with several tunnels large enough to roll carriages through in many directions.

Dayne said the first thing that came to mind.

"Why didn't we come here that way?"

"I don't know how to get here from that direction," Maresh said. "Blazes, who knows where those even go?"

"All right," Dayne said. "But where do we go?"

"That way," Maresh said, pointing to the widest, largest tunnel. Just seeing that made Dayne breathe easier. "Southwest, under the river."

"Under it, incredible," Hemmit said.

"Near as I can reckon, this underbridge runs almost exactly under the Grand Maradaine Bridge, but that was only built twenty years ago. Right?"

"This is all much older," Hemmit said.

"The current bridge was built using the support buttresses of the old Keller Walk Bridge," Dayne said. He looked over to Jerinne, a warm smile on his face. "Built during Cedidore's reign. This might have been done at the same time."

"Tyrant kings do get things done," she said.

"Thank you," he told her.

"Always."

"Everyone," Lin said, pointing down the passage. "We're not alone."

Dayne pivoted, catching the shield that Jerinne tossed to him. He stepped up to the passage entrance, shield high. Jerinne took a stance next to him.

The passage was dark, but there were definitely two figures a few hundred feet away.

"Hello?" Dayne called. "Identify yourselves. We mean no harm."

"Is that a good idea?" Hemmit asked.

"We don't," Dayne said. "No need to provoke something."

Lin increased the intensity of her light. Not enough to see too far down the underbridge, but enough to better make out the two people.

Only for a moment. They both ran off into the darkness.

"Well, that was troubling," Lin said.

"You spooked them," Dayne said.

"I was spooked by them," she said. "Did you see them?"

"I didn't get a good look, no," Dayne said. "Two men, but they ran off."

"Men?" she asked. "Maybe in the darkness, but their bodies were misshapen, out of proportion. Like no men I've ever seen."

"Yeah," Jerinne said. "What I saw wasn't . . . normal."

Dayne wasn't sure what to make of that. "Perhaps a trick of the light. Perhaps something else. But we shouldn't just stand here."

"Right," Hemmit said. "Ever forward. Even with . . . odd residents."

"But Jerinne and I will take the lead," he said. "Shields up, at the ready."

"Right," she said. "No telling what else we'll find down here."

Dayne smiled, finally able to let the muscles in his neck relax, find an easy rhythm to his lungs and heart. "Whatever it might be, we face it together."

"Always," she said with a sly grin. "Let's stop wasting time."

Chapter 9

"THIS IS A WASTE OF time, Trick."

Satrine waited at the gates of the Callwood Estate in East Maradaine, while Kellman was still getting out of the wagon. Kellman was dragging his heels even more today than most days, which was saying something. "You have a few too many beers last night with that clerk from the Protector's Office?"

"Nothing like that," he said, a slight blush creeping to his cheeks. "Just . . . we got a few cases on our desk, so why are you fired up on this one?"

"Instinct," she said.

"That's some Minox sewage," he said. "Sorry."

"Nah, it's fine." She rang the gate bell. "But you've got to admit, this smells hinky. Break in at a rich manor house, and they call in the Constabulary because they want the thief found and caught, but no one is talking about what was taken? Doesn't that stoke a little fire in you?"

"It's odd, yeah," Kellman said.

"So, we'll do a show about checking out the scene. Looking for boot prints, all that."

A servant was coming up the lane to open the gate. "Call in Leppin and his crew?"

"That might be more show than we need. We won't crack this with boot prints."

"What's the plan?"

"Follow along," she said quickly as the servant reached them.

The servant—a young woman in a housemaid uniform—opened the gate. "Terribly sorry for making you wait," she said, in an accent that sounded back country, from a village outside Solindell in the northern part of the Sharain. "You've come back here to investigate the robbery?"

Satrine matched the accent. "Right on that, miss. Hoped to save everyone here some trouble, we were, but I'm fearful we're going to have to turn this place right upside down." She walked down the lane to the house, patting the girl on the arm. "I know it's frightful business, and I'm proper sorry about the upset it'll all be."

"If that's what needs be," the girl said, her darting eyes betraying her confidence. "I'm sure his lordship will be very grateful for your service."

"It's what we do," Kellman said, raising an eyebrow at Satrine.

"The real shame of it is, we've got so little right now," Satrine said. "But you know how these things go."

"I have no idea how these things go," the maid said.

"Oh, of course," Satrine said. "Because you're a good and decent girl, aren't ya? I bet everyone in here loves you, and you are so fond of each of them."

"We—" Her voice faltered a bit. "We are proud to serve the Callwood family as best we can. Everyone here."

"And Lord Callwood loves all of you as well, I'm certain. I know how a noble soul like him knows his duty is to look out for the people below him."

"It'll kill him to have to fire someone," Kellman said.

"Fire, what?" the maid asked.

"I mean, we have to do this formal-like," Satrine said. "Sit with his lordship, and then interview each person on the staff with him. Get down to the bottom of things."

"Each person?" the maid asked. "What do you mean?"

"I mean, and I know how frightful this sounds, but we're going to need to get to the bottom of things, and that means . . ." She paused for dramatic effect, giving a glance to Kellman. "He's going to ask some indelicate questions, miss. That's just the nature of it. We're going to have to figure where everyone was at each hour of the night in question. Where they were, who they were with, what they might have heard. Secrets will come out, and his lordship will have to take steps."

"Secrets?" the maid asked. They were now at the back door to the kitchen. "I mean, these are goodly people who work here. None of them—" Her voice cracked for a moment. "None of them deserve to have their personal matters turned upside down."

"I agree with you," Satrine said. "I mean, I would hate if someone lost their position over some . . . personal matter that isn't related to this investigation. But of course, as these things go, that's sure to happen."

The young woman's face flushed, and her hand reached out to Satrine's arm, quivering ever so slightly. "Perhaps—" she said, and then started again with her voice a bit more under control. "Perhaps you could have a discreet word with Mister Jescint in the stables before you begin all that. That might . . . it might . . . illuminate your investigation."

"Perhaps we should," Satrine said. She pointed behind the house. "Are the stables over there?"

"Yes, ma'am," the maid said. "Shall I let the head of staff know you are here?"

"Please," Satrine said. "But we'll have that discreet word first."

"Very good," the maid said, and went inside.

Kellman let out a low whistle. "You are an evil woman. How did you know she knew something?"

"I really didn't," Satrine said. "But everyone has secrets they don't want getting out, and everyone is afraid to lose their job. A little pressure, and some time is saved." She led the way to the stables.

"So, is Jescint our thief?" he asked.

"Doubt it," Satrine said. "If anything, he was either bribed or blackmailed to facilitate something for the real thieves."

"Like leave a back gate unlocked for them?" Kellman asked. He clucked his tongue uncomfortably. "Yeah, that tracks."

"Let's find out," she said, raising her hand to knock on the stable door.

"One thing," Kellman said before she knocked. "Let's give him a chance to be clean with us, and if he does, otherwise leave him be. He's the small fish."

"Why, Kellman," she said gently. "You're kinder than you let on."

"He's a working guy, like us," Kellman said quietly. "Let's give him a chance."

"Sure," she said. "Let's see where this takes us."

Minox was definitely out of his element, and far from his comfort. He stood outside the Blue Hand Chapterhouse—abandoned, by all outside appearances—ready to commit what was definitively an act of trespass, in the company of a young woman—a stranger—with an army blade on her hip.

And yet he felt calm and certainty. This was what was necessary.

Miss Nell also seemed calm about what they were about to do. Her sober demeanor had briefly dissolved when he rode her on the back of his pedalcycle—her

whoops and shouts a combination of fear and excitement—
but now that she was back on her feet and the pedalcycle
secured out of sight, she was once again tranquil.

"What we are about to do is in violation of the law,
Miss Nell," he told her. "I want you to understand that."

"Everything about these Blue Hand bastards is a violation," she said. "Vee said they were gone, but—"

"They seem to be," he said. He pointed to the steps
of the stoop, the handle of the door. "The level of dust
and debris indicates that, if nothing else, no one has
come or gone in months. At least using the front entrance. Hardly definitive, but notable."

"So do we kick the door open?" she asked.

"It would have a certain degree of satisfaction," he
said. "But I insist on some measure of legal appropriate-
ness, despite everything we are doing." He climbed the
steps and knocked loudly. "Hello, is anyone about?"

She followed him up to the door. "Isn't that going to
give us away?"

"If one of them is in residence, I'd prefer a frontal
confrontation over being taken by surprise, where they
might have advantage over us."

She shrugged, and pounded on the door herself.
"Hello, I've got a complaint to lodge with you kidnapping, creepy, rabbit-wearing bastards!"

"Rabbit wearing?"

"It's a long story," she said.

"I'm satisfied we've fulfilled the requirements of decency, if not law," Minox said. "Now, let's see if I can
manage some subtlety."

He channeled just a hint of magic, a bare fraction of
the torrent that flowed through his hand, and with it
reached into the latch of the door and twisted it. The
door slowly creaked open.

"Nice," Miss Nell said. "I thought you were Uncircled."

"No formal training," he said, stepping across the

threshold. "But my current situation demands I learn control over every aspect of my power."

"Because of your hand?" she asked.

A flash of anger coursed through him, but he tamped it down. It was not reasonable to be angry at this young woman for her deduction. "How did you know?"

"Vee—Veranix. He told me that it's changed somehow. He could connect to it like he can the rope he carries. And you could connect to the rope."

"There is some—resonance there, yes." The antechamber of the house had a level of dust that indicated no regular occupation for several months. A glance about the sitting room revealed the same. And the scent pervading the place was inhuman.

"So did your hand become napranium?" she asked.

"Become what?" That was a term he was wholly unfamiliar with. "I suggest we focus our search of the house on finding a basement."

"Why a basement?"

"I have specific suspicions of how the kidnappers are operating—specifically using underground tunnels—so the basement is a logical point of examination."

She glanced about. "Most houses like this, the way down is from the kitchen, which is usually back that way. Do you know what napranium is?" She took the lead walking down one hallway.

"It is not a term I have come across before."

"All right, first of all, Veranix should do better by you, given what you've done to help him. Get you some Magic Theory books. When we're done with whatever this is, I'll see what I can do about that."

Minox stopped mid-step. "You would do that?"

"I mean, I've done some reading. A lot goes over my head, like about how gemstones—especially cut ones—can divert and alter the flow of *numina*—"

"*Numina*?"

"The—" She turned and looked at him. "The energy of magic. Did you not—sorry. Rude of me. We're definitely going to get you some books, Inspector."

"Thank you, Miss Nell."

"Napranium is a metal. It's what the rope is made of. Or, more correctly, very thin fibers of it have been woven into the rope. And the cloak he wears." She entered the kitchen, which stank of filth and decay. Clearly, when the Blue Hand had left the house for the last time, no one had taken the care to wash dishes or put things away. Plates and bowls covered in mold, and no aspect of the original food was remotely recognizable.

"It's a metal with magical properties?" he asked.

"Not exactly, but it . . . as I understand, it draws *numina* to itself, focusing it, and accepts it more readily. That's why Veranix can control the rope so easily. With a normal rope, it would be much harder."

"Intriguing," Minox said. Not wanting to linger in the fetid kitchen, he went to the door that should lead to the basement. It was notable because it was reinforced with iron, and a large bolt-latch held it shut. "That is troubling, to say the least."

"I wonder what they wanted to keep down there," she said. "Saints knew they were up to some strange business."

"As many people in this city are," he said. He drew up his crossbow. "I once encountered a bear someone was keeping in a dug-out pit in a back room."

"You think there's a bear down there?" she asked, her voice cracking.

"I think you should draw that sword and be prepared for any eventuality," he said. He lifted the heavy metal bar of the latch and slid it open with a hard clanging sound that echoed through the house. Cautiously he opened the door, revealing a wooden staircase that descended into darkness.

"Do you have a lantern?" she asked.

He held up his left hand and made it glow, while training his crossbow down the steps. He went down slowly, with her right behind, until he reached the landing.

The room was chaotic madness. Slateboards with scrawls and writings that made Evoy's ravings seem sane. Shelves filled with jars of chemicals of every color, and more jars with bizarre objects suspended in liquid. Another shelf covered with a heavy tarp. Several tables with copper shackles on them, and other devices of metal and gear work that made Minox's blood run cold.

"By every blessed saint," Miss Nell said in a hoarse whisper. She walked over to the shelves, peering at the jars. "Are these dead animals? Is this a rat or a toad?"

Minox went to examine what she was looking at. In all honesty, the dead creature floating in the jar could be either one, or neither, or both at the same time.

"Some wicked business has been done here, that is certain," he said.

"Magical experiments?" she offered. "They were the ones who had commissioned the rope and the cloak in the first place, and it was for some ceremony to create a creature of pure magic."

That was interesting. "How so?"

"I don't know, exactly, but—that was the bit with Lord Sirath wearing the dead rabbit on his head. Veranix stopped it and . . . well, they're all gone now."

"All except for Ithaniel Senek," Minox said. On one of the tables he found a stack of journals, all of them with "I. Senek" emblazoned in gold lettering on the spine. Opening the top book, he found pages filled with notes and sketches and symbols.

"Who is he?" Miss Nell asked.

"He is why we came," Minox said. He thumbed through the notebook, and on immediate inspection, most of what was written was beyond his understanding. "My partner rescued a group of kidnapped children who were to be delivered to him. You said you've read some Magic Theory, yes?"

"I've gleaned a little," she said, looking over his shoulder. She stopped him from turning a page, mouthing out the complicated words on the page. "But this is nothing I'm familiar with."

"Do you know anyone who would be able to make sense of this?"

"Professor Alimen?" she offered. Minox remembered that man screaming at him on campus last month.

"Not my preference."

"Delmin, maybe," she said. "I know a couple others who could really break it down, but they're no longer in Maradaine." She turned a few more pages, revealing anatomical sketches, drawings of human bodies with lines, circles, and equations highlighting specific points. Each drawing was more and more grotesque.

Minox glanced around the room in disgust. "Everything in here is evidence of some sinister action. I hadn't thought this through. I . . ." He paced about, emotions churning in his gut. "I am a fool, clearly, thinking I had the tools, the knowledge, to investigate this on my own, outside the bounds of the law."

"Inspector!" she said sharply. He turned to her, and she gestured to his hand.

It was glowing bright blue. He hadn't been paying attention to his magic, letting it churn and embroil in him, bleeding out his hand.

"Sorry," he said.

"No, don't apologize," she said. She pointed over to the tarp-covered shelves. There was a similar blue glow coming from underneath the tarp, and a scratchy, rattling sound came from underneath.

"That is decidedly unsettling," Minox said, approaching the shelf. Miss Nell raised the sword as he pulled down the tarp.

Cages—five of them—occupied by monstrous creatures that were neither cat nor rabbit. All of them glowing blue. All of them were shuddering, like they were having some sort of seizure.

"Blessed Saints!" Miss Nell exclaimed. "What . . . what are they?"

"I'm not sure," he said, noticing that his hand was glowing stronger, despite his attempts to pull in the magic flowing into it. "I think I'm affecting them. Or they're affecting me."

All five started smashing their heads against their cages. Minox jumped back, away from the shelf.

"Should we do something?" Miss Nell asked, daring to move closer. "They're suffering."

"They could be dangerous," Minox said. "Or even diseased."

She glanced at the tarp. "The dust on that, it's covered the shelf for weeks. How are they even alive?"

"A disturbing mystery," Minox said as the smashing of the cages grew louder. The doors of the cages were about to snap. "Miss Nell, move away."

She stepped away, but only to grab a leather glove off one of the tables and put it on.

"What are you doing?" he asked.

"Something foolish," she said.

One of the creatures broke out of its cage and leaped to the floor. She snatched it out of the air with her gloved hand. It shrieked and squealed, and attempted to bite her hand with its wild, misshapen teeth. Its blue glow grew more intense.

"What are you hoping to accomplish?" he asked.

She held it up, far enough from her face that its paws couldn't reach her. "I've seen a lot of animals, and I've never seen anything like this."

He moved a bit closer, cautiously, and looked back to the dead creatures in the jar. The beast, whatever it was, seemed decidedly unnatural. Its left legs did not match its right. One ear was definitely lapin, while the other was feline. "It's like two different animals were shoved into each other."

"Maybe that's exactly what it is," she offered.

"Dark, twisted magic," Minox said. "I wonder if we can safely bring this creature, and some of this other material, to the examinarian at my stationhouse."

"I thought this couldn't be used as evidence," she said. "We're outside the law."

"We are, but Mister Leppin is the sort who would allow his curiosity to trump the statute. He might have insights we—"

The other cages all broke open, and the creatures bounded to the floor. Minox braced himself for an attack, but none came. Instead, all of the beasts scrambled to the same spot on the floor, and worked furiously at clawing and scratching the boards there.

"That's very curious," Miss Nell said. Belting the sword, she glanced around until she spotted a broom. "Get ready to check it out."

With the one creature still in her gloved hand, she pounced at the others, broom at the ready, and swept them from the spot on the floor. She kept them away from the spot with well-placed bats, and Minox moved in quickly to the area of the floor that had their interest. A quick inspection revealed what was interesting about it: a trapdoor, almost imperceptible. Minox opened it up, revealing a dark stairwell going deep into a stone corridor.

The four creatures hurled themselves down the steps into the darkness, their blue glow fading out of sight.

"Well, that's quite disturbing," Miss Nell said.

"I concur," Minox said, getting to his feet. She still had the one creature in her hand, struggling and squirming to get out of her grasp. "But I feel we would be remiss in not pursuing this new lead."

"You mean—go down there?"

"I do," he said. "Those creatures may have been . . .

activated by my magic, but they're definitely drawn to something specific. And as much as it terrifies me—" And fear was clawing at his heart at the idea of what he was about to propose. "Whatever Mister Senek and the Blue Hand were involved in, how it connects to abducted children and—"

Children. He looked at the tables.

"Saints above and sinners below," he said in a horrified whisper.

"What?" she asked.

"The tables. Their size. Where the shackles are placed." Perfect for a small child.

Her face went pale, and then she looked at the creature in her hand. "Do you . . . do you think he started with animals and then . . ."

Anger had flooded over the fear. This monster was taking children to perform unspeakable horrors upon them.

He knocked over one table, and then another, and then tore open drawer after drawer on the shelf.

"What are you doing?" Miss Nell asked.

He found what he needed. "Looking for this," he said, taking out a long piece of cord. He tied it around the neck of the strange creature and held onto the other end. "Let it go."

She did so, and it surged forward to the stairs leading down, straining at the cord.

"All right," he said. "I'm going to see where it wants to go. I welcome your company, but I understand if you are not inclined."

"Blazes to that," she said. "I've got your back."

"Appreciated," he said, wrapping the cord around his left hand, which was still glowing blue. He attempted to mute the magic flowing through it, but that was to no avail.

"Inspector," she said cautiously. "Does your hand normally do that?"

"It will illuminate with magic at times," he said. "Though usually only from my intention or negligence. I am troubled that I am unable to dampen it."

"I'm more troubled, given where we are, that you have a blue hand," she said.

So obvious he hadn't even thought of it. "Of course. Something in here is affecting me, like the creatures were. Perhaps it is connected to the larger ethos of this particular Circle."

"Perhaps you should explain what happened to your hand," she said. "It'll be a good distraction as we follow a twisted rabbit-cat down a dark underground cavern."

"Very well," he said as he let the creature lead them down. "It started with a murder case four months ago . . ."

Jerinne found the tunnel that Maresh called "the under-bridge" far more disturbing than any of the narrow passages they crawled through to get here. This was a marvel of engineering, hidden under the city. The idea that something like this would have been built and then nearly forgotten boggled her mind.

But it was also disturbing because it was almost a straight mile, with no side passages, with the roar of the Maradaine River overhead.

"This has stood for centuries?" she asked.

"It would seem," Dayne answered. He glanced at the roof. "But something about that sound makes you think it'll collapse any moment, right?"

"Right," she said. "I'm sure it's fine."

"Nothing to worry about."

"Absolutely secure."

"My heart isn't slamming a Yoleanne beat right now."

"I'm completely calm."

"Both of you, hush," Hemmit said. "Have you seen those two . . . people at all?"

"No sign," Dayne said. "Of them or anyone else."

"Though this tunnel, it's definitely in use," Lin said. She waved her hands, and the light she emanated shifted from white to purple, and the floor lit up as well: footprints, wagon wheels, animal tracks. "Used a lot."

Jerinne couldn't help but notice the size of some of those footprints. "Look how huge those are. They make your feet look tiny."

"I'm more noticing how small all of those are," Dayne said. He pointed to a whole set of them. "Possibly a dozen children driven through here. So we're on the right track."

That, at least, was heartening. Coming down here wasn't some wild horse chase.

"Do you hear something up ahead?" Lin asked.

Jerinne turned her head to listen. "I'm just hearing the rush of the river. But . . . is it getting louder?"

"I think so," Dayne said. "What does that mean?"

The answer revealed itself in a few hundred feet. The passage opened up again, and Lin increased her brightness. The chamber was bisected by a raging river that came out of one cavern and poured into another. A narrow bridge of wood and rope spanned the river to the other side of the chamber, where there were dark tunnels leading off in several directions.

"A rutting underground river?" Maresh exclaimed. "How?"

"There are so many 'how' and 'why' questions at this point," Hemmit said. "But it's clear we need to cross and then figure out which direction to go."

Jerinne went to the bridge and tested her weight on the board. "Seems all right, but I don't think we should all cross at once."

"Wise," Maresh said.

"I'll bring up the rear," Dayne said. "If it's going to break on any of us, it'll be me."

Jerinne nodded, and took his meaning. She started

across, feeling the sway and creak of each step. It held, but she definitely found her nerve being tested as she went on, especially with the roar and crash of the rapid water below her. She reached the other side and let out her breath. "Good," she said. "Come on."

Maresh called something to her, but she couldn't hear him over the rush of the river. She just waved for him to come, and he started crossing. As he made it to her side, Lin started her traverse. Dayne paced about anxiously as they went about it. She knew he was uncomfortable down here, and she hoped they would find what they were looking for and get out of this bizarre underground network beneath the city. Where even were they at this point? Somewhere near Keller Cove? Or Inemar?

Lin finished crossing, and Hemmit started when Dayne looked over to Jerinne and shouted something. She couldn't hear, but his face told her everything. She spun about, shield and sword out.

At least a dozen people, all in dark robes, carrying blades and cudgels. Jerinne stepped forward to put herself in front of Maresh and Lin. Hold these people off. Give Dayne a chance to cross. Protect the others.

Four of them came pounding on Jerinne. She blocked with her shield, parried with her blade, dodged and ducked, but while she was able to avoid getting hit, she couldn't press them away, couldn't get a shot back at any of them. Holding them off was all she could manage.

"Dayne!" she called out. She risked a glance across the river.

Dayne wasn't waiting, charging out onto the bridge while Hemmit was still part of the way across. Jerinne couldn't keep her focus on that; she had to keep fighting off these robed people.

A thunderous crack filled the chamber with a blinding flash, and several of the figures stumbled away from Lin. Lin swooned, and while Maresh caught her before she hit the ground, the robed figures grabbed the two of them.

"No!" Jerinne shouted, slashing out with her blade. She caught the robe of one of the men, tearing it off.

He wasn't a man.

She didn't know what he was.

His head was tilted to one side, and his face looked like it had poured off onto one shoulder; like his flesh had been a candle, half melted down. And his skin—purplish-brown, covered in boils.

Jerinne screamed and smashed him in his misshapen face with her shield. She had to get to Lin and Maresh, who were being dragged away. Maresh struggled vainly; Lin looked like she had no fight in her. Jerinne had to get to them, had to save them. She took the blows coming from the beasts, hitting back hard and fierce.

"Dayne, I need you!" she called.

"I'm—" Dayne shouted. One of the robed horrors charged onto the bridge into Hemmit, and the two of them fell back onto Dayne. One of the ropes holding up the bridge snapped, and the whole structure flipped. In a moment, Hemmit, Dayne, and the robed figure tumbled into the rushing water. A moment later they were swept out of sight.

"Dayne!" Jerinne shouted.

Three of those beasts grabbed her, but she was not about to let them get hold of her. Savagely, without grace or form, she spun on them and slashed with her sword. They pummeled at her, but she didn't care. Days and days of training with Vien and Amaya, pushing her body to its limit, had made pain a familiar companion. She pushed through it, ignored it. She didn't care about the fist crossing into her jaw, and she returned the blow twice as hard. She couldn't do any less. She had to stop these monsters, put them down.

She hammered one with her shield while driving her sword into the gut of another. She pulled out the blade and cracked it against his skull. Then again. One more grabbed her arm and she paid that back by snapping it clean with a blow from the shield. Then a kick to the knee, dropping him. Then another to the skull. And another.

And—

That was it, he wasn't moving.

None of them were.

It was just her, with four of those beasts dead at her feet.

Just her.

Everyone else was gone. Hemmit and Dayne swept off in the river, and Maresh and Lin dragged away by these horrors.

She closed her eyes briefly and offered prayers to Saint Julian and Saint Benton, to watch over Dayne and Hemmit. She had to trust they'd be well, that she couldn't do anything for them.

Lin and Maresh needed rescuing. That was her duty, and she would not fail it.

Not again.

Chapter 10

AMAYA WENT TO SEVEN BARS along the Trelan Docks, asking about where to find a fellow
named Braning. This mostly resulted in a few steves and
skells offering to buy her a drink, or to show her what a
real man could do. The first four bars were a complete
waste of time. At the fifth, one man said he could tell
her where to find Braning if she could beat him in a
strong-arm, which she did rather easily. He claimed she
had cheated, and after pressing, admitted he really
knew nothing about Braning.

At the sixth bar, one old fellow told her she was going
about it all wrong. He said that since the man she was
looking for was a sewer man, she shouldn't be going to
dock man bars, she needed to go to a brick and pipe bar.
He told her to go to the Bitter Candle Pub, two blocks
away from the river. She thanked him and paid off his
tab, since he had been the only decent sort she had met
in those six bars.

The Bitter Candle was the seventh bar, and it was

definitely a place frequented by men who worked in the sewers. The place had a rank air to it, accented with the subtle notes of stale beer.

She didn't want to waste much more time with this. She noticed there was a bell over the bar—something for the tender to get everyone's attention at the end of the night, most likely—and went straight to it. She grabbed the string and rang it hard several times until all eyes were on her.

"Listen up," she said in her best commanding voice as she stepped onto the bar. "I'm not here for a drink or to find a husband, and certainly not here to take anyone home with me. I am armed and skilled in those arms, and I have had a very annoying day. So believe me when I say, do not test me."

"What the rut you want, slan?" someone yelled. More of them shouted jeers with that.

"I'm looking for a man named Braning. Does anyone know him, know where to find him? I will pay for the trouble."

The jeers went quiet. Eyes darted back and forth uncomfortably.

"Ain't no one here named that," one man said.

"But do you know him?" she asked.

"I said, ain't no one—"

From the corner of her eye, she saw someone slip into the kitchen. A few other men gave their attention to the kitchen door. She jumped down and went to follow, and three men tried to grab her.

They barely even touched her. She flipped one of them onto his back and cracked the other two into each other. If anyone else had made a move on her, she didn't even notice as she was out through the kitchen, into the back alley.

The fellow was running hard out to the street, and she sprinted after him. He turned onto the street, crashing and careening into things. He only made half a block before she caught up, and he was winded and wheezing.

"Not fair," he said as she grabbed him. He made no attempt to struggle with her.

"True," she said. "I run five miles every day. I don't think you had a chance."

"So, you got me. Going to take me into the marshals?" He looked resigned, even dejected.

"Wasn't my plan," she said. "You are Braning, yes?"

"That's the name my father gave me, and he didn't have anything else to give."

"All right, let's go," she said, pulling him out of the way of the carriage traffic.

"So, you a bounty hunter? Hired to drag me to the marshals?" he asked. "I can't imagine I'd get a fair trial."

"I'm not interested in a trial," she said.

"Ah, so this is personal," he said. "I knew I should have stayed out of it."

Amaya almost felt bad for him. She pulled him off the street corner and into an alley. "And have you been?" she asked. "Staying out of things?"

"I ain't been partnering with folks like Tharek Pell, that's for damned sure," he said. "I said, live straight and clean, and I am."

"Good," she said. "So maybe you can help me."

"I don't see how."

"Kemmer," she said. "I'm given to understand you can find him."

"So you can drag us both in."

"No," she said, a bit frustrated. She wondered if she should try to trust him, to gain his trust in return. "He's been digging into something. A group of people. I'm looking for the same people. I think we can help each other."

Braning scowled. "Who?"

"I don't—"

"I know who he's been looking into," Braning said. "So you tell me, who do you think he's looking into?"

Amaya lowered her voice to a whisper. "The Grand Ten."

Recognition crossed his face. "And how do I know you aren't with them?"

"You think they're trying to get him? Get you?"

"I know they are," Braning said. "That's why there's a plan in case—" He stopped short.

"In case he's killed?" she asked. "Smart. Well, I think I know who might be The Warrior in this Grand Ten. And maybe The Mage. Is that information worth the risk?"

He scowled again. "I know who you are. You were the one who caught Lannic. And part of that whole thing with the ballots."

"Yes, that was me," she said.

"Aren't you a Tarian?"

She nodded. "But like you said, this is personal."

"Who told you to look for me?"

"Hemmit Eyairin. Of *The Veracity Press*."

"Oh," Braning said. "Mister Yand, the spy." He chuckled. "He was a good sort, even if he did trick us. And I do keep reading his paper. And those pamphlets he put out as well."

"He is a good sort," Amaya said.

"All right," Braning said. "Kemmer is staying in room seven above the Hard Whistle Pig, over on Cosky Avenue."

"Thank you," Amaya said.

"And if anything happens to him, the word is ready to go," Braning said, pointing a finger at her. "Every paper will have the Grand Ten as their headline tomorrow."

"That's good," Amaya said. "But all the same, I hope to find him in good health, and intend to leave him that way."

"Good," Braning said. "After all this business, he . . ." He stumbled for a moment. "He's pretty much all I got."

Amaya nodded. "I appreciate it."

She left him and made her way toward Cosky, his last words striking a chord in her. What did she have? The Order? If her suspicions were true, it had an indelible stain on it. Hemmit? Dayne? Jerinne? Friends, but . . . she wasn't sure what they were to her. She had kept all of them at something of a distance. She had kept everyone at a distance. And with Master Denbar dead, she had no blood kin still alive worth speaking of.

If things did go poorly today, who would be there for her? If she died, who would mourn her?

She shook those thoughts out of her head. She had a mission, and she had a lead, and she would see it through.

On to Cosky Avenue, and hopefully, to Kemmer.

Veranix had lost all sense of direction. Following Asti and Delmin through the tunnels under North Seleth— which were a lot cleaner and better engineered than he had expected them to be—had brought them around several curves and spirals down.

"Are we still headed north?" he asked Asti.

"More northeast," Asti responded. "But we've gone down another twenty feet or so."

"How can you tell?"

"I'm just paying attention."

"Shush!" Delmin stopped cold. "This is . . . unexpected."

Veranix drew and nocked an arrow.

"Easy," Asti said. He moved up to Delmin, holding up his lamp. The passage opened up to a large chamber, where it looked like someone had been doing new construction. Tools, stacks of wooden beams and iron rods, gear work machines.

"No one here," Asti said.

"Is that just for now?" Veranix asked, taking a step inside. "I mean, if this is here, it means—"

"Whatever work they're doing isn't done," Asti finished. "So we have to presume they'll be back. Unless—"

He went over to a set of wooden stairs leading up to a passage blocked by rubble and timber.

"Unless what?" Delmin asked.

"Saints, Thorn, do you know where we are?"

"I really don't," Veranix said.

"I'm pretty certain we're under the Firewing House. Or, at least, where it was before you tore it down."

"This is what they had beneath the basement?" Veranix asked. "Does this mean they're the ones kidnapping kids, working with the giant?"

"Can't say," Asti said. "I mean, they're done. We killed them."

"I only remember two of them being dead," Veranix said. "The one with the flaming wings might have slipped off."

"Flaming wings?" Delmin asked.

Veranix nodded. "Rather gaudy, if you ask me. If you're gonna fly, just fly."

Delmin got on his knees. "Of course, that Circle might have had members who didn't live at that house. There may have been more going on than we're aware of. What is this?"

"What?" Veranix asked. Delmin was running his hand along the floor, where some sort of metallic lattice work had been laid in.

Asti crouched down and touched it. "Maybe something like a cart track? I mean, some of these tunnels date back a few centuries, digging out the stone and ore that built half the city."

Carts to haul out ore. Made sense. "But is this old?"

"No, no," Delmin muttered. "This is new and yet . . ." He stood up, spreading his hands. "Saints, Vee, you aren't feeling it?"

"Feeling what?"

"It's. . . . It's like . . . like the storm gutters, drawing the rainwater out of the streets and down and down and . . ."

He held up his hand, charged with *numina*, and threw the energy down to the ground. The magic danced and skipped, charging the grid at their feet with light.

"Oh, that's . . . that's incredible." Delmin laughed for a moment, and then that laughter turned into short, heaving breaths. "No, that's . . . where is it?"

"Easy, Del," Veranix said. He put the arrow back in the quiver and put up his bow, and held his friend's shoulder. "You all right?"

"No, I . . . I sent magic in there. Wherever that goes. What was I thinking?"

"The real question is what were they building?" Asti said, walking around the chamber. "Thorn, look at this. Water tanks."

Veranix patted Delmin on the shoulder and went over. "That makes sense for the work, right? You've got a work crew down here, they need water."

"No, these are boil tanks, with steam valves," Asti said, kicking one of them. "Heavy steel. This would take a dozen men at least to carry down here. Nothing you would use for just provision."

"What would you use it for?" Veranix asked.

Before Asti could answer, Delmin shouted, "It's gotta be stopped!" and ran out one of the other passages.

"Del!" Veranix shouted, running after him.

"Saints, that kid," Asti muttered as he caught up with Veranix. The two of them charged down the passageway, all the while Delmin could be heard shouting ahead of them, yelling something about magic and danger. Veranix couldn't make out exactly what he was saying.

"Does he usually act like this?" Asti asked as they ran.

"Not at all," Veranix said. "Something must have spooked him. I don't know what—blazes!"

The passage split in two. To his ear, Delmin's shouts came from both directions.

"Which way?" Veranix asked.

Asti scowled. "Can't tell. Maybe there's other passages that connect."

More of Delmin's shouts. Calling for them to follow now.

"What do we do?" Veranix asked. He had brought Delmin into this. He wanted to kick himself. This was all his fault.

"Each take a tunnel and hope for the best," Asti said. He took a piece of chalk out of a pouch and made a mark on the wall. "You find him, drag him back to here. One hour, back here, regardless."

"What?"

"No matter what, be back here in an hour. Last thing we need is all three of us wandering lost. And if we're not back, follow the chalk out and get Verci."

"Got it," Veranix said, and with a hint of magic, tagged the chalk mark. Delmin would be able to sense that, get Veranix's scent from it. "Hope you're right."

"Rarely am," Asti said, and he ran off down the left passage. Veranix drew out his bow and nocked an arrow again, making his way down the right passage, and hopefully to Delmin. He didn't know what trouble he might find—Saint Senea, keep that trouble off of Delmin—but he'd be ready for it.

Verci didn't let himself worry about Asti down in the tunnels with the Thorn. They would be fine. It would all be fine. He forced himself to work to keep his mind off of what could happen. But he couldn't focus on jape-toys and music boxes, even though those were selling very well in the past week. Terrentin was just a couple days away, and everyone wanted gifts to celebrate and rejoice with.

Instead he worked on the spring-launcher gauntlet.

He had designed it to have a lot of different options, and it had proven useful in the fights with the Firewing mages a couple weeks ago. Very successful field test. It could launch both darts and hollow brass balls—and Almer Cort had made a few different interesting chemical mixtures to fill those balls with—but it could stand to be a bit more accurate. Though Verci wondered if part of that was he had designed it to be used left-handed, to keep his better hand free. Maybe he needed to just get better with his aim.

He was working on a way to be able to reload it faster when someone pounded on the back door.

Verci grabbed a knife on instinct. No one knocked on the back door to the Gadgeterium. It had a special lock that only he, Asti, and Raych could open. No one else ever came in that way. But Verci was prepared, opening the lens-hole he had installed by the door so he could safely look out to the back alley.

Another pound on the door. Verci looked through the lens; Kel Essin was out there, holding something under his coat and clutching at his belly. His hand was covered in blood, as was his shirt. Essin wasn't a bad fellow—decent enough window-man when he was sober—though he had been part of Lesk's crew. Not someone Verci would trust or consider a friend. But also, not someone he wished ill.

He opened up a vent. "What do you want, Essin?"

"Rynax!" Essin shouted desperately. "You got to help me!"

"I don't have to do anything."

"Please, Rynax, please. I'm hurt bad."

"Show me your hands," Verci said. "What's under the coat?"

Essin, looking pale and clammy, nodded. He pulled out a small green statue from under his coat—with four arms and a horrific face.

Verci threw open the door and pulled Essin inside,

slamming the door and latching it right away. Essin fell to the floor, panting and wheezing.

"Where did you get that?" Verci asked.

"I just did this job, went totally left. Please." He held out the statue like it was a peace offering.

Verci snapped it away from him, putting the thing on the worktable. "I've got some bandages and such, but you need a proper sew-up."

"No, no, just here," Essin said. "I'm in some trouble, man."

Verci looked at the statue. Even though it was a small thing, it was definitely the same style as the one he had stolen from a carriage a few months back, delivering to the mysterious buyer Josie had arranged. And at Lord Henterman's home, Liora Rand had taken a small one like this. Perhaps this very one.

"Tell me," Verci said as he grabbed his bandage kit. "And talk fast."

"Things have been bad since the brawl at the mage house. Without Lesk, it's been a mess. So I took a gig with this crew from Keller Cove."

"To steal this statue?" Verci asked. "You know what it is?"

"No clue," he said. "They needed a window-man to get into this swell's house in East Maradaine. Gig itself went fine. They had someone on the staff leave a back gate open, I was in and out quiet. Real clean."

"You stayed sober for it." The wound was a pretty vile slice across Essin's belly. Verci could sew it up, but he knew it would probably turn green then black in a few days.

"I ain't had a drink for months, man."

"Good," Verci said. "You sure you don't want Gelson or someone for this? It's not going to heal well under my care."

"It's fine." He winced in pain. "Just patch it up for

now. I gotta lay low. I don't know who's not a part of it. Figured you were safe."

"Part of what?" Verci asked. He got to work on sewing the wound, for all the good it would do. "What's up with this statue? Is Josie involved in this?"

"No clue," Essin said. "Gig didn't come from her. Like I said, it all went clean at the swell's house. In easy, cracked the box that was in, and back out like butter."

"You cracked the box?" He didn't know Essin was also a box-cracker. But he didn't know Essin had stopped drinking either.

"Nah, someone named Raimond. Never worked with them before. Decent sort, good hands. We got that and made our way back to the safehouse in Keller Cove to meet up with the rest of the crew, get our cut. And we got our cut, all right."

"They turned on you?" Verci asked.

"Turned," Essin said before he fell into a fit of wet, hacking coughs. Blood coming from his mouth. "There was nothing turned about this. These cats were part of some cult or something."

"A what?"

"I'm telling you, we get there, they were all in robes, and were saying stuff about the holy vessel, and then to dispatch the unfaithful. Next thing I know, Raimond gets a knife in the gut, and two of those tossers are coming for me."

"And that's how you got this?" Verci asked, pointing to the wound.

"No, thank the saints! I held on to that thing and ran out of there, fast as I could. Was able to give them the slip by roof topping and window dropping. Hid for a bit, and then made my way to one of the flops we used with Lesk. I get there, Ren is already there." Ren Poller, Lesk's right hand when he was starting up his new gang. "He had his knives out."

"Ren did this to you?"

Essin nodded. "He saw the statue and his eyes glazed over. Just jumped on me, whispering about the Brotherhood would be grateful for this gift of blood."

"Ren Poller?" Verci asked again. The Brotherhood again, like Tarvis had said. What the blazes was that about? "You got away from him?"

"I smashed his skull with that thing," Essin said. "That's a rutting gift of blood."

Ren Poller was dead. That was a bit to take in. "So you came to me."

"Rynax, I knew Ren for *years*. If I couldn't trust him, I didn't know where else to go," Essin said. "I figured . . . I know you and your brother don't like me or nothing, but I was certain you'd be straight, if anyone was."

"Yeah," Verci said. He'd done what he could, stopped the worst of the bleeding, but there was no way he had done much other than keep Essin alive for another couple days. "I don't know if I did you any favors here."

"I just need a place to rest, Rynax. Whatever you want, let me rest."

"Fine, there's a spare room upstairs," Verci said. He picked up the ugly statue. "But I'm holding on to this."

"If you want. I just wanted to get away from those bastards, but my gut told me they shouldn't have that."

"I'm inclined to agree," Verci said. "So let's get you in the spare room upstairs, and then you can tell me where in Keller Cove to find these bastards."

Chapter 11

THERE WAS NOTHING BUT DARKNESS and water as Dayne's body was battered and smashed against rock after rock. He had barely managed to get a breath before he had been swept under the current. No sense of anything, other than the rush of river.

Something smashed into him. Soft. Human.

Hemmit.

Dayne instinctively grabbed and held on.

He had to get them out of the water.

Holding on to Hemmit as tightly as he could with one arm, he reached out, trying to get hold of something. Rocks slipped through his grasp, tearing at his fingers. His lungs were burning, he couldn't last much longer. It had to be too late for Hemmit.

He crashed into a large rock, and that pushed him up, above the surface. He gasped, getting as much air in his mouth as water, but still there was air. He struggled to hold on to that rock, to plant his feet, to get his bearings, get Hemmit out of the water.

He managed to get his feet under him, brace himself on the rock and push himself up. Air, sweet air, at last. And the dimmest of light.

He was in another wide chamber that the river cut through, and in the dim, he could see the current slacking off and forming a pool to one side. Forcing himself to hold strong, he hauled Hemmit over his shoulder and took a step into the current, then another, and another, until he reached the pool. From there, he was able to pull himself and Hemmit onto dry stone.

"Hemmit," he said, touching the man's face and chest. "Talk to me, man."

Hemmit groaned.

"You all right?" Dayne asked.

"Got . . . pretty . . . smashed," Hemmit said. "I just need a few minutes. Let me lie here a bit."

"Sure," Dayne said. He let himself give a prayer of thanks to Saint Julian for this small miracle.

"Where?" Hemmit asked.

"Not sure," Dayne said. He made himself stand up, get a sense of where they were. A wide cavern, which looked like it was partly natural, and partly carved by human hands. The strangest part was the soft glow of the whole place. The walls were luminous green. "We need to—"

"Lin and Maresh," Hemmit muttered. "Got to get to them."

"I agree," Dayne said. There were several passages out of this chamber, each definitely manmade. But with no sense of how far they traveled, which direction was where, he had no idea how to get back to their friends. There was no way to get upstream from here. "I'm still shocked by the depths of this whole place."

"We need . . ." Hemmit wheezed out.

"You just rest," Dayne said. "We'll find them."

"Who's crying?" Hemmit asked.

"What—" Dayne started, and then heard it.

Crying. A young voice.

"The children."

Hemmit craned his neck to look at Dayne. "Go. I'll be fine."

Dayne followed the sound down one of the passages. It was surprisingly clear, leading Dayne to a wide, round chamber with a tall ceiling and multiple passages in every direction. Again, Dayne was astounded by the engineering on display. This place was as much a marvel as the Parliament or the Royal Palace. Not merely the scope of it, but the craftsmanship. There were tall columns in the center of the room, intricately carved with designs.

Sitting on the floor in a ball was a small boy, crying softly.

"Hey," Dayne said as gently as he could.

The boy looked up at Dayne and screamed.

"Hey, hey, no," Dayne said. "It's all right. Are you lost?"

"Stay away from me!" the boy yelled. He spoke in perfect, educated tones for a little boy.

"Are you the young baron?" he asked. "Vollingale?"

The boy's eyes went wide. "How do you know who I am?"

"Your father, he told me you were missing. I'm here to find you."

"No!" the boy shouted. "You're here to take me!"

"I swear, I'm not," Dayne said. "Look at my uniform. Do you know what that is?"

"No," the boy said.

"I'm a Tarian," Dayne said quietly. "We're here to protect people. That's what I want to do."

Dayne reached out to the boy, but then he heard the twang of a bow. He pulled his hand back just before a pair of arrows whizzed through the air between them.

"You stay away from him," someone shouted. Out of one of the other tunnels, a hooded figure in a crimson cloak charged in, drawing another arrow and nocking it. "Saints help me, giant, I'll not let you hurt him."

Before Dayne could speak, the cloaked man loosed the arrow.

The trail led to Keller Cove. Satrine and Kellman had put some pressure on the horse groom, and he quickly confessed to leaving gates unlocked and lamps blown out, having been forced by a gang in Keller Cove.

"We're gonna be fair with him, right?" Kellman asked as they rode in the Grand Inspection Unit's carriage to Keller Cove.

"They threatened his sister and niece," Satrine said. "I'm not inclined to make his life any worse."

"Good," he said.

The groom had been more than happy to offer details on the thieves, giving them an exact address to the basement flop of a tenement apartment right next to the charred remains of Tyne's Pleasure Emporium.

"I'm surprised we haven't seen more of a surge of gangs and robberies in this part of town," Kellman said as they came up. "This place employed a lot of people, and Tyne kept a lot of the street bosses in check."

"Maybe that's where this gang popped up from," she said. "But I've got my doubts."

"Why?"

It was moments like this that Satrine desperately missed partnering with Minox. He would pick up on exactly what she meant, which went back to why this case was far more interesting than any of the others on their plate right now. This wasn't some random break-in. These people targeted Lord Callwood. Their goal was specific. Something so specific, something so secret, Callwood didn't want to talk about it.

How was that not a burning curiosity?

"Street gangs that pop up from a fallout like Tyne, they don't get ambitious. They stake down territory, they lick their wounds. They don't plan a heist on the east side of town."

"Unless it's a huge score," Kellman said. "I mean, I still know folks who know folks in westtown. There's talk that the Old Lady of Seleth—"

"Maybe," Satrine said, cutting him off. "But if this is some common gang, I'll give you a crown."

"Deal," Kellman said, going down the steps to the basement door. He gave it three hard pounds, and announced his presence according to protocol. "This is the Constabulary, we have lawful Writs of Entry and Search. We shall be entering the premises immediately."

Courtesy and legality attended to, he kicked in the door.

Satrine was not ready for the sight inside.

The room was filled with candles, meticulously arranged on the points of a nine-pointed star drawn on the floor. Three men sat on the floor, each on a point, while three dead bodies lay in the center of the symbol.

The stench hit her full in the face, threatening to upend her stomach.

"Stand and be held!" Kellman shouted, clearly finding his voice before Satrine had hers. She managed to bring up her crossbow with him.

All three men grabbed knives off the floor, and Satrine focused her aim on the closest one of them, shooting on instinct. Her blunt-tip bolt struck him in the hand as his knife went up, forcing him to drop it. The blade skittered out of his reach. Kellman's bolt knocked one of the others in the chest, but it didn't deter him.

The two who still had their knives went right for their own throats.

The third got to his feet and went for his knife, but Satrine stepped forward, putting herself between him and it. He swung at her, a wild punch. She easily dodged and brought up her handstick, landing a shot across his jaw.

Kellman had a whistle in his mouth, calling for Yellowshields. Not that they would be able to do a damn thing for those two. They had already bled all over the floor, and no Yellowshield or doctor in the city was going to be able to save them.

Satrine locked her handstick under the third man's arm, twisting him around and down to the ground. "You will be ironed and delivered," she said, getting her irons out and on his wrists. "Charges will be laid upon you, including and not limited to murder and robbery."

"I fear not your charges," the third man said. "I fear not your iron. Nothing can hold me while I serve."

"You're going to serve in Quarrygate," Kellman said. "But first, by every saint, you're going to explain what the blazes this all is!"

Satrine turned the man around. He was smiling broadly, eyes wild and crazed. Laughing, he said, "By every saint. You cling to this false faith, praying to emptiness that will never hear."

"And this is a real faith, this horror?" Kellman asked, shoving the man back.

"Derrick, easy!" Satrine said.

"This isn't faith," the man said. "It's truth, pure as the wind." Despite being ironed, he charged down a hallway to a back stairwell.

"Rutting saints," Kellman said, chasing after him. Satrine ran right behind, reloading her crossbow as she went.

Up four flights of stairs they chased him, all the way to the rooftop of the building.

"Nowhere to go," Satrine said as she came out into the daylight. She leveled her crossbow at him. "Let's come along and you can tell us all about this faith."

"There's nothing to tell," he said, turning toward

them. "For you are heretics, and you will never understand."

He took a few steps backward, to the edge of the roof.

"Hey, easy!" Kellman shouted.

"But it does not matter," he said. "Soon this city, and every life within it, will belong to the Brotherhood."

He took another step back, and plummeted to the street, landing with a sickening crunch. Screams immediately rang out from down below. Satrine raced up to the edge to confirm it with her own eyes: he was definitely dead, his head cracked open.

Kellman walked up next to her, and silently handed her a coin.

She took it and pocketed it, but her attention was already elsewhere. Amid the crowd gathering around the body, there was a familiar face. Perhaps just a coincidence, but her instinct still told her no.

The trapmaster, the one who disarmed Sholiar's device in the Parliament. He looked up and met her gaze, giving the barest of nods.

In his eyes, she saw it: that burning curiosity.

Veranix no longer heard Delmin. He had definitely taken the wrong passage, and had gotten so turned around he wasn't sure how to get back to where he had split off from Asti.

Stupidity.

The passage he had found himself in was slightly different—still a manmade tunnel, but the style of the brickwork changed, the wood used to make the support beams—those had changed. And to Veranix's eye, to something slightly familiar. It now looked like the Spinner Run, the tunnel to the university carriage house that Veranix had often used to sneak out of the dorm buildings. Were these built by the same people, or at the same time?

Also, the walls here gave off a low, greenish glow. Veranix touched a spot of the wall with a particularly strong glow, and the brick felt soft. He scraped it with his fingernail—some sort of moss, by the look of it. He wondered what Professor Yanno would make of it. Veranix had only started the naturalism courses he needed to earn his Letters, but he had to admit he found it an interesting study. Yanno was specifically a Master of Plants, so an underground glowing moss was definitely pertinent to his interests.

A tearful cry cut through the air, snapping Veranix out of his thoughts. That was a child.

Then: "Stay away from me!"

Veranix drew two arrows as he charged down the hallway. He had heard it clearly: there was a boy, in terror. When Veranix reached the mouth of the tunnel, it was clear why: a giant fellow was trying to grab the kid. Veranix fired the arrows as quick as he could to let the kid get away.

"You stay away from him!" Veranix shouted. The giant fellow stumbled and looked at him with a stupid expression. And it wasn't just any giant fellow. That one. The one in the Tarian uniform from Fenmere's. Veranix could feel that magical tag he had put on him.

Veranix was a wellspring of rage, and he let it overflow. "Saints help me, giant, I'll not let you hurt him." And he nocked and loosed another arrow. This was one of the special ones Verci Rynax had mocked up for him with his chemist friend.

"Get clear, kid!" Veranix yelled.

The Tarian brought up his shield to block the arrow, which exploded in flame and smoke, knocking the brute back. Veranix took the moment to put up the bow and whip out the rope. He wrapped it around the kid in a cradle and pulled him away from the blast.

"Don't you dare—" the Tarian shouted, as he tried to get to his feet.

"I got you, kid," Veranix said. "Don't worry."

The Tarian charged at Veranix, shield down. Veranix jumped high out of the way, releasing the kid from the rope as he sailed over the brute.

"You're not going to touch him," Veranix said as he landed. He willed the rope around the Tarian's arms, entangling him. Despite being roped up, he dropped the shield and tried to reach the child with those monstrously huge hands. Veranix poured magic into the rope and his legs, to anchor himself to the ground.

"I'm not going to let you take him," the Tarian said. He flexed his arms, and despite Veranix magicking the rope to be iron-hard, he yanked it out of Veranix's hands. He turned on Veranix, anger in his eyes. His arms were still bound, but he moved like a cat.

"Well, you can't have him," Veranix said. "I'm firm on that." He shrouded himself and jumped high, sweetening the jump with magic. Bow out, arrows nocked and loosed: one, two, three. No tricks on these, just razorsharp tips to bury into the brute's huge chest.

The Tarian spun and dodged; none of those arrows found their target. With a great shout of pain, he wrenched one arm free from the rope and picked up the shield. He hurled it, flying out of his hands like a runaway horse, to the exact place Veranix was landing. Veranix took the shield full in the chest, and with no footing on the ground, was knocked into the wall. He barely had a chance to push out magically and cushion the blow. It still hurt like blazes.

"That's how you want to be, Tarian," Veranix said, kicking the shield away. "Then let's really bring the fight."

"I don't want to hurt you," the Tarian said.

"Feeling isn't mutual," Veranix said. "I won't let you take any more children." He nocked another arrow, despite his chest screaming as he drew back.

"Take children?" the Tarian said, looking aghast. "I'm trying to rescue them!"

"Then why are you working for Fenmere?" Veranix held the arrow back, but he slowly fed magic into his arm, into the arrow, so when it flew it would go as fast as lightning. No dodging this time. It would tear through the Tarian like a stone in the water.

"I'm not! Whatever he's doing, I want to stop!"

"Then who's the giant stealing children, if not you?" The arrow was full of magic, ready to send this bastard to meet his sinners.

"Gurond!" A horrifying voice bellowed from one of the other tunnels. A lumbering body to match it came pounding into the chamber, a beast that easily towered over even this Tarian. The boy, huddled in a corner, screamed and ran off. The creature came full into view—gray skin, twisted mouth, inhumanly muscled. "Gurond will take children for the Brotherhood!"

Veranix didn't hesitate to let that killer arrow fly at the beast. It shot out faster than Veranix could see, so fast the room echoed with thunder, and slammed into Gurond's chest.

It didn't even slow him down.

Chapter 12

JERINNE FOUGHT DOWN HER INSTINCTS to do something stupid.

She knew which tunnel Lin and Maresh had been taken down—these beasts weren't exactly trying to hide their trail—and she wanted to just charge after them and take down every one of the bastards to rescue her friends.

That would be stupid, though.

Time to think it through. What would Dayne do? What would Amaya do?

Fight smarter. That's what Amaya would do.

First step was to assess herself, what she had, how she was. Be ready for the next fight. She went through her pack, as well as Lin's, which she found on the ground. Two canteens of water, some bread and dried meat. She had no idea what time it was—at least five or six bells— but she was hungry. Drink one canteen, eat the food. Keep her strength up.

Lin had brought a rope, lamps and oil, strips of cloth.

For bandages. Rutting blazes, Lin was thinking. Why hadn't she been?

Jerinne checked herself. She had taken a few hits. Her jaw ached, but none of her teeth felt loose. Bruising on her left side, but not too tender. Shallow slice on her right. She cleaned the wound and wrapped it as best she could. She had hurt her hip somehow. She took a moment to remember the stretches Raila had taught her, work the joint. After a few stretches, she heard a satisfying pop from her hip, and a fair amount of the pain faded. As good as she could hope down here.

Raila. What was she doing right now? Back at the barracks? At the baths? Wondering where Jerinne was?

Jerinne's thoughts were filled with the icy realization that she could very well die down here, deep underground at the hands of some horrific misshapen creatures. She might never see Raila Gendon again. Never even try to kiss her. She still had no idea if Raila would welcome that, or react with as much terror as Jerinne had to these beasts. Jerinne would probably be kicked out of her Initiacy for that. Was that what had happened to Fredelle Pence?

No, Raila was nothing if not kind. At worst, she would demurely, respectfully break Jerinne's heart with quiet words of disinterest.

That was what would most likely happen. Jerinne had never seen anything but friendship in Raila's eyes. Certainly not the excitement or electric joy she saw every time she talked to Rian.

Saints, Rian Rainey. The thought of not seeing her again made Jerinne's heart almost stop.

No, she'd get on her feet, she'd go down this tunnel and fight every blasted beast and man she had to and save Maresh and Lin. She would find Dayne and Hemmit, they would rescue the missing kids, get back up to the sunlight, and *by every damn saint* she would kiss Rian Rainey the next time she saw her.

The worst that would happen there is Satrine would smack her. She could live with that.

She left the lamps in the bag. Her eyes had adjusted to the near dark, and now she could see the soft glow on the tunnel walls. A luminescent moss of some sort, probably. She strapped the bag tightly onto her back, coiled the rope on her belt, and checked her shield and sword.

One last touch. She checked the dead beasts—they truly were misshapen horrors. How was that possible? Were they born that way, was it done to them? After a bit of a search, she determined which robe was the least bloody and put that on. She was going to have to be stealthy right now, figure out what she was up against before she just charged in.

Fight smarter.

Satisfied that she was sufficiently disguised, she went off down the tunnel.

She didn't have to follow down it very long before it opened up to an enormous cavern, larger than she even thought possible. At least the width of four or five city blocks.

It was filled with tents and huts and buildings. Saints, it was a village.

A village filled with the robed figures. All of them going about their own business, like it was any other part of the city.

Who were these people? How did they live down here? What did they do, why were they here?

None of them had taken note of her. It was good she hadn't lit the lamp; she would have been announcing her presence to all of them. She cautiously walked around the encampment, eyes and ears open. Looked for signs of Maresh and Lin. Where had they been taken? A few of the buildings were rather sizable. Was one of them their Constabulary House where they would take prisoners?

Saints, what if these poor wretches were just innocents who saw Jerinne and the rest of them as invaders?

No, they were taking children. They may be a lot of
things, but innocent couldn't be one of them.

There were no children in this village, not that Jerinne saw.

Nor was anyone talking.

She passed by one tent where a pair of the robed figures were cooking. Again, no talking, and the smells
coming out were atrocious. Jerinne held back her urge
to retch. There was one notable thing about the cooks:
from what she could see of their hands and faces, they
were not the same sort of misshapen creatures that she
had fought.

But others in the village were.

What was going on?

Bells rang in the distance, from the tallest building in
the center of the encampment. That building was dark,
foreboding and even . . . unholy. A twisted set of tall,
thorny spires. Like something out of a nightmare. As
soon as the bells started, every person around Jerinne—
human and beast alike—stopped what they were doing
and made for that building.

A church? Or whatever the opposite of one was.

Jerinne wasn't sure, but whatever it was, answers
were probably within. And more than likely Maresh and
Lin. It certainly was worth investigating.

Jerinne kept her head down and followed along.

The Hard Whistle Pig was the exact sort of place where
someone who wanted to avoid notice would want to stay.
No one would ever walk in here unless they had to. It
was a pit of a pub, in absolute shambles on the outside.
The door was hanging loose on one hinge and couldn't
even close. Stepping inside was like being punched in
the nose: the rank stench of rot and human waste was

overpowering. A few patrons slumped in the taproom. When Amaya entered, some didn't react at all, others winced at the sunlight streaming onto their sallow faces.

"What ye want?" a barman asked. This fellow looked like everything but his hair had died a month ago, and his beard had taken on a life of its own.

"Looking for a tenant of yours," she said.

"Ye the law?" he asked.

"No," she said.

"I ain't telling nothing to the law."

"I'm not the law."

"You can't just shove in here. Ye got writs on us?" This fellow seemed daft.

"Just here to talk to a friend," she told him. "I'm not a constable or a marshal."

"Yer armed. What are ye, bounty hunter?"

She had grown weary of this conversation, having had too many like it over the course of the day. There was no need to belabor it.

"Room seven," she said firmly. "I presume that's up the stairs."

"You can't go up without a writ!" he yelled at her as she ascended.

"Stop me."

The scent was no better upstairs. The reason why was clear, as right at the top of the steps there was a broken water closet with no door. Amaya held down the bile that surged up her throat.

Nothing short of fire could cleanse this place.

She held her breath as she made her way down the hall to room seven. The door was open, and for a moment she assumed that it was yet another door in such disrepair it couldn't close properly.

Then she noticed the cracked wood. The splinters looked fresh. The door had been kicked open.

Cautiously, she pushed the door and went in, hand on the hilt of her sword. The room was a mess. Papers strewn everywhere. The bed flipped over. Drops of blood on the ground.

And no Kemmer.

Clearly there had been a fight—and of course no one downstairs had even noticed. Would that barman or any other employee even care if a tenant was abducted? Or killed? It wasn't like the scent would stand out.

She looked through the papers—there were quite a lot, both on the floor and affixed to the wall. Newsprint articles. Notes of account from goldsmith houses. Maps and sketches. Lists with names, each one headed with The Lord, The Soldier, The Duchess, The Man of the People, and so on.

The Grand Ten. Kemmer had been hunting them down, and it looked like he had narrowed down some of them. At least four of them he had narrowed down to one name. The rest, he had several candidates.

His list for The Warrior wasn't helpful. He had written, "Spathian? Tarian? Could it be Tharek? Or Dayne Heldrin?" So he had no idea. He didn't even suspect Grandmaster Orren.

Amaya examined the rest of it. There was a method to the arrangement, all focused on a map of the city on the wall. A few different locations were marked, but the one he had circled strongly, with several lines pointing to it: the Grand Druth Opera House. It had been closed for repairs for nearly a year, owned by Duchess Leighton of Fencal. From Kemmer's notes, she was his prime candidate for The Duchess.

She looked back to the rest of the disarray. There had likely been a tussle here—the drops of blood on the floor started by the overturned bed, and then led out the door. Not much blood at all—consistent with someone getting sliced on the arm, but still able to walk out on their own power. Someone had come for Kemmer, but left his notes and evidence here. Perhaps he fought the person off, perhaps they grabbed him and took him away. She had no way of knowing.

All she had was a place, and an instinct that she would find what she was looking for there.

She gathered up the papers and made her way back to the chapterhouse. It was getting late, and her absence would be noticed.

"So you aren't *really* moving your hand? Or feeling it?" Miss Nell asked as they continued down the twist of passageway, the horrifying hybrid animal leading them along. She had had the foresight of grabbing a piece of chalk off one of the slateboards and marking the walls so they could find their way back. While she was no Inspector Rainey, he found her a companion of excellent wit and temper. He could see why Veranix worked with her on his vigilante mission.

"Moving, no. I'm controlling entirely with magic. I do have sensation, but . . . I confess that I cannot tell if it is the natural sense of the body or the application of my magical senses."

"And you don't know what it is?"

"I know what Mister Olivant of Lord Preston's Circle called it," Minox said. "He said that it was 'a menace beyond the scope of my comprehension.'"

Miss Nell let out a low whistle.

"He also told me, 'I will likely spend the rest of my nights lying awake terrified, praying you don't lose control of the unholy power you use to wiggle your fingers.'"

"Is that an exact quote?" she asked.

"Someone tells you something like that, it stays in your memory," Minox said.

"Yeah," she said quietly. "Dim the light on that, something up ahead. Hear that?"

Minox covered his hand with a glove, which mostly

muted its blue glow. He was deeply troubled that he couldn't completely turn it off, that he had lost that level of control. Was this just down here, with the cat-rabbit in proximity? Was something else triggering it? Would his control return once they returned to the surface? He had no idea.

Low bells were ringing up ahead, a deep, resonant clang that echoed through the passage. Their path led them toward the sound, and the passageway opened up to an enormous cavern, lit with a dull green glow from all the walls. The cavern had an entire encampment of tents and huts, centered around a large building with several high towers that touched the roof.

The building was the source of the bells.

"Well, that's disturbing," Miss Nell said.

"I'm inclined to agree," Minox whispered, which was all his voice was capable of at the moment. "How could something like this exist?"

"Look," she said, pulling him behind one of the huts. "People are going in there."

"Then we need to do the same," Minox said. He immediately regretted this, and corrected himself. "That is, I intend to investigate it. I will not impose upon you."

"I've got your back, Inspector," she said. "Stop doubting that, all right?"

"I don't want to presume or abuse your assistance," he said.

"You haven't yet," she said.

They slipped through the encampment, Minox noting that all the residents had gone into the building. The bells must indicate obligatory attendance. Who were these people, and what was this—church? Temple? It certainly wasn't like any of the sainted houses of the Church of Druthal, or even the Racquin-influenced Church of Saint Veran outside the city that his mother favored. As they got closer, he saw that the structure was built out of wood—blackened as if by fire—but the wood was raw and twisting, as if it had grown this way of its own accord. That was, of course, impossible, but that was how it looked.

Miss Nell gingerly touched the wall, pulling away after running her finger along it. "It's thorned."

"You work with plants, Miss Nell," Minox said. "Are you familiar with a wood like this?"

She crouched down to look at where the wall met the floor. "It has roots that dig into the stone," she said. "If I were to guess—" She paused and shook her head.

"I welcome your guesses, however absurd."

She looked at the creature, which was rubbing its grotesque form against the building, as if doing so gave it pleasure. "If I were to guess, the same sort of twisted magic that was done to this animal was done to several trees."

"To what end?"

"Is 'make a creepy building' not an end to itself?" she asked.

"I reject that such an effort would be expended on aesthetics alone." Minox went to touch the wall himself, but felt his hand surge with power. Like it was drawn to it. "They all went inside. I would like to know why."

"And I yell at Veranix for doing stupid things." She pointed to an opening. "Let's try to stay out of sight."

"I concur," Minox said.

The inside was like a maze of brambles, walls formed of dead, entwined vines and branches, leading them to a large congregation surrounding a stone dais and altar. The residents—dozens upon dozens of them—were all in dark robes, but it was clear that some of them were not human. Like the creatures in Senek's lab, these people had been twisted and disfigured into mockeries of humanity.

"The results of his experiments?" Miss Nell's hot whisper burned in Minox's ear. "Were they the children?"

"Possibly," Minox said, making sure they were hidden behind one set of brambles.

Two robed figures came up to the dais, carrying a third person. No, a body . . . an unmistakably dead man with his head caved in. They placed him on the altar.

"Our brother is fallen," one of them said. "He is fallen, and the Brotherhood is lessened of him."

Moans of lamentation filled the congregation.

"We would wish him joyous rest, having sunk to the waiting love of the Nine. That unburdened of flesh, his soul could pass through the deep stone to them."

"Blessed be the Nine!" someone from the crowd yelled.

"May the Stone be cracked, so they can rise to us!" another called.

"Yes, indeed," the man on the dais said, gesturing for them to be quiet. "We would love to mourn our brother, that he might touch the divine before we all. But we cannot. We must call him back to us, so he can share with all of us his news."

"Call him! Call him!" the crowd shouted.

"Call him back!"

"Only the High Dragon can perform this great and terrible duty," the man on the dais said. "Please, High Dragon, Holder of the Fervent Fire, we beseech you, your people need your guidance!"

A man stepped out from behind one of the other bramble walls. A young man—no older than Minox, at least—with rich, dark hair and immaculately manicured beard. Racquin, like Minox, by the look of him. He was not wearing a robe, but rather a gentlemen's shirtsleeves with red suspenders and cravat. He looked like he had just walked out of a north city theater, rather than being part of this dark, underground cult.

"The High Dragon is here," he said, his voice easy and untroubled. "As I am always on hand to guide my shepherds, my faithful, my dear Brotherhood." He walked over to the body on the altar. "Oh, my beloved friend, we will bring you home."

"Blessed be the Nine!" the crowd called. "Blessed be their High Dragon, Crenaxin!"

It really was a giant. Dayne couldn't believe his eyes. Nine feet tall at least, and skin like gray leather, and a monstrous face. It charged at the hooded archer, not slowing down in the slightest when it took an arrow in the chest. It smashed its giant fists onto the archer, who only got away with a series of rapid backflips.

Whoever that archer was, he certainly was nimble.

"You're the one," Dayne said. "The child thief."

"Gurond is taking children, yes," the giant—Gurond, clearly—turned his attention to Dayne. Was this the same Pendall Gurond that Vollingale spoke of? How was that possible? "You cannot stop Gurond!" He swung a punch at Dayne. Dayne dodged out of the way, despite still being entangled in this damnable rope. How did it feel like iron?

"Gurond needs to learn personal pronouns," the archer said. He shot another arrow at the beast's feet. This arrow didn't penetrate the creature's skin, but instead exploded with some form of paste. The archer waved his hand, and it and the paste both glowed crimson. A mage as well, it would seem. The beast tried to step forward, but his foot was stuck to the ground. He howled with rage.

"Tarian," the archer called, jumping over to Dayne. He grabbed one end of the rope, and it uncoiled off of Dayne's arms. "Sorry for thinking this guy was you."

"Accepted," Dayne said, moving away from another wide swing from Gurond's massive fists. The giant kept pulling his trapped foot, and the paste was cracking. "I don't think that will hold him."

"I'm never that lucky," the archer said. Who was he? What was he down here for? He was trying to protect the boy, so Dayne wanted to assume the best of him, that he had the same mission as Dayne.

Gurond pounded the floor.

"Where are the children?" Dayne asked him, moving around Gurond's range to get to his shield. "Why did you take them?"

"Really, now?" the archer asked.

"I want to know why," Dayne said. But the beast was about to be free. Dayne had to think of what to do. How did Amaya usually beat him, when he had size and strength over her? Used his strength against him. Pins and holds. "But get ready to bind him."

"Fine," the archer said, drawing another arrow.

Dayne had his shield, and Gurond wrenched his foot free. He looked at each of them, for a moment unable to decide who to attack. One punch would destroy the archer.

"Come on!" Dayne shouted. Gurond charged, and Dayne dropped down in a crouch as the beast punched, driving his shield up into his belly while also knocking him in the knee.

Saints, it was like hitting a tree.

Even still, the beast stumbled forward, and Dayne heaved up with all his strength, flipping the creature and slamming it back-first into the wall.

The archer fired, and with a wave of magic, Gurond's whole back was stuck to the wall. Gurond, upside-down, flailed his enormous arms, and the archer flung out that rope, wrapping it around the beast's wrists.

"None of that, big fella," he said. "You're going to answer his questions, now."

"Gurond not answer!"

"Come on, old boy," the archer said. "I, me, mine. It's not that hard."

"Where are the children?" Dayne asked.

Gurond's attention was entirely on the archer. After a moment his inhumanly black eyes narrowed. "I remember."

"There you go," the archer said. "That's much more helpful."

Gurond struggled with the rope, veins straining against his moist, leathery skin.

"Where are they?" Dayne said. "What did you take them for?"

"I remember," Gurond said again. "I remember . . . this fancy rope . . . can't hold me, Thorn."

The archer stumbled back away from him. "What the blazes?"

At the same time, the sound of bells—deep, resonant ringing—echoed through the passage.

"And I remember!" Gurond shouted, pulling his arms hard. It was as if the bells had given him newfound fury. The rope came flying off, almost hitting the archer in the face, knocking him to the ground. His image shimmered, and the shadow over his face faded. Terror washed over his young face—young, easily Jerinne's age or younger.

"Who—" the archer said, scrambling away.

"I remember you!" Gurond screamed. Even upside-down, he smashed his arms and legs against the wall. The stone cracked and shuddered at the impact. "I remember you're a *goddamned mage!*"

He smashed the wall again and again, and a horrifying sound filled the room. Once more, Gurond kicked, and with that he came free.

As did the roof of the chamber.

Huge slabs of rock came plummeting down. Dayne did the only thing he could think to do: put his body over the archer, holding up his shield while tons of stone fell on them.

Chapter 13

ASTI EXPECTED TROUBLE. THE HAIRS on the back of his neck were up, the danger was in his nose. He knew that whoever had taken Tarvis and who even knew how many other children were evil bastards. Following that Delmin kid down this tunnel, he was certain he was dealing with nefarious people, a depravity deeper than he had suspected.

The metallic tracks were imbedded into the passage floor, and steam pipes along the ceiling. He and Verci had been tracking the people behind the Andrendon Project, the people who had burned down their home and shop to claim the land on Holver Alley, and he believed what was being built beneath the Firewing house had been a part of that.

But this, whatever it was, was something else altogether. He knew these tunnels went deeper and farther than anyone in Maradaine suspected, and perhaps the Andrendon folks were just a front for whatever was going on here.

The tunnel suddenly dropped out, revealing a wide chamber below. This room had machinery—no, a machine, an enormous one with several pieces. Verci had told him about the death machine on the Parliament floor, and this put Asti in that same mind. Titanic and dark in purpose. The metal lines and the pipes fed toward it.

Whatever it was, it was quiet for now. Asti shuddered to think what it would do when fired up.

The kid had scrambled down to the machine floor, sputtering and swearing.

"Kid!" Asti wasn't sure if it was safe to shout, and tried to yell and whisper at the same time. He didn't see anyone else here, but that didn't mean they wouldn't be heard. "What the blazes are you doing?"

"What are they doing?" the kid said, looking up to Asti. "I mean, it boggles me."

"They?" Asti wished he had brought a rope instead of just knives. Not that he couldn't get down there easily enough. Getting back out would be harder. Getting out with folks after them, near impossible. Even still, he started to work his way down.

"Whoever built this," Delmin said. "I mean, it's fascinating. The way the *numina* swirls and pools, and then is drawn up through the big statue, redirected through the little ones, and then is sucked into the spikes."

"Statues?" Asti asked, having reached the floor. He looked up at the machine and saw. "Great rutting saints."

There were eight statues, all green jade: the one in the center of the machine, at least the size of a man, and the ones around the perimeter, each only a foot tall.

Asti had seen one of those small ones. Liora Rand had taken it out of Lord Henterman's lockbox. And the large one, that had to be the one they had stolen in that first gig after the fire.

"What the rutting blazes is this?" he asked.

"I wish I knew," Delmin said, coming back over to

Asti. "I . . . I had fed just a hair of *numina* into it, well, a centibarin, if we're being specific, which was not enough to actually activate it—thank Saint Marian—but enough for me to see how it all flows and pools."

"What would activating it do?" Asti asked.

"Nothing good," Delmin said. "I mean, there's parts that have nothing to do with the *numinic* flow at all—those copper cages, the gear work, and those pipes?"

"Steam pipes," Asti said. "Verci could explain it better, but if there's a water source and a firebox, you can push steam through the pipes, and use that to push parts of the machinery." He went over to one of the copper cages and gently pushed it. It was on some sort of moving gimbal. Perhaps when fired up, those parts would all spin. But why?

"That might explain why here, Mister Rynax," the kid said. He knelt on the ground, placing his palm on the stone. "Feel that."

Asti did. It was hot. "What's going on?"

"Parts of the city are over natural hot springs. That was why the Kieran Empire built the city here over two thousand years ago, for the hot baths."

"Why do you know that?"

"I study history," Delmin said. "The bathhouses on the University grounds are fed from those same hot springs, as are a few others around town."

Asti remembered the one Verci liked to go to, at Larton's Bath and Shave. "So that's the same heat?"

"A natural source," Delmin said. "The rest, I can't even fully fathom. But I noticed—it's incomplete."

"How?"

Delmin pointed to one section. "There should be another spike and statue here. The *numina* is bouncing and pooling in these perfect geometric shapes everywhere except this spot. Here it just becomes a mess."

"So that means—"

Delmin's voice grew agitated. "It means whoever built this knows what they're doing and they—"

Asti grabbed him and covered his mouth. He heard something down one of the other hallways, coming from the east. Delmin protested, but Asti dragged him through another doorway on the north side.

"Quiet!" Asti told him. "Someone's here."

Delmin nodded. He looked like he got it, and Asti released his mouth.

"Maybe they're coming to finish the machine," Delmin whispered.

"Let's see what's happening," Asti said. He peered out of the doorway. A thin, damp man with stringy black hair came into the machine chamber, flanked by a cadre of beasts.

That was the only way to describe them. Almost a dozen, all of them inhuman in their own ways. Skin unnatural colors. Limbs of every size.

"Saints almighty," Delmin said. "That's a mage. A potent one."

"You can sense that?"

"Like I can see you," Delmin said. He stumbled away and vomited in the corner of the room.

Asti couldn't blame the kid. He was of half a mind to do that himself. The last thing he wanted to do was tussle with a mage and a squad of horrors.

"Stay quiet," Asti said. "I'm going to look for another way out."

"How?"

Asti shook his head. "Best I reckon, we're under Saint Bridget's Square. The church should be over there. They've got cellars, maybe it connects."

"I should—"

"Kid, it might be that the only way out is the way we came in," Asti said. "You say you're a mage, so ready yourself to get us back up to that tunnel. You hear?"

He nodded.

Asti followed down the hallway—and it was a hallway. The machine chamber and the tunnel from under the mage house, that had been rough-cut stone. This was more like Josie's passages. Properly built, with real walls and doors. Asti cautiously checked a few of the doors. Empty sleeping cells. Looked like no one was using this place. But dead ends.

Asti checked another door. Empty again.

But not without sound. Crying. Moaning.

Children.

A quick scan of the room showed where that was coming from. A ventilation shaft at the top of the wall. So the kids were somewhere on the other side.

Asti went back to the hallway, seeking the best way to reach to the kids. If he could find them, find a way up to the surface from here, then that would make all this worth the trouble. He went around the next corner, spotting a grand doorway. Drawing out two knives, he pushed the door open. If the kids were here, and he was going to have to fight to save them, so be it.

There were no children. Instead it was far more disturbing. The room held ten glass cases, in a circle. Sarcophagi. Four of them were occupied by sleeping women. Sleeping, pregnant women.

"What in—"

Hands grabbed his head. Liora Rand's face appeared right in front of him.

"You cannot be here!" she said.

He knew she was a figment of his broken mind, but by Saint Senea, she *felt real*. He could smell her.

"Get out, get out, you stupid man," she snarled at him. "You can't see this."

She pushed him away, and he swiped at her with his knife.

He swung at open air.

"Asti!" Delmin was lumbering over to him. "Did you find a way out? Are you all right?"

"I—what just happened?" Asti asked. He was standing in the middle of the hallway.

"You were just stabbing . . . nothing."

"I saw—she . . ." Where had he just been? He had heard something, or . . . seen . . . an image of something troubling was just on the edge of his mind, but he couldn't reach it. No, he had just been searching the hallway, and found nothing peculiar at all.

"Did you find a way out?"

"No," Asti said. Dead end sleeping cells. That's all there was. That was all he had found, he was certain.

Wasn't he? He looked back down the hallway, as if he expected to see something else. Had there been another door? No, of course not. Nothing, nothing at all, no need to look again.

"Then we need to get out," Delmin said. "I don't know what that machine does, but I do know that mage is building up *numina* to do *something*, and I don't want to be here when that happens."

The examinarians came, the bodies taken, the rooms searched, but no revelations that made everything suddenly make sense. Satrine had hoped these fellows, who chose death over arrest, had some sort of journal or ledger or something she could read through and understand it all. But there was nothing.

Nothing except the trapmaster, who had slipped off into the crowd. She didn't even really think he was a part of this, or knew anything. She knew he lived near this part of town; he might well have been just another gawker. She might be putting more weight on his presence just because this whole thing spooked her, and she was trying—needing—to find some sense out of the chaos.

But then she remembered how Sister Myriem had pointed her toward him, exactly when Satrine needed to find him. That couldn't be a coincidence. Unless it was, and she was convincing herself that a random hunch meant . . . what? A greater power helping her? Her prayers were being answered in the form of an angry girl in a cloistress dress?

"There are better prayers you could answer, Saint Marguerine," she said to herself as she stepped out of the apartment into the dusky twilight of the Keller Cove streets.

"What now?" Kellman asked her.

"Just talking to myself," she said. "Sorry this was a waste of time."

"I'd hardly call it that," Kellman said. "I mean, these were three sick bastards who clearly were going up to terrible business. We're definitely better off with them gone."

"No argument on that," she said. "But we still don't know what they stole, why they stole it, or who they were with. Because whatever the blazes this was, they were part of something bigger."

"The Brotherhood," Kellman said, frowning. "I remember hearing that once before, can't remember where."

"Think on that, it might matter," she said. It was well after sign-out time, and she was overdue at home. She waved over a page. "Go run to Inemar, sign-out for Inspector Rainey for the night. You too, Kellman?"

"Nah, I've got the dark watch tonight," he said. "I'll head back and see if I can find that Brotherhood thing in my notes."

He went off with the page.

Satrine should go home, she knew that. But there was an itch she needed to scratch: check in on Minox. In all his unresolved cases, he might have heard something about this Brotherhood. Plus, she was curious what happened in his day investigating as a civilian.

The Welling house was only a few blocks away, after all.

She walked cautiously to the house, not sure how she would be received. It's not like the other Wellings were particularly fond of her. But even still, she walked up to the door and knocked.

A woman of middle years opened the door, shook her head, and closed it again. Satrine started down the steps when it opened again, and a young man in Constabulary uniform with lieutenant stripes came out.

"Inspector Rainey?" he asked. "Are you here in a professional capacity?"

"Not entirely," she said. "I had hoped for a word with Minox."

"He's not available," the young lieutenant said.

"You're Oren, his brother, right?"

"That's right. I came out here when no one else wanted to, on the off chance that you actually had official cause to come here. Since you do not, I'll tell you to walk off. You knock on our door again without a writ in hand, you'll be met with crossbows."

"Now just a damn—"

His hand snapped in front of her face, his pointing finger just inches from her eye. "My sister left here on her last ride with you, Missus Rainey. You didn't even have the decency to bring her body home."

"I . . . I'm sorry."

"Imagine how little I care," he said, going back inside and closing the door. Satrine turned around and made her way back to the street.

"Inspector! Here!"

She turned to see a wild-looking fellow, peering around the side of the house. He gestured for her to come closer. Cautiously she approached.

"Yes?"

"Inspector Rainey," he said, smiling a blackened-tooth smile. His hairy face looked beyond sickly, with his beard matted down with sweat. "Sorry, I . . . I'm not fit for company, I . . . Evoy Serrick. *South Maradaine Gazette.* Or, you know, I was. They don't have me in their employ anymore."

"Evoy?" she asked. Minox had mentioned his cousin Evoy in passing, usually in the context of a person to be pitied. She could see why. But also with a certain fondness. Minox would collect newsprints around the city for him. "Can I help you?"

"Minox didn't come home yet. He . . . I told him not to go alone, I did. I'm pretty sure he went with someone. But not home yet."

"I'm sure he'll be all right."

"I'm not," Evoy said, shaking his head. "I mean, a few months ago—the first case with you. You saved him from that Plum fellow. You remember?"

"I do," she said.

"He wrote me a note. I have plenty of my own notes, I read everything in this city, and I read between the lines, but there is not one newssheet that mentions the Brotherhood of the Nine."

That got her attention.

"What is that?"

"I don't know, but Minox knew. Knew they were connected to Plum. To his eight pins. And the pins led to his hand, and he went to the Blue Hand, and the Blue Hand faced the Thorn. And you met the Thorn. But I don't think the Thorn is there for Minox, so who would he ask for help? I don't even know."

"Slow down," Satrine said. "Who is the Brotherhood?"

"Whispers beneath us," he said. He knelt down and pressed his ear to the ground. "Maybe right beneath us. But also rotting through the city. Touching everything. The children, the robberies, the election, the scandal, it's all the Brotherhood. They are here, and Minox cannot stop them alone."

"He's not alone," she said. "I'm with him in all of this."

"Right, right," he said. "Be vigilant tonight, Inspector. Something is moving, and I feel it in my bones. I think he's going to need you before the night is done."

She nodded. "Jace isn't home yet, is he?" If anyone in the Welling house still had any kind thoughts for her, it was him.

"Jace?" He looked confused. "No, no, I . . . there's too many of them in there for me to track their coming and going. I don't . . . I don't go in there anymore. Not in the house."

"If Minox doesn't come home, let Jace know to tell me."

"I . . . no, I don't go in there. Don't talk to any of them. Just Minox. Maybe Ferah. But, no, just Minox. Only he understands."

"This is for Minox," she said.

"No, no," Evoy said. He started looking up at the night sky. "I should have . . . I should have learned the moons and the stars. They're probably . . . knowing that would help. I wonder if I have an almanac. I think I do. I think I do." He wandered to the barn behind the house, closing himself in.

Satrine sighed. At least she knew that Minox was aware of the Brotherhood, and hopefully he would know more. She would have to believe he knew what he was doing. She needed to get home, see her girls, check in on Loren. Tomorrow she would work on this more.

The sound of falling rocks had stopped, and Gurond's mad howls had faded into the distance. For a momentary eternity, there was nothing but darkness and silence in the hot, close crush of stone.

"So, I didn't catch your name."

"What?" Dayne asked. He could barely make sense of anything, save the terror clutching his heart, and the pain in his arms, bracing his body and the shield, keeping the ceiling from crushing their skulls.

A soft red glow formed in front of Dayne, showing the young man—the archer. What had Gurond called him? Thorn? Why was that familiar? Something Hemmit and the rest had written?

Hemmit. He was nearby. Hopefully not also caught in the collapse.

"I didn't catch your name," he said. "I mean, I've never been quite this intimate with someone without first exchanging names."

"Intimate?" Dayne asked. "We've been caved in."

"And your body is pressed on top of mine," the Thorn said. "I mean, I'm flattered, but . . ."

"We're lucky to not be dead, and you make jokes."

"I can assure you, I wouldn't if we were dead."

Absurdity.

"Can you move at all?" Dayne asked him. "We need to find a way out of this."

"Right now, I'm focused on keeping us from being crushed," he said.

"My shield is doing that."

"No, your shield is helping," the Thorn said. "I used it to envelope us in magic, which is probably why we aren't dead."

"So can you magic us out?" Dayne asked.

"It's all a bit delicate. I didn't want to get started until we assessed the situation. Like who I'm dealing with."

"Who am I dealing with?"

"I asked you first, pal."

"Very mature," Dayne said.

"Well, few people accused me of being otherwise."

Dayne sighed. "You're called the Thorn, apparently?"

"So you have heard of me."

"I heard Gurond call you that."

The Thorn shook his head. "I don't know how he knew that. He . . ."

"He knew you. How?"

"I've never seen that monster before," the Thorn said. "I have no idea."

"Surely—"

"Look, an hour ago I thought you were the giant taking the kids, so let's not dig that useless hole."

"How could you think a Tarian—"

"There is nothing that surprises me anymore," the Thorn said. "So, great Tarian who does not kidnap children, who are you?"

"Dayne!" Hemmit's voice could be heard through the rubble. "Dayne, are you there?"

"So, it's Dayne," the Thorn said.

"Yes," Dayne said. He called out to Hemmit. "Are you all right?"

"I'm not under the rock, if that's what you're asking," Hemmit replied. "I heard the ruckus and came over, but I'm not in great shape right now."

The Thorn called out, "Do you see a giant creature, nine feet tall with oily gray skin? Answers to Gurond?"

"What?" Hemmit said. "I only see this pile of rock covering half the room."

"Well, if we're lucky, Gurond buried himself in the collapse," the Thorn said. "If we're not, he's out and about in the hallways."

"Hush," Dayne said. His heartbeat was going faster, and his whole body felt cold and clammy, and he could only see the Thorn's stupid, cocky face. "We have . . ." He couldn't breathe. "We have . . ." He couldn't hold the panic in any longer, and screamed.

"Hey, hey, Dayne," the Thorn said. "Easy, big guy. My magic is keeping us from being crushed but you're still doing a lot of the work. And pretty soon you'll be doing all of it. So keep your head on."

"Dayne?" Hemmit called.

"Hey, friend," the Thorn called out. "What are we looking at here? You said half the room is buried. So half isn't. You can walk around?"

"Yes," Hemmit said.

"You happen to see any bits of us? Feet or cloth sticking out of the rubble? Maybe a rope?"

"Nothing," Hemmit said. "How many passages were there out of here?"

"Six!" Dayne shouted. Saying that word took every ounce of will he had.

"Looks like one is completely covered by the cave-in. Another is mostly covered. Then four more."

The Thorn closed his eyes. "All right, the one the kid ran down is one of the blocked ones. Hopefully not the same one Gurond went down."

The boy. Dayne remembered. "We have to get that boy safe. If Gurond—"

"Yeah," the Thorn said. "Can you move at all?"

Dayne shook his head.

"All right, brace yourself, Dayne. I'm going to reach a bit to my right. I think my rope is still there."

"What good is a rope going to—"

"This rope, plenty," the Thorn said. His hand moved, sliding past Dayne's chest. "If I can get it, it might make all the difference."

"Magic," Dayne said.

"Right," the Thorn said. He inched his hand over a bit more. "Got it."

Suddenly a snake ran up Dayne's body. The last bits of self-control fell apart, and Dayne shouted. He dropped his arm and collapsed entirely on the Thorn. The rocks fell as well, and they were surely crushed—

But they weren't. They had shot out through the rubble into the passageway, wrapped together in the rope. The rope uncoiled from them and Dayne pulled himself off, getting to his feet.

The Thorn stayed on the ground, panting and heaving.

"Are you—" Dayne started.

"Took—a—lot . . . too fast . . ."

Dayne looked about. They were in the passage that

had been fully blocked by the cave-in. "Hemmit! Can you hear me?"

"I can!" Hemmit said. "It looked like the pile collapsed. Are you clear?"

"Clear but trapped. Unless we can move this stone . . ." He looked to the Thorn. Maybe he could magic it to get them out.

The Thorn shook his head. He crawled over to the wall and propped himself up against it. "That would take a lot, and I don't have that much left in me. Not if I want to be ready for another round with Gurond."

"We're stuck in this tunnel," Dayne called to Hemmit. "The boy—"

"Went down the other way," Thorn said. He dug into one of his pockets and pulled out a sandwich wrapped in cloth. "Good thing I came prepared."

"You're going to eat?" Dayne asked.

"I have to," Thorn said, taking a greedy bite.

"Makes sense," Hemmit called from outside. "You say there's a boy down the blocked passage?"

"Yeah," the Thorn said.

"It's Vollingale's son," Dayne said.

"Hey, kid," Hemmit called. "Er . . . your grace? Are you all right?"

"Go away!"

The Thorn gingerly pulled himself up to his feet. "Hey, kid, you know what?"

"Go away!"

"Hemmit, can you get to him?" Dayne asked.

"No, but maybe he can get through there if he's small."

"Kid," The Thorn said. "Guess what day it is?"

"Shut it!"

"It's two days to Terrentin. Just two days. I bet you're going to get all sorts of gifts at home."

Silence for a moment. "I wanna go home."

"I bet," the Thorn called out. "Do you know the story of Saint Terrence? Why we give gifts on Terrentin?"

"No."

"Terrence was a toymaker in his village. He made toys for all the children in his village, but one day a horrible warlord abducted the children, and brought them to work in his mines. They were trapped underground. Just like you!"

"I don't want to be trapped."

"I know, but Terrence, he was smart, because he was a builder. He knew that if it rained, the mines would flood, so the warlord would have to open the gates, and then the children could be free. So, he prayed for rain, and the rains came. But the warlord still didn't open the gates. He refused. So Terrence went into the mines himself, through the flooding tunnels, to open the gates, and the children were free. He yelled to the children, Rejoice, Rejoice, for you are free!"

"And what happened to him?" the boy asked. "Did he get out?"

"They say he closed the gates again, to trap the warlord, and he held him down there to drown."

"So he drowned too?"

"No one knows," the Thorn said. "But two nights later, the people in the village woke to find toys next to every child's bed, and wet footprints in the room. And some say, in those mines, you can still hear him call."

"Rejoice! Rejoice! Rejoice!" Hemmit called out.

"He's here!" the boy shouted. They could hear a scramble of rock and stone.

"I've got you," Hemmit said. "You're safe."

"Hemmit, you've got to get him out of here," Dayne called. "We'll find another way around."

"How?" Hemmit asked.

The Thorn spoke up. "You take that passage to the left of the one he was in, and you follow it down about a quarter of a mile. You'll reach a junction with a chalk mark on the wall. You should be able to follow chalk marks all the way to a sewer exit in Seleth. And if you find a fellow named Rynax—"

"Asti or Verci?" Hemmit asked.

That startled the Thorn. "Asti. You tell him the Thorn is going for the giant."

"Dayne, what about everyone else?"

"I won't leave them down here," Dayne said. "But you're hurt and that boy needs to get home. Take care of that."

"All right," Hemmit said. "Come on, son. Let's get you home for Terrentin."

The sound of their feet receded in the distance.

"You have others down here?" the Thorn asked. "I know there's more than just one kid."

"Other children, other friends," Dayne said. "I don't know about you, but I'm not leaving without every single one of them."

"What a coincidence," the Thorn said, the shadow of his cloak covering his face again. The rope coiled up at his belt, and he took up his bow. "I feel exactly the same way."

Chapter 14

"BLESSED BE THE NINE!" THE crowd called. "Blessed be their High Dragon, Crenaxin!"

From her place at the back of the crowd, Jerinne was not the focus of anyone's attention, thankfully. Else they would have noticed that she was not calling out with the rest of them.

Under her bloody robe, her fingers were wrapped around the hilt of her sword, so tight she could feel the blood pooling in them. She couldn't make herself loosen her grip. If these zealots noticed her, if they went for her, she wouldn't have a chance. There were easily a hundred of them. She kept her eye on the exits, noting how many robed figures were between her and escape, should things go wrong.

Crenaxin stepped away from the altar and the corpse, looking out to the crowd. "We must call him back, and for that, we must feed the fervent fire."

"The fire must burn!"

"Who will step forward?" Crenaxin asked. "Who

will take their place in the furnace of the world? Who will burn for the Nine? Someone must feed the fervent fire so . . ." He turned to one of the other men. "What was his name?"

"Poller," the man said. "Ren Poller."

"So that Ren can be called. So he can share with us his final secrets."

One of the people from the crowd—one of the misshapen grotesques—came forward. They knelt at Crenaxin's feet.

"Worthy soul," Crenaxin said, placing his hand on their head. "You have already sacrificed so much, being a vessel for the great and terrible power. You were broken, but your faith is strong." Crenaxin knelt down next to the beast. "I am humbled by your courage. I wish that you were enough, dear friend." One hand still cradling the creature's face, he reached out to the crowd. "I need more, please."

Three more stepped forward, all reaching out and putting their hands on Crenaxin.

"Thank you," he said, tears falling from his eyes. "I will hold on to this, dear friends." He touched each of them, kissed them on the head, and then walked slowly to the altar.

As he approached the corpse, his body started to glow, like the last embers of a fire when blown upon. The glow filled his arms, and as it did, the four creatures on the altar began to smolder.

They all screamed as smoke poured off their bodies. One of them held up their arm to the air, and Jerinne watched in horror as it turned gray and ashen, and then crumbled into dust.

They all crumbled into dust, and the smoke that had poured off their bodies pooled and swirled around the altar, and then flew high in the air before jetting down Crenaxin's throat.

Crenaxin's skin swirled with light and color, as if a

raging inferno burned underneath it. He bent back his head and opened his mouth impossibly wide, and then leaned forward to the corpse.

Fire spewed from his mouth, engulfing the body.

Jerinne screamed.

So did the rest of the congregation, but theirs were in elation and ecstasy. Jerinne dug her fingers into the hilt of her sword, hoping the feel of the weapon in her hand could stop the trembling fear in her body.

Crenaxin dropped to his knees, coughing and weeping.

Then the dead man started coughing. The flames cooled down and ebbed, then died down completely. The dead man coughed and jerked, and the two robed figures on the dais rushed over and helped him to his feet.

The dead man stood. His head was still caved in, and his eyes were cold and glassy.

But he stood.

Jerinne's heart hammered so hard, she heard only the thunder of her pulse in her ears.

Crenaxin got to his feet. "Ren Poller," he said quietly. "We drag you from your rest. You have something to tell us."

"The . . . statue . . ." Poller said, his voice sounding like it had been scraped against a stone.

"Where is it?" one of the robed figures asked. "Where can we find it?"

"Essin . . ." he said. "Essin . . . killed me."

"The thief we hired, High Dragon," the robed figure said.

Crenaxin nodded. "And where would Essin go? Where do we find him?"

"He . . ." Poller's face twisted into a mockery of thought. "He would hide."

"Where?"

"Nowhere for him," Poller said. "Every safe hole . . . gone."

"Ren, please," Crenaxin said, touching the man's face gently. Jerinne fought the urge to retch—the man's head still oozed blood and pus. "If he had nowhere else to go, where would he hide? Who would he seek?"

Poller's dead eyes looked at Crenaxin, and his face turned into a horrific sneer. "Rynax. Essin . . . always liked him too much."

"And where is Rynax?"

"Gadgeterium," Poller said. "Let me . . . let me . . ."

"You can rest now," Crenaxin said.

"Let me go there," Poller said. "Let me kill them."

Crenaxin stepped away, a broad smile on his face. "Oh, dear brothers, hear that? Even from beyond death, he serves with faith and loyalty! Who else will serve? Who will go with him, and reclaim that which is ours? Nearly the last piece we need?"

Hands went high in the air.

"No, my troubled ones," he said to some of the grotesques. "The world above is not ready for you, not yet. Very soon." He pointed to a few of the humans. "Go with Poller. Get the statue. The time is ripe and we are nearly ready to crack—"

A loud boom echoing through the congregation chamber interrupted him, as one of the walls of twisted vines exploded in blue flame. As it burned away, it revealed two people not in robes, and for a moment Jerinne's heart leaped, hoping it was Maresh and Lin. Or Dayne. Or anyone she could call a friend.

And it was, at least one of them. She didn't know the dark-skinned girl with the sword, but the man—mad, impossible as it was—was Inspector Welling. His hand was engulfed in blue fire, and his face was filled with rage.

"I will not abide!" he shouted as he raised up his crossbow with his other hand. "Stand and be held in the name of the law!"

Crenaxin simply laughed. "He amuses me. Kill the girl, but take him alive."

Immediately, the congregation swarmed at Minox Welling and the girl. With all these zealots and beasts between her and them, Jerinne was incapable of helping them before they were overrun.

Still, she drew out her sword. She would be damned if she didn't try.

Minox had lost control.

His temper flared at seeing this unholy madness, and he lost control. His hand had surged with magic, destroying the wall they had been hiding behind. Exposed, and still full of anger, he did the only thing he knew to do.

"I will not abide!" he shouted as he raised up his crossbow. "Stand and be held in the name of the law!" He doubted these beasts and malefactors would respect the rule of law, but by Saint Veran, he would at least honor the words.

Crenaxin laughed, hollow and empty. "He amuses me. Kill the girl, but take him alive."

The beasts and zealots charged at him.

His hand was still full of magic, pulsing and screaming to be set free, so let it. He slammed his fist onto the ground, quaking the floor in a wave of force that knocked them all down.

He was about to tell Miss Nell to run, but she had proved adept at determining that course of action on her own. He raced right behind her, his hand now eased down to just a throbbing blue glow. He was amazed that Olivant thought he could destroy the city, when that knock alone had been enough to leave him nearly spent.

"Get back to the tunnel!" she shouted. She ran with her sword in hand, which was probably not the wisest decision, but proved useful when one zealot leaped into her path. She hacked at him with more power than skill, but it was sufficient to discourage his further pursuit.

"My thought exactly," he said. He pivoted in his sprint, firing his crossbow at the closest zealot. He shot true, taking that one down, but that left several dozen still. He spun back to resume his stride, hoping they could beat their pursuers, either with speed or endurance.

He feared he did not have enough of either.

"I can't believe . . . you actually . . . told them to stand . . ."

Minox struggled to reload his crossbow as he ran. It would hardly make a difference, but he would at least make the attempt.

"They're going for the Blue Tunnel!" someone shouted. "Get the gate!"

Minox saw two of them up ahead, running for a wheel. The wheel connected to a chain, the chain to an iron gate, the gate at the tunnel entrance.

Simple deduction. The gate would close before they made it. They would be trapped. They would capture him and kill Miss Nell.

Only one course of action available.

He filled the hand with magic, as much as he could gather.

They were turning the wheel. The gate was closing.

"My apologies, Miss Nell," he said.

"What?" she asked, looking back at him.

He held up his hand and, with everything he had, pushed her across the hollow. Her sword skittered to the ground as she went flying into the tunnel as the gate slammed shut. Safe on the other side.

Minox nearly collapsed from the effort, but scrambled to pick up her sword. If he was going to be taken, he would at least make it hurt.

He only got a few good swipes in before hands were all over him, pressing him down to the ground.

On his knees, a dozen zealots and beasts holding him down, he said the only thing he could. "You will be charged with violations of the law, including and not limited to assault on an officer of the law, assault on a citizen, attempted murder, and murder times four. I shall see—"

"I love his spirit," Crenaxin said, walking calmly up to him. "I mean, even now, he's so righteous. It's very interesting."

He knelt down next to Minox, and ran a finger along Minox's hand, now glowing with just an ember of blue within the hard, dead black.

"But this, oh, this . . . I think this is something Mister Senek will be very interested in, indeed."

Kaiana didn't know what had happened. She had been fighting with those creatures, those bastards, trying to escape with the inspector, when suddenly she had been hurled off her feet, tumbling down the passage. She had lost her sword—Dad's sword—in the process.

She got to her feet and brushed herself off. She knew where she was—the same passage they had come from. She could get back to the Blue Hand house relatively easily, go for help. Maybe Veranix was back. She could get him, bring him back through here, hopefully in time for Inspector Welling.

Welling.

She realized what he had done. He had saved her, sacrificed himself so she would get away. She had to go back for him, get him out of there. It's what Veranix would do for him. It's what he would do for anyone.

Though Kaiana wondered what she, an unarmed groundskeeper, could possibly do to rescue Welling from a blazing army of mad cultists and deformed monsters.

Not a damned thing.

What would Veranix do?

More importantly, what would she *want* Veranix to do in a moment like this?

Why Veranix was constantly doing stupid things became abundantly clear to her.

She resolved to go back for him. It was the only decent thing to do.

She started back down the tunnel toward the encampment, all the while forming a dozen different apologies to Veranix. Not that she would actually tell him any of them. That boy's head was big enough without being told he had been right. But she'd think of them.

After only a short walk, two figures came out of the darkness. Robes, wicked blades and wickeder smiles. She screamed and almost fell back, just barely keeping her footing.

"There she is," one said.

"Time for a gift of blood for the Brotherhood," the other said.

Before Kaiana could even respond, a whistling sound cut through the air. Then the clang of metal on stone, metal on bone, then again. Both those zealots had been suddenly walloped out of nowhere, and a young woman jumped into view, catching the shield flying through the air.

She landed, sword high, shield raised, a look on her face of someone who was both very angry and very happy to find a target for her anger.

"Time to rethink your choices, boys," she said.

The zealots turned to her and charged, but they were out of their league. Their blades and punches missed every mark, while the girl—this saint—made quick work of cracking their skulls about. Without even quickening her breath, she flattened them both.

"You all right, miss?" she asked Kaiana, sheathing her sword as she approached. She was in uniform, but not one Kaiana had ever seen before.

"No," Kaiana said. "I mean, I'm not hurt, but . . ."

"I understand," the girl said—saints, now that Kaiana saw her up close, she was young. Same age as Veranix. "My name's Jerinne."

"Kaiana."

"How'd you get down here with Inspector Welling?" Jerinne asked.

"You know him?"

Jerinne nodded. "He got captured, but when I saw them coming down the tunnel after you, I figured . . ."

"Thank you," Kai said. "He was investigating something with missing children in Dentonhill, and wanted someone to come with him, and . . . it's complicated."

"So you're not with the Constabulary in any way?"

"Not at all," Kaiana said. How could she explain who she was or why she had been down here with Welling? "I'm . . . I'm an associate of the Thorn. Do you know who that is?"

Jerinne nodded. "I've read a couple things in the newssheets, talk in the Initiate barracks. I didn't . . . I didn't think he was a real person."

"He is," Kaiana said. "But he was . . . he was already gone, looking for the missing children with someone else."

"Seems to be the thing to do today," Jerinne said. "All right, can you walk? Are you all right?"

"More or less," Kaiana said.

"I've got some other friends in trouble down here, so I'm going to go back for them and Inspector Welling. Can you find your way back up to street level?"

Kaiana nodded. "Yeah, I marked the way from where we came in."

"Smart," Jerinne said, her smile practically lighting up the tunnel. "Where are you going to come up?"

"Dentonhill. North side of it."

"Saints, I've gone far underground," Jerinne said. "All right, get over to the Inemar stationhouse, look for Inspector Satrine Rainey. No one else."

"Why—" Kaiana started.

"Because there are people up there who are working with these bastards down here," Jerinne said. "Satrine can be trusted."

"What about the Thorn?"

"Maybe he's already down here in this mess," she said with a smile. "If you can get him, I'll take it. But make sure you tell Satrine Rainey. Tell her what happened. Tell her about Welling. Tell her I sent you— Jerinne Fendall."

"Jerinne Fendall," Kaiana repeated. "What if she's not at the stationhouse?"

"Then you find her at home. Fourteen Beltner, in High River."

"Fourteen Beltner. All right." She took a deep breath. "Anything else?"

"She'll know what to do," Jerinne said. She hesitated for a moment, and then wrapped Kaiana up in an embrace. "Good luck."

"Thanks," Kaiana said, not sure how to react to that. Jerinne released her, a shy, awkward smile on her face, and then ran off into the darkness.

Kaiana turned around and started to make her way back to the Blue Hand house, hoping that Jerinne was right, and Inspector Rainey knew what to do.

Verci had tried to be patient. He tried to wait it out.

Seeing that fellow jump off the roof to his death didn't help one bit. Nor had seeing that Waishen-haired inspector on the scene. Whoever had hired Essin to steal that statue, they were part of the Brotherhood, and they were ready to die rather than let themselves be taken by the constables. He had heard the examinarium saying the other two had slit their own throats.

He didn't stick around longer. That inspector had stared at him a bit too long for his comfort. As curious as he was, he didn't want to get wrapped up with the constables.

So he went back to the Gadgeterium and closed things up. He checked in on Essin—sleeping fitfully— and focused his energy on preparing dinner. Raych came home from the bakery, carrying little Corsi, and he kissed them both and ate quietly. Raych told him about her day, but his attention was on the empty chair and plate where Asti should be sitting.

They finished and cleaned up, and the sun had definitely set into night. He played with Corsi and then settled the boy down to sleep.

Asti still hadn't returned.

He had waited enough.

"What do you intend to do?" Raych asked him when he started getting dressed.

"Don't try to tell me not to go," he said.

"I'm not," she said. "But I am going to say, don't go stupidly." She got up from the bed, pulling her dress on.

"You're not coming."

"Don't you tell me what I'm not doing," she said. "But whatever we do, we're going to do it smart." She pointed to the statue, sitting in the corner of the room. "You think that's a part of all this, right?"

"Right," he said.

"So, whatever we do, keeping that secure has to be a part of it. Right?"

She was spot on about that. "Right. Plus we need to remember that Essin is sleeping in the next apartment."

"You don't trust him, right?"

"Not a bit, but I believe his story. And I doubt he'll live to Terrentin."

"All right, let's think about his story. He went to . . . who was it?"

"Ren Poller."

"Someone he trusted. But he was mixed up in this

business, too. So we need to think. What are we going to do? Are you planning on going into the tunnels alone?"

He actually had, but she was right. "No, of course not."

"So who are you going to ask to help you?"

Names rattled through his head. Plenty of people he could call on. Helene and Julien. Helene had made herself scarce of late, spending her nights with Lieutenant Covrane, and Verci wouldn't take Julien on something like this alone. Jared Scall had been walking around with his mace, hungry for a chance to use it. Jhoqull and her cousins. Going into the tunnels with a small army of Ch'omik warriors definitely had its appeal. He could even go over to campus, get Mila.

But did he trust them? Trust them not to be . . . compromised, like Poller was? He wanted to. He thought he ought to be able to. But Essin's story gave him pause.

The shop bell rang below.

"Who is at the door?" Raych asked.

"That's a very good question." No one should be ringing the shop at this hour, though Verci had to think about what might happen if things went wrong underground. What if the Thorn or his scrawny friend were the only ones who got out? Wouldn't they come, and ring the bell?

Raych went over to the peek mirror he had set up in the apartment and had a look. "Well, that's odd."

"What?"

"It's a cloistress."

"For real?" Verci asked.

"Well, that's how she's dressed."

Verci grabbed three darts and palmed them. "Stay here, lock behind me."

"For a cloistress?"

"Just be safe."

He went down the stairs to the front door, leaving the floor bolt in place as he opened it. Unless she was as strong as Julie, she wouldn't be able to force the door open more than the crack he was allowing.

As Raych said, a cloistress—young blond girl. She was staring at him with intense, disturbing eyes.

"Can I help you?"

"Blessed Saint Terrence! Builder and toymaker! Savior of children!"

"I, er . . . well, I make toys, but, I don't know about . . ."

"You do, blessed saint. And that is such vital important work. I know—I know right now you want to turn your eye to other work, but it is *not yet time*."

"I . . . what do you mean?"

"Terrentin is coming, dear saint," she said, tears coming to her eyes. "And soon you will bless the world with your toys. But *right now*, no, it is not the time. Now you need to be here, doing this work."

Verci had no idea what to say to that. Who was this girl?

"But—"

"Trust in God, good saint. Wait for the time, it will be clear."

She nodded and walked off. Verci shut the door and latched it, then went back up.

"What did she want?" Raych asked.

"To spook the blazes out of me, I think," Verci said. "And . . . it worked." He took his boots off. "I . . . I think I need to wait here for now."

Somehow, that made him feel calm, at least for a moment. That he was making the right choice.

He just hoped Asti could wait.

Chapter 15

ASTI WAS OUT OF CHOICES. Big magic machine, the gears and gimbals spinning. Mage so powerful, it was terrifying this kid out of his mind. No less than ten creatures, misshapen horrors that might have once been men. Asti remembered what Tarvis had said. Skin his knives couldn't get through. Was that what these were? Unkillable monsters.

"All right," Asti told Delmin. "You're a mage, right?"

"I mean, yes, but—"

"I don't want to hear you saying 'but.' You are, yes?"

"Not a good one."

"Kid," Asti said. "You're good in school, right?"

"Top marks."

"Well, this is your exam." Asti snuck a peek back at the machine chamber. Fortunately, the beasts and the mage had their attention on the machine. "We're going to slip our way out here, behind the machine to the tunnel we came in, and you're going to get us up there fast. Got it?"

"And what if they see us?"

"Then I'm going to start taking those bastards down, and you're going to get us up there fast. I want you to say, 'I'm going to pass this exam, Professor Rynax.'"

"Professor is a rank bestowed—"

"Say it!"

"I'm going to pass this exam, Professor Rynax." Delmin looked over to the door. "Things are heating up. All right, now or never."

Asti pulled out two knives. "You still got that knife I gave you, right?"

"Yes, but—"

"Just keep it in your hand. Let's hope it doesn't come to that. No matter what, you get up there. And you *run*."

Asti creeped the door open, and slipped into the machine chamber. Mouse quiet. He'd done a dozen sneaks harder than this. They were going to make it.

A steam piston extended on the machine, and the rings around the cages started spinning.

Delmin winced and stumbled. Asti grabbed him before he fell. Then he saw something new with the machine.

The machine was occupied. There was a metal platform in the center, where two people were shackled together: a man and woman. The man was wiry, hairy, with spectacles; the woman, Asti had seen before. The reporter he and Verci had met a few months back.

And the cages each held a child.

Asti swore under his breath.

"Change of plans," he told Delmin.

"What are you going to do?" Delmin asked.

"Something stupid," Asti said.

"Wait," Delmin said. "The *numina* is building up. Maybe I can do something about that. So, my stupid plan, then your stupid plan." He set his jaw.

"What's your stupid plan?"

"Make a ruckus even the Thorn will hear."

Suddenly a green glow surrounded him and the machine, and the glow around the machine grew sickly as his became brighter.

"What is happening?" someone on the other side of the machine shouted.

Asti dove toward the machine, going for the cages. The rings were spinning too fast, he'd be torn to pieces if he tried to get close. He had to figure out how to stop them. That meant the machine controls, and the dozen hairy grotesques between him and them.

So be it.

Delmin held his hands out and yanked them in close to his body, and as soon as he did the entire room shook and echoed with thunder. And with a terrible pop, Delmin vanished from sight.

"Kid!" Asti shouted. He was skunked now, that was certain. As the creatures started to lumber over, he ran over to where Delmin had been.

"Look out!" a tiny voice said at his feet. He looked to the ground, and there was Delmin, the size of a mouse.

"What—" was all Asti had a chance to say before one of the monsters was on him. Its horrible hands, swollen and shrunken at the same time, grabbed onto him, as its half-mouth roared. Asti drove both blades into its throat.

Fortunately, this one did not have skin that Asti couldn't stab through.

"Help!" Delmin's tiny voice called.

Asti pulled his knives out of the dying beast's neck, and threw one knife at the next monster. But they were coming too fast. Asti dove in a roll to get out of the way of one of them, scooping up tiny Delmin in the process. "I got a crazy idea, kid."

"What's that?"

Asti focused on dodging out of the way of the creatures so he could get to a place where he could see the tunnel they came in. He just needed to hold out a few seconds, and then he could tear his way through these bastards. Or die trying.

He placed tiny Delmin on the hilt of his knife. "No matter what, get out, get help. You hear? Hold on."

"Hold on what?" Delmin shouted. Then he seemed to get the idea, and wrapped his arms and legs around the grip.

Asti flipped the blade once in his hand, and then threw the knife as straight and true as he could at the tunnel opening, twenty feet above him. He heard it land and skitter inside the tunnel.

Then a fist smashed his head. He went flat down to the ground. That massive hand picked him up by the skull and lifted him off the ground.

"Asti." The delusion of Liora Rand was in front of him again. "Asti, you have to survive."

"What is this interloper?" he heard someone else say. Asti was carried by his head around the machine—he saw it was stopped again, so that was something—to a thin and dark-eyed fellow who just looked evil. Even the way he spoke was filled with malice.

"Just looking out for the neighborhood," Asti slurred.

"Asti, you will die, listen to me," the imaginary Liora said.

"This fellow has no power in him," the man said. "He couldn't have done that."

"I'm full of surprises," Asti said. He drew another knife, despite being suspended by his head, but the evil man just waved his hand and the knife flew away.

"Petty thing. Feel free to kill him."

"Asti, listen," Liora pleaded. Asti was shocked. He had never known Liora—especially this vision of her that haunted him—to do anything but taunt him. "If you want to live, you have to say—"

"I don't have to—" he slurred. He was hurled onto the stone ground. Now he saw—the great oily giant was above him, as well as several of his monstrous friends.

They all raised their arms to pummel him into nothingness.

"I demand an audience with the High Dragon of the Nine! Say it!"

Somehow, before they smashed him, he found his voice and repeated her words.

They all froze.

"What did he say?" the evil man asked.

The giant spoke. "He demanded—"

"No, I heard." The evil man crouched next to Asti. "Then I suppose we'll comply with his demand."

Amaya had spent the evening hours at the chapterhouse completely restless. The Initiates had all had dinner and were starting Contemplation Exercises, and Jerinne was nowhere to be seen. Amaya was a bit worried for her safety, but not much. She was with Dayne and Hemmit and the others, and the girl could handle herself.

But the curfew for Initiates had passed. There was no way to pretend that Jerinne was just elsewhere in the chapterhouse. Her absence in Contemplation had surely been noticed by the other third-years, and her empty bunk would definitely be once they went back to barracks.

That was all drumming through her mind, as were the revelations of Kemmer's place. That man had made discoveries, and been disappeared for it. She was certain.

Something needed to be done. Amaya could barely think of anything else. Two thoughts kept driving through her brain. Find Jerinne. Find Kemmer.

She went to the Contemplation Exercises herself, joining the Initiates in the back of the room. She strove to follow the same instructions she had given when she ran the exercises, to focus her thoughts on the candle, her breathing, calm her nerves.

The exercises ended, and she was no calmer. Especially with Vien looking put out. As the other Initiates filed out, Vien came up to her.

"Fendall is missing. I know we don't exactly put a close eye on her . . ."

"That's what not having a proper mentor will do," Amaya said. "I had put her on the armory, but I didn't check up on her."

"I looked there during dinner," Vien said. "She hadn't been there for hours. It's not like her."

"No," Amaya said. "I . . . I have my suspicions of where she is. Tell the other third-years I have it handled, and let's keep it between us."

"What about the Grandmaster? Shouldn't we—"

"I will handle it, Candidate," Amaya said, perhaps too sharply. "Your duties are to the rest of the Initiates."

"Yes, Madam Tyrell," Vien said. She looked put out, but went off.

Amaya went to the training room. Maybe she could sweat out these feelings, even though she continued to have the pounding need to do *something*. If not for Jerinne, then for Kemmer. She grabbed a practice sword off the wall and went through her maneuvers, working through positions, wanting someone to aim her energy at.

She knew where to go. Hemmit had told her where to start.

The Opera House.

That thought kept coming up.

"Everything all right, Amaya?"

The Grandmaster had come in, barefoot in just his cottons. It was odd to see him dressed so casually out of his study. He rarely came down not in uniform.

"Just—had something to get out of my muscles, sir," she said.

"I very much understand," he said with resignation.

"Usually you're doing your exercises before the dawn, not after sunset."

"Today—today has been—" She wasn't sure what to say to him. Even now, she looked and saw the kindly face of the man who had been guiding the Order for as long as she had known. But yet there was a shadow over him.

"Trying, yes," he said. "I find that to be the case for me most days. All the little things to . . . keep this place in line. It's quite the burden."

"I'm sure you shoulder a lot, sir," Amaya said, placing the training sword back on the rack.

"You have no idea, Miss Tyrell," he said. "I really hope you never will."

"Even still," she said, coming closer to him, looking into his dark eyes for some sign of deception. "No matter what the weight, I won't waver from following what my heart knows is right."

He blinked and looked away. "I'm sure you wouldn't. But we all . . . we always think we're making the right choices in the moment." He took a few steps away from her, running his hand on the rack of practice weapons. "But the important thing, the most important thing, is that we endure."

"With honor," she said.

"Honor is a vice of the unburdened," he said coldly. "It matters little when all your choices are terrible. I just wish . . . I wish you could understand that, Amaya. What it means to navigate through all that darkness."

"I understand," she said, her thoughts about Jerinne and Dayne and Kemmer and the Grand Ten all coalescing into a single course of action. "But that's why it was on you to be a beacon in darkness."

"Was?" he sighed. "Have I failed in your eyes?"

"I just . . ." She found the words coming together, finding voice to her surprise. "I just know when I am doing the right thing, the light is clear. And I will follow that light."

And it clicked in her head. She couldn't just wait in here for things to resolve themselves. She had to take action.

The Grandmaster's head went up, as if he had heard that very click, but it was just the dark-haired servant coming into the training room.

"Sorry," she said. "I need to clean this room now."

"Of course," the Grandmaster said, his voice now subdued and flat. "We all must do what we must. If you'll excuse me." He stalked off.

Amaya waited for him to be gone, and then hurried to her room. She would do what she must, what she could do. She would find out what happened to Kemmer, find the Grand Ten, and get to the truth. No matter what the cost.

Dressed in her civilian clothes, sword at her belt, she slipped out of the chapterhouse, making sure no one took note of her. She moved now with purity of purpose, certainty leading her toward the Grand Opera House of Maradaine.

The Thorn had led the way down the passage, claiming he could feel where they needed to go. Dayne was dubious, but he didn't have a better solution. Still, he couldn't help but feel he was getting even farther away from Jerinne, Maresh, and Lin. He prayed they were all right.

"How can you feel it?" he finally asked.

"Mage," the Thorn said, as if that said it all.

"What do you mean by that?"

The Thorn sighed, and turned back to Dayne. "*Numina*—magical energy—is all around us, flowing and moving. I'm attuned to that. I'm not great at sensing it . . ." He looked down the hallway, pursing his lips. "I'm actually pretty bad at it."

"So why—"

"Because there's something happening up ahead that's making enough noise that even I can hear it."

"Noise?"

"As good a word as any," the Thorn said.

"All right, and then what?"

"Then what what?"

"What do you intend to do once we get to whatever that is?"

"We'll see when we get there. Hopefully find the people who have been taking these children and putting a stop to them."

"Putting a stop to them?" Dayne asked. "Meaning, what? Filling them with arrows, like you tried to do to me?"

"The thought occurred to me. And I rather liked it."

"What are you?" Dayne asked, grabbing the Thorn's shoulder before he walked away again. "Some common goon?"

"I think I'm rather uncommon, thank you," he said, brushing Dayne's hand away.

"Thus the whole costume."

"Says the man wearing an outfit from two centuries ago."

"This uniform has a history of honor and respect—"

"So much respect you can walk in and out of a drug lord's house."

"You mean Fenmere? He's—"

"He's a killer."

"And you aren't?" Dayne asked. "I saw you back there. Shooting to kill. At me and at Gurond."

"Oh, I'm sorry I tried to kill the unstoppable giant who's *kidnapping children*!" the Thorn shouted. "What was I thinking?"

"It really is that easy for you?" Dayne asked. Did he not understand? Was nothing serious to him? "Taking a life?"

"What do you have that sword on your belt for?"

"Defense. Disarming. And even then, only when it's necessary. There are other ways—"

"Other ways," the Thorn scoffed. He stalked down the passage.

"Do you ever think about the people you've killed? Or is that another joke to you?"

The Thorn turned back on Dayne. "Do you know what I think about? I think about how I go out there, every night, to stop someone from getting that dose of *effitte* that leaves them dead in the gutter, or burned out and left in Trenn Ward. And even then, *even then*, every day someone still ends up that way." The shading over his face flickered and vanished, showing his hot tears. Saints, he was so raw, so angry. "That's someone I didn't save. That . . . that's on me. I carry that *every rutting day*. So spare me your moralizing."

Dayne was silent at first, feeling the Thorn's burning gaze on him. "No, I get it," he finally said quietly. His own guilt was a weight on his heart. "I . . . I'm haunted by the people I didn't save. And for me that . . . that means trying to save every life. Even maybe the ones who don't deserve it."

"Hold on," the Thorn said. "You're the one who stopped the killer at the Parliament. Who captured him alive."

"Guilty," Dayne said.

"Madness," he said. "You've got to—"

He turned his head sharply, looking down the hallway, his shading coming back over his face.

"What?" Dayne asked.

"Something big just burst down that way. I think—" He started to run.

Dayne chased after him, barely able to keep up. They rounded a few corners, the Thorn moving with absurd confidence, until they came to an opening, overlooking a wide chamber that was dominated by a monstrous machine. The thing made Sholiar's creation in the Parliament look like a child's toy. And like that atrocity, there were people trapped in it. Children in cages, and Lin and Maresh shackled to a platform on top. Several other people were on the ground—most of them the same misshapen horrors that had attacked them at the bridge. Two were men—one of them clearly in control of things, the other being held by the creatures. The man in control—a man who seemed to embody vileness—was lecturing to the other, though Dayne couldn't make out the words.

"Where is he?" the Thorn asked.

"Who?"

"My friend, he . . . he shouldn't have come down here. I felt him, but . . . he's not there."

"Maybe he escaped?" Dayne asked.

"I hope so," the Thorn said. "Children. Not all of them."

"I see them."

"And that's Rynax. He came down with me. If those beasts were able to capture him, they're tough customers."

"Like Gurond."

"Hold on," the Thorn said. He waved his fingers, and then Dayne could hear the man as if he were standing right next to him.

"—since you are so interested, I will show you. Time is short, of course, as the ripe moment is upon us. Right before the sunrise will be perfect. But I can't resist another experiment."

"Like these?" Rynax asked, nodding at the grotesques.

"These poor friends . . . they were part of the learning process. But none of them came out as well as my crowning achievement."

"Gurond?"

The vile man's eyes went wide with excitement. "Yes, indeed! You are familiar with my work. He is a marvel, you must admit."

"I really mustn't," Rynax said.

"Well, he's my masterpiece, which I've not yet figured out how to repeat. Some factor made him work so perfectly when no one else did. But we learn through failure! So now to these two." He went over to the machine and raised his hands. It started moving: gears turning, rings spinning, steam belching.

"Those are my friends," Dayne told the Thorn.

"And that guy is a mage," the Thorn said. "A powerful one."

"So is she," Dayne said, pointing to Lin.

"I've got an idea," the Thorn said. "One that suits your peculiar urge for other ways."

"Which is?"

"You get his attention—talk to him or some such— and I'll get those kids and your friends out."

"How?"

The Thorn grinned, and then the whole color of his body shifted so he blended into the wall. "Magic."

Nearly invisible, he leaped out of the tunnel into the open air. Dayne couldn't see where he went at first. Then he saw just a shimmering outline on top of one of the cages. Amazingly, he had managed to slip through the spinning rings. Dayne needed to do something before the vile man took notice himself.

"Hold!" Dayne shouted, stepping into view from the high tunnel. He rested his hand on the pommel of his sword, trying his best to emulate the painting of Xandra Romaine that hung in the chapterhouse. "I demand you stop this wicked act, and release those people who are clearly being held against their will!"

Dayne had never felt more stupid.

"Why am I beset by interrupting fools today?" the vile man asked. "You, sir, are you here with an army or something?"

Dayne decided if he was going to have to play the fool for this, he'd do it to the hilt. And the Thorn was getting one of the cages open. Best keep attention away from the machine.

"I'm Dayne Heldrin of the Tarian Order, and I am commanding you to stop this horror!"

"I grow weary of this," the vile man said. "I am trying to conduct critical research before we attempt to crack into the very fabric of reality." He looked over at Rynax like he was a confidant. "I mean, we only have hours." With a wave of his hand, Dayne came flying out of the tunnel, and then was hurled down to the ground.

"Dayne!" Lin shouted from the platform on the machine.

"Oh, I see," the mage said. "You know them. Now it makes some sense." He started waving his hands over the controls of the machine. "None of this is right."

Dayne forced himself onto his feet.

"You can still make the right choice," Dayne said. "No one else needs to be hurt."

The mage sighed. "I mean, something is wrong. Everything is out of balance. Is one of you a mage? If so, it's messing up the experiment."

Maresh looked up. "She is. Let her go!"

He waved to one of the creatures. "Go get her down."

"Sir!" Dayne said. "I insist—"

The mage frowned. "No, something else is wrong. That cage is open. And—ah. Now it makes sense."

Another indifferent wave, and the Thorn was fully visible. The Thorn leaped over the mage and the monsters, firing arrows like a blur. "Switch jobs, Dayne!" he shouted.

Dayne jumped over to the machine, where the rings were still spinning about. How did the Thorn get through them? Dayne couldn't worry about that. He jumped into their path, holding his shield ahead of him. Then one spinning ring slammed into the shield, knocking Dayne back.

"Adorable," the mage said. He threw a blast of green fire at Dayne, which burst over his shield.

Dayne looked up at the machine. The children looked terrified. Maresh and Lin were the same, struggling with their shackles. Dayne couldn't fail them.

"Thorn, hold him off!" Dayne called back. But he looked back to the Thorn and saw how useless that was going to be. Gurond had come into the room through grand double doors. The Thorn hadn't seen him, and landed right in front of him. "Look out!"

Too late. Gurond's massive fist knocked the Thorn across the room like a doll.

"Stop, Tarian," the mage said, grabbing Dayne magically and lifting him off the ground. "This is truly pointless."

"It is, Senek." A well-groomed man with a manicured beard strolled in, looking oddly out of place compared to every other denizen in this place. "Whatever are you doing?"

"I have time for another experiment," the mage said. He must be Senek.

"You said the ripe time was right before sunrise."

"Thus a few hours," Senek insisted. "And look at all these new toys to play with."

"Fascinating day this has been," the well-groomed one said. "Who are they?"

"He asked for an audience with you," Senek said, indicating Rynax. "I'm not sure about the Tarian and the baby mage, but they seem to be friends."

"They're with me," Rynax said.

"Fascinating," the groomed one said. "Well, by all means, bring them to my sanctum. It seems to be a day of surprises."

"But . . ." Senek said, gesturing to the machine. "My experiment."

"I would prefer you not waste the fuel, Senek," the groomed one said. "Besides, further testing should not be necessary. We will soon have all our missing pieces in place."

"Missing pieces for what?" Dayne asked, still suspended in the air. "Who are you?"

The man came over to Dayne and gently touched his face. "Rejoice, friend. You are most blessed. The Nine wait below, and you will have the privilege of audience with me, their High Dragon."

Chapter 16

THERE WAS NO SIGN OF Rynax. Hemmit couldn't
wait, not with the little boy, who was clearly hungry
and exhausted. Despite his own pain, he carried the boy
down the tunnels. Fortunately, the chalk marks were
there and easy to find. After pushing himself, forcing
himself to take each step, he found an exit to the
open air.

Both he and the boy laughed and whooped once they
realized they were out, even though it was clearly late. It
took him a bit to get his bearings—he was somewhere in
North Seleth. After a bit of searching, he went to the
one place he really knew in the neighborhood: Kimber's
Pub. By the time he got there, the boy, spent, had fallen
asleep in his arms.

It was a quiet night, only a smattering of patrons. Or
perhaps it was just that late.

"You can't bring that boy in here," the matron of the
place said as he came in.

"Ma'am," Hemmit said. "You probably don't recognize me, but I was here the night of the riots? The election?"

She shook her head. "I'm afraid not."

Hemmit frowned. "I was meeting with the Rynax brothers. And that boy was hit in the head?"

"Of course I remember that," she said. "Still, you—"

"Apparently one of the Rynaxes went searching for missing children in the tunnels underground today."

She shook her head and sighed. "Oh, Asti."

"This boy was one of the ones taken. But there are more. And I think Rynax is still down there. As are other friends."

"You were down there?" she asked. "I mean, sir, you look a frightful mess."

"I feel it."

"Let's take the boy to a cot in the back, and then work on finding his parents or such in the morning. You should do the same."

It was awfully tempting. He wanted to lie down and not move. His whole body was hurting.

But Dayne was still down there. Jerinne and Maresh and Lin. He couldn't just walk away. He couldn't rest now.

"I wish I could," he said. "Take care of the boy, and if you see the other Rynax, let him know—"

"I will," she said. She went to the bar and came back with cup of water. Hemmit took it gratefully. He never was so happy to drink water.

"Are you going to be all right?" she asked.

"Not yet," he said. "But I have to help everyone else, or I couldn't live with myself."

Finishing the water, he handed her the cup back, and went into the night.

Sleep was not going to come easy. Satrine had embraced that fact. She had come home, had dinner with the girls, checked on Loren, and chatted for some time with Rian. Rian was insisting she could handle her last year at prepatory and hours at the Majestic. Satrine wasn't thrilled with the idea of that, but had to admit, Rian's income had made things so much easier. Especially since Rian had marks that could easily get her into the Royal College of Maradaine. That would cost a lot, but Satrine really liked the idea of her continuing her education just a few blocks from the apartment.

Rian went to sleep, and Satrine lay out on her couch, not wanting to bother going to her own bed. In her state, she'd just disturb Loren.

She couldn't shake the idea that something was very wrong. The night was trouble.

The knock on her door, after she had dozed off well after midnight, solidified that feeling.

She went to the door, crossbow in hand, in case the trouble was coming for her.

Instead it was a dark-skinned girl, likely Napolic or Turjin descent, who looked frightened out of her mind.

"Can I help you?" Satrine asked.

"Are you Inspector Rainey?"

"Who's asking?"

"My name is Kaiana Nell . . . I'm a groundskeeper at the University of Maradaine, and . . . Inspector Welling is in trouble."

Satrine grabbed her by the wrist and pulled her inside. "Start at the beginning," she said while getting her boots and gear.

"Well, he came to campus because he was going to search the chapterhouse of the Blue Hand Circle, and he wanted . . . he wanted the Thorn to go with him."

Satrine picked up on that. "You know the Thorn."

"I do. And he had already gone off earlier to chase a lead about children being taken by a giant."

"Welling was doing the same. The Blue Hand Circle?" She got her boots on.

"The chapterhouse led us to underground tunnels, where there was a strange cult and monstrous creatures, and they spotted us and Welling was captured."

"Captured?" Satrine said. "But you got away?"

"Only because there was a girl also down there—she told me to find you. Jerinne Fendall?"

"Wait, wait," Satrine said. "Did she go down with you?"

"No, she was already there. She rescued me, told me where to find you."

"Saints preserve us," Satrine muttered. She knew there was trouble in the air tonight.

"And I went looking for the Thorn first, but he never came back. If they're both down there, both in trouble—"

"I hear you," Satrine said. She wasn't even entirely sure where to start. Call in the Constabulary, a full Riot Call to go into the tunnels? She wondered if that was the right idea. She knew there were deep veins of corruption throughout the Constabulary. Calling a show of color might warn these people. She had to be careful.

She stopped for a moment. "You said you're a groundskeeper?"

"Yes," Kaiana said. "Why?"

"As in a gardener?"

"Sometimes." Kaiana looked very confused. "How is that—"

"Listen to the gardener, seek answers when she calls," remembering the mangled passage that Alana had read to her earlier. A notion crossed her mind—a wild, impossible notion—and she went over to her coat, taking Sister Myriem's copy of the *Testaments of the Saints* out of the pocket.

"What are you doing?" Kaiana asked.

"Bit of a mad hunch," Satrine said. She thumbed through the book to reach the Testament of Saint Jessalyn.

Myriem had crossed out words and written in others and drawn symbols and it didn't make a lick of sense, but Satrine was compelled to turn the page. It was the same madness, but as soon as she saw the words and symbols, they bore into her eyes, each one of them slammed across her brain sideways. Memories overwhelmed her.

She was Trini Carthas again, in a dirty tenement on Jent and Tannen. Protecting Lannie Coar. Standing in front of five angry, overeager boys, holding a piece of broken glass to fend them off.

She was Quia Alia Rhythn, finishing her education at an exclusive school in Maradaine, taking a history lesson on Druth kings.

She was Agent Satrine Carthas, fighting for her life against Pra Yikenj in an Imach boilhouse.

She was all three at the same time, and yet still Inspector Satrine Rainey.

Lannie Coar wasn't Lannie—she was Sister Myriem. Pra Yikenj was Sister Myriem. The history teacher was Sister Myriem.

All as Satrine remembered it.

As each of them, she spoke, words that echoed in Satrine's head.

I'm sorry
   —sorry—
   I had to reach you
   —reach you—
Too much
   —your mind was already prepared—
   Receptive
The only way—
   I can't say the words when I'm awake
Too much
   —can only tell you here—
   In your yesterdays
   —From my tomorrows—
Too much
—I only know in my dreams—
   You can't go alone

—You can't trust anyone—
The Brotherhood is everywhere
   —Trust is a weapon—
   Today is the moment.
Seek the champions you need.
   —Listen to the gardener—
Be ready to stop them
   Today we need you.
   —seek answers when she calls—
Remember everything
   Eyes and ears open
   —The city will fall without you—
Find the trapmaster
   Find the trapmaster
   —Find the trapmaster—
He'll die without you.
   They'll die without you.
   —They'll die without him—
   This is the day
   —This is the moment—
It has to be you
   —Find him!—

Pra Yikenj's fist smashed into Satrine's face, and she dropped hard. She almost crashed to the floor, were it not for Kaiana Nell catching her.

Kaiana. Her own apartment. Late at night. Here, today. Herself again, half on the floor, half in Kaiana's arms.

"Are you all right?"

"Decidedly not," Satrine said, getting to her feet. She belted her crossbow and handstick, as well as extra bolts. She left a note for the girls, apologizing for not being there in the morning. She knew—*she knew*—that this was going to take her all night. "You coming with me?"

"Yes, ma'am," Kaiana said. "Back to the Blue Hand?"

"No," Satrine said as she went out the door. "To North Seleth."

Dayne's feet didn't touch the floor until he was brought into a warm chamber lit by hundreds of candles. Senek pulled him through the air, and the beasts took his shield and sword. They dragged in Rynax and relieved him of several knives, and Gurond carried in the Thorn. He was out cold and placed in a chair, his weapons and rope taken from him. Gurond stared at the Thorn's face and growled for a bit, until the well-manicured man—this High Dragon—waved him away.

"I know, my friend, I know," the High Dragon said. "In due time. Bring in the other one."

"Other one?" Dayne asked. They had Lin and Maresh; where was Jerinne? Had they captured her as well?

The High Dragon ignored him and went to a chest and took out a pair of shackles. "Cannot take too many chances with this one, I think." He bound the Thorn with them, and then gently slapped his face until he came to.

"What, where?" the Thorn asked.

"There he is. Sorry about your head, but Gurond is . . . well, he is Gurond."

Rynax raised an eyebrow. "And you're Crenaxin. The High Dragon."

"You asked to see me," Crenaxin said. "And that was enough to earn your lives—briefly—while I sate my curiosity about you interlopers. Seven in all, I think."

"Seven?" Dayne asked.

"Yes, you three, the two that I'll let Senek play with, the girl who got away, and this one."

Two men in dark robes dragged in Minox Welling, shackled and trying to pull himself out of their grasp.

"Minox!" Dayne exclaimed.

"So you are together," Crenaxin said, rubbing his hands together. "How glorious."

"Heldrin," Minox said when he saw Dayne. His captors brought him over and placed him in a chair with the three of them. "And Mister Calbert as well."

"We'll find your dark girl as well, soon enough," Crenaxin said.

That got the Thorn's attention. "Dark girl?" He looked over to Minox, who just gave him a small nod.

"She's surely well out of here, and sensible enough to bring help."

"Help?" Crenaxin said with a mocking tone. "Members of the Constabulary? Perhaps a contingent of Tarian elite? The army? Or you?" He pointed at the Thorn. "Yes, you're the one who started that trouble for the Blue Hand a few months back."

"I'll show you trouble," the Thorn said, trying to stand. He then screamed and fell back down.

"Yes, you'll find that what you and your friend there are wearing are far more insidious than the mage shackles the Constabulary uses. I imagine that was rather painful."

"The machine is more than magic," Rynax said. "But it's not complete."

"Very good, sir. Observant one, you are."

"Machine?" Welling asked.

Rynax nodded. "There's a machine in the other room, combines magic and science, I figure. To make people into those monsters they've got walking around here."

"Monsters?" Crenaxin said. "You say that of our faithful brethren, who have given so much of themselves in the hope of being worthy vessels for the Nine?"

"What are the Nine?" Dayne asked.

Crenaxin smiled. "They are the truest faith. Truer and older than you can even know. Beings of pure power and knowledge, fueled by and fueling all the churning energies in the world."

"Magic," Welling said.

"Beyond magic. Beyond science. Beyond faith and

will and the focus of . . . they are the force of every-thing."

"And you're their High Dragon?"

"The vessel of their blessing. Filled with their power."

"Full of it is right," the Thorn said weakly.

"He's not bluffing," Minox said. "I saw him bring a dead man to life."

"He what?" Dayne asked.

"That's impossible," the Thorn said.

"Impossible is nothing but your limited mind, young man," Crenaxin said, placing his hand on the Thorn's head. "And soon that dead man will complete his mission, come back with the final statue . . ."

"Tell me about the statues," Rynax said.

"Fascinating, aren't they?" Crenaxin said.

"What are they called? *Tazendifol?*"

That took Crenaxin by surprise. "Very good, sir. But do you know what that means?"

"They're sacred idols of a forbidden religion. This 'Brotherhood of the Nine' business, clearly."

"Not entirely correct. Though they are forbidden where they came from, Poasia. That's where the truth of the Nine came from. It was a faith they knew . . . millennia ago. But the faithful were hounded and killed, and only a handful kept it alive, hidden beneath their civilization. And then our soldiers took Khol Taia. The *tazendifol*—and the faith—came here."

Dayne couldn't believe his ears. "Why would you subscribe to a Poasian religion? One that even they rooted out?"

"Because it is a source of pure power, Tarian," Crenaxin said. He went over to the trunk and pulled out a book, finding his page. "'And now today, the day wakes in the sword, with a sliver of white and three children ahead. Now is the day, and we will tap into power—real, true power—that will make Maradaine tremble before us.'"

"And why are you telling us?" Thorn said.

"Because I want you to know," Crenaxin said. He went over to the Thorn and grabbed his head. "For you are going to **Serve the Brotherhood**."

His words came with a weight, and the Thorn screamed. He shook his head wildly for a moment. "What the blazes—" he snarled.

"Mages are always a problem," Crenaxin said with disappointment. He went over to Minox. "But I hope you will **Serve the Brotherhood**."

Minox grit his teeth and then spit in Crenaxin's face.

"No matter," Crenaxin said. "You're going to be useful, regardless. But you—" He went over to Rynax. "You will be very useful, I think. And you will **Serve the Brotherhood**."

Rynax screamed, a scream of pure animal rage and pain. Then he became oddly calm, looking up at Crenaxin. "Blessed be the Nine."

"Blessed be the Nine, my brother," Crenaxin said. He came over to Dayne. "And as for you, Tarian."

"I will never—" Dayne started.

"But you will," Crenaxin said. "You will **Serve the Brotherhood**."

The words hit with a power that filled Dayne's bones. He remembered the words, the power, of Ret Issendel, but that had been a gentle stream in comparison. This was an ocean, washing over Dayne, filling his heart, breaking his soul, demanding his—

Clarity.

He looked up to Crenaxin. It was so clear.

"Blessed be the Nine," he said.

"Blessed be, my brother," Crenaxin said. "Now let us be about things. Take the constable here. He will be useful."

"Of course," Dayne said. He grabbed Minox and threw him over his shoulder.

"Heldrin. Heldrin! What are you doing? Stop! Fight

it, man, fight it!" Minox tried vainly to fight back, but in his bound state, he wasn't very effective.

"Now let's bring him to Mister Senek, my brother," Crenaxin said. He picked up a large knife and handed it to Rynax. "As for you, I would love it if you would carve out all his bones." He looked over to the Thorn. "His meddling caused so much pain, and I would love to have that repaid."

Rynax nodded. His face made it clear he understood. He examined the knife with meticulous care as he approached the Thorn. The Nine were glory, and he served them. Dayne served them, served the Brotherhood, whatever the High Dragon would need.

"Asti, no," the Thorn said. "Asti, wake the blazes up. Asti!"

"Come, my Tarian brother," High Dragon Crenaxin said. "The power and the blessings of the Nine await us."

He left the sanctum, and Dayne followed happily, the futile screams and protestations of the Thorn fading in the distance.

Chapter 17

THE OPERA HOUSE HAD BEEN a marvel of eleventh-century architecture, one of the many grand buildings in North Maradaine of white stone with tall columns and windows of colored glass that had been built during the Renewal after the Reunification. The Renewal had brought a resurgence of art in all forms, and while the plays of Darren Whit and his contemporaries had remained popular since then, opera had fallen out of favor in Maradaine for the past sixty years or so. The opera house had been shuttered, abandoned, and boarded up for decades.

Amaya shouldn't have come alone. She knew she shouldn't have, but with Dayne and Jerinne both out, she wasn't sure who else to trust.

Amaya had been vaguely aware of the news surrounding Duchess Erisia Leighton of Fencal buying the building, and starting the work to reopen it fully restored in all its original glory. She had the goal of reestablishing opera as the pinnacle of art and culture in the city. She would mount the classics, she would commission new works.

That had been four or five years ago, and the outside of the opera house had shown many signs of the restoration moving along: painting, scaffolding, laborers going in and out for months on end. But then the news slowed, and when asked about the status of the opera house and its expected opening, Duchess Leighton would just answer there had been "unexpected delays."

The rumors were that she had run out of money.

But now that Amaya was here outside the dark building, she wondered if the real reasons were far more nefarious. The place was spectacular, a testament to the hard work and dedication that had been put into the restoration. Posters had been pasted to the walls touting the productions of *Demea* and *Canus and Inama* and *The Kingship Cycle*. Amaya had no idea what those last two were, but the posters were dynamic and dramatic.

She circled around the building twice, trying to decide just what she was looking for. She had her suspicions, fueled entirely by Kemmer's notes. He thought the Grand Ten were meeting here, that was why the opera house had stayed closed for so long. She wanted to get inside, but to what end? It wasn't as if they would be meeting right now. What was she here for? Proof?

Proof of what? And reportable to whom?

This might have been a waste of time. The certainty that brought her here at this hour bled away.

Just as she thought that, she noticed a back door that was slightly ajar. She was nearly certain it hadn't been that way when she first circled around the building. Was someone else here?

Maybe this was a chance for answers.

She slipped into the open door, moving as quietly as she could while carrying a shield. She drew her sword, knowing that she couldn't rely on stealth at all right now, so she might as well be ready for a fight.

There were voices in the distance. Someone else was here. At least a few people. Down the steps. She followed cautiously.

"Why aren't we just killing him?"

"Those aren't the orders."

"That's absurd, you know."

"I do know, but still, those are the orders."

Amaya crept to the bottom of the stairs, to a hallway that stretched the length beneath the stage. Dressing rooms, storage, props and sets, by the look of things. Voices were coming out of one of the dressing rooms. Two men came out, and Amaya slipped into a costume room before they saw her.

"Just leave him there?"

"He's not going anywhere, and it's what the boss wants."

"Fine by me. Let's go get some crisp and crankers, I know a place."

Their voices receded down the hallway, and Amaya went over to the door they had come from. Unlocked. She went in, ready for anything.

A man, bloody, bandaged, and blindfolded, tied up in a chair.

She went over and knelt by him. "Sir, are you all right?"

"Who . . . who's there?" he muttered.

"Let's get you out of here," she said, working at the knots binding him. "My name is Amaya, who are you?"

"Kemmer," he mumbled. "Amaya who?"

Blazes, she had found him.

"Did the Grand Ten attack you?" she asked. "Is that why you're here?"

"What—" He tried to pull his hand out of the binds, but couldn't. "How did you know—"

"I've been looking for them. Looking for you. Trying to—"

Before she got any further, the door slammed shut,

and then she heard the sound of it being barred. Trapping her in this small room with Kemmer.

"The blazes?" she said.

"Thank you, Miss Tyrell," she heard someone on the other side of the door say. "You've made things so much easier for us."

Verci woke to the bells ringing.

Someone had tripped the spiderwires down in the shop.

Intruders.

"Raych," he whispered, touching his wife on the shoulder. "Wake up."

"What is it?" she asked blearily.

"Someone's in the shop." He got to his feet, quickly pulling on pants and boots. He pulled a box out from under the bed, taking a crossbow out. He quickly checked it, cranking and loading it before putting it on the bed.

"What?" Raych asked, getting out of the bed. "What do you think—"

"I'm going to go out there to check," he said. "You take that."

"What am I going to do with that?" she asked.

"Hopefully nothing. But I want you to have it anyway."

She pulled on her nightcoat and picked up the crossbow. He grabbed a shirt and his bandolier of darts. The gauntlet was down in the workshop. Damn and blazes. Drawing two darts, he went out to the kitchen. More bells were ringing. He heard a twang and a snap from downstairs, and a man screamed. One of the security traps.

Maybe that was it.

Feet up the stairs. A lot of feet. At least ten pairs.

"That door is double-latched, right?" Raych asked.

"It's still just wood on brass hinges," Verci said.

A crunch of wood. Door kicked open. Things being knocked over. A search.

Asti's apartment.

Another crack. The door to the spare apartment.

Essin was in there.

"Hey, what—" Essin shouted. "You . . . you . . . how?"

Then a scream.

Raych grabbed Verci's shoulder so tight, he thought her fingers would dig into his bones.

"Rynax has it!" Essin screamed. "He's got it!"

Then another scream. Then silence.

"My love," he whispered, taking the crossbow from her. "Go back into the bedroom, push the bed in front of the door."

"But—"

Pounding started on the door. The wood cracked, but the double-latch held.

"Gather Corsi and go out the window. Just like I showed you."

"I can't—"

Another smash on the door. Again and again. It wouldn't hold much longer.

"I'm going to buy you time," he said. "Just go."

She went into the bedroom, closing the door behind her.

One of the hinges broke free.

Verci brought up the crossbow. He wished he had prepared better. More traps, more defenses. There hadn't been the time. He should have made that a priority. He had been hopeful that it wasn't going to be necessary, that here they would be safe.

The door smashed again, the top half of it coming free, revealing the hallway. Several men out there, pounding and smashing on the door. He took the shot, hitting one of them. That man dropped, but the others were not deterred in the slightest. Verci quickly reloaded, but as soon as he was ready, the door came completely open.

He fired again, putting down another one of the bastards before they poured into his home.

They came in, most of them toughs, just the sort of bruiser any gang or boss would use to break legs and smash skulls. Except the eyes. They were dead in the eyes.

And then one more stepped through, making Verci's blood curdle.

Ren Poller. Ren Poller, his head smashed in, blood caked to the side of his face. He raised a finger and hoarsely rasped, "Rynax!"

"The blazes you want?" Verci yelled, palming his darts.

"Where is it?" Poller asked. "The Brotherhood wants it."

The statue. Verci would be blazed if they would get that. Every instinct he had screamed that their getting hold of it would be the worst thing ever.

But his eyes had gone to it in the corner of the room, and the bruisers all noticed. Two of them dashed for it.

Verci flashed two darts, as he went for the statue himself. He put one of them down, only wounded the other. He grabbed that one as more of them came for him, pushing the bruiser onto his companions.

"Kill him," Poller hissed.

Verci scooped up the statue with one arm, drawing and throwing two more darts with his free hand. Two more of the bastards wounded, at least.

"Nowhere to go," one of them said.

"Never," Verci said.

This he had been prepared for, reaching up to the knob above the window. With a hard yank, the window opened and Verci jumped back. He dropped down to the street, holding on to the knob and the rope attached to it that uncoiled from its wheeled housing in the apartment. It jarred his shoulder when the wheel locked, but that was better than cracking onto the pavement.

Perfect length, he was just a foot above the ground. He let go of the knob, and the spring-powered wheel retracted the rope as he landed.

He had a powerful urge to wave back at the bruisers up in the apartment before running, but as he looked up, they were all jumping out the window. As if none of them gave one damned blazes about breaking their legs.

At least two of them did break their legs on the landing, as Verci heard horrible snaps. But not one of them stopped. They came at him, stumbling and lurching, but relentless.

He turned to run, but two more of them were there behind him. He jumped back, avoiding a knife coming for his belly, but lost his grip on the statue. It tumbled out of his hands, and one of the bruisers caught it. Those two ran off with it as fast as they could.

Verci was about to give chase when several hands grabbed hold of him. He turned around, swinging punches and driving darts into each of these fools. Two of them down, more coming. Another knife came for him, but Verci twisted out of the way. Verci kicked at that one in his bad leg, but only caused the man to fall on top of him, forcing Verci to the ground. Still he was able to drive that knife into the man's neck.

Two more came on him, and Verci tried to hold them both off with each hand while they choked him.

Ren Poller came down to the ground and ghoulishly stumbled toward him, a nightmare given form. Verci struggled to hold off the other two while Ren drew out his knife.

A crossbow bolt exploded through his crushed head, and he dropped to the ground. One of the two on Verci looked up, and got another bolt in his eye for his trouble. That gave Verci the chance to grab a dart and slam it into the neck of the one on top of him. The man died, but his dead weight fell hard on Verci's chest.

Verci struggled for breath as he tried to push the

dead man off of him. Someone walked over and pushed the man off, and then offered a hand to pull Verci to his feet.

"Looked like you could use a constable," Inspector Rainey said. "Good thing I was around."

"Asti, you've got to fight it, whatever it is, you can't let it beat you."

Bound in the mage shackles, all Veranix could do was scramble back to the wall as Rynax approached, wicked blade in hand, with a grin to match, as Dayne left the room with Crenaxin.

Whatever Crenaxin had done, it had burned at his brain, but couldn't find a way in. The same couldn't be said for Asti and Dayne.

Asti pounced on him, knife high. He leaned in and whispered.

"Scream, kid, they didn't shut the door." Veranix looked up at Asti, and he winked at him.

Saints almighty, the bastard winked.

"You're all right?"

"Scream!" Asti shouted.

Veranix obliged, giving his best bloodcurdling, knife-in-his-belly scream, better than any of the Cantarell Square Players.

"Nice," Asti whispered. "Let's get this damn thing off you." He started to work the knife into the lock of the mage shackles.

"How?" Veranix asked.

"Keep screaming."

Veranix did as instructed while Asti worked.

"I don't know. He did that business, and part of my head, it was all in. Ready to follow him and praise the Brotherhood. But that part . . . it was already broken off. Everything in my head is broken."

Veranix nodded. "Whatever the blazes he did, it

couldn't make purchase on my mage brain, or your broken one."

"But that Tarian friend of yours is another story."

"Unless he's faking, like you were."

"Doubt it," Asti said. He twisted a catch in the shackles, and they popped open. Veranix was more than happy to get them off. He felt completely drained. He needed to eat, rest, anything. But it didn't look like there would be much chance for either. Asti hung the shackles on his belt and checked the rest of the room. "Look, we know these people have kidnapped children, using them in that machine. Delmin said it was swirling with magic."

"Where is he?" Veranix asked.

"Hopefully he got out. Though he was . . ." Asti trailed off as he went to peek out the door.

"Was what?"

"Extremely tiny?" He held his fingers an inch apart. That was surprising. "How?"

"I think he was trying to fly and something went wrong. Anyway, with any luck, he's going to bring Verci and whatever help Verci can muster. I say we find our gear, get ourselves in position, and wait for that."

"We may not have much time," Veranix said. He was running over all the things Crenaxin had said. "They were talking about only a few hours. The day wakes in the sword, all that."

"What was that nonsense about?" Asti asked.

"Astronomy, I think. Taking a course on it right now. Today the white moon—which is a crescent—and three of the planets are visible just before sunrise. I was supposed to be at class, actually, to observe that. And the constellation those, and the sun, are all in is—"

"Lexin, the Sword," Asti said. "Is that real magic stuff, or just bunk?"

Veranix shrugged. "I can tell you that the position of the moons definitely can have an effect on the power of magic. I wouldn't discount it."

"So waiting for a rescue plan from Verci is not going to work." He swore under his breath. "All right, those kids are part of their plan, so let's make it ours. We find our gear, get those kids, and get them the blazes out of here?"

"And Welling and Dayne? And those two prisoners in the machine?"

"I don't know if we can do anything for them."

Veranix didn't like that answer at all, but he understood it. "First step is our gear?" He wasn't very good at sensing magic, but his connection to the rope and the cloak was far more attuned than most other forms of *numinic* activity. "I think I can get us to it."

"First step is blending in," Asti said. "Two zealots in robes down the hallway. Give me a really good scream."

Veranix let out a gut-wrenching scream of horror and terror.

Asti winked and poked his head out of the door. "Brothers, could you assist me? My task would be easier with you holding him down."

Asti gave Veranix the nod, and Veranix moved to the side of the doorway, building up a charge of *numina* in his body. The two zealots came into the room.

"So where—" was all one got out before Asti pounced on him, hand over his mouth. In a flash, he sliced open his throat with that wicked knife.

Veranix channeled the magic into speed, and dashed at the other zealot, landing three punches before the man had even turned around. The zealot managed to draw his knife, but at Veranix's speed, he was able to grab his wrist and disarm him.

Then Asti was there, jamming his knife into the man's neck.

"Saints, Thorn, kill them, don't dance with them."

"Sorry," Veranix said. "I thought I was doing fine."

"If by fine, you mean taking too long, sure." He stripped the bodies of their robes and threw one to Veranix.

"This is the bloodier one, isn't it?" Veranix asked.

"Probably," Asti said, putting on the other one. "Take his knife in case we have another fight before we get to our stuff."

"I'm not much of a knife fighter," Veranix said, taking the weapon.

"It's the most basic weapon there is," Asti said, glancing out the door again. "I mean, you've got a bow, and the staff, and that rope . . . honestly, it's like you're trying too hard."

Before Veranix could respond, Asti went out in the hallway. Veranix followed after him, swearing to himself that he would stop falling into these sorts of partnerships.

"That rope is why we're going to find our stuff," Veranix said as he caught up. "It's that way."

He followed the sense of the rope out of the hallway to a huge, open, underground encampment. Obviously where the zealots and beasts lived. It was mostly tents and ramshackle buildings, but at the center was a large twisted tower of thorny black.

"Tell me it's not there."

"Don't think so," Veranix said. "That group of large huts, I think."

"Good," Asti said as they crossed over to it. "Because the broken part of my brain, it . . . it wants to go over there."

"That's not disturbing at all," Veranix said. "Tell me you have a handle on that."

"Chained up hard," Asti said. "I can hear it, but it doesn't get the reins at all."

Veranix found that reassuring, oddly enough. He pointed out the hut he was feeling the rope in. "This one right here."

Asti had his knife out, and Veranix held his own, mimicking Asti's grip. If he had to learn how to knife fight, he might as well follow a master.

They opened the doors and went straight in, Asti taking the lead. He tore through three of them before Veranix was even through the doorway, but when he leaped at his next target, he was met with a heavy shield in his face.

Dayne stood there, armed with his sword and shield. Asti went red-faced, attempting several fatal blows on Dayne, but Dayne held him at bay with his shield. Asti couldn't get around it. Dayne smashed Asti again with the shield, knocking him to the ground.

Veranix saw that all of his gear was on the other side of the room, with Dayne between him and it. He had to get through to it.

Dayne raised up his sword, bringing down a blow that would have cleaved Asti in two. Veranix threw his knife, which only clanged on the shield, but it proved distraction enough to slow Dayne's attack, enough so Asti could scramble away.

"Traitors!" Dayne snarled. "The Brotherhood shall have blood and the glory will be yours."

Veranix scanned the room for anything he could use. Supply storage, mostly crates. But there was a broomstick leaning against one wall.

"Glory?" Veranix asked. "Bet you can't even touch me."

Dayne charged at him as Veranix dove for the broomstick. He wasn't sure what his full plan was here, beyond hopefully getting past Dayne and getting to his gear. He was already so spent, if he didn't get a hold of the cloak or the rope, and their *numina*-drawing abilities, he'd pass out in a minute.

He grabbed the broomstick and leaped up on a crate, planning to jump and flip over the big guy, scoring a knock across the skull along the way. Maybe that would shake Dayne back to his senses. If that was at all possible.

Instead, Veranix found himself flipping right into the

shield. Dayne held it up high, and slammed it into Veranix, knocking him to the ground.

Every saint and sinner, that hurt. When he had fought Dayne before, the Tarian had been holding back, fighting defensively. Now he was hitting full strength.

Now he was going for the kill.

"Dayne, come on," Veranix said, scrambling out of the way of the sword. "What happened to not killing? What happened to finding another way?"

"The way is the Brotherhood," Dayne said. He brought down his sword so hard it cut through the stone floor where Veranix had been standing.

Asti jumped on top of Dayne, screaming wildly, blood gushing from his nose. He was ready to drive his knife into Dayne's chest, but Dayne dropped his sword and grabbed Asti's arm. In a fluid motion, he pulled the small man off of him and slammed him into the ground.

Asti groaned and didn't get up.

Dayne picked up his sword and prepared to run Asti through.

Veranix dove in, charging himself with as much *numina* as he could pull, pouring it into his arm and the stick. Swinging like he was going for a Triple Jack, he connected the broomstick with Dayne's chin.

The blow echoed through the hut, and knocked Dayne away from Asti. But only a few steps. He shook it off and rubbed at his chin, looking to Veranix with pure murder in his eyes.

He whipped the shield at Veranix, knocking him off his feet. Dayne brought down the sword on him, and Veranix held up the broomstick, channeling the last bit of magic into it that he could muster, forming a weak shield of *numina* around himself. With heaving, desperate breaths, Veranix forced all the strength he had into holding that up. It was the only thing he had between him and death.

Dayne rained blow after blow onto the stick, until it snapped and the *numina* shattered.

Veranix could barely even breathe, uselessly holding up his hands as the killing blow came down.

It didn't land.

Someone had jumped in, straddling over Veranix with a shield held high, placing herself between him and harm.

PENULTIMATE INTERLUDE

BROTHER MERGOLLIET HAD NO IDEA what was wrong with Reverend Halster, but his behavior had grown more and more erratic over the past few months. At first it was little matters, like the time Halster had insisted on bringing that violent man inside the church, giving him sanctuary and a place to sleep off his madness. Then it was insisting that the Brothers of Saint Bridget seal up sections of the old catacombs. Mergolliet had asked Reverend Halster why it was necessary, and the old man only said, "God commands it so."

That was his answer for so many things.

Mergolliet would not have minded were it not for the fact that Halster had grown so negligent in his daily tasks. Mergolliet had found himself acting as the Reverend of Saint Bridget's Church in all things but title. He had been respectful of the Reverend Halster and his place and position—Halster was a man of advanced years—but he felt he would need to write to the bishop soon.

Especially since Halster had brought in Sister Myriem to join them, which made no sense whatsoever. There were no cloistresses at Saint Bridget's, no order of sisters for her to congregate with.

And in two days, she had been nothing but difficult.

First, she was supposed to arrive at the noon bells the day before yesterday. She did not come until well after sunset. She was assigned her own quarters, since it was plain she should not sleep in the bunks with the brothers, but yet she ended up sleeping in the narthex under the statue of Saint Bridget that night. She ignored everything Brother Mergolliet said to her, going off on her own throughout the day, occasionally praying with Reverend Halster when he was supposed to be leading services or ministering over the brothers.

Now, before even the sun was up, she was in her chambers, screaming and pounding the walls.

Mergolliet told the other brothers to try to go back to sleep, and he went to check on matters. He found Reverend Halster kneeling calmly in front of Sister Myriem's door.

"Sir," Mergolliet said as he approached. "This is madness, you know that?"

"I do," Reverend Halster said. "But should we not tend to the mad, Brother Mergolliet?"

"But why are we—"

"Because God commands it so," Halster said. He sighed, looking at the closed door. "Why do we pray to the saints, Brother?"

"For them to intercede to God on our behalf," Mergolliet said. He didn't understand why Halster would ask such a basic question.

"And why not to God directly?"

"For we lack the worth to question God." Halster gestured for him to continue. If he wanted Mergolliet to recite basic theology, then Mergolliet would comply. "God sees all, is all. They are aware of the grand design in ways that we, mere mortals of weak flesh, could never comprehend."

"So I ask you, can God comprehend us?"

That was a heavier question than Mergolliet was ready for at this hour.

"God is infinite, God everything," Mergolliet said. "They are—"

"Consider that God, in their infinite greatness, cannot understand what being a mortal of weak flesh even means. What our petty limits are."

"Which is why we ask the saints to intercede. They are touched by the divine, they—"

"Touched by the divine, hmmm," Reverend Halster said. "Imagine what a toll that would put on our weak flesh." He tapped his finger on Mergolliet's head. "To have just a sliver of the infinite slice into your very finite mind."

"I hadn't thought about that."

"Consider, Brother, the grand design God might have. All of yesterday, today, and tomorrow in a tapestry. Imagine trying to live all those days at once." He touched the door tenderly. "Madness would be the least of it."

The screaming and pounding stopped, and in a moment, the door opened. The young sister looked out, her face full of suspicion. "Where am I? This is not my cell at Saint Limarre's."

"That is true," Reverend Halster said. "You are no longer posted at Saint Limarre's. Do you remember?"

She scowled. "No. But that's good. Most of them hated me. This is Saint . . . Alexis's?"

"Saint Bridget's," Mergolliet said. "You arrived the day before yesterday."

"Do you know what day it is?" Halster asked.

She scowled again. "No, I . . . the last few weeks have been such a haze. My dreams, they . . . I never know if I'm . . ." She looked around the hallway, confused.

"It's Oscan the twenty-seventh," Halster said. "In the year 1215. Tomorrow is Terrentin."

Mergolliet had no idea why Halster had included the year. Surely the girl was not that addled.

"Oscan the—" she started, and then suddenly she began crying. "I'm not ready for it to be today."

"What?" Mergolliet asked. "What about today?"

She touched Halster's face. "I'm sorry. Why am I sorry? Why am I crying? What is it I'm so—"

Halster took the girl into an embrace. "Shh, I know."

Her sobs quieted as she buried her face in his robe.

Halster looked to Mergolliet. "Wake the brothers and prepare a simple breakfast."

"It's still a bit early."

"Even still. Then be prepared for a service. The people of this neighborhood will need our ministrations today."

"What is today?" Mergolliet asked. "I don't understand."

"I don't either. None of us do." He sighed as he caressed Sister Myriem's head. "But we do as we must, for God commands it so."

"As you say, Reverend," Mergolliet said. "And you?"

"I will pray with Sister Myriem," he said. She pulled away and looked up at him, a gentle smile on her face. Saints above, she truly was just a child, to be so tormented. "While we still have a little time."

Mergolliet nodded and went to wake the brothers. But before he was gone, he heard Myriem say one more thing.

"So very little."

Chapter 18

DAYNE WAS REALLY TRYING TO kill this guy. Jerinne had been scouting the camp, finding her way around, trying to figure out what was going on in this place, find Maresh and Lin. She realized the tunnels extended off in every direction, but the folks down here—both the zealots and the grotesques—were most concerned about a set of tunnels leading west.

She knew she should bide her time until help came, unless something happened that required immediate action. Being unable to find her friends in the camp, and knowing that going down the western tunnels would likely result in getting caught, she decided to lay low.

At one point, she saw the giant. Saints, he was exactly how the kid described him. Thick, shiny skin. So tall he dwarfed Dayne. He walked across the camp, specifically going to various grotesques and touching their heads. When he passed by Jerinne, she heard him say one word to a grotesque.

"Soon."

More and more of the residents were going down the western tunnels. The camp had almost emptied. Something was happening, and she might not be able to wait any longer. She made her way cautiously toward those tunnels, passing one large hut where she heard a fight.

Not just a fight, but a powerful crack that echoed through the camp. It would have brought several people running if the place wasn't already empty.

Jerinne went into the hut, to see Dayne wailing powerful blows on a young man with a broomstick. Another man was in a lump on the ground. Dayne was slamming his sword down over and over; it was amazing the broomstick had held up under that punishment. And Dayne's face.

Rage. Bloodlust. Murder.

She didn't even think Dayne was capable of that.

The broomstick shattered on Dayne's blow, and he raised up his sword once more for the kill.

For the kill.

Something was very wrong.

She dashed in, shield raised to take that blow for the young man. The sword slammed into her shield, a hit so hard it made her bones rattle. But she took it.

"Dayne," she said. "What are you doing?"

"Serving the Brotherhood," Dayne said. He whipped his sword around at her, which she quickly parried. He switched up to a flurry of feints and attacks, driving Jerinne back.

"Serving who?" she asked. "Have you lost your mind?"

"I finally see clearly," he said. His attacks were relentless. Jerinne wasn't able to do anything but draw him away from the two people he had been about to kill. She had no idea who they were, if they were legitimately bad people or not, but she knew that Dayne—whatever had happened to him—would not forgive himself if he had killed them.

"Clearly about what?" she asked, watching Dayne's

feet, watching his wrist, following his technique. In the months of training and sparring together, she had never seen him fight like this. On the offensive, using all his strength. It put him off his usual rhythms.

Whatever was going on in his head, his body didn't know how to fight like this.

"The divine truth of the Nine," Dayne said. "They are the way, and the Brotherhood shall be empowered as they rise."

"That's some blazing bunk," Jerinne said. "You were trying to kill? For the Brotherhood?"

"I serve as I am needed," he said. He overextended his attack. Jerinne parried and then locked her sword into his hilt, followed by a slam of her shield into his wrist. He let go of the blade, and she was able to send it flying across the room, disarming him of that.

She was rewarded by his shield smashing into the side of her head, sending her reeling.

"No," she said, forcing the words through her haze. "That's not how you serve, Dayne."

He smashed his shield on her again, but she was able to get her own up to take the blow. Even still, the sheer power he had, stronger than she had suspected.

"I serve the Brotherhood!" he shouted as he pummeled again and again with the shield. She kept hers up, blocking every blow, even if each one forced her back to the wall.

"You don't serve death," she said. "You—"

Another blow. She still had her sword. In his fury, he wasn't even defending himself. She could stop him. She could end it.

But that wasn't who she was. She was a Tarian.

And no matter what had been done to him, so was Dayne.

He would have to remember.

She would make him remember.

He hit her shield with his once more, and when she

blocked it, his massive fist came at her chest. She had never been hit as hard in her life. It was like a team of horses. The blow knocked her off her feet, landing near the two men, who were crawling weakly toward each other.

"Now you all die," Dayne said.

Jerinne hopped back on her feet. Five-mile runs with Amaya, morning training with Vien, sparring every day, all that had shown her what she could endure. She would put that to the test, no matter what.

Dayne hurled his shield at her, which she deflected with her own. Then he charged at her, fists raised, shouting a primal scream.

She shouted right back at him.

"With shield on arm and sword in hand!"

Punches rained on her shield.

"I will not yield but hold and stand!"

Blow after blow, relentless.

"As I draw breath, I'll allow no harm!"

The punches slowed.

"And hold—" Dayne muttered.

She dropped down and swept his leg, knocking him off balance. He landed on his back, and Jerinne sprang on top of him. She planted one foot on his arm, pressed her whole body with her shield on his chest, pinning him down.

"And hold?" she asked.

"And hold . . ." It was as if the words were hurting him to say, but he struggled to get them out.

"Say it!" she shouted.

In almost a terrified whisper, he said, "And hold back death, with shield on arm."

He started saying the entire oath, repeating it again and again, faster and faster, as tears formed at his eyes. His whole body relaxed as the fight left it. Jerinne cautiously took herself off of him, while he quietly repeated the oath.

"Is . . . is he all right?"

Jerinne whipped her attention behind her, sword up. The two men both quickly raised their hands up, even though they were nearly holding each other upright. The younger one looked like he could barely stand.

"Who are you?" she asked.

"The Thorn and Asti Rynax," Dayne whispered.

"I take it you're a friend of his," the older man said.

"Dayne," Jerinne asked. "Are you . . . you?"

"I don't understand . . . how I . . . ." Dayne started to cry again.

"I definitely think he's all right," the young one said.

Jerinne got up completely. "Do you know what happened?"

"The High Dragon of the Brotherhood," the older one said. "He's got this way of, I don't know, reaching into your head and twisting your soul."

"It didn't take on us," the younger said. "Apparently it doesn't work on mages."

"Or people whose soul is already twisted enough."

"I'm such a fool," Dayne said. "It all . . . it all seemed so clear."

"Wait," Jerinne said. Dayne's introductions suddenly made sense. "The Thorn? Did Kaiana send you here?"

"Kai?" the young one—clearly the Thorn—asked. "You know her?"

"Well, I helped her get away, and she went to get help. I thought she was going to get you."

"No, I was already here with him," the Thorn said, pointing to Asti. "We got separated, I met Dayne, who I thought was the giant, then we tried to stop that mage Senek with his machine, got taken to the High Dragon, and then he turned Dayne into . . . well, you saw."

She looked to Dayne, who nodded, even though he couldn't look her in the eye.

"And Inspector Welling, did you see him? What about Maresh and Lin? Where's Hemmit?"

"Welling!" Dayne said. He got to his feet. "They're going to use him in the machine."

"Make him into one of those creatures?" Asti asked.

"No," Dayne said. "They're going to use him to power the machine."

It took a good half hour of whistleblowing before Satrine got a couple of night patrol constables to show up with a bodywagon and take the corpses away. Apparently, North Seleth was hardly patrolled at all, with only an understaffed Loyalty Waystation in the area. The patrol regulars were oddly unperturbed by several dead men in the middle of the street, and several more in the upstairs apartments of the gadget shop. All it took was her assurance that it was a GIU matter and she would come to the Keller Cove stationhouse later to sort the matter.

By the time that was done, she went into the gadget shop, to the back room, where Verci Rynax—shirtless with several bandages on his chest—was going through a satchel of weapons and devices. His wife was helping him sort things with a quiet calm while Kaiana Nell held their baby.

"Well, that's settled," she said as she came in. "In as much as nearly a dozen dead men in your shop can be."

"I appreciate it," Verci said. "Now how about you explain why you showed up at my shop in the middle of the night, exactly when I needed help."

"A message from God?" Satrine said, even though she wasn't sure what it was.

"I'm going to ask for a bit more than that," Verci said. "Given everything I've seen today."

"Same," Kaiana said. "I was with her and I don't understand it."

"You remember how I found you last time?"

"You said something about a cloistress giving you a pastry."

"Yeah," Satrine said. "I know it makes no sense, but right when I needed your skills, I also happened to look at the bakery bag, and I followed the hunch and found you. The same cloistress who gave it to me, today she left me a mangled copy of the *Testaments*."

"Mangled?"

"Written over, blotted out. Madness to look at it. But one of the first things it had was a rewritten passage about 'listen to the gardener when she comes.' And this one shows up at my door tonight."

"The Thorn's friend," Verci said. "Where's Mila?"

"Probably asleep in her bed like a sensible person," Kaiana said. "I thought about getting her, but I didn't know how to do that without creating a scene in her dorm."

"I'm happier that you didn't. She doesn't need to be in this mess," Verci said. He looked back to Satrine. "So that led you to me, because you saw me at that cult thing this afternoon?"

Satrine wasn't sure how much to explain. "It's more complicated than that, but roughly, the sister left a message only I would be able to understand in the book."

He nodded, then his eyes went wide. "Wait, this sister. She wouldn't happen to be a young blond girl, a bit wild in the eyes and spouting nonsense?"

That described Myriem fairly well. "Rather."

He laughed like a fool. "She came here. She came . . . right when I was about to take off to chase Asti down the tunnels."

"She did?"

"She called me Saint Terrence, and said my work was here . . ." He gasped, and looked at his wife. "If I had gone, those bastards would have killed you and Corsi."

"Message from God, indeed," his wife said, kissing her knuckle and touching her forehead with it. Acserian benediction.

"So you know the Thorn, and he went into the tunnels here with your brother . . ." Satrine remembered the message she had received from Major Grieson about Verci's brother. "Former agent, right? He's why Grieson knew you."

"And Grieson knows you," Verci said. "How about you, girl?"

"Kaiana," she said. "And I don't know who that is. I got sent to her by a girl in a Tarian uniform."

"Jerinne," Satrine said. "She works with Dayne, the big fellow at the Parliament."

"He's in this mess as well?" Verci asked. He finished his adjustments to one device, and then started looking through a selection of brass balls. "Here's what I know. Those zealot fellows in Keller Cove arranged for a statue to be stolen from some fancy house in East Maradaine."

"Lord Callwood's Estate," Satrine said. "What kind of statue?"

"Green jade, four arms. The two bastards who got away tonight made off with it."

"How did you have it?" Satrine asked. After a moment of hesitation from him, she said, "In the interest of expedience, by my authority as an Inspector Second Class, I deputize you, Verci Rynax, as a Character of Material Information and statements you make regarding infractions of the law connected to your information will not be used to prosecute you for past misdeeds. Do you require a counsel from the Justice Advocate Office for your statement?"

He started to laugh. "Thank you, Inspector, but I was just thinking of the best way to explain it. But I appreciate that. The window-man the zealots hired, Kel Essin, he ran off with the statue, and when he found his friends had also been influenced by this . . . Brotherhood, he came to me. He knew I didn't like him, but he figured I was safe. Shows what he knew."

"The dead man upstairs," Satrine said.

Verci nodded. "But I know about two other statues

like that. One stolen from Lord Henterman's place a few months back, and one—a much larger one—stolen from someone else out east, sold to unnamed parties."

Satrine raised her eyebrow at that but didn't comment.

"So why do they want the statues?" she asked.

Verci perked up at a sound out front, and grabbed one of his darts. A skinny young man, filthy and wild-haired, stumbled into the room and fell to his knees.

"Delmin!" Kaiana shouted, rushing over to him.

"Kid, what happened?" Verci asked.

"Machine . . . horror . . ." the young man said.

"Who's this?" Satrine asked.

"He's a mage," Verci said. "He went down with Asti and the Thorn."

"I . . . I . . ."

"He needs food," Kaiana said.

Raych Rynax ran up the stairs, but Satrine reached into the pouch on her belt. She had long maintained the habit of keeping dried meat and nuts on hand for Minox. "Here."

Delmin ate that greedily, and then took a cup of water from Verci. "I'm sorry, it took me so long—I screwed up, it took everything I had to figure out how to get normal-sized, so I had to walk so far."

"Don't worry about that, Del," Kaiana said, stroking his head. Satrine remembered him now—Delmin Sarren, the witness she had interviewed in the fake Thorn attack. Of course, he was the Thorn's associate.

"Mister Sarren," Satrine said. "Can you tell us what's going on?"

He nodded. "There's a machine down there, that the Brotherhood has built. It's science and magic and who knows what else. Those statues . . . they're part of it. They channel the magic, through the spikes—"

"Spikes?" Satrine asked. Saints, were they the same spikes from the Plum murders? "To do what?"

"I don't know, but it feels . . . twisted. Tainted."

"I'm confident in thinking nothing they plan is good," Verci said.

"Same," Satrine said.

"Where's Veranix?" Kaiana asked, before covering her mouth.

"I already knew," Satrine said gently. "What happened down there?"

"Asti was able to stop them using the machine on two people, at least for a bit . . ."

"On two people?"

"Two people were shackled on a platform. And there were two cages with . . . with children in them."

"Why?" Verci asked.

"I'm not sure, but the *numinic* flow seemed like it was going through the cages, to the platform. At least what I saw."

"And Asti?"

"Last I saw, he was held captive. Same with the Thorn, and that big Tarian fellow."

Raych Rynax came back down with bread and cheese and wine, which Delmin happily took. "Thank you, Missus Rynax."

"Least I can do," she said. She looked to her husband. "And what are you going to do?"

He started loading the copper balls into the device he had been working on and gathering a few other tools and gadgets. "I'm going to go after my brother, unless there's another message from God that says I shouldn't." He looked upward. "So this is the moment, huh? Let me know!"

The ground rumbled for a moment.

"Well, then," Satrine said.

Delmin placed his palms on the ground. "This . . . they're starting it. And there's something more going on now."

"More?" Kaiana asked.

He nodded. "Like . . . like the night of the Winged Convergence. But . . . different. Uglier."

Verci started packing things in his satchel. "I'm going for my brother."

"With a plan," his wife urged. "And not alone."

He sighed. "Inspector?"

"We both have partners in this," she said. She took out her crossbow and checked it was loaded.

"Well, then," he said. "Let's give you something proper." He went under one worktable and came up with a case. "A Rynax Boltsinger Mark II. Only one of its kind."

He opened the case, revealing a gorgeous piece of work. He took the crossbow out and handed it to her.

"Half over again the range of that Constabulary issue, with double strings and triggers. Faster cocking and reload, and steel reinforced enough that you could crack it over someone's head and not move the aim alignment a hair."

Satrine looked it over, liking the weight of it in her hands. Even though it was heavier than her usual, it felt right, and she could still use it one-handed.

"Then let's not dally," he said, getting his shirt on. He then went into a satchel and pulled on a heavy leather coat, like the ones the patrol used for riot patrol, and draped his bandolier of darts over it. "Girl, you coming?"

"You call me girl again . . ." she groused. She helped Delmin to his feet. "Someone's got to keep an eye on this one."

"Back to the tunnels?" Verci asked.

"I don't think so," Delmin said. "It's a lot of twists and turns down there. We . . ."

"Can you lead us to where their machine is from up here?" Satrine asked. "Maybe there's a more direct way down from there."

Verci put the satchel over his shoulder, and then put

the one device over his left hand, like a gauntlet. "Then let's be direct."

Dayne felt nothing but burning shame. What had he become? How had that happened?

And why was the clarity of Crenaxin's touch so . . . seductive? He almost craved it compared to the confusion and guilt he felt now. Under the man's influence, everything was simple.

Which meant this power—the same sort of power that he had seen Ret Issendel use, he was certain—was dark and unholy, and must be stopped. He was certain of that. How many of the zealots down here, the people and the altered grotesques alike, were good folk whose souls had been twisted by Crenaxin.

He had to be stopped, and brought to justice.

"Do you know what he's got planned?" Asti Rynax asked. Dayne was impressed that this small man was undeterred from moving forward, despite the beating he had taken at Dayne's own hands. He was going through the storeroom, claiming his own weapons, as well as the army sword he had found among the gear.

"Put Welling into the machine?" the Thorn asked. He looked the worse for wear, but he had gathered his weapons and gear, and was back on his feet, eating a sandwich.

"How many of those did you bring?" Dayne asked him.

The Thorn looked at the sandwich. "This was, I think, in Inspector Welling's bag. Acserian spiced pork. Highly recommend. He might be upset I ate it, but if I can't get him out of the machine, he won't care."

"Put him in what machine how?" Jerinne asked.

"Do they want to change him?" Asti asked.

"Or do they need his hand?" Thorn asked.

"What about his hand?" Jerinne again.

"I'm not entirely sure," Dayne said, holding his head. "I'm still . . . everything is a mess in here."

"Yeah," Asti said, coming up to Dayne. "Listen to me. That mess, you have to just accept that it's there. You focus on it, you'll lose everything. Find the thing you can focus on, keep that in front of you. Get the job done, drive forward."

Dayne understood. There were people who needed saving. He would save them. "Right. Minox, he . . . they're going to use him to power the machine. His hand, specifically."

Asti double-checked his weapons. "I'm not clear on his hand. He's a mage?"

"Yes," the Thorn said. "But untrained. Raw and potent, especially his hand. It got changed somehow, so it's almost made of magic."

"They were going to use him, do one final test, and then they would . . . 'tap' into the power."

"Those words, exactly?" the Thorn asked.

"And most of them went to the machine," Jerinne said. "The camp here is nearly abandoned."

"What about the kids?" Asti asked. "We need to save the kids."

"Save the kids," Dayne said. "Save Minox, save Maresh and Lin." He looked to Jerinne on that, who nodded.

"And burn everything else here to ash," the Thorn said.

"Saint Senea hear you," Asti said back to him.

"They were leading some of the kids to the machine," Dayne said. "They're . . . part of how the machine works." He shuddered, even though he wasn't sure what that meant.

"Some, but not all?" Asti asked.

"They need them all for the tap, though," Dayne said.

"You know where they are?"

Dayne nodded.

Asti paced the room, rubbing at his chin. "All right, I've got a good sense that the two of you are capable with those swords and shields. But you, big fella, you're less keen on using them to hurt people. Mind games notwithstanding."

"Right," Dayne said.

"Thorn, you've really got no qualms along those lines. How are you feeling?"

"Ready to tear it down," the Thorn said.

"And what do you have left in the quiver from Verci?"

The Thorn looked at his arrows. "Four smoke powder, three boom powder, two knockout. Plus a couple dozen sharp, pointy ones."

"No acid?"

"Acid?" Jerinne asked.

"Used them against some dealers."

"Acid?" Jerinne asked again.

Asti bit at his lip. "All right, down here, those boom powders should be a last resort. Don't want to bring the roof on us."

"He's right," Dayne said. "You already did that once."

"That was Gurond."

"Probably because you weakened it."

The Thorn scowled, and focused on organizing his arrows in the quiver.

"We can presume the kids will be guarded, but a majority of the Brotherhood are near the machine, as are Crenaxin and Senek."

"And Pendall Gurond," Dayne said.

"You know his full name?" Thorn asked.

"I think that's his full name," Dayne said. "He kidnapped the Vollingale boy because of a grudge between their families, and—"

"Pendall!" the Thorn shouted. He started to laugh, "Oh, that's who he is. No wonder he's mad at me."

"You tangled with him before?" Asti asked.

"When he was, well, not like that. Big strong guy, worked with two other assassins. But strong guy like

Dayne, not a . . . half-human monster. I thought I had killed him, actually."

"We're wasting time," Jerinne said, looking out the door. "I can hear something in the distance."

Asti went over to her. "That's the machine. All right, fast and dirty plan. Dayne, you and I will go to the kids, handle any guards, and lead them to the fastest way out. You, girl—"

"Jerinne."

"You're with the Thorn. Thorn, you lay down some chaos, let her carve her way to the machine, get those people out. Then you shred the machine."

"You know what I like," the Thorn said. He looked to Jerinne and nodded approvingly, which she rolled her eyes at.

"That's your whole plan?" she asked.

"Don't let Crenaxin touch you," Dayne said. "I think he needs to do that much to . . . change you."

"Good tip," she said. "All right, let's move, 'Thorn.' Do I actually have to call you that?"

"Friends call me 'Vee.'" He had grabbed a tool from the corner and knocked the end off, making an improvised quarterstaff.

"Fine, Thorn," she said. She came over to Dayne and grabbed his hand. "You good?"

"No," he said. "But I'm ready, and that will do."

"Go get those kids," she said, taking him in an embrace. "See you on the other side."

"Be careful," he told her. "We didn't train for anything like this."

"Doesn't matter about the training. We're Tarians," she said. "We do what's needed."

"Jerinne," the Thorn said. "Let's move."

She winked one more time at Dayne, and went out the door with the Thorn.

"Let's be about it," Asti said. "Like I said—"

"Focus on the job," Dayne said. He put that in his head. Innocents needed him. He would do whatever it took to save them. No matter the cost.

Amaya did not remember falling asleep.

But she woke up with her face flat on a wooden floor. Immediately she startled to her feet, checking her surroundings. She had been locked in the room in the lower tunnels of the opera house. Locked in there with Kemmer, who had been dazed. Clobbered over the head.

But then what had happened? It was a blur. Someone taunted her through a door? She had a vague memory of that.

She was surrounded by light now. Great burning torches all around, with a grand lens focusing their light upon her. And seats. Rows and rows of seats.

She was on the opera house stage.

She turned around and almost vomited. Dead bodies were strewn out on the floor around her. Six of them, with Kemmer tied up in a chair in the center.

"What happened?" she asked, taking a heavy step forward.

Heavy.

She was in a mail shirt, full uniform. Shield strapped to her arm, sword at her belt. She definitely was not dressed that way when she arrived last night.

"It looks like you happened, Miss Tyrell," a woman's voice echoed around her. "It looks like this intrepid young man discovered your dark secret, and so you killed him, as well as your co-conspirators, in order to avoid further consequences."

"My what?" Amaya had no idea what was going on. "I don't have a dark secret."

"I didn't say what it was," the voice said. "I said what it looked like. This will very much look like there was a Grand Ten, undermining the interests of the city and the crown, meeting in secret in this opera hall to discuss their nefarious plans."

"What?" she called out.

"And it looks like the Grand Ten will be revealed in their death. Behold, The Man of the People—former City Alderman Willman Strephen."

One of the lights swept over to one of the bodies on the floor. Amaya realized he had been stabbed several times. The light swung around, illuminating the other bodies.

"The Lady: Baroness Kitranna. The Lord: Earl Estminton. The Priest: The Archbishop of Sauriya. The Soldier: General Dougal Moorin. The Mage: Larian Amelie."

The light swung onto Amaya.

"And The Warrior: Amaya Tyrell. The young woman whose strange and rapid rise in the Tarian Order is explained so easily now. She had powerful friends who facilitated her ascension. Gave her a step up so she could aid them. Unfortunately, you all were discovered by this Kemmer fellow."

"None of this is true!" Amaya shouted, not sure where she should be shouting it to. There was no source to the voice, no body she could aim her anger at.

"I didn't say it was true," the voice said. "I just said . . . that's what it looked like. And when Mister Kemmer does not report to his friends today, they will bring his findings—these findings—to several newssheets. And when the marshals discover this definitive proof of this conspiracy, the newssheets will accept it. The people will believe it."

The direction of the voice coalesced to Amaya's left. She turned to face it, sword drawn. Colonel Altarn stepped out of the shadows.

"It will become truth."

"How dare—" Amaya started.

"Of course," Altarn said, holding up a hand that was

charged with light. "Such a tale will require a bit of verisimilitude to make it easy to accept. We were able to alter some of Mister Kemmer's findings, but he had already discovered too much truth, shared that with his colleagues, that some choices were unavoidable."

Voices came from the other direction. Amaya turned to see two older men and a regal-looking woman walk onto the stage.

The woman was speaking, clearly incensed. "I don't understand why we've returned here, or what was so urg—"

Her diatribe was cut short by a sword quickly depriving her of her head. Grandmaster Orren came out of the shadows.

"But what—" one of the men managed before the sword found a home in his heart.

The last old man looked about, his eyes finding Altarn. "How dare you!" he shouted. "I created this, and you would be noth—"

His last thoughts would not be heard, as Grandmaster Orren's fast sword took his life.

"Leighton, Pin, and Millerson. Necessary sacrifices," Altarn said. "But not hard ones."

Amaya ignored her, focusing all her rage on the Grandmaster. His face was completely neutral, devoid of emotion. "How could you, sir? Whatever made you think you could be a part of this?"

"I do what is best for the Order," he said, his voice with that same empty flatness as before. "I accept the damnation upon me, but the Order will survive."

"On a foundation of blood," Amaya said. "Built with deceit."

"But," he said, "it will survive."

Amaya extended her sword, crouched in a defensive stance. "I'd rather it burns down in truth than survive like this."

"Such are the ideals of youth," Orren said, walking around the dead bodies calmly. "I wish I still had such righteous fury. The burdens of command, of responsibility . . . I wish you understood, Amaya. I wish Master Denbar had understood."

"He would never—"

"Indeed. Which is why he had to go. And now you."

"Not easily," Amaya said, raising up her blade.

"Oh, she wants to fight," Altarn said. "This will be spirited."

"I don't want to kill you," the Grandmaster said. "But I will, as that's what needs to be."

Amaya understood the odds. She knew her opponents, how dangerous they were. She didn't have much of a chance, so she had to act quickly. She launched herself at Orren, looking to clock him with her shield. But as he moved to defend himself, Amaya spun hard and launched her shield into Altarn's sternum, knocking the mage back, hard and heavy.

It wouldn't kill her. In probably wouldn't even slow her for long. Amaya knew that. But she also knew, if she hoped to walk out of here alive, she had to stop Colonel Altarn.

Whatever it would take.

Chapter 19

MINOX WAS GLAD HE HAD not told his mother not to worry. He said it was his intention to come home, and that had not happened. That was, barring a miracle, unlikely to happen. He would probably not see the sunlit sky again.

She would lose two children in a month. He hoped she would be able to bear it. He hoped that Oren would step up and be what she needed. Jace would be there for her. So would all the aunts and uncles. She had been a constable's wife, she knew what it meant to go out for the last ride.

Bound with mage shackles, hood over his face, told he was going to be used for an experiment of obscenity, it was clear: this was his.

But if he was to die today, he would do his best to deal a wound to the Brotherhood in the process.

"The time is ripe. Let's see what he can do."

Minox was dragged along and then put on his knees before the hood was removed. Ithaniel Senek loomed over him, and behind him: the machine. This horror that was reminiscent of Sholiar's gearbox devices, but even grander in scope than the one in the Parliament. Of all the frightening details, one jumped out above all the others: seven of the magic-draining spikes Nerrish Plum had used in his mage-killing spree. One of those had catalyzed the process that altered his hand.

"I won't do anything for you," Minox said to Senek. "Consider yourself bound by law. Charges will be laid against you. They will include, and not be limited to, kidnap and abduction, in multiple counts, and grave harm and mischief to the body, in multiple counts."

"That's quite a mouthful, my friend," Senek said. He took Minox's hand and lifted it up. It started to give off a faint blue glow, despite Minox's current inability to channel any magic through it at the moment. "Fascinating that you achieved Lord Sirath's dream here. How did you manage?"

"I've no idea," Minox said. "Untrained. Uncircled."

"Incredible. You have no idea what you have here. It's as if a blind toddler scribbled wildly and wrote all the plays of Darren Whit."

"Take off the shackle and I'll show you what I can do," Minox said.

"The fact that the shackle stops you at all shows me how unworthy you are."

"Maybe so," Minox said. "But this will not end with me. This city will stand up against you."

"You are a fool," Senek said. "I wish you knew how easily this city has fallen into our pocket."

"The corruption may be deep," Minox said. "But I will fight you to my end. And so will so many others. Whatever your evil, you will not succeed. This I promise you."

"Very bold, very foolish words."

"You're wasting time, Ithaniel," Crenaxin said. "Mister Welling here does not care one bit about what you think."

"Fine," Senek said. "Gurond! Put him in place."

The giant Gurond picked Minox up and put him in a spot on the machine beneath one of the jade statues, and forced Minox's hand into the hole designed for the spike.

To Minox's horror, his hand shifted and flowed, like water, to fit into the hole perfectly. Like he was a key that just unlocked something. The gears of the machine began to move. Magical energy began to pour out of Minox, like he had never experienced before in his life. Flooding and rushing, more than he could ever hope to control.

The power to destroy the city.

It was too much, more than he could bear, and all he could do was look around, hoping to see something that he could use, something he could do, that would sabotage the plans of Ithaniel Senek and the Brotherhood.

The room was full of members of the Brotherhood, both the robed men and the transformed grotesques. Easily a hundred of them, if not more.

"Stop, please!"

Lin Shartien, the mage reporter from *The Veracity Press*, also in mage shackles. Had she come down with Dayne? Where was he? Had he truly been turned by the dark power of Crenaxin?

And if Crenaxin could do that, and the machine was to give him the power of the Nine . . . what did that mean for Maradaine?

Minox looked up. In the brass cages, several children had been bound, and Maresh Niol, *Veracity*'s artist, was shackled to a platform.

The magical energy was whirling through the machine, through Minox, out of the children, up onto the platform. Into Maresh. Magic and more, things Minox had no name for.

I still have my mind, Minox thought. *I will find a way.*

But as the magic curled and coalesced around Maresh Niol, Minox realized he was almost out of time.

Maresh screamed, with a voice that was in no way human.

"Yes!" Senek shouted. "It's working!"

"The worthy vessel!" Crenaxin said. "It can be done!"

Purple smoke erupted from one side of the room. Then the other. Then a burst of sickly yellow smoke erupted around Gurond.

Minox looked up in time to see a flash of crimson race by, and the crack of wood against bone. The magical energy flooding through Minox suddenly stopped, leaving him breathless and drained.

But still, a smile came.

Veranix Calbert—the Thorn—was standing over Senek, cloak flowing, staff in hand.

"Gentlemen," he said, his voice echoing through the chamber. "You're all out of bed after curfew, and I'm afraid I'm going to have to issue demerits."

Dayne took Asti out of the encampment, through the side hallways to the cells. Dayne remembered having gone down here before with Crenaxin; he remembered being happy about that. He could still feel that, and it repulsed him.

"Rynax," he said. "How did you stay free from Crenaxin?"

"Honestly, I'm not, entirely," Asti said. "I mean, I'm in control of myself, but . . ."

"I don't understand."

Asti paused. "I've already had my brain shattered by Poasian telepaths, who . . . put something in my head that was designed to serve the Brotherhood."

"What?" Dayne asked.

"But I've got it . . . locked away, kept in place by the other broken part of my brain. I'm shattered. And I've . . . I've learned how to live with being shattered because . . . what choice do I have?"

"How?" Dayne asked. "How do you do that?"

"Day to day, hour to hour," Asti said. "It's still a part of you, isn't it?"

Dayne wasn't sure. He remembered being the man that Crenaxin turned him into, wanting to serve the Brotherhood, fulfill their destiny through the tap and becoming grand, worthy vessels of the Nine. He had no desire for those things now, no secret wish to be back to being that man. But still, the memory was there with him.

"There's going to be anger," Asti said. "I don't know if that'll help, but I use it."

They came upon a closed gate. When they came before, Crenaxin called to the faithful, who opened it from somewhere else. But there were no controls here. "Maybe I can—" Dayne grabbed hold of the bars, straining to pull it open. The steel bars didn't budge. "I can't get through here."

"Fortunately, I'm much smaller," Asti said. He climbed up the gate to an opening on the top and squeezed his small frame through it. He pointed down the hallway, to the several sets of doors. "All kids? Any guards?"

"There were faithful . . . zealots in those two rooms," Dayne whispered, pointing to the first two. "Then the children chained up in the next two."

Asti nodded. "Like I said, there's going to be anger. And I use it."

"Asti," Dayne didn't want to yell. "What are you going to do?"

Asti went to the first door, placing his hand on it, and then listened at it for a moment. He stepped back for a moment, and then exploded with a violent kick that knocked the door open, drew out two knives, and jumped into the room.

The door slammed shut.

Sounds of a fight echoed through the hall. Blows and punches and shouts. The door on the other side of the hallway opened up and two men came out, looking confused, and two more in the doorway.

Dayne wanted to cry out, warn Asti, but before he could, the door flew open, one zealot falling out onto the floor. One of the men from the second room came over to him, to be greeted by a chair flying out of the first room, knocking him in the head.

Asti flew out right behind it, landing a punch, followed by a slash of his knife. Without even looking, Asti slammed one foot onto the chest of the man on the ground, and then shoved the man he was engaged with into the one behind him. They both went down, but Asti didn't even stop. Two slashes of his knife, he put them both down, moaning and bleeding, as he pivoted into the two standing in the doorway.

It was horrifying and beautiful, watching Asti fight. It was the most visceral, violent, ruthless he had ever seen a man be. Animalistic. But at the same time, it had the purity of an animal, a wildcat with its prey.

The other men took their shots, landing blows on Asti, but it was like the man didn't even care. He accepted their punches, taking the opportunity to land two back, slice open their bellies.

As he made quick work of the last men in the second room, one stumbled out of the first room, blood pouring out of his throat and belly and he fruitlessly tried to hold it in. He made it three steps before he fell.

Then quiet.

Then the sound of a wheel being turned, and the gate opened.

Dayne wasn't sure if he could take a step forward.

Asti stumbled out, blood on his face and hands, his eyes sparked with madness and joy. Keys in his hand.

He went to other doors and opened them.

"Free, free!" he shouted, dropping to his knees. "All free!"

Then he started laughing. He laughed as Dayne approached, and as he let Dayne take the keys, his laughter turned to tears. Dayne glanced in the cells. Each of them had at least ten children, maybe more, shackled to the walls.

"All free," Asti said, staring at his hands. "A gift from God."

"Come on, Rynax," Dayne said. "Let's get these children out of here."

Asti nodded, getting to his feet. In a moment, he had regained his composure. "Right. Job's not done."

"Gentlemen," the Thorn said, his voice echoing through the chamber. "You're all out of bed after curfew, and I'm afraid I'm going to have to issue demerits."

Jerinne had thought him absurdly cocky, to the point of annoyance, but she had to admit the Thorn knew how to stage a distraction. All the attention was on him, and with the machine chamber half filled with smoke, none of the zealots of the Brotherhood of the Nine were going to be noticing her slipping around the edge of the wall.

The Thorn moved like a rabbit, knocking the zealots with his staff, never still for a second. Even still, she knew he couldn't hold his own against all of them for long. Time to do her job.

She rushed through the smoke, shield first, toward Lin. Free Lin first—her magic made her an asset in the fight. Then Welling, then up on the platform for Maresh. She charged through, knocking zealots out of her way. Almost to Lin.

The Thorn leaped high, landing in the mouth of one of the high overlook tunnels. From that vantage, he loosed more arrows into the crowd.

"You pest!" Senek shouted. "I will eat your liver!"

"Promises, promises," Thorn said. "Come have a taste."

Jerinne pushed through, reaching Lin, clocking her

guard with the shield. She grabbed Lin's shoulder, and at first Lin swung her shackled fists at Jerinne.

"Lin," she said, grabbing her arm mid-swing. "It's me."

"Get Maresh," Lin said. She held up her shackled hands. "I'm useless."

"Got to get you out, too."

"Maresh, please!" Lin cried. "Look!"

Jerinne looked up on the machine, to Maresh on the platform.

"Sweet merciful saints," she whispered.

Maresh's body had been twisted. Half his face green and scaled. One arm the size of the rest of his body. His back bent at an impossible angle.

Crenaxin was climbing up the machine to the platform. To Maresh.

"Come on," Jerinne said, pulling Lin along. She had to get to him, no matter what.

Crenaxin reached the top, and casually yanked Maresh out of his shackles, then pushed him off the platform to fall to the floor.

"Maresh!" Jerinne screamed.

But the Thorn was there. He had flung out his rope, and wrapped it around Maresh midair, pulling him up to the tunnel.

"Enough!" Senek shouted. A blast of magic flew out around him, and the smoke all cleared. The zealots and monsters were all around Jerinne, drawing weapons. Closest of all was Gurond, the towering giant, though he looked dazed and groggy.

"This is the time!" Crenaxin shouted, now standing tall on the top of the platform. "We are ready to tap open our power! Make me your worthy vessel! **Bow down before the High Dragon!**"

The words slammed through Jerinne's bones, and it took all her will to stay upright. Everyone else—the zealots, the monsters, Senek, even Lin—dropped to their knees and prostrated themselves toward the machine.

"We are ready for the blessings of the Nine! We are ready to tap into their power. We are ready for a bright new day!"

Jerinne moved toward Minox, forcing herself with every step. Her whole body wanted to obey Crenaxin.

"Begin, Senek! **Begin!**"

Senek stood and the whole machine began to move again. All the wheels, rings, and gimbals spun, whirling around the outside, faster and faster. Too fast for Jerinne to see. The spinning rings were right over Minox, but there was a narrow path to get to him. None to get to the men in the cages.

Men.

Those were children before, but now they were men, looking Dayne's age. How was that even possible? What was this machine doing to them? What was it about to do?

Something shifted, and Jerinne could move again. She pushed forward, shield above her head, under the spinning rings that threatened to slice her to oblivion. More than once sparks flew as they scraped the shield.

"Can you move?" she asked Minox.

He nodded. "But I cannot extract myself from this infernal device."

Jerinne grabbed hold of his waist and tried to pull him. His hand wouldn't budge from the machine.

"Worthy vessels!" Senek shouted.

"Worthy vessels!"

Blue and purple lightning sparked all over the chamber. Jerinne looked up and saw that it surrounded Crenaxin, surrounded the old men in the cages. The entire room, as the lightning struck all the grotesques as well.

The Thorn appeared behind Jerinne. "I've got your friends secured away in the tunnel. We need to move."

"He can't!" Jerinne said.

"Leave me," Minox said. "Maybe I can—"

"Not an option," the Thorn said. He touched Minox's wrist and furrowed his brow. "Come on!" Then he yanked his hand away, like he had been burned.

The lightning sparked and popped all around, forming chains of fire between each of the grotesques. All of their bodies began to shift and change. Lightning sparked back to the machine, knocking Jerinne's shield.

"I've got an idea," the Thorn said. His rope coiled around Jerinne, up to her shield, and back down around Minox. "Hold on."

"What are you—"

"This might get uncomfortable."

A green and red nimbus surrounded the three of them, as the purple and blue lightning exploded in fire, but none of it touched them. The light of it all was blinding, and the Thorn and Minox both screamed.

Then in a flash, it stopped.

Jerinne looked to Minox, whose hand was free of the machine. Both he and the Thorn were breathing hard, but the Thorn had a smile on his face. Then he looked past Jerinne and his face fell.

"We need to move quickly."

Jerinne turned and saw. The grotesques were no longer misshapen abominations. All of them had become beasts similar to Gurond—monstrosities with wide jaws, spiky skin, and clawed hands. All of them looked up and howled.

"Worthy! Worthy! Fuel for the fire!"

Jerinne lowered her shield and raised her sword. She would get these two out of here.

Whatever it took.

"Come on, come on," Dayne told the kids as they moved through the dark tunnel. "We have to hurry."

"Where you taking us?" one of the kids whined.

"Why should we go with you?"

Dayne remembered the Thorn's inspiration to get the young baron to move. "Tomorrow is Terrentin. We need to get you home so Saint Terrence can find you."

"He never finds me," one kid said.

"I've never gotten a Terrentin present," said another.

"You're definitely getting one now," Asti said. "We're getting you out of there, getting you safe, and hopefully getting you home."

"I ain't got a home," one of them said.

"We can't trust these guys," another said.

"Yeah, we can," one kid said. "That's Mister Rynax. He's a tough bastard, but he's a good guy."

"Telly?" Asti asked. "That you?"

That kid stepped forward. "Yeah."

"Tarvis sent me to find you," Asti said. "All of you."

"Tarvis is all right?"

"He's up at Kimber's," Asti said.

"Let's get you all there," Dayne said. "Bet she's got a Terrentin Eve feast planned. You all are hungry, right?"

"Starved," Telly said.

"Then let's move," he said. He could hear echoes of thunder, deep booms of power and magic raging in the distance. He wanted to turn back, help Jerinne and the Thorn, but the kids were his charge right now. Trust in them. Protect the children.

Asti took the point, finding the path he had marked on his way in. He led with quiet confidence, an odd calm, despite the blood on his face and hands. Dayne took the rear, expecting a rush of zealots, or even Gurond, coming to reclaim the stolen children.

"Someone's ahead," Asti said. "I'll take him down."

"Wait," Dayne said. He moved a little ahead, calling out, "Drop any weapons you have, you'll be treated fair."

"Dayne?" a voice called back in the darkness.

"Hemmit?" Dayne called back.

Hemmit came up to them, looking exhausted and haggard. "Thank every saint you're all right!" he said.

"Alive and uninjured," Dayne said.

"And you found Rynax," Hemmit said. "And the children!"

"Where's the baron's son?" Dayne asked.

"Safe at Kimber's," Hemmit said. "I got him there, and came back to help you all."

"We've got to get these kids out of these tunnels," Asti said. "You're not lost, are you?"

"Not at all," Hemmit said.

"Good," Asti said. "Get these kids out, get them to Kimber's. Tell her I'm on my way."

"What are you going to do?" Dayne asked.

He tapped his head. "This part of my skull is screaming about going to the Dragon, and I can hear something awful happening back there. I bet the Thorn is in over his head. I'll go pull him and the others out."

Dayne nodded. Jerinne was there, and as good as she was, Dayne knew she wasn't prepared for what was happening down here. She needed help. Maresh and Lin and Minox Welling—especially Minox Welling—needed help.

"Get them out, Hemmit," Dayne said. "Tell them a story about Terrentin."

"Got it," Hemmit said. "Come along, all. We're going to be free and rejoice, rejoice, rejoice!"

"Let's go, Dayne," Asti said. "Time to be a hero."

Dayne didn't know about that. He certainly didn't think he deserved such a title. But people needed help. If what he understood about that machine and Crenaxin's intentions was correct, and the Brotherhood wasn't stopped, the whole city would need it as well.

Chapter 20

"EXPLAIN TO ME WHY YOU aren't calling in every damn constable in whistleshot," Verci asked Inspector Rainey. Not that he had any fondness for the Constabulary, including Rainey, but if any time seemed like an opportune moment to call them in, this was it. Assuming Delmin and Kaiana weren't delusional, there was a literal army of zealots and monsters—monsters, the girl had said—beneath the city, and a giant magical machine that was about to launch some bad business. And all he was doing was following an off-duty inspector down Bridget Street.

"Matter of trust," Rainey said. "The Constabulary has been infested with corruption, and it ties to the Brotherhood, to Senek, to the Blue Hand, all of it."

"And you said Crenaxin?" Verci asked Kaiana, who was a few paces ahead, helping Delmin walk as he led them by his magical nose.

"That was his name."

"Mean something?" Rainey asked.

"Friend of mine met a bounty hunter who was looking for him," Verci said. "I'm inclined to help her collect."

"I think the law might have an interest," she said. "But if he ends up in a small box, and they throw the box away, I'm all right."

"This way," Delmin said. "Toward the plaza—"

They walked into Saint Bridget's Square, with the rising sun right behind the church's bell tower. As early as it was, the square was already a bustle of activity: people going to and fro, opening up their shops, getting ready for another day. Verci felt more than a little conspicuous walking in broad daylight, fully armed, even if he was with a constable.

"Verci, what's going on?" Kimber came up to him, leading a little boy.

"Kimber," he said. "I'm not entirely sure, except something terrible and magical is happening below the city—"

"In the tunnels, missing children, yes. That reporter showed up with this boy, and left again."

Rainey knelt down in front of the boy. "What's your name?"

"Lord Aston Vollingale, son of Baron Vollingale."

"Sweet saints, he's nobility?" Verci asked.

"I know!" she said. "I was bringing him to the church; they would know what to do."

"Oh, very, very big," Delmin said, kneeling on the ground in the middle of the square. "It's all happening."

"What is?" Rainey asked.

"It's coming up."

"Hey!" A dirty man with a beard came running toward them, leading a large group of children. As he approached, Verci realized he was that reporter from *The Veracity Press*.

"Mister Eyairin," Rainey said. "Are you all right?"

"Fine," he said. "I got the kids. Came up out of a tunnel hole in the creek over there. But something—"

"Something is definitely happening," Delmin said. "We aren't safe."

Verci did not like that particular combination of words.

"All of you, go in the church," Verci said. "I'll track that tunnel. Inspector, are you—"

Before he finished that thought, the earth shook, harder than he ever imagined it could. Everyone in Saint Bridget's Square, Verci included, tumbled to the ground.

He started to get back to his feet when Inspector Rainey grabbed him and pulled him back. He was about to yell at her when he saw why she had done that.

The cobblestone had cracked, and began to open into a wide chasm across the square.

Dayne chased Asti down the tunnel, toward the sounds of screams and grinding gears and fighting. Everything was going wrong down here.

"I hope you're ready to bring the fight," Asti said. "Because it's here."

"I'll draw the fight to me," Dayne said. "Hold them off while you help get the Thorn and the others out of here."

They rounded the corner, and almost fell over Lin. She was slumped on the ground, weeping next to one of those grotesques. That creature lay on the ground, unmoving. Possibly dead.

"Lin!" he said. "Are you all right?"

"I . . . I tried to save him . . . I . . . I couldn't . . ."

"What do you—" He looked at the creature. Despite its misshapen head, it was wearing spectacles. Horror and despair flooded into Dayne's heart. "Maresh?"

Lin nodded. "They . . . they changed him with the machine. They made him into . . . I tried . . . but . . ." She held up her shackled hands. "I was powerless."

"It's not your fault," Dayne said.

"Dayne, this is some trouble," Asti said, looking over

the tunnel precipice. "Your girl is fighting like blazes down there."

"Stay here," Dayne said. "We'll . . . we'll take care of things."

Dayne came to the edge and saw. The machine was fully engaged, and Crenaxin stood on top of its platform, surrounded in energy and light of every color. Jerinne, Minox, and the Thorn were together, pinned up against one part of the machine, perilously close to rings spinning absurdly fast. Jerinne was in front, shield high, pushing her way through zealots and beasts. The misshapen monsters had somehow transformed into great beasts with massive claws and teeth, and Jerinne was doing her best to hold them off, while the Thorn fired arrow after arrow to take them down. Both of them seemed to be protecting Minox.

"More!" Crenaxin shouted. "More fuel for the fervent fire! Bring them to me!"

Dayne noticed something else about the machine. The brass cages—the ones that were holding children before—held only the withered corpses of old men.

"Bring the fuel! Bring it!" Senek shouted.

Gurond stood in the doorway. "The children are gone! They escaped!"

"Impossible!" shouted Senek.

"You!" Gurond shouted, pointing up at Dayne. "Gurond will—" He shook his head. "I will make you pay!"

"Get the fuel!" Crenaxin shouted. "Now!"

Jerinne was fighting for her life, holding off the great-fanged creatures that tried desperately to eat her shield whole.

"Jerinne!" Dayne shouted. "I'm coming!" He just needed a way to slide down.

"Stay there!" the Thorn shouted. "Catch!"

His rope coiled around Minox Welling's body, and with a sudden snap, flung the man up to the tunnel. Dayne reached out and caught Minox, pulling him to safety.

"Don't you—" Minox started.

"My head is clear," Dayne said. "I'm very sorry."

Minox took that in. "Forgiven. I'm glad you reconciled yourself."

Asti looked to the shackles on Minox's wrists. "Let's do something about those."

"Please," Minox said.

Dayne's attention was back on the floor. Jerinne was flanked on both sides, as Gurond was barreling down on her. He knew she couldn't possibly take one of his punches.

"Get out of there!" Dayne shouted.

The Thorn grabbed Jerinne's waist and flung up his rope toward Dayne. Dayne grabbed hold of it, planting his feet and anchoring one arm to the side of the tunnel. He held on as strong as he could as the Thorn and Jerinne came flying up at him, just as Gurond was about to slam a massive fist into Jerinne's shield. Dayne wasn't sure even a Tarian shield could hold up to that.

"You good?" he asked Jerinne as she landed.

"You?"

"As much as can be."

"Minox," the Thorn said. "You holding up?"

Asti had removed the shackles.

"Ravenous," Minox said.

Thorn pulled a sandwich out of the pack and handed it to him.

"This was mine," Minox said.

"I know."

"There were two."

The Thorn looked sheepish for a moment. "I did save you."

After a moment, Minox nodded. "Fair."

"Last part of the plan?" Jerinne snapped.

"Right," the Thorn said, helping Minox to his feet. "I'm guessing a bunch of angry zealots are coming this way."

"Worse," Asti said, looking out over the room.

Dayne looked back to the machine, where Crenaxin was screaming.

"They've been taken! Taken to the surface! Taken to the sky!"

Senek looked up at Dayne and the others, and smirked. "Then we will do the same. Reclaim our prizes, our fuel!"

"Yes, now!" Crenaxin shouted. "Now this city will see!"

"Now!" the zealots and beasts shouted. "Now!"

Senek laughed and raised his arms high. "Rise. Rise! **RISE!**"

The ground beneath their feet shook, and the floor of the chamber cracked. Then the ceiling split open above them, revealing the bright blue sky. The sudden burst of light stabbed through Dayne's eyes, and he winced, looking away.

Then everything in the chamber—the floor, the machine, Senek, the zealots and beasts—all rose higher and higher. The stone floor rushed up at them, pipes cracking as it came, shooting steam at everyone. The Thorn's rope coiled around Dayne and Asti and pulled them out of harm's way.

"Saints," Jerinne said. "They just went to the surface. Where?"

"Saint Bridget's Square," Asti said, horrified. "We have to get up there. Now."

He was already running, and the Thorn and Minox were right behind him.

"Time to hold back death," Jerinne said, running after.

"Sword in hand and shield on arm," Dayne said to no one, following behind them all. He had never seen anything like this atrocity, and he feared that he and the other four would not be enough to stop it.

Lin was still on the ground, crying over Maresh. He wanted to weep with her, Maresh deserved to be properly mourned, but this was not the moment. He scooped up Maresh's misshapen body.

"Can you walk?" he asked Lin.

She nodded. "If nothing else."

"Then come on. We're going to get out of here."

A juggernaut of metal emerged from the wide gap that split in the cobblestone, rising up to blot the sun out in the square. Satrine barely had time to pull Verci Rynax out of harm's way from its ascent, and she lost sight of Delmin and Kaiana, as well as Hemmit and the children.

Verci found his footing quickly, jumping back perching on the low stone wall that enclosed the square. Satrine instinctively blasted a Riot Call as the thing continued to rise, gripping her handstick in her off hand. Now she could see the whole thing. Copper and steel intertwined and connected as massive rings spun at impossible speeds around it. Huge spherical cages sat in the center, with a raised platform on the top. A man stood on the top of the platform, arms raised triumphantly as he was surrounded in swirling light and energy.

"He seems very pleased with himself, doesn't he?" Verci asked.

"Rather," Satrine said. "Eyes up."

The rise finally stopped, and a small army arrived with the base of the machine. Dozens of people in dark robes, dozens more that were not even human, and one howling, hairy madman.

The tallest, scariest of the unhumans bellowed out. "Get the children! Fuel the fervent fire!" The army all ran in every direction in the square. Four zealots charged directly at Satrine and Verci.

Satrine was ready with the crossbow, pulling the first trigger as she aimed dead at the heart of the first zealot. He went down and she immediately shot the second, clipping him in the arm. He closed the distance, and was met with the cocking stirrup in his face.

Verci had made short work of the other two with a combination of darts and kicks.

"I presume my deputization protects me from murder charges," he said to her.

"If I get to keep this crossbow," she said, quickly recocking and loading it back up. "They're going for the kids; we need to get to them." She hadn't heard any response to her Riot Call. Not that anything could be heard over the racket of all this.

"Right," he said. He raised his gauntlet arm and shot one of the brass balls. That section of the square filled with smoke. "Let's go."

"We can't see the kids now," Satrine said as she followed him into the smoke.

"Neither can they," Verci said.

"Small comfort." Something fleshy and spiky barreled into her, knocking her to the ground. She rolled with the fall, moving out of the way as a clawed hand swiped at her. What were these things? When she was a kid, there had always been rumors—more childish taunts—about horrors that lived in the sewers, but she had never really believed such things. She couldn't deny the reality trying to sink its teeth into her face, though. She swung up her handstick, wedging it into the fangfilled maw coming at her. Another clawed hand grabbed her, dragging her and the beast along with her, out of the smoke, out of the square.

This beast looked down on her, hunger in its eyes. "Not child," it said.

"Nope," she said. She brought up the crossbow and fired both quarrels at once at it, while bringing up her knee into the crotch of the other. It squealed and fell off her while the first dropped dead. At least these things, whatever they were, still had tenders and other weak spots.

She got back on her feet and drove her boot into the face of the creature, then a second time for good measure. She recocked the crossbow again—saints, this thing was a beauty—but before she could finish reloading, Verci came hurtling out of the smoke. He managed to land on his feet, but started to scramble away as soon as he did.

"Giant!" he shouted.

The largest beast—the one with scaly gray skin, thick and oily, lumbered out of the smoke holding a lamppost like it was a club.

"Constables," he said in a lumbering voice. "Hate constables."

The lamppost came swinging down on Satrine, but it didn't hit her. Instead she was surrounded in blue energy, which pulled her back, away from the beast.

"Apologies for the abrupt action, Inspector Rainey."

Minox Welling.

Minox looking like he walked through the blazes and fought every sinner in the canon, but still: Minox Welling. She'd have embraced him if she didn't know he'd hate it. Instead, she responded to him as he would appreciate.

"Apology accepted, even if you are late."

The beast charged at them, only to be intercepted by Jerinne Fendall, knocking him in the knee with her shield, throwing him off balance.

"I would argue it was you who has missed a majority of events," he said.

Blasts of wind filled the square, followed by surges of fire and lightning raining down. The wild, hairy fellow was clearly the source of that, sowing chaos all around. People throughout the plaza screamed as they attempted to get away, but zealots and beasts were grabbing them, running farther into the streets of North Seleth. Satrine pointed to a pair of zealots who had pinned some shopkeepers into a corner.

"Fill me in while we rescue them," she said, running over there.

"I would also argue for some form of tactical withdrawal to discuss strategy, were it not for the immediate danger," he said. He raced over to the first zealot, knocking him down with a magically charged fist. While Satrine knocked down the other, he said, "I find myself without a call whistle. Summoning a show of color would be prudent."

"I don't disagree. My calls haven't gotten a response yet," Satrine said. She turned to the shopkeepers. "Lock yourself inside until you hear a Clear Call." She took out her whistle and blew a series of blasts. Emergency call. Call for any and everyone in the loyalty to come, spread the call.

"You're wasting your breath." A small greasy-looking man came up to her and Minox. "There's not likely to be any sticks within five blocks of here."

"You are?" she asked.

Her answer came when Verci Rynax jumped on him, embracing the man. "Asti, thank Saint Senea. I thought you were—"

"We still may be," he said. He looked over to the machine. "This job is well and truly skunked."

"Take cover!" Minox shouted, pulling them behind a pile of rubble. Blasts of lightning and fire came at them.

"We need to do something," Asti Rynax said.

"I'm open to suggestion," Verci said. "But magic and monsters are out of my league. What happened to the Thorn?"

Veranix didn't know where he was when he came out into the sunlight—was it already morning?—but there was no time to dwell on that. The zealots and monsters were running in every direction, grabbing children and other people, while Crenaxin and Senek still worked whatever twisted plot they intended. There was no time to think about anything else.

He jumped at a group of zealots who were dragging children toward the machine.

"None of that," he shouted as he leaped into the center of them, staff whirling. No time for panache or style. Just knock them down and clear them out.

"Run to the church!" he yelled to the kids. "Hurry, go!"

The kids all started running, and the zealots gave chase. Veranix thought for a moment it would be easy to just whip out the rope, magically yank them back, but he had to pace himself. He only had so much magical strength left in reserve. Too much going on, and he couldn't track it all, and saints only knew what he needed to do next.

Right now, just muscle and bone. Punch what was in front of him. Solve the immediate problems. Four zealots chasing after the kids.

He whipped the staff at one of them while taking up his bow. Draw, nock, and loose. Again. Again. Three put down, the fourth tripped up.

"Get off him!" a far too familiar voice shouted.

Veranix spun and saw Kaiana hammering punches at one of the monsters, which was dragging Delmin toward the machine. What the blazes were either of them doing here?

No time. He pulsed a hint of magic into himself, into speed, and ran at them, firing two arrows and scooping up his staff to smash the beast's face in at the same moment the arrows found their mark. It fell away from Delmin.

"I think we missed curfew," he told Delmin lightly.

"You think?" Delmin shot back.

Kaiana grabbed Veranix in a hard embrace. "I thought you were dead."

"Came too close," he said, quickly squeezing her back. "You two need to get out of here."

"And where will you be?"

He drew and fired two more arrows at an approaching monster before answering. "Stopping this. But I can't if you guys are in danger. Go in the church."

"We're not leaving you alone," Delmin said.

"I'm not alone," he said, glancing around. "Look, constables, Tarians, Rynaxes. It's a party."

"Veranix!" Kaiana said.

"They want the kids who ran into the church. Go and keep them safe. Please." He spotted another monster going after a pair of kids on the church steps. He launched another arrow—he was running low at this point—taking it down. "Those two. Get them inside. Protect them, Kai."

She looked to the kids, and nodded, pulling Delmin off with her. Veranix looked back to the chaos, spotting the first major situation. Gurond was hammering at the Tarian girl—Jerinne—and she was buckling under his strength.

"Hey, Gurond!" he shouted. "Why are you wasting time with her? I thought you wanted to play with me!"

Gurond looked up at him and grinned. "Goddamned mage." He threw a dismissive swipe at Jerinne, which hit her shield and sent her skidding away. Then he ran at Veranix.

Veranix drank in the *numina* swirling around the square, sending it to his legs, filling the cloak, waiting for the exact moment when Gurond's massive hands were about to land on him.

Then he jumped, rocketing up to the sky as far as he could go, while shrouding himself with the cloak. Gurond crashed into a wall.

Satisfying, but a drop in the bucket. Too much happening. No chance of stopping it alone. He didn't even know where to start. He needed a plan.

He aimed his descent to land right by the very people who might have one.

CHAPTER 21

DAYNE LEFT MARESH'S BODY IN the mouth of an alley, as far from the chaos as he dared to go. "Stay here," he told Lin.

"What are you going to do?" she asked.

"I don't know," he said. "But I have to do something. Be safe."

"I'll do what I can," Lin said. She twisted her hand—her wrists were completely raw—and pulled it out of the shackles with a subdued cry. "I should have kept him safe. I should have—"

"Not now," Dayne said, squeezing her arm. "We will . . ." He fought the tears that wanted to flow. This was not the time. "We will mourn him and honor him after we stop these evil men."

"Go," she said.

He ran over to the square, not even sure where to start, what he could do. Then he saw Jerinne get knocked to the ground right in front of him, while Gurond charged off in another dirction.

"That guy's got a punch," Jerinne said, pushing herself to her feet.

"How are you?" he asked.

"Really looking forward to spending the whole damn day in the bath after this," she said. "Let's put these bastards back in the ground, hmm?"

"Let's figure out how," Dayne said. "I'm out of my depth." He spotted Minox and Satrine Rainey huddling behind a pile of rubble with Asti Rynax and another fellow. "Let's go."

He and Jerinne ran over there, knocking down a couple of the beasts that were running after the citizens of this neighborhood. Even still, Dayne wished he didn't have to resort to that. These beasts, they had been human, altered in body by Senek, and twisted in soul by Crenaxin. Perhaps there were still good people in there, people who could be saved.

"This is a horror," he said when he got behind the rubble.

"That's the truth," Asti said. His attention went to another part of the square. "Jared! Get out of there!"

The Thorn landed behind them all, bow out. "Well, this is far more interesting than class would have been."

"This isn't a joke," Jerinne said.

"Levity is his weapon, Miss Fendall," Minox said. "Let him use it."

"We need every weapon," Satrine said. "I called the Riot Call, the emergency call, but I haven't heard any returns yet."

"There's rarely any loyalty in this part of town," Asti said.

"And when that machine broke through, the tremors were probably felt for blocks," the man next to him said. "Any who are nearby probably have their hands full."

"We're on our own," Satrine said.

"Still, we take appropriate action," Minox said. He stood up from behind the rubble and shouted. "Attention, malefactors! Consider yourself bound by law! Accept arrest peacefully or further force will be required to subdue you!"

Three monsters leaped at him, but they were met with savagery from Asti, Satrine, and Jerinne before any of them touched him. Satrine pulled Minox down.

"Was that really necessary?" she asked him.

"It eases my mind about the lethal force we'll need to use," he said.

"I'm fascinated by this use of 'we' here," the other man said. Dayne finally took a good look at him.

"You're the one from the Parliament," Dayne said. "Who disarmed Sholiar's machine."

"It's a whole reunion here," he said. "Let's all get a few ciders after."

Satrine sighed. "We don't have time for this. Verci and Asti. Satrine and Minox. Dayne and Jerinne. And Veranix in the hood."

"Hey!" the Thorn said.

"Glad everyone knows each other," Jerinne said. "So how do we stop this?"

It was too much, screaming and yelling and chaos and blood. Fire and magic and violence. Everyone needed to be saved. Dayne didn't even know where to start. But he knew he couldn't do it alone.

"Together," he said. "Anyone have a plan?"

"Asti," the Thorn—Veranix—said, nocking an arrow. "That's your department." He loosed it at one of the monsters.

"Ask me, take out that mage first," Jerinne said. "Then mop up the rest."

"Mister Sarren said that machine is fueled by steam and magic and I don't even know what else," Satrine said, loading her crossbow.

"We're wasting time," Minox said.

"Hush," Asti said, holding up a finger. "You're all right. That machine and the mage are the key."

"Then let's break that key," the Thorn said, selecting two arrows. "Been saving these all day." He nocked and loosed them; arrows flew out toward Senek and the monstrous machine. Before they struck, Senek turned, and with a wave of his hand, the arrows stopped midair.

"That's not good," Verci said.

Senek smiled. "So very convenient."

The arrows started to glow, bright hot white, and turned toward the seven of them.

"Plan?" Satrine asked.

"Shields high," Dayne told Jerinne, and he stood in front of the others.

"That's not going to hold it," Veranix said. "Minox, grab the rope!"

Minox did as instructed just as the hot-white arrows flew at them all. The Thorn's rope coiled around Dayne and Jerinne, and then around the straps of their shields.

The arrows smashed into the shields, erupting in a ball of fire as bright as the sun.

But the seven of them were surrounded in a nimbus of light, red and blue and green, spreading out from the shields. Nothing touched them.

"Soon as this clears, we move," Asti said. "Verci, you get to that machine and shut it down, sabotage it, whatever you can."

"Fun," Verci said.

Asti handed a sword to Minox. "Constables, you escort him in, and watch his back. Block those bastards from getting any more kids into the machine." He handed the shackles on his hip to Satrine. "Slap these mage irons on our friend if you can."

"My pleasure," Satrine said. Minox said nothing, but a pulse of black energy shone from his onyx hand.

"Thorn, you've got speed and range. Get high, and corral those creatures back to the square. Keep it all here, away from the rest of the neighborhood. Get someone to run for constables. Girl—"

"Jerinne!"

"Get any civilians and children into the church and hold the door."

"I should—" Dayne started.

"You've got one job, friend," Asti said. "Keep that giant busy."

"And you?" Veranix asked.

Asti drew out two knives and grinned. "I'm going to welcome these bastards to my neighborhood."

The fire subsided, and the nimbus shielding them dropped.

"Go!"

Hemmit had lost track of everything in the chaos. When the ground cracked, and the machine rose up, he had gotten separated from everyone else, pinned, hiding behind rubble while the zealots and the beasts tore through Saint Bridget's Square. Terror had paralyzed him, terror and shame for failing to be of any use to anyone.

He was still of no use.

Go, Hemmit thought. *Run for more help. Do something.*

But his legs refused to do anything. His whole body rebelled at the thought of taking any action.

A bright blast of fire filled the square. Hemmit wasn't even sure where it came from, but instinctively looked toward it, covering his eyes from the glare.

The fire faded, and in a shimmering spectrum of light, there they were.

Saints.

Champions.

Dayne Heldrin and Jerinne Fendall, their Tarian uniforms a mess, their shields scorched and seared. But still standing strong, refusing to yield to these villains.

Inspector Minox Welling, sword in one hand, the other glowing with magic.

Inspector Satrine Rainey, in the red and green of the Constabulary, crossbow in hand.

The Rynax brothers. Asti in his patchwork coat and knives at the ready. Verci, leather coat over suspenders and shirtsleeves. Darts in one hand, metal glove on the other.

And the Thorn—Hemmit could barely believe he was real—with his crimson cloak shimmering with magic as he leaped into the air, drawing back his bow.

They all launched into action, moving as one.

Asti Rynax was out in front, charging into a pack of the beasts. He fell upon them like a wolf upon deer, slicing through them with easy, fluid movements of his blades. Like a poet of death, he was perfect. No fear, no hesitation, like he had become a machine himself, one made to stop these creatures.

Satrine Rainey and Minox Welling moved toward the machine, on either side of Verci Rynax. He slipped and dodged his way past the zealots who tried to grab him, firing shots from his gauntlet as he went. The zealots who went for him found themselves facing Minox's sword or Satrine's crossbow. Minox fought with precision and care, as if each opponent was a book he had already read, anticipating their moves before they were even made. Satrine was the opposite, scrapping with each one wildly, impossible for them to predict or match.

The Thorn had landed on a lamppost, scanning the chaos and homing in on targets. He spotted a group of zealots and monsters charging off toward Frost Street. In a flash he was off, bounding after them.

Jerinne went for zealots dragging children to the machine, bashing them with her shield, wrenching the children free. She fought through to a pair of civilians caught between two monsters, pulling them out while knocking the monsters into each other. She pointed each person she rescued toward the church, working her way closer with each person she saved.

Dayne—bless him, that man—he ran straight toward that great giant, the largest beast of them all. He went at him, hands open. Hemmit couldn't hear over the din and madness, but he could see that Dayne was doing what he always did. The thing that made him Dayne.

He was trying to talk to the giant.

The giant threw a massive punch, which Dayne blocked with his shield. The sound rang out through the square like a church bell. The giant punched again and again, but Dayne held his ground and took the blows.

And kept talking. Because he was Dayne.

These saints. These champions. These people fighting so hard for this city, for the people in it.

Hemmit prayed it would be enough.

The church was filled with terrified people. Kaiana was no exception, but she wasn't going to let it show on her face. She made Delmin sit down in one of the pews, as he looked like he was only making himself stay on his feet as a point of pride.

"What's going on out there?" one of the brothers asked. "What can we do?"

"I'm not entirely sure," Kaiana said. "But those . . . people. They want these children. They need to be kept safe."

"They will be," the reverend said, coming up to them. "You all are safe in this house, daughter." He looked to Delmin. "You look decidedly unwell."

"I am," Delmin said, looking back toward the narthex and the doors leading outside to the square. "That power is building to something, I can feel it."

"Something dark and unholy," a young cloistress said, walking down the aisle. "Something so . . . contemptible, so abhorrent the ground itself shudders in its horror."

"Sister," the brother said. "Perhaps we should look after the children, the flock. We should—"

"I am not here to tend to children," she said vacantly. She turned to the reverend, her face a puzzle. "This is really today, isn't it?"

"It is," he said. "We're ready."

The sister's eyes found Kaiana. "You're the one who tends to things. To keep all the . . . you help . . ." She shook her head. "I'm sorry, I'm made of memories I've lived too many times, but I haven't lived yet. I'm just so very grateful to you and can't understand why."

The brother gently took the cloistress by the shoulders. "Maybe these children are hungry and we should—"

That was as far as he got before she swung her arm hard and knocked him down.

"Do not!" she snarled. Then her face went calm again, looking to Kaiana. "Watch. Remember. Listen."

She turned and walked down the aisle to the door.

"Sister Myriem!" the reverend called out. "You're certain?"

"Of nothing," she said, looking back. "But necessity still calls."

Kaiana looked at Delmin, who was rubbing his temples. "It's going further," he said. "The machine, it's magic and science and . . . life. I can feel it all, and she—" He looked down the aisle to Sister Myriem, now in the narthex. "She prayed with Vee yesterday."

"He's going to need her prayers," Kaiana said. "Maybe ours as well."

"Praying is always good," the reverend said. "I will look to the children." He glanced to the brother, still insensate on the floor. "Watch over Brother Mergolliet, please. He . . . he does not understand what today is."

"What is today?" Delmin asked.

"The worst day," the reverend said. "For so many of us."

"This is how I see it," Sender said, lighting his pipe while standing on the walkway outside Grandma's North Seleth flop. Bell had fled Dentonhill and had been crashing at Grandma's with his cousin Sender for the past week, and they knew she would kick them to the street after the holiday. He and Sender didn't push it, so they had been making a habit of slipping outside for a smoke, and whatever it was that shook the whole building was a good excuse to step outside. Bell had been enjoying spending time with family. Sender was good people, even if he insisted on staying out in westtown. "You're on the outs with Fenmere. My crew is almost all in the wind. The time is ripe for us."

"For us to what?" Bell asked.

"I got a few muscle boys who are still loyal to me. Access to a couple warehouses with merch. You must have a few guys. Some knowledge of buyers, of movers?"

"Yeah," Bell said, though he struggled to think of who, exactly.

"Between the two of us, we build something. Maybe not here, definitely not in Dentonhill, but maybe if we go deep westtown, where there's no real bosses?"

"And no real money."

"Maybe. But maybe being the kings of the Old Quarry is better than in the gutters here."

"I don't—" was all Bell managed to say when some blighter tackled him to the ground. Bell didn't even know what was going on, just suddenly had this bastard pinning him to the ground, about to drive a knife in his neck. Bell managed to grab hold of the guy's wrist, keep the knife away. He looked up to Sender, but he was just as busy—two of them holding him against the wall as he struggled to avoid getting stabbed.

Then one of the blighters on Sender went flying. A rope suddenly wrapped around the neck of the other one, and he was yanked off of Sender, followed by the satisfying crack of wood on bone. Two more of those hits came, and the robed blighter on top of Bell slumped over.

A hand grabbed Bell's and pulled him to his feet.

He was face to face with the Thorn. Or his shaded mask of a face. Bell instinctively let go of his hand and stumbled back. This bastard, this kid, he had been the cause of all of Bell's troubles. The arrow in his leg, the loss of his position with Fenmere, the near exile from Dentonhill . . . it all stemmed from the Thorn. Bell's hand balled into a fist, ready to strike him in that smug smirk on his face.

"Get off the street," the Thorn said. "Get in and lock the door."

"How dare—" Bell started.

In a blink, the Thorn drew his bow and fired an arrow that buzzed past Bell. He turned and saw the arrow found its mark in a creature—like a bear and a man put together—that had been charging down the street. Bell couldn't even believe it was real, except there it was, dying a few feet from him.

The Thorn had just saved him. Twice.

"Really, get out of here. It isn't safe." He leaped up onto one of the street lamps, and from there to a second-floor windowsill.

"Thorn, what the blazes is this?" Bell asked.

"The worst thing I've ever seen," the Thorn said from the windowsill. "But I couldn't have them killing my favorite."

"Where's this coming from?" Sender asked.

"Saint Bridget's," the Thorn said. "If you want to make yourself useful, run for the constables." He flung out his rope to an outcropping on the roof across the street. "Saints all know we'll need them." With that, he leaped off and was gone.

"Gran, lock the door 'til we get back," Sender yelled into the flop. He shut the door. "Let's go."

"Go where?" Bell asked. "To get the sticks?"

"I don't know," Sender said. "All I know is that guy has every reason to put arrows in the both of us, and instead he saved us." He gestured to the insensate men in robes, the dead bear-man. "Whatever this is, it scares him, and it's happening where I live. So, let's go."

Bell scowled. "I think the nearest stick house is in Keller. We better get running."

Amaya was surprised how much of a fight Grandmaster Orren had brought. Of course, he had been a Tarian for decades, training the people who trained the people who trained her. But at his age, she did not expect him to be as strong, fast, and nimble as he was. He had been able to cross the stage and keep Amaya from driving her sword through Colonel Altarn's heart.

"Why, sir?" she demanded, pushing her offensive on him. He might have skill on her, but there was no way she couldn't beat him on endurance. If she had all the time, she could hold him back until he tired, and then subdue him.

But she didn't have that kind of time.

She had no idea how powerful a mage Colonel Altarn was, but assumed she was only briefly dazed from the shield blow. She would recover shortly. She would bring her power to bear. Amaya had only moments.

"You wouldn't question me if you knew," he said, parrying her blows with casual ease. "I've done what anyone would do in my place."

"Not Master Denbar," Amaya said, feinting low and then swiping at his right side. Get him to dodge left. Move away from Altarn.

"I wish he had understood," Orren said. "I wish you did."

"I will never," she said. He had left an opening, and Amaya leaped, driving her boot onto Altarn's chest.

That kept her down, but Orren was able to land a swipe that sliced through Amaya's arm.

"We are saving this country!" he shouted.

"From who?" Kemmer shouted. "You all were behind the Patriots. Behind Chief Toscan. Behind Tharek Pell."

"And saints know what else," Amaya said, grinding her heel onto Altarn while holding off Orren's attacks. Altarn grabbed Amaya's foot and twisted, forcing Amaya off her. Amaya stumbled back a few steps, losing any advantage she had pressed on Altarn and the Grandmaster.

But she had stepped next to her shield, lying facedown on the floor.

She stomped on the rim of it, sending it up in the air, and slammed it with the flat of her sword like it was tetchbat. The shield hurtled across the stage, knocking into Altarn just as she got to her feet.

Amaya had only seconds. She dashed to Kemmer, slicing the ropes that bound him.

"Run," she said. "I'll hold the line. Go tell the truth."

He scrambled out of the ropes and ran off the stage. Amaya turned back to Altarn and Orren. What happened to her didn't matter, if Kemmer got out the door.

She ran and dove at the both of them, arms wide. In the same moment, Altarn snapped her fingers, and bolts of red lightning flew across the opera hall. Amaya crashed into her, into Orren, and all three of them went tumbling off the stage into the orchestra pit. They landed with a resounding thud.

Amaya didn't let herself wallow in the pain. She had to get up, get on her feet, put an end to this. She forced her way up, glancing around through dazed hazy vision. Her sword and shield were on the ground. She grabbed them quickly, ready for whatever happened next.

"Too late," Altarn said from the floor.

Amaya glanced back. There in the aisle, the scorched body of Kemmer.

328 Marshall Ryan Maresca

Grandmaster Orren moved in a flash, and Amaya didn't react fast enough to stop him from slicing her side. She knocked his blade aside with her own, knocking him back with her shield. Altarn blasted more red lightning, which struck and danced on Amaya's shield.

Kemmer was dead. She was bleeding. Altarn was getting her wind back.

There was no winning this fight. If she died here, Altarn's lies would become the truth.

There was a trapdoor to her right, for the musicians to slip out below the stage unseen. Amaya dashed for it before either Orren or Altarn could take another shot at it. She slammed it shut and wedged her sword and shield into it to barricade it.

Then, hand to her bleeding side, she ran. On instinct, she pulled off her mail shirt and tunic, leaving them on the ground as she went. Around the corner, down another hallway, through a costume wardrobe. She grabbed a coat and threw it on as she stumbled her way around another corner. Out the door. Into the sunlight. Down an alley.

She couldn't go to the chapterhouse. There was no chance it was safe. She was too hurt to get too far, and she had to believe that Altarn was right behind. She had to believe the woman had eyes everywhere.

She had to hide. Get help from someone she could trust.

Only one place to go.

CHAPTER 22

THE SPINNING RINGS WERE TOO much, too fast, making getting close to the controls of the machine impossible. Verci wished that was his only problem. The zealots were fiercely guarding the only path to the machine that didn't involve being torn up by the rings, as that was the route they were using to bring the children they caught into the cages.

And they were.

Verci watched in horror as each child they threw into the cages became engulfed in the same energy as the rest of the machine, and rapidly aged to adolescence, to adulthood, to elderly senescence, and then to dust.

"I do admire a futile fight," the mage said. "There's something invigorating about watching doomed people try." He hurled balls of flame at Verci, but Minox was there, using his odd black hand like a shield.

"Consider yourself bound by law," Minox said to the mage. "I will enumerate your crimes fully."

"That'll really stop him," Verci said.

"What've you got, deputy?" Satrine asked. She was doing a damned fine job holding off the zealots who were trying to grab her, using their position near the spinning rings to keep them from being swarmed.

Verci looked at the rest of the machine. What surprised him was, despite the fact that it was clearly more about magic than technology, the whole thing made a kind of twisted sense to him. "Well, those nine ugly statues are probably directing the magical energy somehow. Don't know how that works, but I do know how to break things."

He cocked the spring load on his gauntlet and dialed in one of the boom powder shots. Aiming at the base of the machine, he launched one, and then quickly repeated a second.

The explosion knocked him back, tumbling into Minox and Satrine. The zealots all fell over, as did the mage. Minox scrambled to his feet and pulled up Satrine, but their opponents were back up just as quickly. From the ground, Verci drew and threw darts at as many zealots as he could, giving Satrine an opportunity to reload.

The smoke cleared away from the machine.

Not even a scratch on the bronze.

All the while, the madman up on the platform cackled and howled.

"I wish to point out that he has been up there for some time," Minox said, shielding them with magic on one side while defending with his sword on the other. "I can only presume the longer exposure to the magics of the platform will generate an abnormally large effect."

"Great," Verci said. "Well, I can't get closer with the rings spinning, and the source of that energy is the magic. I don't think we can do anything until we take that mage out of the equation."

"Then I will gladly remove him," Minox said. "Stay vigilant and take your moment."

"My moment?" Verci asked.

Minox was already stalking toward the mage.

"More kids," Satrine said, pointing to the three beasts who were dragging children toward the machine. More of the monsters were charging toward the church.

"The kids are the fuel," Verci said. "If we can't turn off the machine, let's stop them from throwing more logs on the fire."

"The church?" she asked.

"Asti's on it," Verci said. He saw Asti moving like a whirlwind of knives through the zealots and the monsters. Laughing. For once, he was letting himself let go completely, and it was terrible and glorious.

Asti was, for once, at peace. His body was a fury, acting with pure instinct and skill as he cut his way through the mob of villains who had dared to come here—come to his neighborhood, his church—and unleash these horrors upon those he loved. He had no mercy for any of them as he carved a path of blood. Knowing what he needed to do brought clarity.

The beast was quiet. Right now, they both wanted the same things. Justice. Vengeance. Death.

Liora was quiet. The part of his mind that served the Brotherhood was quiet. Drummed out for the moment by his rage, by his purity of purpose.

He heard a scream. A scream he knew.

Driving his knife into the throat of the zealot leaping at him, he looked to see another group of zealots cornering a handful of people. Asti's people. Missus Hoskins and her granddaughter. Almer Cort and Doc Gelson. Jared Scall, trying to hold the zealots off with that old army mace he always carried. And Kimber.

All the saints would cry and the sinners laugh over what Asti would do if they hurt Kimber.

Asti tore his way to them, not caring what he had to

fight through to reach them. One of the beasts jumped at him, all teeth and claws. Asti didn't even pause. One knife in its belly, another in its heart, he pushed it down to the ground. He barely even noticed it had gotten a piece of his arm. That didn't matter.

Five more steps, he was on the zealots threatening his friends and neighbors. With quick swipes of his knives—heart, neck, eye, kidney—he dispatched the zealots.

Kimber dove in on him, grabbing him in a warm embrace. No fear of him, of the slaughter he was capable of, of the blood he was covered with. Nothing but gratitude and grace.

"Are you hurt?" he asked.

"Are you?" she countered. "You're bleeding."

"Nothing that matters," he said. He looked to Almer and the others. "You need to get out of here."

"Not sure where," Gelson said.

"Get in the church," Asti said, pointing the way. "See the girl with the shield? Go to her." Missus Hoskins and her granddaughter didn't hesitate, and Almer pulled Gelson along with an understanding nod.

"And you?" Kimber asked.

"I'm going to end this," he said. "I have to."

She nodded.

"I can help," Jared said, holding his mace. Asti wanted to believe that, would have welcomed it. But despite Jared's strong arms, his hands quavered. His eyes weren't focusing. He was already drunk. Or still from the night before.

"Help in there," Asti said. "Stay with Kimber. If something goes wrong—"

Jared grunted in assent. Kimber squeezed Asti's arm one more time, and then the two of them ran to Jerinne.

Asti couldn't watch them go in. Another group of zealots had smashed down the doors of a tenement, and were dragging people out into the street.

Not today.

Not in his neighborhood.

Knives out, Asti dove in.

Minox needed contact. As crude as it was, he had a need to engage in pure physical altercation with Ithaniel Senek, to take down this twisted architect of horror. He charged at the man, balling magic into his fist and knocking a powerful blow against his skull.

Senek smiled as the magic burst off Minox's hand, and the black and white energy pooled around him, swirling into an impossible blade that formed around Senek's hand. He brought the blade—looking like lightning and shattered fire—down on Minox. Minox blocked with the sword he was carrying, holding it with both hands. He pushed the magic into his own blade, holding it together, holding off Senek's attack.

"I told you," Minox said. "You would be thwarted. Your plans would be denied."

"I see nothing being denied, Inspector," Senek said. "You fools are providing a brief moment of entertainment until our ascension is complete. We will be transformed. We will be exalted."

Minox kept at him, with sword and magic, but to no avail. Every blow Minox struck was blocked, and every bit of magic he threw at Senek, the man just took and reshaped to his own end.

Senek knew his craft, on every level. He was a master mage. Minox was an untrained fool. He would not defeat him with magic. Not directly.

But maybe he didn't need to defeat the man. Maybe he just needed to distract him long enough for Inspector Rainey and Mister Rynax to disable the machine.

He would need to be controlled. He would need to contain his magic.

Pulling in with all his will, he drew down the magic in his hand. Every ounce. Make it like a dead piece of stone. Without the magic, he couldn't move his hand or his fingers.

Which is why he had left it as a fist.

He was a Welling. His family's blood had served the streets of the city, served the Constabulary with loyalty. He would not fail.

He pushed in, remembering his training as a cadet. Remembering the wrestling spars with Oren and his cousins as children. Remembering the first arrest he made as a horsepatrol, the fight that alley rat had made.

He pushed in, knocking Senek's magical blade out of his way with his sword, and hammered his dead fist at the man. His hand that felt nothing. He slammed it again and again on the man, unleashing brutal punishment on him.

Senek brought the blade on Minox, driving it into his shoulder. It did not cut him, but pierced him with fire that ran through his body, holding him frozen.

Minox screamed, but he would bear the pain.

He had to bear it.

He brought his hand down on Senek once more, and this time he drew magic into it.

All of it.

Senek screamed as Minox pulled every bit of energy he could, dissolving the magic blade.

"No!" Senek screamed. He grabbed Minox's hand. "You don't deserve this!"

He tried to draw and take control of the hand, but Minox pushed back.

Too hard. No control.

The energy burst forth, throwing Minox away from Senek and knocking them both on the ground.

"More! More!" Crenaxin shouted from the platform. "The fuel is in the false church! Tear it down! Take them all! Bring them to me!"

All the beasts howled, and then charged at the church,

where Jerinne Fendall stood alone on the steps, ushering the last civilians through the door.

The beasts all went right to her.

Dayne had never been hit so hard as he was by Gurond. Even though he blocked every blow with the shield, each punch still knocked Dayne back.

"Pendall!" Dayne urged. "You don't have to be a part of this."

"Why do you call me that?" Gurond said, continuing to hammer on Dayne. Dayne didn't know how long he could stand it, how long before the shield would be dented into nothing, but he would hold. Every moment Gurond was focused on him, he wasn't hurting anyone else. Keep his attention while the others saved the children, stopped the machine.

"It's your name," Dayne said between blows. "You are Pendall Gurond. Son of Lord Gurond of Itasiana. Born to a noble house."

"Noble?" Gurond shouted. "Gurond is not noble!" He slammed both fists on Dayne, knocking him to his knees. "Our name is nothing now. Nothing!"

Gurond raised up his arms wide, showing his great full height, his sinewy, shiny body. He laughed, which sounded bizarre with his gruff voice and over-toothed mouth.

"Make it noble again," Dayne said. "You still can."

"I am only this now," Gurond said.

"You are still a man," Dayne implored. "No matter what was done to you, that remains true. You are a man that can reason. You can choose."

Gurond grabbed Dayne's shield and wrenched it from his arm. "I choose the Brotherhood."

"Even after—"

Gurond's massive fist pounded into Dayne's face, knocking him to the cobblestone.

"I was near dead," Gurond said. "I remember it all now. The Thorn nearly killed me. Senek saved me. Made me stronger. Better."

Dayne pushed himself up, spitting out blood. "You aren't better. Better is standing up for something."

Another punch knocked him down. "You aren't standing."

"I will keep getting up," Dayne said. "And when I can't, someone else will."

"No," Gurond said, hammering another punch onto Dayne. "You will all stay down."

"This city . . ." Dayne said, forcing his arms to push himself to his knees. "Is full of people who will stand up to you."

"I only see the cowering, the hiding," Gurond said. "The fear."

"We . . . will . . ."

Gurond smashed him down to the ground again. "You have no 'we.' Just you, lonely Tarian." Gurond grabbed Dayne by the front of his uniform and raised him high in the air. "And now you will die alone."

He hurled Dayne down, to smash him on the cobblestone. But Dayne didn't hit the ground, instead he was cradled and protected, then pulled out of the way before Gurond's massive fists smashed onto him.

Pulled away and deposited on his feet by a rope.

"Hey, Gurond," the Thorn said, landing next to Dayne, staff in hand. "Thought we should have one more dance before the party ended."

"Get the doors shut!"

Jerinne slammed into one beast with her shield, knocking it out of the church doorway. She pushed with her shield, holding it against the wall, while the last two children ran inside.

The creature swiped at her, its claws raking into her

side. She cried out, stumbling away from it, and it dashed into the church. She pressed one hand onto the wound, hot blood seeping through her fingers. Saints, it was deep. It didn't matter. Those children—all the civilians in the church—would be slaughtered by that thing. And she would stand between them and harm, no matter the cost.

Step by agonizing step, she pushed her way into the narthex. The beast howled and was about to grab one of the children.

"Not today!"

A grizzled old man, bald with a shaggy beard, charged up on the creature, battering it with an army mace. He slammed it again and again, while it clawed at his arms. Jerinne raised up her sword and drove it into the beast as hard as she could, just as it closed its massive maw on the old man's head. Both the creature and the old man fell over, dead.

Jerinne looked back outside. At least five more creatures were galloping up the church steps. With the last bit of strength she had, she pushed the massive church door shut. She threw down the wooden bar to latch it just as the beasts slammed into it, making it shudder at the hinges.

"You're hurt."

A Cloistress of the Blue was there, taking Jerinne's arm, leading her away from the door, as the beasts howled and pounded on it.

"Barely a scratch," Jerinne lied. She forced herself to stay on her feet, but dropped her shield. "That door isn't going to hold. Get inside and shut the door to the narthex. I'll hold it here."

"You won't survive," the cloistress said.

"It doesn't matter," Jerinne said. "I'll stand between you and them."

"You won't survive," the cloistress said again. She pulled Jerinne over to the bell tower entrance. "But you have to survive. You aren't supposed to be here, this isn't your place."

"My place—ow!" The cloistress had torn open Jerinne's tunic to look at the wound.

"It's deep. You need to—you need—" The cloistress took a few steps away, looking around the narthex. "Why are you even here, this isn't . . . you were supposed to be at the chapterhouse . . . no . . . at the opera house . . . but if you didn't go there, if . . . if . . . if . . ." She started pounding on her own head.

Jerinne didn't have time for this nonsense. The cloistress needed to get out of here. She tried to reach out to her, but her strength faltered. She could barely even take a step.

"Close the door between here and the nave," Jerinne said as her feet gave out. She slumped to the floor. "You all have to stay safe."

The cloistress turned around, and looked at the people in the nave. "Do as she says. Shut it, barricade it, and hide yourselves. Now!"

Whoever she gave those orders to obeyed. Jerinne couldn't quite see, everything was going hazy, and her head was pounding.

No, the pounding was on the door. Each slam knocked the hinges a little looser.

But the doors to the chapel were shut, and the people in there were safe.

Except the cloistress was still there, in the narthex.

"What are you doing?" Jerinne asked.

"I don't even know," the cloistress said, kneeling next to the dead old man. "I've remembered today so many times, but this isn't how it ever went. I'm still not sure this is really now. You shouldn't be here."

"You shouldn't," Jerinne said. Where could she hide this girl, protect her? Was the bell tower safe?

"I've remembered today so many times, as the person I am tomorrow. And you're not supposed to be . . . you are supposed to be with her . . . but it's today, and you're here. Why . . . why do I remember all the wrong todays?"

She picked up his mace, looking at it with confusion. "I know this isn't mine, not the one that I . . . I know this isn't who I am, not today. But I'm here, today, with this in my hand. Even if it isn't mine, I need to take it up."

Jerinne tried to get back on her feet, slumping against the wall in the base of the bell tower to stay upright. "Sister, you have to get out of here."

The cloistress let the mace fall and came back into the bell tower. "I don't have much time. Now if you're the one in the narthex, you will die. And if you die today, no one—" Her eyes glassed over for a moment, as she looked up to the top of the bell tower. "No one will be there to save her."

The main doors were splintering. Those things would be in here any moment.

"I have to—"

The sister cupped her hand around the back of Jerinne's head. "You have to live, Jerinne." The other hand went to the wound. "You have to live."

Suddenly the wound burned, scorching hot, and Jerinne couldn't hold back her scream.

"Listen to me," the cloistress said, her words intense, her face full of fear. "I have to fix this. We weren't supposed to meet until Erescan, Jerinne. I thought if I changed the path of today, I could end it all here. But I think I got it all wrong, if you're here now. I'm so sorry. You have to live."

Jerinne could barely hear, barely think straight, as the fire of the cloistress's touch seared through her body.

"You have to live," the sister said again in a whisper. She pushed Jerinne to the ground and went back into the narthex. "And I have to become who I was tomorrow."

The doors cracked open. Another blow and they would fly apart.

Jerinne tried to get to her feet, but she had no strength to do so. She barely could breathe through the burning pain in her side. She was on fire.

The sister picked up Jerinne's shield and the old man's mace, and looked back to Jerinne. Her expression changed. No fear on her face.

"This is for tomorrow."

With a sudden, assured motion, the sister spun and knocked the door to the bell tower closed.

In the same moment, the front doors flew open, and at least six of those horrible monstrosities poured in. The last thing Jerinne saw before the door slammed shut was the cloistress turning toward them, shield high, mace at the ready.

Then the pain exploded through Jerinne, burning through her whole body, knocking all sense out of her as her world went dark.

CHAPTER 23

"THORN," GUROND SAID, THE WORD rolling through his throat. "You came to die as well."

"Not really the plan," the Thorn said.

Dayne did his best to stay on his feet, but the pummeling he had taken from Gurond made that almost impossible.

"You can't take him," Dayne said. "He's too—"

"I probably can't," Thorn said. He flashed a quick smile. "But five crowns says *we* can."

Gurond charged at them, and the Thorn jumped out of the way, staying out of the reach of Gurond's massive fists. He bounced and flipped, always too quick to be touched. He went over the man, planting his staff in Gurond's face, then landed far behind him. Gurond spun around, enraged. It was like watching a rabbit fight a bull, though Dayne feared one wrong step would get the rabbit gored.

A bull.

"Hey, Thorn," Dayne called. "You ever been to Lacanja?"

"Yeah," the Thorn called back as he adroitly dodged the massive fists. "Great fish crackle there. And the oysters! Though when we finish this up, there's this Fuergan place—"

"I was thinking more the Blood Shows."

"Shut it!" Gurond shouted. "I'm going to give you a blood show!"

The Thorn dodged another blow and nodded. "I got you," he said, and tossed his staff to Dayne. Then he ducked another punch and slipped under Gurond's legs. With a roll he ran over to Dayne. "I figure I'm the Zany and you're the Burly."

"Makes sense," Dayne said. He had only gone to the Blood Show once when he was in Lacanja—Master Denbar insisted he take in the local culture—and he couldn't stand to watch such casual cruelty to an animal in the name of entertainment. But he remembered it well enough.

"Hey, Gurond, hey, hey, Gurond," the Thorn said, waving his hands and making magical sparkles. "Weren't you always going off on how strong you are?"

"I am the strongest!" Gurond shouted, charging at him. The Thorn blasted him in the face with the sparkles as he leaped away from the charge. At the same moment, Dayne burst forward, sweeping low with the staff and knocking Gurond off balance. The great giant went flying and landed on his face.

"Look where that got you," the Thorn said when he landed. "Turned into a freak!"

"I will tear you both apart!" Gurond shouted, turning to Dayne as he got up.

"And what about your friends?" Thorn called quickly. "Samael and Coleman? You know what happened to them?"

Gurond turned his attention to the Thorn again.

"You know what I did to them?" the Thorn taunted. Gurond howled and charged at him. The Thorn dodged him again, jumping high, slamming a kick onto Gurond's head before landing next to Dayne.

"We need to end this," he said. "Beasts are breaching the church, the constables are losing at the machine. We can't play with him forever."

"We need to subdue him," Dayne said. Even now, he loathed the idea of killing Gurond.

The Thorn looked up. "I got an idea for that. Keep him busy." He drew out an arrow—the last one in his quiver—and aimed high before firing.

Gurond was turning back to them. "When I catch you—"

"You'll fail," Dayne said, holding himself as tall as he could, despite every part of his body hurting. "You'll always fail."

Gurond didn't run this time, instead walking at a deliberate pace toward Dayne. The other fights in the square echoed and thundered around them, but Gurond's rage had turned calm and cold. "When I catch you," he continued, "I will tear the two of you limb from limb and wear your arms as a necklace."

"You will fail," Dayne said, tightening his grip on the staff. He glanced at the Thorn, whose focus was still up high, hands raised. "Because there will always be another Tarian, another constable, another friend, another neighbor. Another champion to fight you."

"None of them can stop me," Gurond said. "None of you can stop me."

"Please," the Thorn said through gritted teeth. "I've stopped you before."

"I remember," Gurond said. "I remember you most of all."

"And yet, once again," Thorn said, his voice rising with effort and strain. "You forgot I'm a goddamn mage!"

The Thorn pulled his hands down hard, and with a deafening *clang*, the grand church bell from the tower of Saint Bridget's landed over Gurond.

The Thorn swooned, almost cracking his head on the cobblestone before Dayne caught him.

"That was a lot," the Thorn said woozily. His facade over his face had faded, showing he had taken a few solid hits. Blood trickled from his nose, an ugly bruise on his cheek. Even still, he managed a weak smile on his very young face.

"Well done," Dayne said. From under the bell, Gurond bellowed and pounded fruitlessly. "Took him alive."

"I mean, fine," Veranix said as Dayne helped him back on his feet. "Wasn't fully the plan or anything, but if it makes you happy."

"It should hold him while we take care of the rest," Dayne said. "What do you have left in you?"

Veranix took a deep breath. "Just give me a moment."

Dayne's shield came flying toward them, which Dayne didn't realize until it nearly hit them. He reached out and caught it, noting where it was coming from.

"What are you standing around for?" Asti Rynax yelled. "Get those bastards off of Verci and the constables."

Dayne handed Veranix his staff. "Ready for the next?"

"Not even remotely," Veranix said as he took it. "But bring it."

Satrine was out of bolts, but there seemed to be no end to zealots and monsters. After cracking one of them over the head with the crossbow—saints, what a beauty that thing was—she kept at it with her handstick and the irons Asti Rynax had given her. She just hammered anyone in front of her with the chain of it.

Minox was on the ground. Two zealots were going for him.

"We're losing this," she told Verci. "Clear me a path to Minox, get over to your brother, regroup."

"But the machine," he said.

"Can't do much if we die. Go!"

He shot from his gauntlet, laying down smoke. Satrine dashed to Minox, ready with her handstick. She couldn't see through the smoke, but she had a good sense of where she was, where Minox was, and where those two zealots were going. She relied on her memory, on her ears, as she slammed her handstick into someone's chest. She brought it down hard on them, knocking them to the ground, and then did the same to whoever was right next to them.

"Minox!" she called.

"Here, Inspector Rainey," he said. She reached down and grabbed him, pulling him up and out of the cover of smoke.

"Are you all right?"

"I do not think I can defeat Senek," he said. "He is too adept in his magic. I do not have enough control."

"Then don't have any," she said. "You have the power. Remember what Olivant told you."

"I never forget that," he said. "I cannot risk . . ."

"You have to lose control, Minox. Let it all go, and we'll be here to bring you back." She grabbed him by the shoulders. It would make him uncomfortable, but she needed him uncomfortable right now. "Use your anger."

"I don't know if that's enough."

Satrine knew what to say to make it enough. "You've been plagued by one unresolved question for the past couple weeks. Senek knows the answer."

His eyes flashed black, looking just like his hand for a moment. He turned and looked to Senek, who was again focused on the machine, and his voice dropped to a growl.

"I should go ask him."

Black energy pulsed and seeped out of Minox as he stalked over toward the hairy, wiry man. Two more zealots jumped on him, but Minox brushed them off with a wave of his dark, magicked hand. They both went flying.

"Senek!" Minox shouted as he closed the distance. He wound back his left arm and delivered a punch that sent waves across the square, all while shouting his question.

"Where is my sister?"

He kept pummeling, punctuating each blow with a word. "Where! Is! My! Sister!"

Energy of every color, even impossible ones that Satrine could never describe, swirled around Senek as he blasted back at Minox, but nothing deterred him. The magical energies rose and bloomed, surrounding the both of them, the machine, filling the square.

The Thorn stumbled over Satrine, Dayne right behind him. "I've never seen anything like that! There's no way Minox can control that!"

"He's not," she said. She pointed to the rope on his belt. "I was hoping you could anchor him back down."

"Maybe," he said. "But—"

"Just be ready," she said, taking one end of the rope, quickly wrapping it around her waist. She held the shackles ahead of her and went toward Minox and Senek. The magic slammed at her, but went around the shackles like it was a rock in the river.

She just had to push upstream.

Seven steps. Every one of them impossible. It didn't matter. She had to push through, save Minox. Stop these bastards. Make this city safe for her daughters, for Loren, for everyone.

Another step. She was right next to Minox and Senek, both of them with hands around each other's necks. Only one thing to do to save her partner.

She grabbed Senek's arm, even though it was like grabbing a snake made of fire. She held in the scream, held in the pain. She just needed another second.

She brought up her other arm and clapped the irons on Senek's wrist.

Now it was his turn to scream.

She pulled him off Minox and drove him to the

ground. Knee on his back, she latched the other half of the irons on his other wrist.

Still the tempest of magic did not cease. Minox was the center of the storm, spiraling around him.

"WHERE?" he shouted. "TELL ME!"

She unwrapped the rope from her belt, and prayed to Saint Deshar that Veranix Calbert was up to the task. Taking a deep breath, she lashed it around his hand.

The storm of magic exploded to the sky, and it was all Satrine could do to stay on top of Senek, to grab hold of Minox's body, keep him anchored.

Then the storm came rushing down, all pulling into Minox's hand, sinking into it like water down a channel.

And then it was all gone.

Saint Bridget's Square was near silent for a moment, save for Minox's heavy breaths. She glanced over to the Thorn, holding the other end of the rope, being held up by the Rynax brothers and Dayne. All of them looked like Satrine felt. Impossibly spent.

Then the silence was broken by a beautiful sound. Constabulary whistles cutting through the square. Emergency calls. She looked and saw dozens upon dozens of Constabulary regulars run up, grabbing zealots, tackling the beasts to the ground.

"Let's hear it for the Green and Red," she said to Minox weakly.

"Indeed," he said.

"Hey," Veranix called. "I don't know about you, but I am famished. There's this great Fuergan place—"

"Wait," Minox said. Then a look of horror crossed his face, and he looked up to the machine.

The rings were still spinning. It was still glowing. And Crenaxin still stood on top, pulsing and surging with energies.

"**Come my children!**" he shouted in words that sliced across her bones. "**Come to me and feed the fervent fire! COME!**"

Several of the constables stopped struggling with zealots. They all let go of each other and charged at the machine, diving at the cages. They clamored to get inside the cages, and as soon as they did, aged into dust with a look of rapture on their faces.

And to her horror, Satrine almost—*almost*—wanted to join them.

Asti and Verci ran over and pulled Satrine and Minox back to the rest of them.

"What is this?" Dayne asked.

On the platform, Crenaxin's whole body began to shift and change. It grew to ten feet, twelve feet, fifteen feet tall. His skin became scaly and blackish-green. His face stretched and his mouth became full of teeth, as great wings burst forth from his back.

"Come my vessels! We shall ascend! The Nine will rise! The world will burn for them!"

Several of the beasts stood up, surrounding the machine as the magical energies flooded into them. Eight of them, one in front of each statue. Their bodies began to roil and shift as more of the zealots and constables and other civilians all fought each other for the privilege of throwing themselves in the cages.

"Well," Veranix said. "I guess we have to wait on the Fuergan place."

CHAPTER 24

DAYNE COULD NOT COMPREHEND WHAT Crenaxin had become—scaled, winged, fanged, and the size of a house. In no way human anymore. And the beasts on the ground, linked to each other and the statues with beams of light, were starting to change as well.

"So that's the High Dragon," Asti said.

"Aladha va calix," Minox said. He glanced over to Veranix.

"Thought the same thing," Veranix said. "I guess this is on me to finish."

Minox chuckled darkly. "I didn't mean to imply that."

Dayne raised an eyebrow at them, but he didn't have time to think about what they were talking about. The constables, the zealots, other civilians—they all were trying to get in the machine, sacrifice themselves to it. Crenaxin's voice had driven them to it. The same sort of power that Ret Issendel had used at the Constabulary House, making everyone stop. But here they obeyed him to their death.

"Why not us?" Dayne asked. "Why are the six of us immune to his power?"

"The three of us already were," Asti said. "And maybe you've beaten it."

"Doesn't explain your brother and Inspector Rainey," Dayne said. "Everyone else in the square is trying to kill themselves."

"Maybe that's your answer," Satrine said, looking over to the church.

A cloistress—no, the same young woman from Saint Limarre's the other evening—stood on the church steps, holding up a mace and a shield. Jerinne's shield. Why did she have Jerinne's shield? And she was screaming something, words Dayne couldn't make out.

"Her?" Veranix, Asti, and Verci asked in unison.

"Sister Myriem," Satrine said. "I think she . . ."

"No!" Minox yelled, running over to the crowd of constables climbing into the machine.

"That's his brother," Satrine said. "We need to stop them all before—"

Crenaxin spread his wings and leaped off the platform, landing on the cobblestone with a resounding crash. Then he stalked toward the church.

"Keep them out of the machines," Dayne told Satrine and the Rynaxes. "Thorn—"

"I know, I know," he said. "I just need—there." He dashed off to one of the shop stands that had been knocked over in the carnage.

Dayne didn't have time to wait, running over to the church steps. Crenaxin was almost on top of the girl, who, to her credit, didn't budge from her position. Dayne closed the distance as fast as his legs would take him.

"I abjure you!" she shouted. "I abjure you and your unholy doctrine! By Saint Alexis, I abjure you! By Saint Justin! By Saint Benton! By Saint Jesslyn! By Saint Deshar! By Saint Jontlen! By Saint Terrence! **You shall be abjured!**"

Crenaxin roared and reared back, as if her words caused him pain. Maybe they did. Then Crenaxin swiped at her with his great clawed hand, in as much as it was still a hand. It scraped across the shield, tearing gashes in the metal. Jerinne's shield. Where was she? Had she been killed? Did this girl pick up her shield when she fell?

Myriem stood her ground.

Then Crenaxin opened his mouth, and a blast of fire poured out of that giant maw.

Dayne could abide no more. He drew his sword and drove it into Crenaxin's side.

It just scraped against his scaled body, but it got his attention. He turned his colossal head toward Dayne.

"Ever the protector," Crenaxin said, his voice now a deep rumble. "You could have been such a worthy vessel."

"Never," Dayne swore. "I will stand to my last breath against you."

"Of course you will."

Dayne risked a glance to the church steps. Sister Myriem, despite the scorch marks on the shield, was unharmed. Good.

But now Dayne needed to fight. For Jerinne. For Maresh. For the children lost to this lunatic. For the Tarian Order.

For Maradaine.

With shield on arm, with sword in hand. He would defeat this Dragon or die in the effort.

A handful of goxies from the knocked-over stand had been enough to keep Veranix from passing out, but he had no idea how he was going to stop this thing. And yet, he knew—deep in his soul—he knew, somehow, it was on him. With three words in Sechiall, Minox had reminded him.

Aladha va calix. The cursed beast from the old Kellirac story Veranix's mother would tell him so many nights. *Dark as the night, with an impenetrable hide, sharpest claws and wings of leather. The Dragon of Moshkar.*

Aladha va calix terrorized village after village. The warriors of Moshkar fell one after another to his might, until he was stopped by the mythical figure of Kellirac legend. The Kellirac demigod, the trickster who bound Aladha va calix. Pulled him to his cave and trapped him there.

Veranix.

This was the real story, Mother had said. The Druth church had corrupted the stories, changed them around to the Testament of Saint Veran, which bore little resemblance to the trickster of legend.

In the story, the warriors had fallen, one after another. Dayne was fighting the thing, but he couldn't last long against it. And if the other eight beasts finished their transformation, there would be nine of them. Worthy vessels of the Nine. An ascension. The constables and the Rynaxes were doing everything they could to stop that, or at least stop the other people from throwing themselves in the machine. They couldn't do that forever.

All of this was above his head. He wasn't going to solve this with arrows and banter. He needed a clear head. He needed Delmin.

Delmin was in the church.

Veranix ran over to the steps. The cloistress was still there, screaming a prayer with her mace held aloft.

"Miss," he said as he approached. "You've got to get out of here, I—"

She stopped and looked at him, her harsh features suddenly breaking into a wide smile, tears in her eyes. She let the mace fall to the ground.

"Veranix!" she said with warmth and joy. "I—I've missed you *so* much."

"You've what? How—"

She touched his face gently. "I know you're scared. I know you think you don't have the answers. But you do. You know exactly what you need to do. Your mother told you the story."

All the fear and doubt in his heart melted away.

She stumbled and stepped away, picking up the mace, but looking confused as she did. "I—I don't know why I said . . . I don't—"

"It's all right, Sister," he said. "I think I understand."

She looked at him again, the kindness all gone from her face. Instead it was righteous fury. "It must be abjured. They cannot ascend."

"They won't," Veranix said. She was right, he knew. It was all clear now.

Dayne was suddenly knocked through the air at them. Veranix whipped out his rope and caught him before he crashed into the side of the church, putting him down on the ground.

"Thorn," Dayne said, panting. "We need . . . we need . . ."

"Easy, big guy," Veranix said. Crenaxin was turning his massive dragon body toward them. "Get over to the machine. Help get Minox and Verci in there. Verci will have to shut it down, but before he does, Minox will have to connect himself to it again."

The sister stepped forward as Crenaxin charged at them, raising the shield and mace high as she shouted scripture.

The Testament of Saint Veran.

Dayne struggled to get on his feet. "But what are you—"

"Just tell Minox to remember what we did with Enzin Hence," Veranix said. "He's going to do that again."

"And you?" Dayne asked.

Crenaxin the Dragon opened his horrible mouth and released a plume of flame. Veranix raised his hand and let the *numina* pour out of him, shaping it into ice and snow. It met the dragon's flame over the sister's head, canceling it in the air.

"I'm going to live up to my name," Veranix said. "Go." Dayne ran to the machine.

Sister Myriem shouted, "And so, vile one, you shall **begone!**"

She slammed the mace into the ground, and it shattered, releasing a blast of pure power that knocked Crenaxin back, high in the air. She flew back to the church doors at the same time. Veranix didn't have any chance to check if she was all right. He had to act.

Veranix filled his legs with *numina* and jumped high, whipping out the rope as he went. Drawing everything he could through the rope, the cloak, his body, he landed on the dragon's back while the rope coiled around the beast's neck.

It was time to drag this bastard back to his cave.

Asti was trying very hard not to kill these constables, who were not extending him the same courtesy. They were all desperate to get inside the machine, to let themselves be drawn in and be drained of life to feed the horrible power. He would have been happy to let the zealots find their death in the machine, if he wasn't certain that the end result would be horrible. He kept his eye on the creatures that were being further altered, and if they completed their transformations . . .

This neighborhood would be the first to suffer, but not the last.

He had already tried killing them, but they were surrounded by a nimbus of magic and power that he couldn't penetrate with a knife.

"Eyes up, agent," Satrine said, pulling another constable away from the machine. She had grabbed a set of irons off the constable and locked him up with it, pushing him into one of the others. "You're drifting off mission."

She talked like Intelligence. "Authorization?"

"Saints, I've been dark for fifteen years," she said,

knocking another constable in the teeth. She had pushed herself closer to Asti, so the two of them were nearly shoulder to shoulder, blocking the way into the cages. Minox was in the back of the crowd, wrestling with one constable in particular, while Verci was using his roof-lines to tie up others, while sticking more to the ground with his paste shots. He wasn't sure how long he and Satrine could hold this line, keep these folks out who were far too eager to die.

"Same," he said. "A little over a year."

She nodded, while using a pair of handsticks to pro-tect herself from the constables and knocking them back. "We need to shut this down."

"Don't disagree. At least get rid of the other beasts that are changing."

"Well, they are not the True Vessels," she said. She then looked at him, like she was surprised by what she said.

No more surprised than Asti was by what he said next. "They do not have the Blood."

"They are not the Infused," Satrine said.

"And thus the Power will be rejected," he said, still not sure where in his head the words were coming from. It was like they didn't exist until she spoke, and then it was like he had always known them.

"It can be taken back," she said. "For the Unworthy shall never hold on to it."

"The Nine must be Contained," he said in unison with her.

"How?" she asked. Then she scowled. "Grieson."

"That bastard," Asti said. She knew his old handler in Intelligence, and whatever just happened must have somehow been his doing. But he also understood. "Whatever this is, it isn't going to hold, but we have to reverse it."

"How?" she asked.

Dayne suddenly barreled in, shield first, knocking

356 Marshall Ryan Maresca

over the crowd of constables like they were eight pins. "We need to shut the machine down."

"You think?" Satrine asked, her annoyance clear. "How?"

Dayne glanced up to the sky. Asti followed his gaze to the dragon creature flapping its wings while the Thorn rode on its back like it was an unbroken horse. "Sweet Saint Benton," Asti muttered.

"Thorn had something. He said Verci should shut it down once Minox connects with it again."

"Shut it down how?" Asti asked.

"The people in the cages are like wood in a firebox!" Verci shouted as he struggled to bind a few constables and zealots together. "Keep them out long enough, no fire, no steam, no power."

"We'll keep them out," Asti said. "You all do what you can. Minox!"

Minox Welling wasn't listening. His full attention was on keeping one possessed constable from killing him.

"Damn you, Oren!" Minox swore. His brother's hands were wrapped around his neck, squeezing with all intent to kill him. "I expected you to be stronger-willed than this."

"The Nine require the fire to be fueled!" Oren said.

There was something of fascinating curiosity to Oren's desperate act of martyrdom. It wasn't just that Crenaxin's dark power had overridden Oren's will so he wanted to throw himself in the machine, he had a *reason* to want to, complete with knowledge of the purpose he was serving. Did the command from Crenaxin that turned all these people into his zealots convey additional information beyond the spoken word? Did they intrinsically understand the dogma and rhetoric of the Brotherhood?

Minox wished he had time to explore these questions

while keeping his brother from killing either Minox or himself.

Oren's hands were wrenched off of Minox's throat, and Rainey was there, throwing irons on Oren. "We need you back in the machine."

"In the machine?" Minox asked. "To what end?"

Dayne shouted above the throng of would-be martyrs. He and Asti Rynax were guarding the gap between the spinning rings that allowed access to the cages and the machine controls. "Veranix said to do the same thing you did with Hence. Does that make sense?"

It did, even though Minox had been little more than a vessel following Veranix's lead at that point. "I'm not certain I can achieve that, but if it can stop this, I will endeavor."

Verci Rynax tossed a wound-up cord to Rainey. "Iron them, tie them up, keep them out." He tapped Minox on the arm. "Come on, specs. Let's save the world."

"That's a definite exaggeration," Minox said. "But we should waste no further time."

On an unspoken cue, Dayne, Asti, and Rainey all grabbed the throng of zealots and constables and pulled them away from the gap. Minox dashed through the gap with Verci, and they were underneath the rings, the cages, and the platform, where both the spikes and statues could be accessed, as well as the gear work.

"I'm guessing the spikes and statues can't be removed," Verci said. "But there's the spike missing."

"Which is where I fit in," Minox said. He focused his intentions on his hand and placed it in the niche for the spike, urging it to flow into the space.

Unlike last time, where Senek had taken control over him and his magic, this time Minox was in full command of his faculties as his hand, and to an extent he, became part of the machine. He could feel the magic and other energies flowing and shifting throughout the device, whirlpools of the spikes threatening to pull him in. The statues like floodgates, letting the magic surge out to the changing beasts.

"What do you need?" Verci asked as he took out a tool to pry at one of the metal panels.

"I need to draw it all in," Minox said. He took a deep breath and tried to pull the magical energy into his hand, into himself. But he couldn't manage it; it was like pushing against the current. The magic wanted to go through and out, and he wasn't strong enough to overcome it.

"What's wrong?" Verci asked.

"The flow is too strong. I can't get it to come to me."

"Flow, like water?"

"An apt description."

Verci looked over the machine, tracing lines with his fingers.

"So we reverse it," he said. "You said it's going out through the statues?"

"Yes."

Verci pulled a pair of heavy leather gloves out of his pack. "Then get ready. I'm about to do something stupid."

"Mister Rynax—"

Verci had the gloves on, standing in front of the first statue. "Don't worry. Stupid's my specialty."

He grabbed it and quickly spun it around to face inward. Minox immediately felt a shift in the flow of the magic. Verci winced and shook out his hands.

"Are you injured?"

"No, but it didn't tickle," Verci said. "Let's keep on it, you keep pulling."

Verci got to work, wasting no time getting the eight small statues turned around. With each one, Minox was able to draw the power away, draw magic out of each monster that was being fed.

"Holy saints, it's working!" Verci shouted. Minox saw that the beasts were changing: teeth pulling back into their mouths, skin descaling, claws shrinking.

Then there was a massive shift in the flow of energy, from the platform. Minox looked up and saw that Veranix was on the platform, trying to pull down the dragon with his rope. Minox had no idea how the young man was able to handle all the magical energies pouring and swirling up there.

"Keep it going!" Veranix shouted. "We need to reverse it all!"

Even with the statues turned around, it wasn't enough to pull all the magical energy back into his hand. At most, he could hold it at a standstill.

"It's not enough!" Minox shouted. "I welcome further ideas."

"Right," Verci said. "I think . . . oh, yes, that's it."

"What?"

Verci pried open one of the panels to reveal the gear work in the machine and peered inside, then looked up at the rings.

"All right," Verci said. "Remember in the Parliament where you stopped the whole machine for a few minutes? We need to do that again."

"If I could, I already would have," Minox said.

"I don't mean completely, just for a minute. Just the rings. We get them stopped for a bit, then I can get in there and flip out the control shafts."

"Which will do what?"

"Reverse the direction the rings are spinning."

"I can't do that and pull back the magic," Minox said.

Verci called up. "Thorn?"

"I'm a little busy!" Veranix shouted. He was holding his cloak over his face to shield himself from the bursts of fire Crenaxin was shooting on him.

"What do you need?" Asti called from the gap.

"The rings stopped."

"That's imposs—"

Asti was interrupted by a horrifying wrenching noise, as the rings suddenly jammed in place. Minox felt a sense of immense relief, as the magical energies began to pool and grow inside him. He glanced over to the gap.

Dayne Heldrin had wedged his shield between two of the spinning rings and was holding it still.

"Hurry!" he shouted.

Dayne couldn't hold the rings in place long. They strained against him, forcing themselves against the shield that he struggled to hold in place.

Verci Rynax crawled into the bowels of the machine. Up on top, Veranix was pulling on his rope, which surged with pulses of green and red energy.

"You lose that and Verci gets torn to shreds," Asti said.

"I'm aware," Dayne said.

Crenaxin squawked and screamed as Veranix kept reeling him in to the platform. **"Save me, children! Save me from these heretics!"**

The words made Dayne's knees buckle, and for a moment he almost slipped, the rings moving only half an inch before he reaffirmed his hold on them. The zealots and constables, who had all been subdued and bound, strained and struggled as if the command had reinvigorated their desire. Some of them tried to break their own arms or legs to get out. Satrine worked to keep them in their places.

But that wasn't the problem. There were a handful of the transformed beasts across the square that rose up and galloped toward the machine. From the look of them, they had all been nearly mortally injured, but Crenaxin's powerful command had been enough to get them back up.

Asti stood in front of Dayne, knives out. "Keep at it. Not one of these bastards is going to touch you."

The beasts leaped at Dayne, but Asti moved fast and

hard, not only striking with savage skill, but taking the blows that would have gone to Dayne. Letting himself take the punishment.

Suddenly there was a shift, and the rings pressed at him from the other direction. It was all he could do to still hold them in place, as the change nearly knocked him off his feet.

But Verci had done it.

"Get out of there!" Dayne shouted.

Satrine dashed through the beasts, Asti, and Dayne to get under the rings, and in a flash her hands were in the panel. She yanked Verci out by the legs. As soon as they were clear, Dayne dropped down flat.

The rings spun with wild abandon in the other direction.

The last beast standing hurled itself at Asti, who ducked and let it crash into the rings, where it was torn apart in an instant.

"Tragic," Dayne said as Asti pulled him out of the way of the spinning rings.

"I won't cry over it," Asti said. "Now?"

Veranix struggled to get Crenaxin onto the platform as the whole machine began to emit a pale white glow, and a high-pitched whine grew louder.

"We have to help him," Dayne said.

Asti held up one of his knives. "Aim for the wings."

Dayne understood. He hurled his shield hard at Crenaxin, knocking it in the wing. Crenaxin screamed in pain, though that was more likely from Asti's knife in its eye.

"You said the wings."

"I told you the wing."

But the distraction had thrown Crenaxin off balance in his attempt to fly away, and Veranix was able to pull him onto the platform.

"Now!" he shouted.

The white glow and the whine intensified, and around the machine the eight beasts collapsed to the ground, now eight naked, normal humans.

Up top, the dragon was melting away back into human form, while Veranix wrapped him further in the rope, holding him down.

Minox screamed and collapsed, his hand falling out of the niche in the machine. Despite that, the rings spun faster than ever, the glow so bright it hurt Dayne's eyes. He could barely see Veranix on the top of the platform, holding down the nearly human Crenaxin.

"Get out of there!" Dayne shouted.

"I need to hold him to it!" Veranix yelled over the whine, which was nearly deafening.

Verci and Satrine dragged Minox's limp form over to the gap, pushing him out to Dayne and Asti. They crawled out next, as the orbiting rings wobbled and shuddered. Verci ran over and embraced his brother, while Satrine helped Minox to his feet.

The glow became impossibly bright, brighter than the sun, as the rings flew loose from their housing.

Dayne held up his shield standing in front of the constables and Rynaxes.

Then a flash of light, a crack of thunder.

Then nothing.

Dayne lowered his shield.

Where the machine had been, there was just rubble and scraps of metal.

"The Thorn?" Asti asked, still holding a tight grip on his brother. "Crenaxin?"

There was no sign of either one.

CHAPTER 25

JERINNE STARTLED AWAKE.

Her hand instinctively went to her side. She should be lying in a pool of blood, but there was almost none on the floor. And no pain from the wound. She looked down—her tunic was shredded, caked with blood, but when she lifted it up: no wound. Barely a scar.

How was that even possible?

She got to her feet, noticing a strange amount of sunlight streaming down on her. The bell was gone from the bell tower, as was half the roof. What the blazes had happened? It was oddly quiet outside.

She opened the door to the narthex. It was strewn with bodies of the beasts. Eight or nine of them.

The cloistress.

Jerinne drew her sword and ventured out the shattered church door. The cloistress was on the ground, holding Jerinne's shield on her arm, the bald man's mace—the head now shattered-- in the other hand. She was just lying there, like she was sleeping peacefully.

The square was a smoking ruin, with a pile of rubble in the middle where that machine had been. The bodies of zealots and creatures littered the square, along with the church bell, sitting overturned on the cobblestone. Over near the rubble, she saw Dayne untying a group of constables, while Minox and Satrine were talking to other ones. To the side, the Rynax brothers—they were brothers, right?—were conferring quietly, looking like they wanted to stay out of the way of the constables.

Lockwagons arrived, and Jerinne watched as zealots were ironed and wagonned. An older man in uniform pulled Minox Welling into an embrace, and then did the same for Dayne, and then gave Satrine an awkward shake of his hand.

The fight was definitely over, and she had missed most of it.

"Dayne!" Jerinne called out.

Dayne looked up, and charged over to the church. The Rynax brothers started to walk over—more like limp—while Satrine and Minox took a bit more time finalizing things with the constables.

"Jerinne!" Dayne said as he bounded up the steps. "I . . . I was so worried that you were—well—"

"I think I almost was," Jerinne said. "I think she—she saved me somehow." She looked down at the cloistress.

"Why does she have your shield?" Dayne asked.

"I was hurt, and she . . . she wasn't making any sense, but she touched me and locked me in the bell tower. And now there isn't a mark on me."

Dayne knelt down and scooped the girl up. Jerinne took her shield back, while the mace felt to the ground.

Asti and Verci came up, both of them taking note of the mace as they approached. "The people in the church?" Asti asked.

"Safe, I think," Jerinne said. "The monsters never got past the narthex."

"Good work, girl," Asti said. Jerinne didn't have the energy to correct him.

"I can't take the credit," she said as they went in. "It was all her. Somehow."

Asti and Verci surveyed the carnage in the narthex. Verci went and righted the statue of Saint Bridget, while Asti knelt down by the body of the bald man.

"Oh, Jared," he said, touching the man's face. "I hope you find some peace, my friend."

"He helped save everyone else," Jerinne said quickly.

"Old fool," Asti said, wiping at his eyes. "He deserved better."

Verci went to the door to the nave and gave it a few knocks. "It's all clear out here. It's over."

A voice called from the other side. "How do we know?"

Asti stepped up. "Is Kimber in there?"

After some murmuring on the other side, a woman's voice called, "Yes?"

"Kimber, it's Asti. I swear on Saint Bridget that it's absolutely safe to open the door."

The door flew open, and a short, stout woman came out and wrapped her arms around Asti. "Thank every blessing," she said. She then reached over to Verci and pulled him in as well. "You are both such blessings."

"Easy, easy," Asti said. "I'm covered in bruises."

"Is everyone all right in here?" Dayne called out, centering his focus on one of the brothers. "The children?"

"Those who are in here," the brother said. "We're all safe. But Sister Myriem?"

Dayne lowered the girl to the ground. "I don't know if she's hurt. She's breathing."

"She saved me," Jerinne said. She was still very confused about what happened in the narthex. "I don't understand how, but she saved me."

Asti took a good look at her. "She was in your pub yesterday," he told Kimber. "She prayed with me."

"She came to the shop, called me Saint Terrence," Verci said. "Who is she?"

"She's Sister Myriem," Satrine said. She came in with Minox, both of them looking an absolute fright. Minox was as pale as curdled milk. Behind them, Hemmit and Lin walked slowly, both looking distraught and out of sorts. Then what happened to Maresh came flooding back to Jerinne. Sudden tears coming, she went over and embraced them both.

"I'm so sorry," she said, almost choking out her words. "I . . . I know I failed you down there. I know I—"

"No," Lin said. "Don't blame yourself. They did this. Only them."

Hemmit tried to hide his tears, but failed. "Maresh . . . the bodywagon is taking him away. He's got . . . I need to write to his mother."

Dayne approached. "Do you . . . can we do anything?"

"We're going to go with Maresh," Lin said. "But . . . stay and make sure everything is set here."

"We'll see you soon," Hemmit said, grabbing Dayne in an embrace. "Thank you, my friend, for continuing to be . . . everything that you are."

"I'm not entirely sure what that is," Dayne said.

Hemmit chuckled. "A champion, my friend." He pointed to Jerinne, and to the Rynaxes and the constables. "All of you."

Lin led him out, and Dayne and Jerinne went back to the group around Sister Myriem.

Satrine was kneeling down next to the cloistress. "Myriem, it's Satrine Rainey. Are you all right?"

The girl didn't stir.

The reverend approached from the back of the church, a group of children behind him. His expression was a cipher as he knelt down next to Myriem. "The sister is our charge, friends, and we will tend to her. It shall be our honor." On his signal, a few of the brothers picked her up and took her back.

From behind the children, a young woman came through. Napolic. After a moment, Jerinne realized it was the same one from the tunnels yesterday. Kaiana.

"Where's Ver—the Thorn? What happened?"

Dayne looked stricken. "Um, he . . . that is . . ."

"Miss Nell," Minox said, stepping forward. He spoke quietly, as if his voice would break if he raised it at all. "Mister Calbert was instrumental in stopping the disaster that unfolded today. We . . . we would not have been able to end this crisis without him. He . . . his bravery . . ."

Kaiana's face fell as the meaning of Minox's words became clear. Her whole body crumpled, and she would have fallen had a skinny young man not been there to catch her.

"We're very grateful to him," Dayne said. "He was—" That was all Dayne managed before he started crying.

"We should—" Asti said haltingly. "We should figure out what do with these children."

"I'm having a wagon come to bring them to the Grand Inspection Unit," Satrine said quietly. "We'll . . . we'll find their homes, and take care of the ones without any."

"Good," Dayne said, wiping his eyes. "This is all a good day. You all will be able to go home in time for Terrentin."

"Indeed!" a voice boomed from the church door. A figure strolled into the church—dressed all in yellow and soaking wet, and every step left a wet footprint. He walked confidently, with a sack over his shoulder. "So Rejoice, Rejoice, Rejoice!"

Kimber fell to her knees, "Blessing upon us, Saint Terrence has come."

"Indeed!" he said, coming closer. "I've come because I heard there were several children here, some of whom have *never* received a gift for Terrentin." He put the sack down and opened it up, revealing that it was filled with toys: jape-snaps and wind-ups and clamor-boxes.

"Wait a minute—" Verci said. Saint Terrence looked up at him and winked.

"So many beautiful, incredible toys for these children," Saint Terrence said, handing them to the children. "For you, and you, and you."

Kaiana looked up and screamed. She leaped on top of Saint Terrence, wrapping her arms and legs around him.

"Does he have a gift for her?" one of the children asked. This one must have been the baron's son, based on his accent.

"I think so," Dayne said.

"Let's let the children enjoy their toys," Asti said, urging everyone to step away. "I'm sure *the saint* has a lot more places to go today."

"Indeed," Saint Terrence said, letting Kaiana back on her feet, though her arms stayed wrapped around him. "In fact, let's adjourn to the back room."

"All of us?" Jerinne asked.

"Yes," Satrine said, her voice dripping with honey. "We're all the saint's helpers today."

They—Dayne and Jerinne, Asti, Verci, and Kimber, Satrine and Minox, Saint Terrence and Kaiana and even the skinny fellow—went through to the back to a small meeting room. Saint Terrence slumped into a chair. "I know, I know, I owe you about sixty crowns, Rynax."

"At least," Verci said.

Saint Terrence sighed, and his features, yellow suit and even his wetness melted away to reveal the Thorn. He looked a mess of cuts and bruises, but he had a wide, if exhausted smile on his face.

"Can you explain what happened?" Dayne asked. "How are you—"

"Not dead?" the Thorn asked.

"You let me think you were dead!" Kaiana said, slapping at him.

"I did nothing of the sort," the Thorn said. "So those last moments on the platform, we had sucked the last bit of dragon out of Crenaxin, and I jumped clear. Except I'm just brimming full of *numina*, so I sort of jump, like . . . how can I explain this? Like, sideways to the world. A direction that doesn't exist. I land about five blocks away from here. And right by your shop. So, I think, it's going to be Terrentin, and my survival was a damn miracle, so why not make the most of it?"

"Seventy crowns," Verci said.

"Fair. Besides, Dayne owes me five."

Dayne broke out laughing. "You did win that bet."

"You fool," the skinny kid said. "Do you know most people go through rigorous study of magic and its effect on the physical world and the body for *years* before even attempting something like that, and you do it by *accident?*"

"Listen," the Thorn said. "I would love to continue this whole conversation with all of you, but I am utterly famished. And I bet Minox is as well."

"That is accurate," Minox said.

"So, I'm telling you, around the corner is this fabulous Fuergan restaurant that is *absolutely* one of the best things you've ever tried. Can we *please* just go there?"

"He's been talking it up," Dayne said. "And I haven't eaten since lunch yesterday. Shall we?"

"Why not?" Jerinne said. "It's not like I'm not going to get in more trouble with Amaya."

Amaya found almost everything she needed at Hemmit's flop. A place to hide, something to bandage her side, and a bottle of Fuergan whiskey to dull the pain.

But no Hemmit.

There had been a bundle of documents already delivered to his flop, though. Evidence of the Grand Ten, the vast conspiracy seeking to undermine the crown and the government, with the ten conspirators named. Including herself as The Warrior.

If he had received it, so had all the other newssheets. Surely interesting enough for those reporters to investigate on their own, confer with each other, contact the Constabulary and the marshals. Before midday they would find the slaughter in the opera house—it was there to be found, after all—and that would surely be proof enough to confirm everything in the bundle.

But Hemmit wasn't here. She had checked first at The Nimble Rabbit with the owners—who she clearly had spooked—but they hadn't seen him, or Maresh or Lin since lunchtime the day before.

It was possible none of them had come back from the excursion with Dayne and Jerinne.

She had no idea how to reach out to either of them. They were the only other ones she trusted right now, or at least trusted enough to listen to her fairly. But they would either be at the chapterhouse or the Parliament, and there was absolutely no way she could go to either of those places.

Where else could she even go?

Someone knocked on Hemmit's door.

"Hemmit? Are you there? No one is in the office."

Lady Mirianne.

More knocking. "Hemmit?"

Amaya had to make a choice. She opened the door, grabbed Lady Mirianne by the wrist, and pulled her inside.

"Amaya!" she exclaimed. "What are you—are you all right?"

"Decidedly not," Amaya said, sitting on Hemmit's bed.

"Oh my saints," Lady Mirianne said, noting the bandage on Amaya's side. It was already seeping with blood, and she'd need to change it. "What happened? Why are you . . . why did you come here?"

"I guess it's not in the newssheets yet," Amaya said.

"What isn't?" Lady Mirianne said. "I had noticed there was a stir of a story in many of the sheets—something about a conspiracy—but I wondered why my own newssheet hadn't printed anything today. I found no one at the offices or at the Rabbit, so I came here."

"That," Amaya said, pointing to the bundle. As Lady Mirianne thumbed through the papers, Amaya went on. "Hemmit and the others went with Dayne and Jerinne on something. They were going to sneak into the Necropolis of Saint Terrence. But maybe they've not come back yet. Maybe they got in as much trouble as I did."

"Oh, my," Lady Mirianne said. "These are . . . this is all quite serious. I presume you deny the allegations in here."

"I do," Amaya said. "There is an actual Grand Ten, but I'm not a part of it. Though Grandmaster Orren and Colonel Altarn of Druth Intelligence are."

"What?" Lady Mirianne said. "Are you certain?"

"Of those two, quite." Amaya nodded, pointing to her injury. "This was the cost of tangling with the two of them. Barely escaped."

"Grandmaster Orren did this?" she asked with incredulity. "He did this to you?"

"After killing three people right in front of me. I . . . I never . . ."

"Three?" Lady Mirianne choked on the word as she sat down. Lady Mirianne let out a deep breath. "Well that . . . that must have been . . . very difficult to see. And you saw Colonel Altarn as well?"

"She taunted me. This was a trap for me that I just walked into, and . . . I had suspected her and the Grandmaster, but . . . to see it? See them both be so savage, it was . . ."

Lady Mirianne got to her feet. "We have not been close, Amaya. I understand if that's at all my fault. I have not been the friend to you that I could have been."

"This isn't the moment—"

"But it is," Lady Mirianne said. "I believe in you, in your innocence in this conspiracy. That you have been incriminated by malefactors who wish to use you as a patsy."

"Thank you," Amaya said. It wasn't much, but in this moment of complete failure, she would take any bit of kindness she could find, even from Lady Mirianne. "I was thinking, I need to get ahead of this. Maybe turn myself into the marshals, or the Parliament, so I can get my side of the story on the record."

"No," Lady Mirianne said firmly. "If this is true, think about it. The corruption is everywhere. Chief Toscan. Chief Quoyell. There are surely people who are working with Altarn and Orren. The corruption in this city is deep, and there's no trusting whoever you might turn yourself over to isn't part of it."

"So what do you suggest?" Amaya asked.

"My carriage is outside," Lady Mirianne said. "Let's get you into it, and from there to my household, and then to my lake cottage in the Sharain."

"You want me to hide?"

"I want you to recover, safely," Lady Mirianne said. "We can assume your reputation is already shredded. But I will make sure that Hemmit and Lin and Maresh believe in your innocence. That they—and Dayne and Jerinne—and especially me, we'll all work to exonerate you. In the name of the law and the public eye. But you will be safe away from all of it, ready to come back when it's time."

Amaya wanted to cry. She had misjudged Lady Mirianne, convinced she was a privileged popinjay more interested in fashion and money than anything else, empty in thought and spirit. But now she saw what

Dayne must have seen in her all this time, why he loved
her so much.

"Thank you, my lady," Amaya said. "Thank you for
everything."

Lady Mirianne took her in a warm embrace, though
she made sure to position her body to not get blood on
herself. "Of course, Amaya. You'll see. We will make sure
justice is done, have no doubt." She stepped back, a warm
smile on her face. "Come. Let's get you out of the city."

Seven of them went to Jonet's Clay Bowl. Kimber, the
sweet woman who clearly had overwhelming affection
not for just both of the Rynax brothers, but all of the
North Seleth neighborhood, stayed at the church to arrange services for Jared Scall, the man who had died
helping Jerinne protect the church. Delmin and Kaiana,
the friends of Veranix Calbert, chose to go back to the
University to lay the groundwork for whatever story
they were telling about Veranix missing classes this
morning, as well as the multiple injuries that were clear
on his face. Before they left, Minox presented Kaiana
with the sword he had used in the fight.

"It's hers," Minox explained as they went into the
Clay Bowl. "Or rather, her father's. But I'm grateful that
it found its way back to her hands."

"Good friends," Veranix said to the proprietors. He
had abandoned all of his trappings as the Thorn, looking just like a normal University student, if one covered
with cuts and bruises. "There are seven of us here, but
feed us as if we are twice as many. We have had a long
night and a longer morning and are deeply famished."

"You again!" one of the proprietors said. "But where
is your lady? Or do you have more ladies and gentlemen
now? Very nice."

"Don't give him a hard time, Gessin," Asti said, stepping forward.

"Asti!" the man said, grabbing him by the shoulders and kissing both cheeks. "You are coming to eat? With your *natir*? I am most honored."

Satrine chuckled. "We aren't all married to each other."

"Because you Druth are very closed-minded. Seven is good number for marriage. Not as good as nine, and truly, eleven is *very* good, I hear. But seven is good."

He led them to a table, and in just a few moments, dish after dish of culinary delights were brought out to them. Veranix and Minox wasted little time digging into them, and while Dayne was not familiar with the cuisine, he was hungry enough to try anything at this point. And, to his pleasant surprise, he found it quite agreeable. Savory and piquant, without the overwhelming sense of burning spice that other foreign dishes he tried usually had.

"Fortunately," Satrine said, "the ranking officers on the scene in all this were Minox's uncle and brother. They were more inclined to believe the story we gave them."

"Which was what, exactly?" Verci asked.

"Largely what happened, though I glossed over the Thorn's involvement," Minox said. "And we painted the two of you as civilians and local businessmen who proved useful in a crisis."

"Not untrue," Asti said.

"Incredibly useful," Satrine said. The two of them shared a knowing look, and then she said, "I think we should stay aware and vigilant about the Brotherhood from now on."

"Really?" Jerinne asked. "I mean, Crenaxin's gone, Senek's in custody—"

"Gurond escaped," Dayne said. He had noticed that at some point the bell had been overturned, and Gurond was gone. Perhaps he did reconsider his loyalty to the Brotherhood, or at least to Crenaxin and Senek, and abandoned them. Still, Dayne worried about the giant, twisted man.

"I don't know how well he can hide," Veranix said.

"He did rather effectively for months," Minox said. "But more to the point, we know that the Brotherhood had infiltrated the Constabulary, and who knows where else."

"Ren Poller," Verci said darkly.

"How do you know they infiltrated the Constabulary?" Asti asked.

"The spikes in the machine," Minox said. "They were in evidence custody from a murder case we worked, and they had been stolen, with all record of their existence eradicated. Seven of the eight spikes."

"So that hole was for the missing one, not you," Asti said.

"We had lent one to a consultant for study," Satrine said. "As far as I know, he still has it."

"We should check in with Dresser regarding that," Minox said.

"Major Dresser?" Veranix asked. "Stern guy, tight hair? Mage?"

"You know him?" Satrine asked.

"He's my new professor."

"Is no one troubled by the various chains of events that led us all here today?" Asti asked.

"Immensely," Minox said.

"I really feel we need to talk about Sister Myriem," Veranix said.

"Yes," Jerinne said.

Dayne remembered his odd encounter with the girl the other night, how her words had put him on the path to share his troubles with Hemmit and Maresh, which then led to them going into the tunnels. After recounting it, the others each had their own story of her, though Satrine was quiet and contemplative for most of this conversation.

"What's odd was," Jerinne said between bites of her third bowl of *sradtikash*, "she acted like I freaked her out more than she was freaking me out."

"How so?" Satrine asked.

"Like . . . she had this whole thing like she was *remembering* today. But that she didn't remember me being part of it."

"You did miss a fair part of it," Asti said.

"More like . . . I wasn't supposed to be here. I was supposed to be somewhere else. And . . . I was a bit out of it, but—she knew my name, and said we weren't supposed to meet until next year."

"You know what else?" Veranix said. "She talked to me like she knew me."

"Well, she did that with all of us," Verci said.

"No, I mean, she . . . for a moment there, she *knew me*. Like I was a dear old friend she hadn't seen in years."

"She kept saying something about being who she was supposed to be tomorrow," Jerinne said, looking to Veranix. "Is that possible? Can magic—or whatever she was doing—can that be used to know the future?"

Veranix paused for a moment. "I'm not the best person to ask about mystical theory. I know that what we call 'magic' is just a small part of the forces that affect the world."

"There's psionics," Asti said. "And whatever the blazes Crenaxin was doing."

"Right," Veranix said. "Maybe she's something else. Maybe time itself is one of those forces, and she can tap into it like Minox and I can with magic."

"Maybe it's simpler than that," Satrine said. "How faithful are you all?"

"I make my prayers to Saint Senea," Veranix said.

"Kimber makes sure I go to services from time to time," Asti said.

Satrine smiled ruefully. "I've been thinking a lot about how what we faced was not just evil, but . . . unholy. It needed to be stopped. And as astounding as it sounds, maybe . . . maybe we were the instruments

God needed to stop it. So God touched the mind of a troubled, angry girl, a great and terrible brush with something infinite. Just enough so she could ensure that we were there."

The table was quiet for a moment.

"I would say that's a lot to swallow," Verci said. "Except you showed up at my shop at three bells in the night, exactly when I needed you. I don't have a better explanation for that."

"Maybe the saints did hear our prayers," Asti said. "And sent her to us. Not the strangest thing I've seen."

"I just hope—" Satrine stumbled on her words for a moment. "I *pray* that the brothers are able to help her. That she'll have some measure of peace when she wakes. If she wakes."

The servers came over with seven glasses of Fuergan whiskey. Dayne raised his up to them all.

"To all of you," Dayne said as he got to his feet. "Thank you for . . . for reaffirming my faith. For being the people this city needed in this dark hour. For courage and cleverness and . . . compassion. I was honored to stand with you all."

They all drank.

"Though," Veranix said, getting to his feet. "I truly hope nothing like this is ever necessary again."

"Well said," Asti said. "We would really like the quiet life of honest businessmen."

"Try to keep it that way," Satrine said.

"I should be getting back to campus," Veranix said. "I might even make it to my theory class."

"We should get to the shop," Verci said, tapping Asti's shoulder. "Someone cleared out our inventory and we need to get building."

"We'll be sending you a bill, Thorn," Asti said.

"I'm good for it," he said. "But speaking of—"

The proprietor came over, "Oh, no. My husbands just told me all the things that happened by the church. It is us who have a debt to you all, so we offer this feast to you as recompense."

"Are you sure, sir?" Dayne asked. "We did eat a lot."

"And you have earned it," the proprietor said.

"I should get back to my home," Minox said, getting up. "I have profuse apologies to offer to my mother. And also my brother. I may have broken his wrist at one point."

"He kind of deserved it," Satrine said. "I get to go to the stationhouse and write up a lot of reports to my captain over this."

"I can aid—" Minox started.

"No," Satrine said. "Formally, you weren't there, and officially, we're still mad at each other. We should still maintain that fiction."

"You fear we've not seen the last of the Brotherhood?" Dayne asked.

"Even if we have, there's an infection they leave behind," Satrine said. She specifically pointed to Asti. "Stay where I can find you if I need you."

"Joyfully," Asti said flatly.

Satrine patted Dayne on the shoulder, embraced Jerinne, and left the shop. Minox walked out behind her, giving only a slight salute. Asti and Verci left without ceremony or sentiment.

Veranix walked over to Dayne's end of the table.

"We did all right, didn't we?"

"For two people who have very different . . . philosophies," Dayne said. "We made an effective team."

"Listen," Veranix said. "I'm not sure how much stock I should put in this, but . . . your friend Maresh, he died right in front of me."

"Oh, I'm sorry," Dayne said.

Veranix shook it off. "Not the first person I've seen die. Won't be the last. But he was talking in the end. He said, 'Tell Dayne, don't trust.'"

"Don't trust what?" Jerinne asked.

"I don't know," Veranix said. "He just said that, over and over, until he stopped breathing. I couldn't tell you what it means, but I thought you should know."

"Thank you, Veranix," Dayne said, offering his hand. "Call on me if you ever need."

"Same to you," Veranix said, taking it. "Jerinne, feel free as well."

Jerinne took his hand. "Give Kai my best, all right?"

He paused at that for a moment, chuckled knowingly, and left.

"And us?" Jerinne said. "We are probably in so much trouble with Amaya, with the Grandmaster, with the Order."

"Indeed," Dayne said. "All the more reason why we should get home."

CHAPTER 26

JERINNE WAS BONE TIRED WHEN they got to the chapterhouse, but she was happy to walk in with Dayne right next to her, the two of them both in their Tarian tunics, shields on their arms, swords at their hips, and covered from head to toe in scrapes, smudges, and scorches.

Today they had been Tarians, and no matter what scourging awaited them when they walked in the door, they had earned every mark, every bruise, and every tear on them. She would wear them with pride, and not one harsh word from Amaya, the Grandmaster, or any third-year Initiates would shame her.

The first people who spotted them were Iolana and her mentor, an Adept whose name Jerinne had never learned.

"Saints above," the Adept said. "What the blazes have you two been digging into? Heldrin, you look like you've fought the whole host of sinners."

"Something like that," Dayne said.

Iolana, meanwhile, was glaring at Jerinne.

"What?" Jerinne finally said.

"Why is it always you?" Iolana asked, and stalked off.

"Sorry," the Adept said. "I'll go have a word with her."

"No need," Jerinne said.

"We should go speak to the Grandmaster," Dayne said. "Let's not belabor that."

He took the lead as they went up the stairs, past the Initiate bunks, past the gawks and stares, and then up to the Grandmaster's aerie. Jerinne had never been up here before, and was surprised how easily Dayne just walked up without invitation or summons.

"Sir," Dayne said as they entered, knocking on the doorframe. "If we could have a moment?"

Grandmaster Orren was at his desk, hunched over a pile of papers with a look of great consternation on his face. He looked up, and for a moment, there was a look of genuine shock on his face.

"Dayne!" he shouted, coming over with grace and speed that belied his age. "Miss Fendall. You both . . . I presume you've been in a situation."

"You could say that," Dayne said. "I want to take full responsibility for Jerinne. She should not be reprimanded for breaking curfew or missing training—"

"I don't care about that," the Grandmaster said. "I'm simply gratified you are both alive and safe. It . . . I presume you are unaware, but the Order has received something of a shock today, and . . ." He stumbled on his words, his throat choking. "I'm just happy to see you home."

"What's wrong?" Dayne asked. "How can I help?"

"Dear saints," Orren said. "You two walk in here, clearly having been through something traumatic, deeply in need of the baths if not the infirmary. And the first thing you do is ask how you can help." He chuckled ruefully. "I am humbled by you, Dayne Heldrin."

Jerinne coughed uncomfortably. "I should go clean up. I'm sure Madam Tyrell is screaming for me."

The Grandmaster sighed. "No, she most is definitely not. I'm afraid Madam Tyrell is not here."

"Is she all right?" Dayne asked.

"I cannot speak to her health, but she has gone into hiding, as she is wanted by the authorities."

"What?"

"I do not have all the details, but it appears that she was embroiled in a conspiracy to overthrow the government. Her crimes were discovered, so she murdered her co-conspirators and fled."

"I cannot believe that, sir," Dayne said. Jerinne didn't say anything, but her instincts matched Dayne's.

"I am struggling to understand it myself," the Grandmaster said. He glanced uncomfortably at Jerinne. "We should discuss this privately. Perhaps, Miss Fendall, your instinct to clean up and join your cohort is correct."

"Of course, sir," Jerinne said, giving Dayne a quick glance that she hoped communicated the depths to which she did not believe Amaya had been involved in any of the things the Grandmaster had just reported. His expression was not as confident, but he gave her a nod to go.

She left, and made her way to the barracks for the other third-year Initiates. Raila Gendon was waiting there for her.

"I see Iolana told you I was back," she said.

"What the blazes happened to you?" Raila asked. "You just vanished and Vien made a stink and then Madam Tyrell told us to quiet down but you were gone all night and . . . saints, look at you."

"I've been in it," Jerinne said, stripping off her torn-up uniform. "What's this nonsense about Madam Tyrell?"

"Can you believe it? It's apparently in all the newssheets. There was this conspiracy where this group calling themselves the Grand Ten were trying to overthrow the government. Like, a member of Parliament and a

Duchess and some general and I don't even know who. But Madame Tyrell was part of it."

"Really?" Jerinne asked. "Madame Tyrell trying to overthrow the government?"

"Well, it makes sense she was into something shady," Raila said. "I mean, come on. She made Adept after one year of Candidacy. That never happens. And why did she stay in Maradaine, where she had her Initiacy, unless to be in a place of power."

"There could be—"

"And look what she did to you. Keeping you on the bottom of the roster, denying you a mentor. Because she was threatened by you. Maybe she thought you and Dayne were onto her. She and Dayne had been close in Initiacy, you know. He'd know if something was wrong so she made a point of keeping him away. Let me tell you, it all makes sense that Amaya Tyrell is bad news."

Jerinne was about to protest how none of that made sense, but Raila went on.

"I'm just saying, she was rude and a bully, and I'm certainly glad she's gone, and glad that if she shows her face again, she'll end up locked away at Quarrygate. Or even better, Fort Olesson."

Jerinne had never seen ugliness of this sort from Raila Gendon. It was more than a little off-putting.

"Saints, look at you," Raila said now that Jerinne was down to her skivs. "You're a right mess, my friend. I want to hear all about your whole adventure. How about we go down to the baths and you tell me all about them? Just you and me?"

Ten minutes ago, that would have been everything Jerinne wanted, but now it was distinctly unappealing.

"You know," Jerinne said. "I'm completely exhausted. I think I'm going to just clean up quick and go to sleep. Figure out everything tomorrow."

"Oh," Raila said. "Of course, I should have realized. I'll . . . I'll leave you to it."

Raila left. Jerinne found her drycloth and got ready to go to the baths. If anyone gave her a hard time about her plans for the rest of the day, she would crack their nose open. Later, she'd find out what was really going on with Amaya, because whatever this story was, it was pure sewage.

Jerinne remembered her last conversation with Amaya, and that seemed like a good place to look for the source of the sewage: Colonel Altarn of Druth Intelligence.

But that was a mission for another day.

Dayne waited as Jerinne left, and the Grandmaster went back over to his desk.

"Tea, Dayne?" he asked as he poured himself a cup. "I think you could use some."

"Rather," Dayne said. "Can you explain further what is going on with Amaya?"

"I wish I could," the Grandmaster said. "I am shocked that she had such secrets."

Dayne scowled. Amaya did have secrets, that was true. He remembered she told him she didn't trust the Grandmaster, especially in terms of how Jerinne was being treated by the Order. How he had kept Dayne isolated and nearly exiled. Perhaps that was coloring his read of this conversation, but something about the Grandmaster was a warning.

He was being too kind.

Perhaps a test was in order.

"You should know that Jerinne and I had been working together on Amaya's request," he said. "She wanted to supplement Jerinne's training, since she never received a mentor."

"Hmm," the Grandmaster responded, as if it was just a curiosity. "And she told you to keep it secret. See, that's another thing. Perhaps she was planning on positioning you and Jerinne as weapons she could use in her ploy. Or perhaps you were her scapegoat if things went wrong."

"Scapegoat?" Dayne asked, taking the tea the Grandmaster offered. "How so?"

"Well, perhaps she then asked another favor. Look into this, chase after that. Something that seems noble and appropriate, but when it went wrong, what would you do?" The Grandmaster chuckled. "I know you well enough to answer. You would take whatever blame there was to protect her. You did it just moments ago to protect Miss Fendall. It's in your nature, Dayne. It's why you're a Tarian."

"Just a Candidate," Dayne said. "And we both know that's all it will be."

"Tell me about this escapade," the Grandmaster said. "Did Amaya start it?"

"Not at all," Dayne said, sitting down. He recounted what he could—Golman Haberneck, the Vollingale boy, the journey underground, the Brotherhood, the Thorn, the battle in Saint Bridget's Square—only leaving out the details that were not his to share.

"If it wasn't for Jerinne, I would have been lost," Dayne said. "I don't understand the power Crenaxin wielded, but . . . I don't know if I'll ever feel clean of it. What I did, what I could have done."

"Yes, I can imagine," he said, his voice haunted. "Like you're a passenger in your own body as it commits horrors . . ."

"Yes, exactly," Dayne said. He was grateful that the Grandmaster seemed to understand. "If Jerinne hadn't been able to crack through to me, I don't know what would have happened."

"Then we are all very fortunate she was there. That you both were there." He sighed. "In light of these revelations about Amaya, I do feel I have made mistakes."

"For what it's worth, sir, I am skeptical that she is

guilty of these things. I've had my arguments with her, but I do not think she is capable of conspiracy and cold-blooded murder."

The Grandmaster smiled. "You truly see the best, Dayne. It's a blessing. I hope you are right, but the evidence is, I'm given to understand, compelling. But I don't want to talk about that."

"Then what?"

"With the new policies of protection for the Parliament being jointly handled by the marshals, Tarians, and Spathians, your position of 'liaison' seems . . . extraneous."

"I was already at odds with that, sir."

"And moreover, I think having you alone over there has left you vulnerable to bad influences. So, I've decided to move you back into the chapterhouse."

"Really, sir?"

"To a specific end," the Grandmaster said. "Amaya's primary duties involved training the Initiates, especially the third-years. I am recalling you here so you can take charge of their training."

"Are you sure, sir?" Dayne asked. "I mean . . . that isn't a Candidate's role."

"Perhaps not," the Grandmaster said. "But I can think of no one better to shape the minds of these young Initiates. Do you accept?"

"Gratefully," Dayne said.

"I'm glad," the Grandmaster said. "I think things will go very well by having you close."

Lady Mirianne had expected treachery. She prepared for it, planned for it. She had smelled it in the air with Colonel Altarn.

Mirianne strove to be prepared for every eventuality she could foresee, which was why she had a plan in place for a whole Scapegoat Grand Ten, and candidates lined up for every position. She had expected Altarn to take her own spin, but to use Miri's plan to actually expose and kill members of the true Ten was atrocious.

Atrocious, but anticipated.

Which is why it was fortunate to have the disgraced Amaya Tyrell all but delivered to Miri. Her rescue and delivery of Amaya had not gone as she planned—she had thoroughly expected for Amaya to go to Dayne and then he would have gone to her for help—but the results were the same. Amaya was in position to be her weapon when she needed it.

She would need it. She would have to be ready for a confrontation with Colonel Altarn, and possibly the others, before too long.

Not that she mourned the loss of Duchess Leighton, High Judge Feller Pin, or especially Chestwick Millerson. All three of them had been trouble, and she had plans at the ready to handle each of them, if needed. But Altarn was definitely an adversary to watch out for now.

As well as the Grandmaster. That was quite shocking, that he would have so willingly been Altarn's pawn. If he was the one who actually held the sword that killed Leighton, Pin, and Millerson, that was a fundamental shift in his very character. She wasn't sure how Altarn had managed that, if her methods of turning him were natural or unnatural pressures, but regardless, it highlighted how critical it was for Miri to be prepared.

She would be prepared for both of them. It was time for action.

She strode into the *Veracity* offices. The lamps were burning low, but both Hemmit and Lin were inside. They had clearly already gone through several bottles of wine.

"Stop wallowing," she told them as she came in.

"Wallowing?" Lin asked as she struggled to stand. "Do you have any idea—"

"I do, yes," Mirianne said. "We have lost gravely today, but that doesn't mean we don't have work to do."

"Work?" Hemmit asked.

"Indeed," Mirianne said. "Though we will also take time to mourn. I am making arrangements for a proper service for Maresh. I will handle the details and expenses. The least I could do."

"Thank you," Lin said.

"But that doesn't mean the truth isn't under assault," Mirianne said. She pointed to the folder that Altarn had so cleverly arranged to be delivered to all the newssheets. "I noticed you didn't print that story like the other sheets."

"Because it's sewage," Hemmit said. "The sort of sewage that is spiced with just enough truth to smell right, but—" He shook his head. "There's no way Amaya was a part of that. No way."

Perfect.

"I agree," Mirianne said. "Which means we need to get to the real truth, clear her name. That needs to be a long-term priority."

"How?" Lin asked.

"That's on you to figure out, my friends," Mirianne said. "And I'll sign off the expenses you need. But I think that's only part of it."

"What else?" Hemmit asked.

"Right now, the story of this 'Grand Ten' is what everyone is talking about. So we need to change the conversation."

"Given what happened in Saint Bridget's Square, it's astounding this is the big story," Hemmit said.

"Right," Mirianne said. "Because no one is talking about Saint Bridget's Square. You need to tell them about it."

Hemmit stood up and stumbled to Maresh's desk, sorting through some pages. "We don't have an artist right now."

"We'll work on that," Mirianne said. "But what can we do?"

Hemmit pulled out pages and thumbed through them. Miri had seen them before—saintly sketches a mysterious reader had sent them.

"I think I know," he said. "Can I get a pot of tea? I need to start writing."

"I'll do better," Mirianne said. "I'll send over a few assistants to handle tea and whatever else you need. You just do what you do best."

If she knew Hemmit, she knew exactly what that would be. He was already sitting down, writing furiously.

Mirianne nodded to Lin and went out. She would have to work hard over the next months, use all of her skills and knowledge, to coax things where she needed this nation, this city to be. For it to be what it could be, what it needed to be.

She knew that was the difference between herself and Altarn. Mirianne was not doing this for any personal glory or aggrandizement. She wanted to make Druthal the best thing it could be. Altarn had her own agendas, and more and more, Mirianne was growing certain those agendas served no master who wished the best for Druthal. So she needed to position herself to stop her, in case that was necessary.

"You've alienated your allies, Colonel."

Silla Altarn didn't need to justify herself to Torla Rassin, but she saw this as a teaching moment. The young dark-haired woman might be a skilled telepath and useful asset for the Brotherhood, but she had a certain naiveté that Altarn needed to squash out of her. While they descended into the catacombs beneath the Central Office was a good enough time to instruct her.

"They were never my allies," Altarn said. "The Grand Ten was a means to an end with foolish goals. I mean, honestly, we nearly achieved their goals in a few minutes by you rewriting a few minds. They want to wrap themselves around convoluted plans when all they need is a well-shot crossbow."

The assassination attempt, of course, didn't matter, beyond being a good field test for Torla's value as a blunt instrument, though she had clearly shattered that servant so he barely understood anything other than a driving need to kill the king and restore the True Line.

The True Line. Like it even mattered who was on the throne. Once the Brotherhood was truly ready, they would be the only rulers of the nation.

Torla was clearly thinking about her performance on that task. "Amaya was easier to influence. She barely needed a nudge to go off on a reckless mission alone." She sighed. "Do you still need me to pretend to be a servant at the Tarian Chapterhouse?"

She had considered it, but Torla was too valuable to waste on that. Grandmaster Orren was now completely under her thumb, thanks to Torla's telepathic talents. She had managed to guide him to act against his principles, believing his loyalty had earned him the things he so desperately wanted for the Order. It truly was a testament to her gifts.

"No, I have a different assignment for you."

They reached the meeting chamber, where Liora Rand was waiting impatiently.

"How is this not a disaster?" Liora asked.

"Should I spell it out for you?" Altarn asked.

"Please," Liora said. "The machine has been destroyed, the statues and spikes lost, Senek arrested."

"You well know that was only the first phase of the Hierarch's plan, a field test of the theories. He's very big on testing theories, after all."

"Asti Rynax found the mothers," Liora said. "Thank the Nine the code phrases to blank his memory still worked."

"I don't understand why you don't just kill him," Altarn said.

"She harbors affection for him," Torla said.

"He's still useful," Liora said. "We don't have all the names on the list, so he might be the only key to getting them."

That was true. Especially now that Grieson had gone into hiding. The bastard. She needed to hunt him down. Soon enough.

"The point is, he doesn't know anything about the mothers, and you had them moved away from there. All is well."

"We were exposed! We lost most of the followers."

"The followers were expendable, by their nature. And the exposure suits our purpose. There had been rumors enough about the Brotherhood for months. Now they've been found and defeated, and then soon forgotten. We will again be in the shadows."

"And Senek?"

"He was always a bit too engrossed in his own peculiar fixations to be truly useful," Altarn said. "Besides, Lord Sirath is nearly recovered. Senek was always a placeholder until that time."

"And Crenaxin?" Liora asked.

"Well, from what I understand Crenaxin is neither arrested nor dead, at least as far as anyone knows. Perhaps he'll turn up. If not, the Hierarch will mourn the loss of his right hand and move on."

"We're all expendable to you, aren't we?" Liora asked.

"You are if you fail," Altarn said. "But it's time for you to go on another mission."

"Who am I marrying now? Or is it just seduction?"

"You're going to Fencal for Colonel Danverth Martindale," Altarn said. "And you'll take Torla with you."

"Why?" they both asked.

"Because Martindale—" Altarn paused to think of the best way she wanted to phrase it. "He will not fall for your particular charms as easily as the others. You're going to need Torla for that extra edge."

"Fine," Liora said. "I guess we'll be off. Come on."

She and Torla stalked off, and Altarn went back up to her offices in the Central Office.

Liora was right, it had been a disaster—mostly due to Dayne Heldrin and the others who had meddled—but in failure, there is opportunity to learn. And the Hierarch of the Brotherhood had been pleased with what they had learned, despite the losses.

Heldrin and his companions would be dealt with soon enough.

Soon they would have the blood, the stars would be ripe, and with the knowledge they had gained, the Brotherhood would unleash the true power of the Nine.

Then all would be theirs.

ULTIMATE INTERLUDE

REVEREND HALSTER KNELT AT THE side of the bed where Sister Myriem remained asleep. A quiet, restful sleep, he had hoped. Saints knew she had earned that, at the very least.

He prayed that she had. He wasn't sure.

"No change?" Brother Mergolliet asked, coming in with a bowl of broth. "I fear we'll have to feed her in her sleep if this continues."

"We'll care for her, in whatever she needs, as long as she needs," Halster said. "Our greatest, most sacred duty now."

Mergolliet nodded and placed the bowl on the table in the corner. He went about the business of checking on Myriem, adjusting her bedding. His face was full of trouble, and finally he voiced it.

"You knew this was coming, didn't you, sir?" he asked. "That she would play a role."

"I did as God commanded," Halster said. Though at

this point, he was full of doubt. "To put us on the path of faith."

He had seen it coming. He knew—he had known for years—the horrors would be unleashed outside Saint Bridget's. His whole life, he had heard the voices, seen the visions, known the saints were whispering to him. He had embraced that, following the path they had laid out for him.

His most sacred duty.

Be ready for the day. Prepare the church, protect it from below. Invite the girl here when it was her time. Sister Myriem had come, and when he saw her, it was like a key had unlocked in his mind. He knew her face was the one he had seen every time he closed his eyes. Her destiny was here, when the horrors came.

And he had been ready for his role.

He had been ready to die.

He had seen it so clearly every time. The giant stormed into the church, snapped his neck. Sister Myriem's heart would shatter, and from that broken heart her power would pour out, filling her body with the light of God.

She would become the Champion of the Faith, vanquishing the Dragon.

She would do that *alone*.

But nothing went as he had seen it.

She had changed it. She had somehow brought other champions to stand with her. To fight for her.

He had no idea how she had done this, or why.

He was supposed to be dead, and he was not. She had not become the champion she was supposed to be, she was here in the bed. Nothing of what he had seen was coming to pass.

He had no idea what this meant, but for the first time in his life, he felt doubt.

"And are we on the path, sir?"

"We are on a path," he said. "The evil came, and

champions stepped forward and vanquished it. But we must remain vigilant, for there is still so much work to be done."

"Of course, sir," Mergolliet said. He whispered a quick prayer over Myriem, and went off.

He had no certainty of the future. Myriem had changed his fate, and he feared, changed the fate of everyone in the city. He was certain that would have a great and terrible cost.

And he feared that she, and her champions, would be the ones to pay it.

CHAPTER 27

AFTER ONLY TWO WEEKS, RIAN Rainey was already tired from trying to balance school and her shifts at Henson's Majestic. She would keep it up, of course, since she knew perfectly well how hard her mother had been working to maintain their household, take care of Father, pay the tuition for her and Caribet. She wouldn't let her mother down. Fortunately, today had been a quiet, subdued shift at the glove counter. Her commissions wouldn't be much, but the rush of sales before Terrentin had put her a bit ahead, so she was happy for the easy day.

"Hey, Rian."

Alexanne and Rowa had never come up to her counter and spoken to her before. She didn't even know they realized she existed, let alone knew her name. The two of them—dress models in the window displays—were both so sophisticated and glamorous. They always got to wear the best dresses and get paid to do it.

"Hi," Rian said, not sure why she was so flustered by their approach. "Were you needing some gloves?"

"Your mother is a stick, right?" Alexanne, with Waishen hair that was impossibly long, asked bluntly.

"And your last name is Rainey, right?" said Rowa, the dark-haired one who somehow seemed ageless.

"Your mother is a stick named Rainey, right?" Alexanne asked.

"Yes," Rian answered, more than a little confused. "What about it?"

They dropped a thick pamphlet on her counter. Rian had seen it being sold on the street corners when she came in, and noticed more than a few customers walking around with it. The cover said CHAMPIONS OF MARADAINE in large, bold letters, with an image of seven saints in silhouette below it.

"That's your mom, isn't it?"

"What's my mom?"

"The Inspector Rainey in there, who rutting saved the city from, like, monsters or something. Is that your mom?"

Rian opened up the pamphlet and read through some of the pages.

The fire faded, and in a shimmering spectrum of light, there they were.

Saints.

Champions.

Dayne Heldrin and Jerinne Fendall, their Tarian uniforms a mess, their shields scorched and seared. But still standing strong, refusing to yield to these villains.

Inspector Minox Welling, sword in one hand, the other glowing with magic.

Inspector Satrine Rainey, in the red and green of the Constabulary, crossbow in hand.

The Rynax brothers. Asti in his patchwork coat and knives at the ready. Verci, leather coat over suspenders and shirtsleeves. Darts in one hand, metal glove on the other.

And the Thorn—I could scarcely believe it, the Thorn was real—with his crimson cloak shimmering with magic as he leaped into the air, drawing back his bow.

"I—I need to read all of this," Rian said.

"It's astounding," Alexanne said.

"I don't fully believe it," Rowa countered.

"I heard from Freya and Macey it's all true. They have cousins who live in that part of town."

"They fought a giant winged serpent?"

"Did your mother fight a giant winged serpent?"

"She doesn't tell me everything about her work," Rian said, continuing to read through it. Mother did all that? Jerinne did that? How was that even possible?

"Well your mother is *very* crush," Alexanne said. "We're dying to have tea or such with her."

"Quite," Rowa said.

"I'll let her know," Rian said.

"Please," Rowa said. "Invite us when you can."

They floated off, leaving Rian to read through the impossible, incredible tale three or four times before she left.

She left the shop out of the employee entrance, and was surprised to find Jerinne Fendall waiting there, in dress uniform with a violet mourning sash draped over it. She looked incredibly dashing, especially since she also wore the gloves Rian had sold her.

"Are you going to a grieving?" Rian asked.

"I am, actually," Jerinne said. "But your mother said you were getting off work so I thought I'd see you."

Rian held up the pamphlet. "Is this real? Did this really happen?"

"It really happened," Jerinne said. "Though it glosses over how I spent half the fight knocked out in the bell tower."

"How?"

"It's . . . one of the monsters got a piece of me."

"Oh my saints!" Rian exclaimed, her hand almost involuntarily reaching out to touch Jerinne's face. She pulled back just before she actually did. "You're all right?"

"Miraculously, yes," Jerinne said.

"I . . . you must have been scared, right?"

"Terrified," Jerinne said. "But not half as terrified as I am right now." She took a step closer to Rian, and Rian suddenly felt her heart race again.

"Why—" Rian cleared her throat, which had become quite dry. "Why are you terrified?"

Jerinne smiled—warm, bright, vibrant—and looked down to the ground for a moment, before looking back up and meeting Rian's eyes.

"Because I want to kiss you. Is that all right?"

Rian couldn't breathe for a moment. When she found her voice, she was astounded by what she said.

"I think you should."

Then the most extraordinary thing happened.

It wasn't the first time Rian had been kissed—there had been Poul Tullen, who had been rough and quick and altogether rushed. Rian had found that rather disappointing, even though her schoolfriends had told her that was just what kissing was like. She had resigned herself to accepting that.

Jerinne was something else altogether. Fierce and intense, confident and strong, soft and giving, kind and tender.

Everything Rian had thought a kiss should be.

Jerinne pulled back. "Was that all right?"

"More than," Rian said. She glanced over to the employee door. Thankfully no one had come out. "Though we shouldn't stand around here like this."

"Right," Jerinne said, flashing another smile. "I'm about to go to this service for a friend. Would you . . . would you like to come with me?" She offered her arm to Rian.

It had been a long day, and Rian knew she needed to go home, read three chapters and study math, but none of that mattered right now. She took Jerinne's arm.

"I'd love to," she said. "Though you're in your dress uniform, I'm in shopgirl clothes. Won't you be embarrassed by me?"

"Never," Jerinne said. "You always look like a princess."

"And so, dear friends, we are here in celebration of Maresh Niol. A man who lived in pursuit of truth, and art, and beauty, and whose loss diminishes us all."

It was a beautiful sentiment, though Dayne did wonder how much Maresh—a man who spoken so strongly against the current government as well as the hierarchies of the church—would feel about Ret Issendel—former bishop, now member of Parliament—speaking at his service.

"He was a man who would probably argue vehemently about me speaking here," Issendel went on. "The few times I met him, he argued with me, and . . . I will miss the opportunity for further arguments. His work challenged us all to look deeper into our preconceptions. I'm pleased to see us here in celebration of him, and the work he did."

The courtyard of The Nimble Rabbit was decorated with Maresh's art—largely charcoal sketches, but a few painted pieces—and filled with an eclectic mix of people. There were writers and artists from other newssheets. There were other artists—eclectic, broke Fenton types as well as tony ones with rich patrons. There were a few Tarians beyond just Dayne and Jerinne, mostly other third-year Initiates. There was a smattering of young nobility—friends of Miri. Two of them—Baron Vollingale and Baron Deeringhill—were making a point of buying Maresh's art for a ridiculously high amount. Vollingale, especially, was unrestrained in his generosity and expressions of gratitude. "The least I can do for the man who died helping get my boy back to me." Hemmit had pledged to send that money to Maresh's mother.

And there were two members of Parliament: Ret Issendel and Golman Haberneck. Haberneck had come with his extended family and friends, all with their children. Children that had been rescued from the Brotherhood.

"So, hold up your wine, or whatever you prefer," Issendel said. "I know that Maresh preferred wine. And ask for a blessing for his spirit, to his memory, that he resides with the saints."

Glasses went up, and most everyone drank. Dayne noticed Lin refraining. Most people were wearing a violet sash or shawl, but Lin was in a long violet dress, shawl, and scarf, looking more like a cloistress than her usual revealing fashion. As Issendel stepped down, and the gathered people started talking amongst themselves, Dayne worked his way over to her.

"How are you managing?" he asked.

"Badly," she said. "He . . . it's funny, a week ago, if you had asked me a defining characteristic of Maresh, 'brave' wouldn't have been a word that came to mind. But when we were captive down there, he stood up to them on my behalf. He . . . died because he made them take him instead of me."

"I have to ask you something," Dayne said. "It might be uncomfortable."

"I'm fine with uncomfortable," she said. "I'll be living with this for a while."

"The Thorn was with Maresh when he died, and apparently the last thing he said was a message to me."

"To you? Whatever was that?"

"Tell Dayne don't trust."

"Don't trust what?"

"I have no idea," Dayne said. "But you were with him until the end. Was there something you heard or saw?"

She frowned. "Nothing I can think of. I'm so sorry. I wish—I wish I had been stronger, better. If I had taken my magical studies seriously, maybe I—"

"Hey, no," Dayne said. "I have been down the path of 'maybe I' so many times. I live with that. I live with it now. Maybe I could have gotten across the bridge faster. Maybe I could have insisted you all went back once we reached the highway. Maybe I could have found a different way. I know how maddening it can be. But the truth is, this is only the fault of the evil people who did this."

"Evil is too easy," Lin said. "I'm not saying they're not, but . . . the world is too complicated to make it that simple." She glanced around the party. "We're surrounded by a thousand little compromises that made this possible. Just look at . . ." She chuckled ruefully. "Look at this event. Even we're compromised."

"But we keep doing our best," Dayne said.

"Thank you," she said, taking his hand. "Thank you for remaining so . . . pure." She took out a violet handkerchief and dabbed at the fresh tears. "I'm going to retreat inside for a while. Discourage people from following me."

She went into The Nimble Rabbit, and Dayne noticed Hemmit watch her go, and then gave a glance to Dayne. They exchanged a silent agreement and continued to move about the event. Hemmit was talking with a group of people Dayne assumed were mutual friends of Maresh from RCM.

Dayne went over to Mirianne—resplendent in a violet suit that managed to be both highly fashionable and somber at the same time—who was talking with Golman Haberneck.

"Dayne," Haberneck said as he approached. "I . . . I feel like I cannot say thank you enough. You did something beyond extraordinary."

"Not alone," Dayne said. "I was fortunate to have help."

"And thanks to you," Mirianne said to Haberneck. "I have to say, most members of Parliament would not have noticed or cared about something happening to the working people of Dentonhill. But you're a real man of the people."

"I'm just a dock steve from Kyst who people listened to," Haberneck said.

"Exactly," Mirianne said. "And that's what this country needs."

"I will do what I can." He looked to Dayne. "Issendel and I are already working on making sure Saint Bridget's Square will be quickly repaired and restored."

"I would love to help with that," Mirianne said. "Baron Vollingale and I can spearhead a movement among the city's nobility to raise funds to that end. Literally the least we can do."

"Thank you, my lady," Haberneck said. "Of course, Dayne is the real hero here."

"I am not comfortable being called that."

"Then 'champion'?" Haberneck produced the thick pamphlet Hemmit had published that morning. Already it was circulating around the city like a fire. Of course, with its flashy title and the seven saintly silhouettes on the cover, it was very hard not to take notice of.

"It's 'Champions of Maradaine,'" Jerinne said, coming over to them. "You'll notice this one is not just about him." She was beaming, in the company of a young Waishen-haired woman who looked surprisingly like Satrine Rainey.

Then he noticed, across the courtyard: Satrine Rainey there, wineglass in hand. Sitting a short distance om her: Minox Welling. Neither of them were in n, and in this crowd looked rather inconspicuous. both subtly raised their glasses to him, which he returned. Then Satrine gave him a small nod in the other direction.

Leaning against one of the trees in the courtyard:

Asti and Verci Rynax. They were both in suits, slightly ill-fitting and years out of fashion, but not looking out of place among the people around them. They also raised their glasses to Dayne.

Then, finally by the entrance to the courtyard, Veranix Calbert was in his University of Maradaine uniform. He had no wineglass, but instead had one of The Nimble Rabbit's famous crispers in hand. He winked and took a bite.

Dayne laughed briefly, in spite of himself.

"No, it's not," he said finally. "And quite fittingly as well. Maradaine is full of people ready to stand up and defend it. Ready to fight and die for it, for the ideals we hold dearest. I'm honored just to be considered worthy to be counted among them."

For once, he was not embarrassed or ashamed of the coverage in the press. He was glad the story was out there, that the public was aware of the truth of what happened at Saint Bridget's Square. But more, he was glad that everyone knew what he always had: that Maradaine was full of champions. If something went wrong, someone would be there. He could count on the people of this city.

"Does anyone need more wine?" he asked. For tonight, for at least one night, he could let his guard down.